A Feast of Small Surprises

by

Corinne Van Houten

Bloomington, IN  Milton Keynes, UK

authorHOUSE

AuthorHouse™
1663 Liberty Drive, Suite 200
Bloomington, IN 47403
www.authorhouse.com
Phone: 1-800-839-8640

AuthorHouse™ UK Ltd.
500 Avebury Boulevard
Central Milton Keynes, MK9 2BE
www.authorhouse.co.uk
Phone: 08001974150

First published by AuthorHouse 4/26/2006

ISBN: 1-4208-5113-6 (sc)

Printed in the United States of America
Bloomington, Indiana

This book is printed on acid-free paper.

Dedication

I dedicate this novel, with love and appreciation, to my husband, Marc, whose enthusiasm and support mean so much to me

Acknowledgements

There are many people without whose support and faith I would have lost courage to continue with this novel. First, there are my children, Mariek and Alex, who have tolerated periods of frustration and despair with great fortitude and good humor, then my parents, Betty and Tom, whose love and support have always been invaluable, my parents-in-law, Michelle and Roger, and my dear friends among whom Rene Detroye, Sharon Greene, Marilyn Kaye, Bob Detweiler, Roslynn Hight, Marianne Gardner, Diane Yowell, Sairan Stanley, Mary Burnett, Peter Supino, and Peg Johnston not only listened when I was down but were willing to read the novel in its various stages of progress. In addition are those friends who were always there to sympathize as I obsessed over re-working a complicated plot; Sissy Ledbetter, Duke and Brenda Jackson, Paulien Veltman, Jean Bried, Suzanne Justen, Tom and Annette Buk Swienty, and my sister, Olivia Van Houten.

I want to give special thanks to my friends, David Frati and Linda Ridings who helped me with Italian phrases and daily rituals centered around food, coffee and aperitifs. I also want to thank my agent, Ron Laitsch, for his belief in this book and my editor, Candy Davis, who helped me regain perspective when I was foundering.

I also want to acknowledge my professors at Emory University, Tom Lyman and William Crelly, who taught me to appreciate and enjoy both the human and the divine dimensions of great artists and great art.

I want to add my deepest appreciation to my friend, Anne Desne, who has so beautifully translated the novel into French. Merci beaucoup!

Finally, I want to express my appreciation to my friend, Irene Belknap, for letting me use one of her beautiful paintings as the cover to this book.

The cover is taken from a painting titled "Continuum," oil on canvas (1990) by Irene Belknap, (415)383-3613. Ibelknap@comcast.net

CHAPTER ONE

"Light reveals but it also conceals, it illumines but it also blinds:
the devastating light of God's presence, the midday sun bleaching
the world of color. Light alters our perceptions as much as it defines
them. Intangible, invisible and yet making all visible, light is the
ultimate paradox in art: essential to it and yet eternally peripheral,
eternally untranslatable. With Caravaggio, light becomes the
painting's darkness, light exposes the shadows of a world of illusion."
(Edward Donant from his guide to Italian galleries and museums)

Valeriano Cerasi squeezed his black Maserati between a battered
BMW and a Ford van. He looked into the mirror and removed a speck
from his eye with the nail of one perfectly manicured hand. It was very
hot in Sicily even though it was only March and, in spite of the car's air
conditioning, he was already sweating in his dark blue, pin stripe suit.
Nonetheless, he straightened his tie and buttoned his collar. Gianni had
told him the padre was impressed by wealth and power, an impression that
Valeriano easily projected. There was no one in the square that fronted
the Church of Messina. It was too hot and everyone had taken refuge in
the cooler and more appealing shade of a café or tree-covered courtyard.
The church itself had a typical Gothic façade, squatter than it's Northern
neighbors but attractive in a quiet, provincial sort of way.

The interior was dim. Father Bassi was standing by the altar, his back
to the entrance. The padre turned and saw Valeriano.

"Si? Posso aiutare, Signore?" Father Bassi walked slowly down the
aisle towards Valeriano.

"Si. Sono Valeriano Cerasi…"

"Ah, si, si. Benvenuto, Signore. Welcome to our humble church. Is it not
very hot? Already in March but it is so much cooler here in the sanctuary."
Father Bassi smiled genially at Valeriano who smiled perfunctorily back.

"The painting?"

"Ah, yes. It is down below the church, in the crypt. Quite a mess,"
Father Bassi said as he led the way. Valeriano followed the father at some
distance, discreetly covering his mouth with his handkerchief. Emanating
from the padre was a potent body odor made more nauseating by the reek
of garlic, which must have been the starring ingredient in Father Bassi's
lunch. When they arrived in the crypt, the padre pressed a switch on the
wall and the dim light from two bare bulbs revealed the disorganized
state of the room. Somber, dusty paintings representing the gruesome

1

martyrdom of one of the innumerable Catholic saints leaned against the walls, a pile of broken glass had been swept into a corner, boxes of books and a partially open wardrobe full of sacramental objects and religious vestments filled the remaining space. Father Bassi had set the painting Valeriano had driven so far to see on a slightly off tilt table so that the crucified Christ looked as though he were going to slide off the canvas. Murmuring his apologies, the priest lifted the lop-sided end, straightened the work and looked expectantly at Valeriano.

Valeriano had grown up studying the masters of the Italian Renaissance and he had confidence in his ability to recognize a masterpiece when he saw one. This painting—he stepped closer to it, frowning for the benefit of Father Bassi—struck him as having that quality, that immeasurable quality of beauty and sincerity that was only evoked by the greatest of artists.

"And how did you say you found it?" He asked the question carefully, suspiciously. It would never do to give Father Bassi the idea that he might have one of the world's great masterpieces hidden away in the dingy basement of his provincial church.

"It wasn't me," Father Bassi smiled apologetically as though confessing a secret to Valeriano. "A man, an artist he described himself, came to me and said that he would like to look through the basement in search of something he thought he might be able to use as a prop for a painting."

Valeriano didn't take his eyes from the painting. He knew all about Gianni, of course. A forger and a smuggler, it was Gianni who had told Valeriano he had to see the work. He had little doubt that this priest had alerted Gianni before to works that he could smuggle out of Italy to the benefit of them both. Turning his head slightly away from the odiferous padre, Valeriano took the canvas from Father Bassi's hands and walked over to hold it beneath one of the bulbs. "Not the best light in which to view a work of art," he commented. "It certainly appears to be old and it's in terrible condition. So you believe that this work could have been lying here for, what, several centuries? Doesn't it seem rather odd that no one has discovered it before?"

Father Bassi raised his eyebrows and spread his hands in an expansive gesture. "It is not only possible, Signore, it is quite likely. There is much down here that is old and forgotten. We do not spend our time on the past but think only of the future and what we may do in the name of the Lord."

"Where did this artist say he found the painting?"

Father Bassi beckoned to Valeriano who left the canvas and followed him through the maze of jumbled debris. "He found it leaning against the wall here." They were at the back of the crypt where the ceiling became so low they had to stoop. "Behind these paintings." He indicated several ancient canvases, their somber hues so darkened with age that Valeriano could barely make out the figures painted on them. "You are welcome to look at these if you are interested."

But Valeriano had already turned back to the painting on the table. Picking it up, he examined the canvas. "Well," he spoke almost reluctantly. "It has some value to those few like myself who are interested in obscure paintings from this particular period. I will offer you two million lire."

The priest looked scornful and they began the inevitable process of bargaining, which resulted in Valeriano removing the painting for the equivalent of twenty-five hundred dollars. He carried it carefully out of the sacristy and into the late afternoon sun. Once he got outside the church, he scrutinized the work, holding it so that the sun fell directly across the grimy surface. He could be wrong but he thought that there was only one man who painted like this and he had been commissioned to paint four works for this very church. It was assumed that none of them had ever been executed. After all, Caravaggio had been a man on the run. But somewhere there was a record that one of them had been completed. He would have to make sure, of course. There were certain preliminary tests that would have to be made.

Valeriano carefully wrapped the ancient, darkened canvas. Christ's eyes gleamed at him as he disappeared beneath the bubble wrap. He couldn't be absolutely positive that the painting was an original. It looked like it might be, he *felt* like it was but whatever the case, of one thing he was certain: this painting was going to be the answer to his prayers.

CHAPTER TWO

"A great painting, like a beautiful woman, is constantly
revealing itself yet remains shrouded in mystery. Look at
this still life by Claesz. The glint of light (where does it
come from?), that glass half full of wine (the forbidden fruit),
that tantalizing peel descending from the lemon. I can
imagine squeezing it onto those luscious oysters, hmmm?
And yet, sumptuous pleasures though we observe, we know
that there has been a drama here, perhaps a *MELO*drama
that is about to unfold with greater violence. The broken
glass, the beautiful jeweled cup tipped so beatifically on
its side. Something's rotten in Europe, in the world of
art and artifice. What a feast of small surprises, hmmm?"
(Edward Donant)

Anne Langlais smashed the soft, beige beret more firmly on her head
as she struggled to drag her bags through the crush of people packed into
the small compartment that connected the train cars. They had left the
Gare de Lyon in Paris at eight o'clock that evening and already she was
regretting the fact that she had not gone first class.

"Oh, mais c'est des fruits et des legumes. C'est bon pour toi."

"Pour moi, il n'y a que le chocolat et les bons bons."

The young couple giggled and Anne regarded them with some
amusement. She had been lucky really. She had to share her couchette with
only this girl and boy who were completely engrossed with each other.
The girl had acne and was overweight, he was tall, thin and snorted when
he laughed but they were happy and she envied them their unselfconscious
pleasure in being with one another.

Anne was a tall, fair-skinned woman with gray-green eyes that flashed
and sparkled as sunlight entering the water trembles opaquely beneath the
waves. She walked with a slight limp, the result of a fall from a hotel roof
in Rome nineteen years before when her pelvis had been pierced by the
flagpole on the hotel facade. Her hair was long and black and pulled back
into a bun at the nape of her neck. Tufts and tendrils of it were continually
working their way out beneath her hat, teasing her by floating elusively
across her eyes. For the first hour she had pushed them away, but now,
growing impatient, she reached up and jerked off her beret, shaking her
head so that the short bangs fell into place. Folding up the soft hat she
stuffed it into a great straw bag.

4

Had she made the right decision to return to Rome? She could, of course, do what she had always done—retreat into solitude and the world of academics but she didn't want to do that any more. Anne had avoided looking at the possibility that her plan could fail but here, on this train speeding to Rome, she was faced with the fact that she was committed whatever unforeseen circumstances might arise. She sat up, her spine straight against the uncomfortable seat back, her book lying face down in her lap. It was strange how John had suddenly reappeared in her life, like some nemesis come to call after all those years.

She looked out of the window as the train jerked into a tunnel—the landscape disappeared, replaced by a dark pane reflecting her face, wan and puffy around the eyes. She wasn't going to be one of those women who aged beautifully, she thought. Anne took a deep breath. Her analyst had told her she had to confront her fear and her anger, that she had to enter her nightmares and vanquish her foes and that was exactly what she intended to do. She pulled out the letter Maya had sent her and read it again.

Dearest Anne,

You can love so many people in so many ways or, an alternative way of putting it, you can present your own rationalization of needs in an attempt to make what you secretly cannot control sound virtuous. I try desperately to make myself a gracious, hard-line, rational, unemotional woman but I'm essentially romantic, passionate and sensitive to any slight of myself as an attractive female. Jealousy is the inevitable result of this combination of the need to be adored and resistance to this need. All of this is just a preface to my confession that Edward and I are getting married and to the hope that you've not been carrying any repressed resentment towards us because we became lovers. I know he still loves you, so I am jealous but not of you, never of you. I'm jealous, I think, of the fact that I can't achieve that coolness which I ache to acquire and which you so naturally possess. It's a grace for you and not a coldness or a pretense to be other than what you are. It's part of your irresistible charm and one that I continually try and fail to emulate. But there, I love you so much and I feel you're such an important part of my life that, much as I love Edward, I feel if only you can forgive, no that's not the word, if only you can understand and accept what I'm trying to tell you, then I can truly look forward to my life with Edward.

Well, I'm off. I'm going to my favorite haunt, "Les Deux Magots," to drink a glass of champagne and see if I can still attract the young men. I'm really not all that prepared for marriage and its accompanying responsibilities, am I? But then, I do so love Edward—perhaps he'll be the one to make me a virtuous woman.

Yours forever, Maya

Anne looked across at the boy and girl. It was so like Maya to believe that her actions bore no consequences. Her letter was guileless, revealing more about Maya's selfishness than it did any love she had ever felt towards Anne or Edward. "That coolness you possess." Anne closed her eyes and leaned back in the seat. If Maya only knew how hard it was for her, how hard it had been watching Edward trying to hide his increasing infatuation for Maya. Anne knew that Edward still loved her, just as she loved him but they really had been impossible together.

"Art is ultimately a male product," Edward had said. "Even the women who produce art are masculine in their sensibilities, in their desires, in their ambition. Women's role is and has always been to inspire the male. It may be a cliché but, like so many clichés, it's true. Women are, by nature, muses and critics, the graces and the harpies." Naturally, this had not gone down well with Anne—"Don't be such an asshole" she had snapped—nor had Edward, in the end, much cared for her role as harpy. Anne shifted uncomfortably in her seat. She should be grateful to Maya for releasing her from such a relationship but she wasn't. Anne felt the familiar tears well up and she shook her head, determined to shut them out. She missed him. She missed their arguments, she missed watching him paint in the cool, brightly lit studio he had set up in the glass conservatory behind their house, she missed the comfortable way that they lived together, knowing what the other was thinking even without speaking. That's not true, Anne reminded herself, wiping an errant tear with a quick motion of her hand. They had not had sex for months before Edward asked for the divorce. He had been cold and distant when she had tried to talk to him, and, what was truly unforgivable, he had abandoned her, like all the men she had ever known. Except John, Anne thought. She laughed suddenly. How absurd it all was. John had really meant to kill her. Anne realized that the boy and girl had stopped talking and were watching her. She smiled at them. They whispered to each other.

"No excuses," Anne told herself firmly and looked out of the window again. This time she was relieved to see, not her face, but the fields parallel to the train passing rapidly in varied shades of green that were turning velvety in the dimming light. The boy and girl had taken out sandwiches and cokes and were happily chewing and drinking. She had brought some cheese, a baguette, and a half bottle of Haut Brion but felt uncomfortable taking them out in front of this couple. In spite of the fact that they didn't offer her anything or include her in anyway, she would feel obligated to share her dinner and she wasn't inclined to do that, not tonight, not with them.

The landscape shifted from day to night, the fields and towns and trees losing color until they metamorphosed into sharp, black edges. In Anne's lap lay <u>Gaudy Night</u>, a mystery by Dorothy Sayers with which she had been trying to stave off her increasing sense of unease. But what, really, could go wrong? She left the book lying face down and stared at her reflection in the darkened windowpane.

***

The train jerked on the track, the lights from the stars disappeared and there came the familiar reverberating clack of iron on iron as the train sped through another tunnel and emerged once again in the soft summer night. Anne started awake, stifling a small gasp. She rested her head against the pillow, breathing slowly to quiet her nerves. She was reclining on the seat, her head squashed between the seatback and the windowsill, buffered by the small pillow. The boy and girl were sleeping soundly on the top bunks so she had been able to leave the middle bunk raised, giving her more space. The stale breath of sleep combined with the dim light above the door to create an oppressive atmosphere in the closed compartment. She felt as though she would suffocate if she fell asleep again. She lit a cigarette and leaned her head back against the headrest.

She had dreamed of Edward. He had been lecturing in a huge auditorium. There had been adoring men and women, dancers and musicians and lights and she had been sitting at his feet gazing at him worshipfully. But then some silly woman had spoken of him scornfully. How small and egoistic and fraudulent he was. And there he was exactly as the woman had described him—a fraud all neatly brushed up and displaying himself coquettishly and Anne had had that same dull, dirty feeling as when he had sat at her table and drunk her wine and brought in his dog, unasked, to lie on her floor and spread fleas in her furniture and in her hair. How she had resented his smug confidence sitting there. Arriving unannounced after he had left her. Gone off on another erotic fling.

Anne turned on her reading light and began to read. After a few pages she closed the book irritably. At one time she had dearly loved Dorothy Sayers and had rather disloyally rejected Agatha Christie as superficial and facile. Now she found Sayers closed-minded and pettily academic as opposed to Christie's gently humorous representation of human foibles. How tiresome it was to constantly re-orient your opinions; about the people you loved, the books you savored, the places you visited.

Anne looked at her watch—six in the morning. She would be arriving in Rome around eleven where Maya had offered to meet her. Did Maya really believe that her engagement to Edward hadn't affected their friendship? Anne thought that she probably did. She sighed as she walked down the aisle of the train towards the dining car. She might as well get a cup of tea. She might as well go on with her life the way she always did. What difference did it make what she wanted anyway?

Three businessmen and two elderly women were sitting at separate tables in the dining car. As Anne ordered tea in her careful Italian, she was acutely aware of the difference between this trip and the last time she had taken the train to Italy. Then she had been twenty-two: very plump, very eager, very young and naive. In the bar, burly Italian men and hawkish French had shared smoky obscenities, twirling between two fingers the phallic ego of a man's world. They had drunk and smoked with avidity, sharing a camaraderie born of centuries of exclusivity: exclusive of feminine wiles, feminine deceit, the hated Pandora.

She had listened to them with a half smile, already tipsy, a bottle of Chianti swinging lazily from the straw loop hooked around her finger. These had been the older men: men of the Mediterranean, of Gaul, of Cesarean troops and glorified homosexuality. She had felt no particular fondness, no admiration for them, but as she had entered the bar, listening to their incomprehensible chatter, brushing past them, her feelings had been fiercely contemptuous, fiercely sexual—they had burned and pricked her thighs. Now, in retrospect, as she observed the sedate behavior of the five persons sitting with her in the narrow car, she wondered at her interpretations of the men she had seen. Had it been she who had been fascinated with male camaraderie, male love of a masculine ethos? Had it been her fantasy or theirs that had filled the car with erotic undertones?

When the train was two hours away from Rome, Anne returned to the dining car for lunch. She ordered cold chicken and fruit, bread and Asiago cheese and a small bottle of white table wine. She had spent the morning reading and staring at the passing countryside, impatient to arrive yet feeling increasingly edgy.

She was looking forward to the private showing in the Palazzo Vecchio in Florence. The discovery of a Caravaggio was rare, exciting if it proved to be the real thing. It would also be interesting to test her knowledge of Caravaggio against Edward's. Edward had written about and studied Caravaggio intensely enough to be considered one of the world's authorities on the great artist. Not that Edward would ever admit that Caravaggio, or anyone else for that matter, was a greater artist than himself. Anne wondered again why the market for Edward's works had dropped so suddenly and, though she experienced a certain satisfaction at the thought of his sudden fall from favor, she was also a bit perplexed. He was talented—there was no doubt about that—so what could have happened to cause this sudden lack of interest in his work?

A distinguished-looking, older man was sitting at a table across from hers reading the "Herald Tribune." Anne placed a slice of cheese on her bread and leaned forward to read the article on the page facing her.

"VALUABLE PIRANESI DRAWING 'DISAPPEARS.'" A Piranesi drawing, which was lent to the Cerasi gallery in Rome, has been reported as having been stolen. The private collector who lent the drawing was notified by Valeriano Cerasi, the well-respected collector and art dealer, some time ago. After making discreet inquiries the gallery has made the disappearance public knowledge in the hopes that the thief may have tried to sell it..."

Anne's heart beat faster. She glanced up to see the man watching her from behind his paper. He smiled at her and graciously extended the paper to her. Anne smiled back and shook her head. "Non, non, grazie. Mi scusi." She turned to look out of the window. So the theft had been made public. There was no turning back now.

CHAPTER THREE

"How do you paint Helen of Troy? How do you
paint the most beautiful woman in the world? You
must look for various manifestations of beauty in
nature and put them all together and then you have
something more beautiful than nature can
produce. Sort of an extracted abstract."
(Edward Donant)

Maya Kelly put on her black, spaghetti-strap Donna Karan dress with
the flippy skirt. She brushed her cropped blond hair back from her brow,
applied lip-gloss, slipped on her sling-back shoes and a leather jacket and
strode out onto the Rue Rambuteau.

It was late June in Paris and the weather was very changeable; cold
and gray, the air redolent with the omnipresent odor of pollution. She
recalled the heady smell of exhaust fumes with which she associated her
Roman adventures—adventures that had been so often recollected as she
stood by a bus stop or crossed a busy road. A dangerous allure—one that
was, like MSG, both irresistible and lethal; nicely symbolic of the games
of passion played daily on the streets.

Maya shivered and wished that she had worn a hat. She glanced
occasionally at her reflection in shop windows, wondering what men
thought of her as she ignored their stares, their murmured compliments
as they brushed past her. Did they really find her beautiful? Did they see
her as a distant object of desire, as some fantastical image of feminine
beauty, as a whore? Did the women see her as vain, as ridiculous, as
enviably lovely? It was different in Amsterdam, in Paris, in Rome. The
farther south you went the more fashionably provocative the clothes, the
more open the sexual assumptions, the more reverential the propositions.
It was an erotic game that was simultaneously sincere and superficially
flattering, genuinely erotic and ultimately meaningless.

It was early and the tables at "Le Jardin de The" were nearly empty.
Maya took one where she could sit close to the Stravinsky fountain and
watch people wandering around the Pompidou Museum. Suddenly,
unexpectedly, the sun came out and the gray fog disappeared. Nikki de St.
Phalle's sculpture of a big-bottomed bather turned her tiny, faceless head
and stubby limbs in Maya's direction, her huge breasts and buttocks a
colorful cousin to the Venus of Willendorf. Two doves, wings silver against
the blue opaque sky, soared from de St. Phalle's rotating striped serpent to

10

the buttress of the church of Parousse de St. Merri. In one graceful swoop they flew from 1980 to 1331, from twentieth century sculptures derived from the capricious humor of modern cynicism to a thirteenth century architectural edifice dedicated to a solemn God and faith in an everlasting life.

Maya removed her jacket and ordered a cappuccino. The light had shifted from metallic gray to metallic blue. Her period was two weeks away and already she was feeling heavy. She drank her cappuccino quickly, adding up the days as she did so. Edward was already in Rome. He had not suggested that she accompany him when he had left the week before and she had been disappointed but she had reconciled herself to the fact that that was how it was with Edward. "You must take me as I am," he had told her when they first moved to Europe, caressing her, half teasing. "And that's no mean feat." She had laughed and thought nothing of it at the time.

They had spent the winter in Amsterdam. A charming city and cold in spite of the brown cafes and the bright strings of lights which illuminated the curving bridges across the canals; the Herengracht, the Prinsengracht, the Kaisersgracht. Edward had insisted they ride bicycles like the Dutch. Scarves wrapped around her throat, up to her nose, breathing in warm wool and icy air, she had gone for wine every afternoon at Cafe Luxembourg. That's where she had met Stephen. Dark, good-looking in a melancholy, slightly ominous way, she had hoped that he would offer to buy her a drink. He had spoken to her twice as he had made his way to the bar but he had given no indication that she could expect him to risk his pride by asking if he could join her. He had surprised her, however, telling her, in a deep, slightly lispy voice, how beautiful she was.

She ordered a bottle of Perrier. The cafe was beginning to fill up. Couples warned one another as they stepped around a pile of dog droppings at the edge of the terrace. Anne should be passing through Paris about now. Maya wondered how they would feel when they saw each other again. Maya had received only a brief note in response to her letter, in which she had made her feelings vulnerably clear. Of course Maya couldn't expect Anne to be really happy about Edward and her but it wasn't like she had done anything really wrong. After all, Anne had told her she was having problems with Edward, that she wasn't happy with him. Edward said Anne wasn't jealous because she wasn't capable of loving anyone but Maya thought it was because Anne was above all the petty emotions like jealousy and envy.

"Madame. Voulez-vous quelque chose?"

Maya started then glanced again at her watch. Twelve-thirty. "Oui. L'artichaut vinaigrette et le filet de Rascasse en papillote, si'l vous plait." 'The bloating begins,' she thought. 'I must try to remain thin without growing weak from lack of food.' When had she last eaten a meal? Twenty-four hours? Thirty? Stephen was late.

An old man sat down two tables away. He turned the pages of "Le Monde" and began to cough. Thin lips opened wide, reminding her of the discs in Duchamp's "Chocolate Grinder." Bright blue eyes turned in their sockets as he hacked. The waiter deposited Maya's artichoke and she ordered a half carafe of white wine, ever conscious of the hacking and coughing such a short distance away. His evident lack of concern over the repellent aspects of his physical distress was completely foreign to Maya whose every move was governed by an imagined male audience. She even ordered and ate according to the men around her. With older, very correct men she took small bites, interspersed with sips of water or wine. With younger, more openly interested men, she took on a thoughtful, semi-erotic manner; picking at her food, looking off into the distance, drinking wine and throwing her head back in a state of abandon. The difficulty was to eat what was necessary for the nourishment of your body and soul without allowing the internal pleasure to be registered externally in any way. After taking a sip of water or wine she had a tendency to cover her mouth as though she had just committed an indecent public act.

There were moments when Maya wondered what it would be like to live a life without an audience, without anticipating the effect she had on others. What would it be like to be "normal," she would think as she sat at a table in a crowded café. To be one of the anonymous group of people she saw enjoying themselves in bars and on the streets, staring at other people, laughing and talking with a freedom of spirit and being that she rarely felt. But, most of the time, she enjoyed the effect she had on others. It wasn't just the vicarious pleasure she took in seeing her reflection in others' eyes, it was the only time she felt truly alive. She thought of Edward and momentarily wished that he were with her. He always made her feel beautiful and secure and he released her from her obsession with her image. It was one of the things she loved about him.

"C'est un jouissance pour moi de faire des bons investissements." The gentleman was young, correct, boring, wearing the inevitable dark suit. He was in conversation with two other men, dressed in the same discreet style. The three of them glanced in her direction. They had ordered two bottles of red wine, which the waiter had displayed reverentially, almost humbly, a certain indication of a good vintage and a high price. Maya fantasized momentarily on the possibility that they would invite her to join them for a glass of champagne.

Stephen wasn't coming. She was destined to have another lonely lunch. The artichoke leaves were emerald green against the pale amber of the vinaigrette. She was thirty-nine for God's sake. She should know better.

De St. Phalle's blue bowler hat whirled on the far side of the twirling heart, Tinguely's metal skeletons spun and spit.

CHAPTER FOUR

"Paint, even when it's dry, never quite forgets its
memory of being liquid. It's like a pot of soup
simmering on the back of the stove—very slowly
its molecular composition changes. Today,
Vermeer would say, 'God, what's happened to
my painting,' you know and Poussin would
faint right away because the dark undertones
of his paintings have bled through."
(Edward Donant)

The train wheezed into Roma Termini, bells and short shrill whistles announcing its arrival. Anne stationed herself with her luggage by the door. The gentleman who had been reading the Tribune assisted her by handing down her two suitcases. She smiled at him. "Grazie." There were no more luggage carts. Settling her hat more securely on her head she picked up the heavy suitcases, half dragging, half carrying them down the long platform to the cavernous entrance. The old wound was aching, protesting against the weight of the suitcases but she couldn't find a porter.

The train station was uglier and louder and surprisingly cleaner than she remembered. All around her rose the unceasing cacophony of incessant voices from various nations—shrill Italian, nasal American, guttural German, clipped French. Disembodied over loudspeakers, nameless, restless, monotonous—they spoke to her sense of adventure and soothed her nerves. Absorbed in reverie, Anne collided with a man.

"I'm so sorry," she exclaimed.

"That's perfectly all right." He spoke English with a slight Italian accent and when he smiled at her she realized that she must look awful after two days of travel. She turned away, then looked back to see him staring thoughtfully after her. Tall and slender, with dark hair and sunglasses, he reminded her, for a minute, of Charlie.

Anne set her bags down to wait, glancing impatiently at her watch. "Good grief," she thought. "Did Maya always have to be late?!" After twenty minutes Anne grabbed both suitcases and, limping slightly, began to lug them in the direction of the taxis.

"Anne! Anne, wait!"

She turned to see Maya running toward her in high-heels and a short dress. Breathless, Maya caught up with Anne and hugged her. Anne tolerated her embrace stiffly before Maya grabbed the bags from her.

14

"No, no, I want to take them," Maya smiled at her eagerly and Anne followed her to the curb where a taxi was waiting. "So…" Maya said as they settled in the back seat.

"Yes?" Anne resented Maya's breathless enthusiasm at seeing her.

"Well, I mean, it's been awhile since we've seen each other and, you know, I was…ummm. Did you get my letter?"

"Yes. I wrote you back, remember?"

"Well, what do you think?"

"About what?"

Maya stared at Anne. "About Edward and me, you know, getting married…"

"Oh, yes. That. Well, congratulations are due I suppose though don't you think marriage might interfere with you meeting other men?" Anne couldn't stop herself.

"What do you mean? Why did you say that?"

Anne shook her head. "I was referring to what you said in your letter. About looking for young men at the café, about not being really ready for marriage."

"Oh." Lines creased Maya's brow as she leaned back in the seat but then she looked up at Anne and smiled. "Well, you know it's true. I've never been too keen on being with just one man. But I think if there is one man for me then it's Edward."

"Well then…" Anne knew that she sounded irritable.

"Something's wrong, I can always tell when you don't want to say something. What is it?"

"Nothing's wrong. Why?"

"Well, you must know that I'm a little afraid that you're angry…"

"Angry? About what?" Anne stared impassively at Maya. She wanted her to say it.

Maya rolled her eyes. "About Edward and me, of course."

Anne lit a cigarette. "Do you mind?" She rolled down the window and took a deep drag on her cigarette. "I've told you before it wasn't because of you that Edward and I divorced. I know you may find this hard to believe but it was really because of me."

"You don't seem very…well, you don't seem too…I mean," Maya stopped, confused. "What I mean is, are you really sure it's okay?"

"I'd already decided to leave Edward when he met you," Anne blew smoke out the window. "And, okay, yes, I wasn't terribly happy that you happened to be the woman he wanted to marry after me."

Maya looked startled. "Really? Gosh, Anne, I'm sorry. I didn't think you minded. I…oh dear."

Anne pulled on the cigarette. "Don't worry. It's not a rational response. It was just one of those things. Anyway, I'm fine now." 'Liar,' Anne thought as she squashed her cigarette in the ashtray and looked out of the window. Although it really hadn't been Maya's fault that she and Edward had divorced. Anne had to admit that that wasn't the case so why should she resent Maya? 'Because she seduced Edward with her beauty,' Anne thought bitterly. 'How could I compete with her? With my scarred thigh, my limp, my ruined womb. Of course he would prefer her. Any man would.' Angrily, Anne lit another cigarette.

As the taxi wound through the chaos of avenues and monuments, buildings and fountains that she only vaguely remembered experiencing so many years ago, Anne felt her anger dissolve into a familiar frisson of pleasure. They passed the Basilica of Santa Maria degli Angeli and then circled the Piazza delle Repubblica where she had had a glass of wine with some man whose name she had forgotten. They turned down the Via Nazionale and Anne saw the team of pawing horses that topped Mussolini's "Wedding Cake" monument. She wondered if they were going to go through the Piazza Venezia but the taxi veered to the right, the horses disappeared and they continued down winding streets until they reached the Corso Vittorio Emanuele II.

She leaned back against the seat. She was tired. Rome, the Eternal City. Had it really been nineteen years since she had last been here? It seemed so familiar as though she had returned home after having left just days before. They crossed the Ponte Umberto I to the opposite side of the Tiber heading towards the Vatican. The sun shone with the same intense, bright light so familiar from her memories of that summer long ago. She could smell the cloying odor of garbage baking in the searing heat that intensified the exhaust fumes on the crowded streets and she wondered why more taxis didn't have air conditioning. Anne finished her cigarette and flipped it out the window. She could feel Maya's disapproval but she didn't care.

The Hotel Alimandi had been recommended by a friend who traveled often to Rome. "It's not the most convenient location but the brothers who run it are very nice and there's a wonderful garden on the roof." Not that that was going to appeal to her, Anne thought grimly. They arrived in the Piazza del Risorgimento. "Risorgimento," Anne spoke up suddenly. "It reminds me of regurgitation."

Maya smiled at her, looking relieved. "That's not what it means, darling."

"Doesn't it? Well, it should. Just look at all those people standing in a line around the walls of the Vatican. Like a line of saliva dribbled from St. Peter's mouth, snaking around a great double chin."

"You always did have a strange way of seeing things, Anne."

Anne laughed suddenly and looked at Maya. "Do you think so? Considering how fat most of the popes were I think it's a pretty good metaphor. Maybe I can use it in my lecture on the Sistine Ceiling."

They arrived at the hotel where Maya insisted on carrying Anne's bags inside. Stiff from the long train ride, Anne limped painfully up the steps to reception. The man who registered her was cool but polite. He handed Anne a note and a small bouquet of flowers. They were from Geraldo telling her he would pick her up at 8:00 that evening for dinner.

"You must be tired," Maya said seeming almost shy.

"I am." Anne hesitated. "Thanks for meeting me at the train station. You didn't have to do that."

"I wanted to. I'll see you tomorrow night in Florence, then." They hugged rather awkwardly.

Anne's room was small with a private shower, a toilet and the inevitable bidet. Anne remembered soaking her feet for hours in this strange bowl trying to cleanse them of ingrained dirt. She had never figured out how to use it properly. Maya had often made fun of her though she had been little cleaner, walking about in her flip-flops and jeans. They had had such fun exploring Rome, fending off the good-natured attempts at seduction, sharing a crush on Edward who had been one of the young professors on the tour and now it looked like they would share him as a husband. Anne sighed. What difference did it make if Edward and Maya were engaged? Even if she did miss him she didn't want to go back, she could never go back.

Anne opened the window wider, showered and hung up her clothes. There was no air conditioning but a ceiling fan stirred the air so that it felt quite agreeable in spite of the heat. She placed the flowers in a small water glass on the table before the mirror across from her bed. The freesias and camellias filled the room with a delicate scent. Sitting cross-legged on the bed, Anne stared at them and at her reflection behind them in the looking glass. She saw dark eyes, puffy from lack of sleep, a large nose, thin lips. Add a skull and a photograph and she could be looking into a still life by Audrey Flack. Shivered glass, a skull, a photograph, doomed flowers—her memento mori seemed a trifle insipid and frighteningly prophetic. She was being characteristically neurotic. After all, what could go wrong? But she still wondered why John had contacted her after all these years. What could be his motive for asking her to help him?

Anne turned away from the mirror. She ordered a taxi to take her to the Spanish Steps. Rising in three levels, topped by the two spires of the Church of the Trinita dei Monti, they provided spacious public seating for people watching, sunbathing, and daydreaming. Palm fronds whispered above the cornice of the building where Keats had died. His apartment was maintained as a shrine to romantic heroes, to poetry, to the melancholy romanticism of the nineteenth century—mostly empty now that tastes had shifted to more immediate and less demanding quests.

Anne sat down in a relatively unpopulated area and spread her skirt over her knees. It had been right about here, on the second tier of steps, that she had met Charlie. It had been her first night in Rome and she and Maya had been accosted by a group of young Italians. Maurizio, a good-looking boy, had claimed Anne for himself but she had been attracted to the mysterious Charlie. Dressed in black, his dark sunglasses hiding his eyes, he had kept aloof from the others. For some reason he and Maurizio had walked Anne and Maya back to the hotel. It couldn't have been solicitous concern. From the first Anne had realized that Charlie lacked the capacity to care for others.

The hotel had had what had been described as a "roof garden" in the brochure but which had turned out to be a flat asphalt terrace on which Claudia had badly burned her breasts when she fell asleep sunbathing topless. The four of them had gone up to the roof where they had seen John and Hawk and Ben sitting on folding chairs, drinking from bottles of cheap whiskey. Big, barely twenty, gaunt and gangly, with greasy brown hair and melancholy brown eyes, John had been in love with Anne since he was seventeen. She had told him, on the train from Paris, that she didn't want to sleep with him anymore. Drunk since they had arrived at the hotel that afternoon, (drunk since she had known him really) John had smashed his fist through the small glass panel on Anne and Maya's door when they wouldn't let him into their room.

John had turned to look at them as they emerged, laughing, onto the terrace. Stinking of alcohol, he staggered over, grabbed Anne's arm and told Charlie and Maurizio to 'fuck off.' Anne pushed John away and pulled on Charlie's arm, trying to get him to go back downstairs. Charlie shrugged her off and picked up a chair in both hands.

"What chou say?" he asked in a soft voice. Maurizio spoke to him in Italian but Charlie spat something back that made Maurizio shut up. The rest of the group waited expectantly.

John smiled sweetly at Charlie. "I told 'chou' to fuck off."

Holding the chair above his head, Charlie swung it toward John but, drunk as he was, John anticipated the move and stepped to one side. The chair smashed and splintered on the asphalt rooftop. Maurizio grabbed an empty bottle and threw it at John, hitting him above the eye. John's two friends picked up their chairs and began swinging them in arcs forcing Charlie and Maurizio back toward the door leading off the rooftop.

"Stop it, John. Charlie! Stop," Anne had said, infuriated with them and with her sense of helplessness.

Turning to go for help, Maya had run into the Hotel Manager who came, puffing and red-faced, up the stairs. Just as he arrived Charlie grabbed one of the chairs and flung it. Missing John, it sailed over the parapet and landed with a crash on the sidewalk below. A couple of cars squealed in the street. John, blood streaming down his face from the gash over his eye, staggered to his feet with one of the bottles of wine, which he smashed on the parapet then waved threateningly in Charlie's direction.

***

A shadow fell across the step where she was sitting and Anne sensed that someone was watching her. Looking up, she emitted a small cry. "Charlie?" she said incredulous.

CHAPTER FIVE

"Let me remind you again that when you are looking
at a picture you can't be like the girls on the Via
Veneto who walk the streets waiting for it to happen.
You have to get off your fanny and *make* it happen.
In Michelangelo's 'Tondo Doni' he plays on the
intellectual division between the sacred and the profane,
between heaven and earth, the spiritual and the material.
He's not just telling a familiar story, he's reinterpreting
humanity in God's image which is male, of course.
Virtue means 'manly' and God is virtuous above all,
at least, in Michelangelo's theological world view."
(Edward Donant)

"Mi scusi."

He must have been standing there for several seconds. Immediately after she spoke Anne realized that this man wasn't Charlie. He was dark and slender with muscular forearms but there the similarity stopped. His hair was too elegantly cut, he was dressed too nicely to be Charlie. Anne squinted up at him, the sun shining full in her face. "You're the man I ran into in the train station this morning."

"Si. I wanted to speak to you then but I was waiting for someone."

"How did you find me here?"

"Purely by accident."

"Oh."

"What did you think? That I had followed you?"

"No, of course not, it just seems odd that I would see you twice in one day."

"These things happen in Rome. Have you visited our *bella citta* before?"

"Yes. A long time ago."

"You like Rome?"

"I love it. Your English is very good."

"Grazie. I don't usually approach strange women but I thought it would be interesting to see whether you were as intelligent as you are attractive."

"Oh dear. A challenge." Anne stood up, brushing off the back of her skirt. "Why can't you just try to pick me up like a normal Italian male?"

"Is that normal? I'm afraid it's not for me."

Anne felt ashamed at her assumption. Of course, not all Italian men went around trying to pick up women. "You're right. That was presumptuous of me. I'm sorry."

He laughed. "Va bene. I actually did want to meet you. I just said that because you assumed I was like 'all Italian men.' We're really not all like that, you know."

She raised her eyebrows. "So, what you're saying is that I was right."

He laughed again charmingly and followed Anne as she walked down the steps.

"What do you do in Rome," Anne asked. "Teach English?"

"You're not far off. I'm a professor at the American University here. But I teach history." He took her arm firmly as Anne stumbled a bit on a step.

"Really! Another coincidence. I'm here to lecture for the University this summer."

He stopped. "What is your name?"

"Anne Langlais."

He laughed again. He had an infectious laugh. "I am Antonio Tani. I'm supposed to dine with you tonight with my colleague, Geraldo."

Anne looked at him curiously. "How extraordinary." He really was very good-looking and he smelled delicious. Anne had a weakness for men who wore cologne.

He smiled warmly at her. "Extraordinarily pleasant."

Anne gently pulled her arm away. "So, why is it that your English is so good?"

"I went to high school in America, in San Francisco."

"That's a beautiful city."

"Yes, but it's not for me. I prefer Roma."

They walked on together. Antonio took Anne's arm lightly again and guided her around a tight group of men. "Did you like the little bouquet we sent you?"

"It was lovely. Thank you."

He accompanied her to a taxi stand.

"Well, I look forward to seeing you this evening." Anne shook hands with him. "It's really funny meeting here like this, don't you think?"

"But very nice," he said charmingly. "A sta sera, see you tonight."

Anne settled into the taxi with a sense of confidence and anticipation that she realized was probably misplaced. After all, Antonio had only recognized her as the woman from the train station, it was natural that he would stop to talk to her and the dinner was just a business affair, arranged so that she could meet some of her colleagues.

21

She raised her head to see the reflection of her face in the rear view mirror. Her eyes met those of the taxi driver who smiled cheerfully. "Bellissima." He had shifted the angle of the mirror so that he could watch her in the back seat. Anne smiled back. She remembered Charlie doing something similar. Regarding her through the mirrored panes of his sunglasses. Always catching her unawares. Antonio had just done the same thing, she realized but this had been a pleasant surprise. He was very sexy, she thought. He was the first man since she had left Edward who had aroused her interest. She straightened in the seat and pressed her lips together. What difference did it make if he was attractive or not? After all, he was just another professor at the University; he had only stopped to talk to her because he had recognized her from the train station. Still, he had said that she was attractive...Anne smiled at the memory, pleased at the thought that they would be dining together that evening.

***

After leaving Anne, Maya went to the Piazza della Rotunda. She shivered as she crossed the threshold between the huge doors leading to the chilly interior of the Pantheon. It had been a mistake to meet Anne at the station. Maya had been so looking forward to seeing her and Anne's coolness had been so disappointing. Not at all what she had hoped for. Tears gathered in the corners of Maya's eyes and she brushed them away.

Standing in the center of the ancient building, Maya gazed around her, her eyes gradually adjusting to the dim light. Built in the early second century AD, its design attributed to the Emperor Hadrian, the Pantheon is an impressive structure in which, like everything Italian, everything Catholic, the sacred mixes with the profane. Originally dedicated to all the gods, the great space soars up to the oculus, carrying with it human aspiration and despair, mythological lust and religious metamorphosis.

Restless, Maya left the temple and walked to the Piazza Navona. She didn't want to think about anything right now, she just wanted to be distracted from all of her confused feelings—about Anne, about Edward, about getting married. She sat down at a small table on the terrace of the Bar Tre Scalini and watched the tourists around Bernini's "Fountain of Four Rivers." A young man in loafers and an open-necked shirt walked aimlessly around the fountain and crossed casually to a bench which was directly in front of Maya where he sat, staring fixedly at her. Maya shifted irritably in her seat, thirsty and out of sorts with this unwanted attention. Where was the waiter in this café? Ignoring the young man, she looked around the piazza.

This had been Domitian's "Circus Agonalis;" for centuries it had remained a stage for jousting, for flooded festivals, and the spectacle of Roman carnality and color. The colors of Rome—the deep golden-baked stone, the brilliant sun, the mauve color of the heat that rose in steaming spirals from the pavement in the early evening, the pale blue wash of sky on stone that turned to deep lilac in the night—these harmonized perfectly with the sounds of fountains splashing, of car horns and shrill sirens, and strident voices raised in conversation. Young men and women on their Vespas zoomed past Maya, the scent of the familiar exhaust fumes adding to the colorful, human circus that now dominated the piazza. A handsome young man appeared suddenly at her side.

"Oh," Maya jumped. "You scared me."

"Mi scusi," he smiled at her, he had a very thick accent that she couldn't immediately place. "I've been watching you. That man over there can't take his eyes off of you. You need to be careful."

"Of what?" Maya spoke coldly as she stood up to leave the café.

"Of men like me trying to pick you up."

Maya laughed at that and turned to look at him. He was very handsome—tall, fair, with broad shoulders and long legs. "You're not Italian. Where are you from?"

"Russia. Come with me. I have my motorcycle over here."

He had just bought the motorcycle, he told her. It had shiny gray paint and a long, black seat. "Do you know how much this cost?"

"Ummm, well, ummm, five thousand? Three thousand? Two thousand?" Maya had no idea.

"Three thousand. *Dollars*. Can I take you anywhere? Have you been to the Borghese gardens?"

Maya looked at him thoughtfully. "I'd appreciate a ride back to my apartment if you don't mind."

"It would be my pleasure. Be careful," he said as she climbed on the back behind him, "You can scratch the paint with your high heels." Pressing her hands against his groin, "I just ate lunch. I'm too full. You must hold me here.

Maya gave him directions to her apartment but he insisted he had to go to his place first. Resigned, Maya clung to him as he sped through the streets of Rome.

"Come up for a minute. You can have a glass of water. I've got to get my tennis racket. I'm playing a match this afternoon."

Reluctantly, Maya followed him up the stairs. She went to the bathroom only to return to find him half nude, waiting for her in his bedroom.

"I don't want to have sex," she told him firmly as he pulled her to him. "I'm engaged."

"I just want to hold you," he said. "So that I can dream of you tonight."

His name was Sergei, he was a model who scorned modeling. "If you want to get anywhere you can't stay in modeling. It's just easy money. Besides they're all gay. If you want to be a singer you've got to compromise yourself with some gay. I hate gays."

"Are there many gay men in Rome?"

Sergei snorted with disgust. "Millions."

"Oh."

This after he masturbated in front of her. Maya turned her head away. He came all over her new dress. She pulled away from him, feeling used and annoyed and a bit afraid.

"Let's make love," he said, reaching for her but Maya shook her head, eager to get out of his apartment, away from him.

"No. I need to go home," she said. "I'll take a taxi."

"No, I'll take you." He zipped up his pants and combed his tousled blonde hair. Maya followed Sergei down the stairs to his motorcycle. "I'm going to be a recording star," he said as they got on the bike. He sang a snatch of Paul Simon's "Fifty Ways To Leave Your Lover" as an example of something. Perhaps he meant she had several ways of leaving Edward or perhaps he meant it in reference to his California girlfriend or, maybe, it was only supposed to exemplify his singing ability. Whatever it was Maya was determined not to see him again. She crushed the piece of paper with his number on it and let it drop as they careened around a corner.

CHAPTER SIX

"Who can resist the exquisite beauty of Raphael's 'Sistine Madonna?' You may be sick of seeing those adorable putti leaning on the parapet, their eyes rolled back in their heads, which have been reproduced ad nauseum on posters throughout Rome, but where else do you find such simple yet compelling images of feminine and cherubic beauty?"
(Edward Donant)

Once again Maya found herself with the day to spend on her own. She and Edward had arrived in Florence late the night before. She wanted Edward to accompany her to one of the museums. "I've got to meet a gentleman, darling," Edward told her. "Why don't you go to the Bargello? It shouldn't be as crowded as the Accademia."

"Oh, Edward, can't you even spend one day with me?" Maya had wrapped her arms around him but he had insisted that he could not.

She had barely seen Edward since she had arrived in Rome until the night before they left for Florence when he had surprised her, bringing home a bottle of Illuminati Riparosso and making spaghetti alla puttanesca. Edward always did the cooking when they ate at home and it was always delicious. He said that he found cooking a rejuvenating act, one that allowed him to transcend the banal problems of the everyday. One of the aspects he had hated most about growing up in an orphanage had been the fact that he had had to eat institutional food, rarely interspersed with meals out and those of the lowest order; McDonald's, Burger King and the occasional meal at Morrison's Cafeteria. "I determined that, when I became independent," Edward told Maya, "I would eat only the finest cuisine. Even if I had to steal in order to do so."

Maya walked to the Bargello, wearing high-heeled sandals and a spaghetti-strap summer dress in a soft rose hue. She always felt mystically romantic when she visited museums, a notion that she avoided analyzing for fear that it would reveal itself as trite. Inside the building, it was cool and dark. The sturdy piers that supported the weight of this medieval building reminded her of the cloistered chambers of Mont St. Michel. She wandered beneath the loggia in the courtyard looking at the big, dumpy statues by Ammanati, one of Cellini's contemporaries.

Walking through the spacious rooms of the thirteenth century building, so surprisingly empty of tourists, Maya passed Verrocchio's statue of "David" before she found her favorite sculpture: the "David" that Donatello had created. Self-satisfied, he looked down at her from beneath the plumed hat that was rakishly tilted across his forehead, his curls carefully arranged around his face. Naturally, although he looked down at her, he didn't see her or acknowledge her presence. His was a narcissistic victory; even Goliath's head beneath his foot was an accessory to his pose rather than proof of his courage. Curiously effeminate, he seemed to toy with the head like some macabre transvestite in a Gothic horror film. It was this strange amalgam of violence and effeminacy, of heroic legend and theatrical superficiality that drew her to the sculpture. What a vast difference there was between this saucy, self-satisfied figure and Donatello's earlier "David" with his vacant, staring eyes and awkward cloak.

It was almost noon when Maya felt that she could justify halting her cultural expedition to find a restaurant for lunch. She returned to the courtyard via the portico leading to the stone staircase and descended it in a self conscious, sweeping motion; her head held high, her shoulders back, her hands almost coquettishly posed by her sides. She noticed two guards watching her, their dark faces suddenly invisible as the glare of the noonday sun nearly blinded her. She liked seeing men watching her but it unnerved her when their faces disappeared. Defensively, she put on her Vuarnets.

Outside the Bargello the heat was pleasant, not too intense and the sun shone in a spotless, blue sky. Maya went to Gilli, the famous café where Ruth Orkin had taken the photo of the beautiful, young American student walking haughtily past a line of laughing, whistling men. Maya had always been fascinated by this image, a copy of which she hung above the toilet in her bathroom. When she had first seen it she had assumed that some man, who had been enjoying a lecherous moment in a piazza at some poor woman's expense, had taken it. It wasn't until much later that she had learned the photographer was a woman and that she had arranged the whole scene with the young student. So that, instead of the young woman being represented as trapped within the clichéd role as object of desire and derision, it had been male desire that had been exposed for what it was—predatory and easily manipulated.

Maya sat at one of the tables outside the cafe. Hedges surrounded the terraced area, separating it from the broad expanse of the piazza that was bathed in a shimmering veil of heat that seemed to have intensified since she left the Bargello. At each opening of the hedge a cypress, twisted like a baroque column, stood sentinel in its pot. Vespas and Fiats maneuvered through the crowds of tourists meandering up and down the Via Roma that bordered the piazza. Exhaust fumes mixed with the more elegant odors of roast chicken and balsamic vinaigrette that wafted from a nearby table. Crossing her legs, Maya watched the men in their business suits leaving their offices for a long lunch. She wondered how they managed it—walking in the sun in their dark suits and jackets: unruffled, unwrinkled, and apparently sweat-free. She herself noticed the uncomfortable familiarity of perspiration beginning to trickle down her armpits. And then there were all of these good-looking young men with longish black hair, black sunglasses, white shirts rolled up to the elbow, white teeth. Voracious, they glanced her way, their reflective lenses passing across her figure like undulating waves.

Her food arrived and, as Maya cut tiny morsels of the mozzarella and tomato, she wondered if she was fated to spend her days in Europe eating lonely lunches. She ate sparingly, stopping often to sip her wine and watch the patrons of the cafe. The terrace was gradually filling up, mostly with tourists; American, French, Italian, Japanese.

She was going to see Anne again that night and she hoped that they would be able to talk. She was such an old, dear friend, she was Maya's only female friend and now...Maya hoped that Anne would fall in love with another man so they could be good friends again. 'I really am awfully selfish,' she told herself but she was distracted from this thought by a sign advertising "Cinzano," which was erected on the balcony across the piazza on the facade of the "Albergo Olimpia." Cinzano had been one of John's favorite drinks, that and whiskey. John had been so in love with Anne, so drunk with love, crazy with love for her. It had been terrible that night when Anne had fallen from the roof. Maya shuddered at the memory of visiting Anne in the hospital. She hadn't known what to say and Anne had just lain there, pale and so thin she looked as though she would break. Anne hadn't said a word other than good bye but her eyes had held a look of such anguish that Maya had gone to the airport feeling guilty as though she had somehow been responsible for the accident. Anne had had to remain in Rome for several weeks after the rest of the group had returned to America. The doctors had been afraid to move her and it had been several months before Anne could walk again.

Maya paid her bill and walked out to the Via Roma that cut along the edge of the piazza. As she started to step out into the street a motorcycle suddenly bore down on her with ferocious intent, the driver invisible behind his black helmet. Shocked, Maya was unable to move before the man leaned over and snatched her purse from her shoulder. Thrown off balance she stumbled on her heels, one of the rosy straps falling from her shoulder. Someone grabbed her, supporting her and asking if she were all right. She looked up confused and angry.

27

"All right!? That man could have killed me! And he took my purse!" She rubbed her shoulder, amazed at the realization that her purse was gone.

"Si, si, I know. Mi scusi, signora." Others around her were nodding angrily, gesticulating and discussing the incident.

"He had a knife," someone was saying.

"He took her purse," another said.

"What a bastard."

"You need to report it to the police. I will call them."

"No, no, grazie." Maya shook her head. "Ma...Grazie. Molto grazie, signore."

"Well, at least let me help you to sit down. You are in shock." Maya allowed herself to be led back to Gilli. "What would you like? Some tea?" Without waiting for her response, he ordered for her.

"But I can't pay," Maya protested. "He took my purse." She felt as though she were going to cry. She hadn't had much money but her credit cards and her passport—they had all been in her bag. She pressed her face into her hands.

"It's no problem, signora." The man paid her bill, assured himself again that she was all right, and disappeared. The maitre'd fussed over her. Maya shuddered as she took a sip of the tea. She had been lucky really. He wouldn't have minded slicing her arm as long as he got her purse. She was unused to such violent disregard of her beauty and it altered a bit her sense of confidence. If men on motorcycles raced by dragging purses from women what did that say about those who walked by with compliments? Was something to be stolen there as well? Maya began to laugh and the maitre'd looked at her in concern. Of course, there was. Wasn't that always the case?

CHAPTER SEVEN

"What is beauty? How do you define the beautiful?
Each century has a different idea. I suppose you
could say health and youth are always beautiful.
But beauty can be old, too. Or is that character?
Sad, how we've separated the two. That same old
duality; spirit and flesh, the beautiful and the ugly,
the immortal and the corruptible. But there's
always a twist. The erosion of the flesh is as
nothing to the corruption of the spirit. One is
temporal whereas the other is eternal."
(Edward Donant)

Anne was shown to a table on the terrace of "Rivoire" in the Piazza della Signoria. Situated directly across from the Palazzo Vecchio, the café was always crowded with tourists and it was no different this evening. She ordered a bottle of Veuve Clicquot champagne, poured a glass and raised it in a salute to Florence. Maya and Edward should be arriving shortly—she needed the champagne to calm her nerves. It had been a year since she had seen Edward and she wondered if he had any regrets about their divorce or about his engagement to Maya. 'Probably not,' Anne told herself ruefully.

She had arrived in Florence late that morning and had spent the afternoon looking at Masaccio's frescoes in the Church of Santa Maria Novella and the Brancacci Chapel. Her thoughts shifted to the Caravaggio the three of them were going to see that evening. Anne knew little about the painting except that it was a depiction of Christ's "Crucifixion" and that it had been discovered in a Capuchin church in Messina where it had apparently lain in the basement for centuries. It was in very poor condition when discovered, dirty and torn. The lower right side of the canvas had been so damaged that it was irreparable. However, after meticulous cleaning and superficial analysis it had been tentatively declared an original Caravaggio and put on view as a possible new masterpiece prior to more serious analysis. Of course, there would be further investigation after it was taken down but there seemed little doubt that it was original. In support of this was the fact that, while Caravaggio was in Messina, he had been given a private commission to represent Christ's passion on four canvases. None of these canvases had ever been seen or described, although it had been recorded that one had been executed and it was believed that this was the work. Why it had been spirited out of sight was perplexing. Anne could only assume that the church had removed it because of some imagined impropriety (just as "The Death of the Virgin" had been rejected by the Fathers of Santa Maria della Scala in Rome) and that it had then been forgotten.

It would be thrilling to actually see the work. She knew perfectly well why she and Edward had been invited. The Italian government wanted the painting legitimized and the presence of many so-called authorities in the field was just one of the means they would use to insure the painting's authenticity. There was always that underlying question of authenticity, which arose whenever a work by a great master was so serendipitously "discovered."

A blue sky arched over the Palazzo Vecchio, magnificent clouds touched by the rose hues of a slowly setting sun appeared like some Baroque fantasy on a limitless ceiling. There were no angels, no chariots or cherubim yet it was permeated with the promise of eternal glory. A stage had been set up in front of the Loggia della Signoria. Vivaldi was playing from loudspeakers while men in jeans and t-shirts checked the sound system and busied themselves on stage. Vivaldi, blue sky, the possibility that she would be seeing a long-lost Caravaggio—suddenly Anne was filled with a sense of anticipation; of endless sensual and spiritual possibilities. She lit a cigarette and savored the moment.

Dinner the night before had been fun. Anne feared that she had drunk too much wine and that she had acted silly. Had it been obvious that she found Antonio attractive? He had been attentive and she had felt ebullient, almost rapturous with the combination of the soft Roman summer night, the wine and the feeling that she was beautiful. But now, as she thought about it more soberly, she realized that Antonio had given her no reason to imagine he was particularly interested in her. Still, she couldn't have mistaken the way he had looked at her while they were drinking coffee. She had turned to see him staring intently at her. The pull between them had been intense and, shaken by the strength of her attraction to him she had been the first to turn away, laughing unsteadily at some comment Geraldo had made.

Anne glanced up to see Maya standing by the hedge that enclosed the terrace. She was dressed in a long silver gown, which looked as though it had been poured over her slender body. Anne stood up and waved to her. Maya grinned and waved back enthusiastically. Anne watched her weave between the tightly packed tables. Staring after her, a waiter tripped over a man's foot and dropped his tray. The man's companion squealed and rose to brush off her dress while the waiter and the man gazed after Maya who arrived at Anne's table impervious to the disturbance she had created in her wake. It was so typical of Maya that Anne laughed as Maya hugged her. "You do know how to make an entrance, don't you darling? How on earth did you get here unmolested in that outfit?"

Maya grinned and struck a movie star pose. "It is a sexy dress, isn't it? But you know how much I love attention. Anyway, one of Edward's friends walked with me so it was no problem."

The waiter brought them another glass and, placing his hand over his heart, sighed melodramatically. Maya laughed and blew him a kiss.

"Where is Edward?"

"Oh, he had a phone call just as we were leaving. He promised he'd come as soon as he could but I came on because I couldn't wait to see you."

Anne smiled skeptically and lit another cigarette. She left it planted in one corner of her lips as she poured champagne into each of their glasses. "When did you get to Florence? How was your trip?"

"Last night. It was actually very nice." Maya raised her glass and clinked it with Anne's. "Cin, cin."

"Did you take the train?"

"No, we drove up in Edward's new toy."

"Oh God. What kind of car does he have now?"

"Not just a car! An adorable Porsche; a 356 restored sc Cabriolet. I found it in Paris and had it shipped to Rome. I bought it for him for his birthday." Maya smiled slyly at Anne. "And for a very good price."

"Really Maya, you shouldn't do those kinds of things." Maya's extravagance often irritated Anne. In all fairness she supposed it was because Maya had never had to work for the money she spent so carelessly.

"What kinds of things? You mean spending money on someone I love? I'd do the same for you, you know."

"I wouldn't let you," Anne flipped the ashes off her cigarette. "And I think it's tacky of Edward to encourage you."

"Why do you say that?" Maya looked puzzled. "He didn't even know about it. It was a surprise."

Anne shrugged. "Well, I'm sure you made him very happy."

"I did." Maya stared at Anne. "But that's not what you mean, is it? You really mean you think he's taking advantage of me."

Anne said nothing.

"You think that Edward's only with me because of my money." Maya tossed her head. "Well, it's not true. He loves me."

Anne puffed on the cigarette. That was exactly what she had meant. "I'm sorry I said anything. It's your money and you should do what you want to with it. And of course, Edward loves you."

"I know he loves me and I love him," Maya said defensively. "But you know how insecure I am—about my money and men and everything. Why would you say something like that?"

"I didn't say anything about him wanting to be with you for your money, Maya. I just said that I thought you needed to be careful about Edward or anyone taking advantage of you. But it's none of my business and you're right, I have no right to say things like that."

Maya sighed again. "It's just…I'm just afraid that I'm not really worthy of him."

"Oh, please Maya." Anne spoke sharply. "Don't be ridiculous. Not good enough for Edward!"

"Do you honestly think he's only interested in me because of my money?" Maya looked vulnerable as she leaned earnestly toward Anne.

"If you're really worried about that then I think what you mean to say is he's not worthy of you."

"No, no. I know it's not true."

"Well, then you needn't worry."

"And I bought the car for him because I wanted to. It was his birthday and I wanted to do something really special." Maya had regained her composure. She smiled confidently at Anne.

"Oh, yes, Edward's birthday. God forbid you should forget his birthday—a sacred day. Well, no one can fault you for being generous." Anne leaned back in her chair and dropped the smoldering butt of her cigarette on the terrace.

"I don't give away anything that doesn't also benefit me." Maya laughed. "You know how much I love sports cars and how much I *hate* to drive. And who else would feel obligated to escort me if not my beloved? So, I guess you can't credit me with generosity but it's a nice thought." The waiter winked at her and she smiled back.

"Did you read about the bombing?" The waiter poured more champagne for each of them.

"Which bombing?" Maya polished one of her fingernails with her napkin.

"The most recent one, just a few days ago. The antiques shop."

"Yes, of course. With all the bombings in Italy I wonder why anyone would want to bomb an antiques shop. All those lovely Meissen and Dreissen and whatever smashed into smithereens. Difficult to find a political motive in *that*."

"Maybe they're radical contemporary artists who want to destroy any connection with the past." Anne lit another cigarette, blew out a ring of smoke and watched it evaporate on the light breeze that had suddenly emerged.

"Or maybe they just can't stand Meissen. Those little figurines—ugh! Oh, sorry," Maya looked suddenly remorseful. "Your mother collected things like that, didn't she?"

Anne blew out a plume of smoke. "You know that I don't share my mother's taste," she said shortly.

Maya waved the smoke away from her face. "Do you remember the first night we arrived in Rome? And Charlie and John got in that terrible fight? I thought they were going to kill each other."

Anne shook her head and, as usual, thin tendrils of her hair fell into her eyes. "John's always been a stupid man."

"I think it was romantic. John was jealous, he loved you." Maya was looking toward the piazza as she said this.

"Good God, Maya, he was *drunk*! That's hardly romantic." Anne followed Maya's gaze to where a couple of men in dark suits were standing, staring at the two women. "Do you know those men?"

"No, but they're awfully good-looking, don't you think? Especially the one with the white shirt." Maya smiled and the men turned to confer with one another.

"Oh, good grief, Maya. Now you've encouraged them."

"I did no such thing," Maya turned her back to them and picked up her glass. "I was just being pleasant."

"You know very well that they think they have the right to talk to us now. Oh Christ, here comes one of them." Anne gritted her teeth.

"Buona sera, bella regazze." The one Maya liked had approached them. "Would you mind if my friend and I joined you? It is so crowded here and there is no place for us to sit." He waved his hand at the packed terrace.

Maya smiled at him. "I wish we could accommodate you but I'm afraid my fiancé would not be pleased to see you here when he arrives."

"Ah," he looked disappointed and then he bowed slightly. "He is a very lucky man."

Nodding at both of them, he returned to his companion who was waiting on the piazza.

Maya smiled at Anne. "No harm done, you see. He just wanted a place to sit."

"Oh, right!"

Maya looked unperturbed. "Really, Anne, you're no fun anymore. And don't pretend that you never did anything like that. What about that night in Florence when you seduced all those guys?"

Anne crushed the butt of her cigarette on the terrace beneath the heel of her shoe. "It was a long time ago."

"You were wandering around the hotel terrace, holding a bottle of wine, flirting with them. I thought John was going to have a fit."

Anne blushed. "I really was awful and proud of myself for being awful. I remember I stopped one of them on the stairs. I was standing above him and I leaned down and kissed him and told him he was 'molto bello.' Holding that bottle in my hand. He must have thought it was an invitation."

"Well, gee, what did you think he'd think?"

"I didn't really think, I just felt like I should be able to flirt and be aggressive if I wanted to. Guys do it, why can't women was what I thought. Of course, I realized later that when men flirt they're usually hoping to or willing to have sex and I wasn't. I just didn't think much further than adjusting the balance. I never thought they'd take it so seriously or that they would attack us."

"And John and Hawk rescued us when those guys forced their way into our room." Maya laughed.

"Poor thing. You didn't even have anything to do with it. I really felt bad. They hated me after that. They'd be sitting on their scooters in the piazza, watching us, waiting for a chance to get even. One of them came into the hotel lobby when we were waiting to go out one night. He grabbed me by the hair and jerked my head back and said something mean. I'm glad I couldn't understand what he said. I'm sure it was something awful." Anne finished the champagne in her glass.

"Ooh, terrible Anne. Tck, tck. Come on, it was funny, really. We had such a good time together." Maya poured out the rest of the champagne. "Isn't it amazing? To think that almost twenty years ago we were both here as students flirting outrageously, never imagining we would be coming back like this: you as a professor and a lecturer and both of us invited to an exclusive exhibition. Of course, I wouldn't be going if it weren't for Edward. Somehow I always knew you would do something important whereas here I am, just wasting my life: eating, drinking, following Edward around. Wouldn't my parents be proud of me." Maya made a lop-sided face at Anne.

"Of course they'd be proud of you. You're beautiful and intelligent. You've done a lot of things," Anne ended weakly, wondering what exactly Maya had done.

"Well, it doesn't matter, I guess. They're both dead now." Maya sounded sad and she looked away from Anne across the terrace of the café.

Anne watched the men moving large speakers onto the stage. Her parents were dead also; well, her father might as well be dead as often as she had seen him in the years since he had left them. She sipped her champagne. The incessant background chatter of Italian conversations soothed her. She looked at the couples seated around them. It was really depressing how you could always spot the Americans, she thought. They were inevitably dressed in drab, unattractive clothes or shorts and loud shirts. They made an unseemly contrast with the impeccably attired Italians. Maya smiled prettily at a man who was staring at her.

Anne looked in his direction. "I met a man at the train station yesterday."

"Aha."

"It was really kind of funny. I ran into him again on the Spanish Steps and it turns out that he's on the faculty of the American University. And, on top of that, I thought, at first, that he was Charlie. He looks sort of like him."

"Really?" Maya looked into a tiny mirror and applied lip-gloss.

"Isn't that sort of bizarre?"

"Are you going to call him? Charlie, I mean?"

Anne shook her head. "I don't even know his last name. I have no idea how to find him."

A pigeon fluttered onto their table and began to eat peanuts out of the bowl. Nineteen years ago Anne had sat at this same café. She was rather ashamed of the image of herself that she retained from that first summer of freedom. How she had flirted and shuffled about, wearing her spangled gypsy skirt and brave naiveté pinned haphazardly about her waist. She had erred when she had first come to Europe, assuming that her youthful ideals would triumph over centuries of intolerance, of prejudice, of moral rigidity. She had trod the cobbled streets in hippy regalia with a nineteen-seventies American optimism that must have astonished the world-weary Europeans. She had believed that the superficial was unimportant; that clothes, shoes, luggage, makeup were negligible aspects of character; not qualities by which she should be judged nor by which she should judge others. But she had been wrong. These are, after all, the indices of status, of class, an indication of a person's sense of self-worth.

She had fallen under Florence's spell the first time she had visited it. Entranced, she had wandered idly through the streets, stopping to talk to vendors, to listen to some Americans playing guitar on the steps of the cathedral. Her only focus, the space to which she had been drawn day after day, was the Medici Chapel. Inside the dim light emanated from a couple of low wattage bulbs. Characteristically, conversation dropped to a whisper as people walked down the stairs and into the small chapel. Anne had stood to one side, sinking into an underworld serenity muffled in soft murmuring voices and echoing footsteps. She had walked around Michelangelo's "Dawn," peering at it from different angles. There were the heavy, fleshy arms and thighs, the stuck-on breasts and those awful wrinkled stomachs. How ugly these women's bodies had seemed to her and yet they were appealing—strength coagulated in thickened folds of flesh. The arm upon which the exquisite head rested, had struck her as strangely tender and soft.

Surreptitiously, Anne had reached out and stroked the forearm, the lips and nose. Immovable, grand beyond any human care, the face had remained impassive and distant.

She had pulled out her notebook and sat on a high step where she had drawn for hours, carefully studying the lines, the shapes formed by the shadows. Ignoring the fact that she had touched the sculptures, the guard had admired her sketches and her perseverance—returning every day to draw the same figures from different perspectives. He had shown her drawings to visitors, demanding that they admire her line, her capacity to capture the image. He had brought her fruit. "You must eat if you want to be an artist." But she had never become an artist, only an observer, a 'deconstructor' of art.

Maya passed a hand in front of Anne's eyes. "What are you thinking about?"

"I was just remembering when I first came here. I was very naïve and very insecure. I felt as though I had to compete with the beauty of Florence. I don't quite know how to describe it. It was, in part, because I was American and, in part, because I was so in love with the city I felt as though I had to triumph over it or it would devour me."

"And did you triumph?"

"No. I'm afraid Florence won. Hands down."

"Speaking of the sinister side of Florence," Maya leaned toward Anne, turning her shoulder so that Anne could see the bruises on her arm.

"Good grief, Maya, how did that happen?"

"A man on a motorcycle stole my purse today. He just ripped it from my shoulder. He had a knife." She spoke almost triumphantly.

"How awful. And how lucky that you weren't hurt." Anne pulled out her pack of cigarettes, frowning.

"What's really amazing is that someone returned the purse to the hotel this evening. All of my money and credit cards were gone but my passport was still there." Maya swung her leg distractedly. "The man at the desk said that the man who returned it refused to leave his name or anything. He said that he had found it lying in the gutter on the side of the street so the guy must have just thrown it away. Oh, there's Edward." Maya stood up and waved as Edward made his way through the crowd to their table.

Putting his arms around her, Edward kissed Maya, then turned to Anne. She turned her head as he brushed his lips across her cheek. "It's lovely to see you, Anne. It's been so long. You must excuse me for being late. I see you didn't save me any champagne. Shall we order another bottle?" He spoke briefly to the waiter in Italian then seated himself between Anne and Maya.

He looked exactly the same. The white hair pulled back in a ponytail, the aquiline nose, the rumpled linen suit, the self-assured complacency. Anne was annoyed by her sense of discomfort. Her pulse had increased and her palms felt sweaty. Surely she hadn't stooped so low as to be jealous just because Edward loved Maya, she thought. She had always considered jealousy the most useless and destructive of emotions but she had been amazed at how intensely jealous Edward could make her. No, it wasn't jealousy, it was just that she hated his careless disregard of her feelings. Not only with Maya but by his comments about other women, his constant appraisal of beauty both male and female, her suspicions of his philandering while he grew less and less affectionate with her. Anne's mouth trembled and she lowered her eyes to look in her purse, pulling out her pack of cigarettes, firmly pushing back the self-pitying thoughts that crowded her conscious causing her brain to freeze. How long was it going to take before she could get out of this destructive mindset? Carefully, she removed and lit a cigarette. She would not give either of them the satisfaction of seeing her agitation. "Have you heard anything new about the exhibition? Have you talked to Valeriano?"

Edward sipped his champagne. "No, I've not had time to contact him but he'll be at the exhibition tonight."

Anne raised her eyebrows. "So I'll finally have the opportunity to meet him."

Edward nodded for the waiter to pour the champagne. "That is correct," he said and Anne thought it wasn't clear whether he was referring to what she had said or to the manner in which the waiter poured.

"I heard about Maya's purse. How lucky that she wasn't hurt."

"Yes, no harm done," Edward smiled genially at Maya. "Her beauty is intact and that's what counts, right, darling?"

Maya stared at him, shocked. "Really, Edward!"

"Speaking of beauty, don't you love Maya's dress, Anne? Don't you think she looks sexy?"

Maya sighed, exasperated. "You told me to wear whatever I wanted. 'Wear something sophisticated. Be as sexy as you want,' that's what you said. Now you make it sound as if I'm some sort of freak."

Edward flourished his hands as though they had come into contact with some contaminated object. "Not at all. I love to see you dressed up. Let's see you compete with Caravaggio. Why shouldn't you amuse yourself?"

CHAPTER EIGHT

"Leonardo da Vinci's 'Madonna of the Rocks' in the Louvre.
There's that beautiful angel again. He really grabs the viewer's
attention. The angel and the rocky background. The Madonna's
hand is poised over his outstretched finger which just touches
the invisible line descending from Mary's extended thumb to the
infant Christ's two raised fingers. It's no longer the simple logic
of a medieval passion play. It's more like a play by Brecht, it
exists on an existentialist plane. You think you've got it but you
haven't. The ever-receding horizon, the ever mysterious void."
(Edward Donant)

Anne almost tripped as she followed Maya and Edward up the stairs
to the Salone dei Cinquecento on the second floor of the Palazzo Vecchio.
A man put out a hand to catch her at the same time that Edward grasped
her arm. Anne caught her balance and pulled away from him. Legions of
men and women, some beautifully dressed, others in jeans and t-shirts,
were climbing the stairs and entering the cavernous chamber. Edward,
Maya and Anne followed two elderly women in furs, "In this heat," Maya
whispered to Anne, and a young man in a tuxedo jacket and blue jeans.

Maya was attracting a lot of attention in her silver dress. Anne had
on a long, black skirt and a black shirt with a high-necked collar. Her
only concession to the celebratory aspect of the occasion was a rhinestone
brooch pinned to her shoulder and rhinestone earrings. They made a rather
odd trio, Anne thought as she noticed people turning to look after them.

The painting was smaller than Anne had expected it would be. It
was set rather theatrically yet appropriately before a large, forest-green
velvet curtain in the front of the huge room. They regarded the work from
various perspectives, each in their own manner; Edward with gleeful
relish, remarking on tiny details, Anne quietly attentive, putting on her
reading glasses to peer more closely at certain points, and Maya dutifully
meticulous but with half an ear and eye perked for the flattering remarks
which were inevitably expressed as someone brushed by.

Several viewers had already commented on the impression that
Caravaggio had represented himself in Christ's haggard features. There
was the familiar bearded visage, the partially opened lips of Caravaggio's
self-portraits which he so often included in his paintings: the figure of the
man in the rear of "The Martyrdom of St. Matthew," and the features of
Goliath's decapitated head in Caravaggio's later work. But he had never

cast himself as a saint, certainly not as Christ—something that, Anne told herself, already brought into question the legitimacy of the work.

Standing back from the painting, Anne was repelled by the idea that Caravaggio could have identified himself with Christ. As though he had ever sacrificed his own desires and needs for the good of others or even cared about anyone but himself. Anne had identified with Christ when she was young. It had given her some consolation in her role as martyred daughter, envisioning herself sacrificing her own happiness and needs in order to make her mother happy, in order to let her father go. She had consciously associated her role with that of Christ because, she now saw, for her to identify with Christ was to idealize what had really been passive acquiescence, turning timidity into a virtuous act.

How dare Caravaggio project himself into the role of sacrificial victim? 'Here, then,' she thought, 'may be the reason the painting was removed from view and buried in the storage rooms of the church.' Anne frowned, looking more closely at the craquelure, the dark foundation, the muddy white of Christ's loincloth. There was something wrong with this painting; there was something not quite in sync with Caravaggio's style.

Edward pressed his hand against the small of Anne's back and maneuvered Maya and her to the back of the room where chairs had been set up. Anne allowed herself to be led by him, somewhat amused at the apparent ease with which he had resumed the role of guide and escort, somewhat annoyed at his presumption. She sat down on one of the chairs that had been placed about the room and looked around her. The hall was impressive, of course, though Anne found Vasari's frescoes, like all of his works, flat and dull. She recognized the statue by Michelangelo of "David with the Head of Goliath" and Donatello's statue of "Judith and Holofernes."

Farther down the room Anne saw the strange statue by Rosso Rossi of "Hercules and Diomedes." Rossi had sculpted two burly men wrestling in the nude. Hercules held Diomedes upside down in a vice-like grip so that Diomedes' huge genitals hung down his belly in a vertical line while he grasped Hercules' enormous member with his right hand. The subliminal sexuality of male contact sports made explicit, Anne thought, uncertain whether the lethal outcome of this encounter sublimated or emphasized the erotic overtones. Once again she found herself pondering the underlying homosexual tension that she often felt in a room full of men and once again she wondered if she were imposing this tension or if it actually existed. She had often wondered if Edward's excessive philandering wasn't a result of a repressed homosexual orientation. He certainly appreciated beauty whether it was expressed in male or female form. Anne realized that

Edward was discussing the composition of the painting and she turned her attention once again to the canvas at the opposite end of the room.

"It's interesting how it's really the reverse of the Impressionist paintings. The closer you get to, say, a Monet, the more abstract it becomes whereas the further away you get from this painting the more you're struck by the abstract composition. It's true of most of Caravaggio's late works."

"Ah, the artist is speaking," Maya murmured.

Edward raised his eyebrows. "Are you questioning my ability to comment on works of art?"

"Never, darling," Maya put her arm through his and gazed at him adoringly.

Irritated by the fact that she was irritated by this show of intimacy, Anne removed her glasses and gestured with them toward the painting. "Did you notice Christ's finger? It's in almost the same position as in his painting of 'The Calling of St. Matthew'..."

"...which was derived from Michelangelo's figure of Adam on the Sistine ceiling." Edward finished for her.

Maya looked again at the painting. "That's funny. I hadn't noticed before, but you're right. There seems to be a line between his forefinger and Mary Magdalene, almost like he's pointing at her."

Edward took two glasses from a tray as it passed and handed them to Anne and Maya. "St. Augustine referred to the Holy Spirit as the 'Finger of God.' Poor Jesus, his whole life was directed by the finger of God. Like the parent who says, 'I wouldn't lift a finger for you,' here you've got the great father who won't even help his son who's suffering on the cross."

Like my father, Anne thought bitterly. She recognized the signs of a bad mood; everything was getting on her nerves. She needed to pull herself together or she would say something she would regret.

"What about Mary Magdalene?" Maya asked. "Is Christ saying he won't lift a finger for her or is he pointing at her as though she's the one who has to bear the burden? Kind of like passing the buck."

Anne put her glasses back on. "In this case it almost looks as though he's pointing to her as though to say 'It's all your fault.' The old idea that through women men are born to suffer. Maybe the artist was expressing a repressed hatred and resentment toward women."

"I think you're projecting a bit there." Edward said. "We assume that Caravaggio had little desire for women but he certainly seemed aware that his suffering stemmed from his own character and the society in which he lived. He's never represented women in a way that would make you think he hated them. No, I think this must be read as a calling as in the painting of Matthew, or as a re-birth."

41

"Do you think it's original?" Maya asked.

Anne put her glass down and lit a cigarette. "I don't know whether the work is original or not but something about it bothers me. And I resent the idea that Caravaggio represented himself in the figure of the crucified Christ. It's really too much. I know the man could be arrogant but...you know I just thought of something. What if it were one of Caravaggio's contemporaries who painted this work? Someone who hated Caravaggio and crucified him in his own style? That would be rather neat."

Edward smiled and shook his head. "It's an interesting idea. I think that I'll withhold judgment on this issue."

"You shouldn't withhold your opinion," Anne said teasingly, "After all, you're the artist."

Edward turned to look at her. "What do you mean?"

Anne laughed. "That you're an artist, you idiot. What do you think I meant?"

Edward smiled. "I feared you were being sarcastic about my profession."

Anne stared at him, curious. Something was bothering him. Did Edward know something he wasn't telling them about this painting?

"Edward!" The three of them turned to see a distinguished-looking, older gentleman pushing his way through the crowd.

"Ciao, Valeriano." Edward shook hands with the man. "This is Valeriano Cerasi. He's the man who 'discovered' me."

"Of course." Anne held out her hand. "I've heard Edward speak of you but we've never met." So here was the man responsible for Edward's sudden success. Again Anne wondered what could have happened to cause Edward's paintings to fall so suddenly out of favor.

Valeriano smiled at Anne. "No, we've never met but I've had the pleasure of looking into your beautiful eyes on the train returning from Paris."

Anne looked at him more closely. "Oh my goodness! You're the man who was reading the paper on the train."

"This is Anne Langlais, my ex-wife," Edward laughed as though this was funny. "And this is my fiancée, Maya Kelly."

"I've heard Edward talk about you," Maya held out her hand but Valeriano had turned to look again at Anne.

"Anne Langlais." He frowned. "You've visited our country before, I believe."

Anne nodded, surprised. "Maya and I both came here a long time ago with a group of students from Emory University."

"Did you know a student named John Audet?"

"Yes." Anne paused as she pulled out a cigarette. "Why do you ask?"

Valeriano leaned forward with a match. "He's my son."

"Oh." Anne pulled furiously on her cigarette. So, this was John's father. How typical of John—he had never told her who is father was. "But I thought John was American."

"His mother was American. We've been divorced since he was three."

"Isn't that amazing, Anne?" Maya interrupted. "Anne and I were just talking about John and now we find out you're his father. What's he doing now?"

"He's living with me in Rome. His mother died."

"Oh," Maya murmured, "I'm so sorry."

"How are you doing, my dear?" Valeriano turned to Anne. "It was such an unfortunate accident."

She smiled stiffly. "Yes. I'm fine."

"So, Valeriano," Edward finished off his glass. "Tell me about the Caravaggio. I hear that you were lucky enough to find it in a church."

"Let's just say that I know someone who alerted me to the fact that he'd found an old painting, somewhat the worse for centuries of neglect. Of course, when I saw it I knew there was no question that it was a Caravaggio. It captures the grandiose melancholy of his late style."

"And, of course, you've taken all precautions to ascertain its validity. As any reputable dealer would do. Not only for the integrity of the profession but to safeguard your own reputation." Edward spoke casually.

Valeriano smiled at him. "We all need to be careful. No one would like to be in the position of promoting a fake."

Anne sipped her wine, trying to control her anger. That had been no accident; John had intended to kill her. She watched Valeriano and Edward. There was something wrong; they didn't trust each other. She wondered why. She was also curious as to what tests had been made on the Caravaggio. It was a bit odd that it had been exhibited prior to being fully tested and what a bizarre coincidence to discover that Valeriano was John's father. She studied him, deciding that the man on the train she had originally thought so elegant was in reality rather cheap and artificial, like the over-dressed criminals she remembered seeing on TV, entering and exiting courthouses during trials of financial fraud.

"Edward, do you remember Lors Svendquist? The Norwegian collector?" Valeriano handed his empty glass to a passing waiter. "He's always wanted to meet you and I received a message inviting me to see him tonight. Naturally, I thought of you…"

Edward shrugged. "I'd love to come with you."

"Good. He's not staying far from Florence. I'm afraid..." Valeriano turned apologetically to Anne and Maya.

"Oh, we have other plans, right Anne? We're going back to 'Rivoire' to pick up a couple of sexy Italian men." Maya stared defiantly at Edward who smiled genially back at her.

Valeriano kissed Maya on both cheeks and bowed over Anne's hand in an old-fashioned gesture. "I'll tell John that we met. He...would want me to send his best wishes I know."

Anne nodded coolly. "Please give him my regards."

"Buona sera. Arrivederci." Valeriano departed in conversation with Edward. Maya smiled at Anne, ignoring two men standing nearby who were commenting on how they didn't need to go to "Rivoire" to meet charming Italian men. "Single women out on the town," she said gleefully. "Like we used to do." She tucked Anne's arm into hers.

Anne glanced at the two men before accompanying Maya down the stairs. "Are you sure you want to get married, Maya?"

"I'm sure I want to marry Edward if that's what you mean."

"I was just wondering."

"What a prude you've become, Anne," Maya said affectionately.

Anne stiffened. "I suppose so."

At "Rivoire," the maitre'd recognized them. "Ah, buona sera. Siete ritornate, signorine. Good evening, you have returned. Venite, venite!" Bowing slightly, he led them to a table near the back of the very crowded terrace.

"Did you hear that?" Anne whispered to Maya. "He called us 'signorine.'"

"Oh, they do that sometimes as a compliment. We're obviously not that young." Maya smiled flirtatiously at him and he smiled regally back. "Isn't that funny that Valeriano is John's dad? Did you know that?"

Anne shook her head. It was very funny. She suddenly realized that that was how John had been able to steal the drawing. It had been in his father's gallery. Of course, he wouldn't be capable of something like that if he didn't have some sort of internal access, Anne thought contemptuously. Maybe Valeriano was also involved. Anne turned the idea over in her head. That might make things a bit more complicated but she didn't see how it would adversely affect her plan.

They ordered cappuccinos and watched the people strolling through the square. A couple of Americans set up a music stand near the café. One of them strummed a guitar while the other sang "Strangers in the Night" in an off key. An appropriate song, Anne thought as she watched the last vestiges of sunlight fade into the night sky that glittered with stars behind the tower of the Palazzo Vecchio. The piazza shone with the brilliance of artificial light and became more animated and dramatic as the darkness deepened beyond its borders. Several people toward the front of the terrace started to laugh, softly, between themselves at first, then more openly.

"Those poor musicians." Anne felt excruciatingly embarrassed as she always did when someone performed poorly.

"Well, it serves them right, singing like that. It's ghastly." Maya stood up. "Oh, look," she pointed toward the front of the cafe. "They're not laughing at the music. It's a mime."

Anne looked in the direction in which Maya was pointing. A tall, heavy-set man, dressed in jeans and a plain, blue shirt, was following individuals across the piazza. His face was moon-like, painted in white, his eyes hidden by what appeared to be sunglasses. As he neared the café Anne saw that he was wearing a mask. Though this rendered his face expressionless, he had an amazing and somewhat unnerving capacity to use his body to capture the gestures, posture and moods of the unsuspecting individuals he chose to emulate. Oddly inconspicuous, he focused on the small vanities or insecurities of the persons he followed, until they turned suddenly to find themselves the butt of his parody. Some of his victims laughed with the crowd, some tried to ignore him and ended up fleeing the piazza ignominiously while he pattered after them walking quickly, his body parodying the fleeting expressions of embarrassment, amusement, resentment or anger. Feeling safe at their table, Anne and Maya laughed, watching as he worked the crowded square.

He turned quickly from imitating a short, fat lady who laughed good-naturedly to follow a tall, handsome man who was walking into the piazza from the direction of the Uffizi. The gentleman appeared to be unaware that he was being followed as the mime strutted importantly behind him.

"Look," Anne pointed discreetly. "Do you see that man? He's really handsome, don't you think?"

"Ummmm. Excuse me," Maya murmured. "I've got to go to the toilette."

Anne watched the man as he walked toward the café. The mime interpreted his dark presence perfectly turning it from sinister to funny, from slightly dangerous to slightly ridiculous. Still oblivious to the mime's presence, the man assumed a haughty sneer, which the mime imitated, arching his back and puffing out his chest. Apparently sensing that someone was behind him, the man turned unexpectedly, almost stepping on the mime's feet. The man flexed his muscles as though he were going to hit the mime but, just as suddenly as he had confronted him he turned on his heel and left the square. The mime gave a barely perceptible shrug and sat down in a chair next to an elderly man, leaning back and crossing his legs at exactly the same angle as the old man.

"Has that mime gone?" Maya slid back into her seat, frowning. "I don't like him. It's cruel and unfair following people and making fun of them like that."

Anne looked at her in surprise. "The mime? He's right over there and I think he's rather good. It's only the people who take themselves too seriously who look ridiculous."

"You mean like me?"

Anne shrugged.

"I think its people who have no compassion for others who find him funny."

"You mean like *me*!" Anne started, staring angrily at Maya. She really was impossible. How could Anne have been so blind to this side of Maya before?

"Whatever you think," Maya began in a peevish tone of voice when they heard a loud noise that sounded like a sonic boom. "What was that?" Maya stood up and Anne turned to look across the piazza. All around them people were rising from their seats in consternation, gesticulating with others while some people pressed their hands to their ears and leaned low as though they were trying to hide.

"I don't know," Anne said. "It was too loud to be a car or a gun."

Suddenly they heard the sound of sirens and people rushed past the tables at the café. Someone came into the café speaking rapidly in Italian.

"What's he saying?"

"There's been a bomb," Maya said. "A car bomb and someone's been hurt."

CHAPTER NINE

"Who is sacred and who is profane? And what is that little
boy doing stretching his hand into the dark waters of the
sarcophagus, its lid half open? Stirring up trouble?
There's always trouble in the past. Titian's a master of
mystery. Even his birth is a mystery. He probably had
a hand in 'The Tempest' and 'Fete Champetre' as well.
Poor old Giorgione. *There's* a mystery. We know
almost nothing about him. Soon he'll disappear entirely."
(Edward Donant)

Anne stared at Maya in total disbelief. "A bomb?"

"Yes, yes," Maya spoke impatiently, waving for the waiter to bring them *il conto*, the check.

"What are you doing?" Anne felt dazed. Of course there were always bombs, cars were bombed, churches were bombed, antique shops were bombed. But it was unbelievable that they would actually be in the vicinity of such a thing. Bombs were something that always happened somewhere else. "Why would someone do something like that?"

"Come on," Maya picked up her purse and wrapped her shawl around her shoulders. "Let's go see."

"What? Ugh. Why should we go see what happened? I don't want to go."

"Maybe we can help."

"What could we do? We're neither of us doctors."

"Well, I'm going." Maya walked off, her shawl swinging from one shoulder.

Anne sighed and followed her. They hurried across the piazza, caught up with the other people, all of them drawn by a morbid curiosity. It was several minutes before they arrived at the scene of the accident where they were jostled by a crowd of people, gesticulating and speaking loudly. Anne and Maya pushed their way through the throng until they were close enough to see the embers flying from the burning car. Blood on the street had spattered in an almost festive manner across the paving stones, pooling darkly near the car's remains. The sweetish smell of gasoline and the acrid odor of burnt metal mixed with an air of shock and bewilderment. A couple nearby spoke to one another and smothered their laughter as they left the scene. Anne thought how odd people were—that violence could elicit laughter—as she stared at the circle of blood and flames, wondering whose car it had been and what had happened to the occupants.

Maya turned to grasp Anne's hand. "A bomb," she said, her face was pale. "How horrible. I wonder what happened to the people in the car."

"Dead, I would imagine," Anne muttered. She felt sickened—by the blood, by the realization that someone had actually been in the burning car, by the fact that someone would actually do this to another human being, by all of the ghoulish spectators like herself and Maya, now being forced back from the scene by the police. "Let's get out of here. We're just like those creepy people who are always fascinated by bloody accidents."

"I don't think you can call them creepy, Anne. It's perfectly normal that people are curious about what happened. It's not like it makes them happy or anything."

They left, walking slowly, almost in a trance. Maya tried to call Edward on her mobile phone but to no avail. "His battery must be dead. He's always forgetting to charge his phone. Come back to the hotel with me and have a drink, will you?" Maya was shivering and her teeth clattered when she spoke.

"Are you all right?" Anne took Maya's shawl and pulled it closer around Maya's shoulders. The bombing had made her forget how they were dressed and it seemed incongruous to her that they were still in evening clothes. A group of men accosted them as they walked down the street but Anne and Maya ignored them, arriving at the hotel followed only by two persistent young men who regretfully left as Anne and Maya entered the lobby.

"Signora," the man at reception called to Maya.

"Would you order me a vodka tonic, Anne? I'll meet you in the bar."

There were only a couple of other people in the bar. Anne sat at a small table. Her hands were trembling so that it took her three matches before she succeeded in lighting a cigarette.

"Anne." She looked up to see Maya standing next to the table, looking pale and strained. "Edward was in that car."

Anne stared at her. "What car?" she said stupidly.

"The car that was bombed. I've got to go to the hospital."

The man at reception had come up behind them. "I have a taxi for you, Signora."

Anne put out her cigarette. She was stunned and unable to think clearly. Why had Edward been in a car that was bombed? What could he be involved in? Was she in danger? Anne felt ashamed of her fears; after all, Edward had been hurt and needed her support…Anne caught herself. But, of course, he didn't need her. Maya was the one he had called, Maya was the woman he loved now. Let them support one another, she thought, annoyed that she had automatically assumed she would be wanted. She sat at the table watching Maya as she walked to the door.

"Anne, hurry up. You are coming with me, aren't you?" Maya turned to look pleadingly at her.

Anne hesitated and then grabbed her purse. "Yes, of course, I'm coming."

CHAPTER TEN

"When you go to Florence you should visit Santa Maria Novella
if only to see Masaccio's 'Trinita,' one of the great Renaissance
works. The holy dove flutters above the hanging corpse of Christ.
The figure of God stands behind Christ and the Holy Spirit, a
skeleton lies on a bier below the fresco. 'IO FU GIA QUEL
CHE VOI SIETE E QUEL CHIO SON VOI ANCO SARETE.'
'I was once that which you are and what I am you also will be.'
In contrast to this powerful image of the frailty of human flesh,
there are tacky scenes of wax figures immortalizing persons
revered in the pantheon of the Catholic Church. Behind panes
of glass you can view lit images of the Virgin Mary with Christ
sitting on a rock or clouds and adorned with pearls and medallions.
These images are reminiscent of the gaudy Fortune-telling
machines you can find in penny arcades though their message
is one of redemption through suffering, not the promise
of sports cars, wealth or true love."
(Edward Donant)

John leaned over Anne, his eyes glinting like the eyes of a reptile, his thin lips opening as though he were going to bite or devour her. She shrank back but she could not escape. Reaching out she pushed against his chest and her hands touched something wet. Flashing lights exposed long, red lines that dripped down his torso, beneath the tattered shirt. He wanted to tell her something. She quit repelling him so she could hear better and he suddenly grasped her throat in both hands. Anne tried to push him away but her hands were stuck to him, pulling him closer as she tried to escape. Suddenly they were falling and she was struggling desperately to find a place to hold on. She flung off the sheets and awoke, her heart pounding, her body sweating in the late morning warmth of the Italian summer. Slowly, Anne raised her hands and turned them over, peering at the palms. There was nothing there, just trickles of sweat running down the lines. She hadn't had the dream in a while—it must have been meeting Valeriano the night before that had brought it back.

Anne lay still, her eyes closed, waiting for the physical fear caused by the dream to recede, waiting for her heart to return to a normal pace. She opened her eyes and focused on the light coming through the window. It took her a moment to realize that the way the bed shimmered in the sunlight indicated that it must be high noon or later. She flung off the covers and washed her face in the tiny sink. She didn't often sleep so late. Anne shivered at the memory of the bomb the night before.

She dried her face on the thin towel supplied by the hotel. The bomb had not been extremely powerful, the police had told them, though it had been forceful enough to destroy the car and remove the lower section of Valeriano's right leg. Edward had escaped relatively unharmed. He had dragged Valeriano away from the flames that had started licking dangerously close to the car's engine. She and Maya had only been allowed to visit briefly with Edward as he was being questioned by the police. Edward's right arm had been broken and they had had to set it but he was supposed to be released sometime today. Valeriano was being treated for shock, the severed limb had left his bones shattered below the kneecap and they had had to cauterize the wound to keep him from losing more blood.

The phone next to her bed rang. "Pronto," Anne said cautiously.

"Buon giorno, cara."

"Edward!" Anne felt an immense relief. "Where are you? How are you doing?"

There was a pause on the other end of the phone. "What? You'll have to speak up, Anne, I can't hear too well. The doctors say it's the noise from the explosion."

"I said, 'How are you doing?'" Anne shouted into the phone.

"Oh, I'm fine. A few cuts and bruises is all. At least I have both my legs."

Anne shuddered. "Don't even say that."

"Maya and I are checking out. We wanted to know if you would like to ride with us back to Rome."

"I don't even know if I want to be in a car with you." Anne was suspicious at this unexpected offer.

"It was Valeriano's car that was bombed, sweetheart. Not mine. I was just an unlucky passenger."

"Why would anybody want to bomb Valeriano's car?"

"What?"

Anne repeated her question.

"That's what the police want to know. We'll pick you up in an hour."

Anne was shocked when she saw Edward again. His arm was in a cast and he had a nasty cut over his left eye. "Can you drive, Anne? I'm..." he motioned to his arm and grimaced, "somewhat incapacitated."

"So that's why you asked me to come along." She set her teeth. "Can't you drive at all, Maya?"

Maya looked at her from her position in the back. She looked tired. With her large, dark sunglasses, pale face and the scarf she had tied about her hair, she resembled a 1950's movie star. "No," she said listlessly.

"Oh, never mind. I'll try." Anne had never driven in Italy before and felt a bit intimidated at the thought of going all the way to Rome. Edward climbed gingerly into the seat beside her. "Is there any difference between driving a Porsche and any normal car?"

"Just don't strip the gears, per favore." Edward leaned back and closed his eyes.

Anne carefully pulled out and immediately a small Fiat drove onto her rear, honked and swerved around her. "Good God, where did he come from?" Anne took the wheel with determination and cautiously maneuvered the car out of town. They drove over the Arno River and she began to relax. It was a relief to focus on something so mundane and pleasant as driving through the beautiful Tuscan countryside.

"Did you see Valeriano this morning?" Anne asked Edward. "How is he?"

"He's still in shock. They won't let anyone into his room. I don't think he realizes he's lost part of his leg. They say that comes later." In spite of his seeming calm, Anne noticed that Edward was gritting his teeth as they drove over the uneven pavement.

Anne looked at the scenery through the windshield. The splendid cypresses of Florence flashed past. "What did the police ask you?"

"Oh, the typical questions: what was I doing in Italy, how well did I know Valeriano, did I know why anyone would want to put a bomb in his car, did I have any contacts with the Mafia?"

Maya giggled in the backseat.

"What's so funny?" Edward cradled his arm and sounded irritable.

"Typical questions. How about 'Have you ever been in a car that was bombed before?'"

"'How often have you been in a car bombing?'" Anne began to laugh.

"'How often do you and Valeriano lose your limbs?'"

"Oh, Maya, that's awful." They were gasping with laughter.

"You find this funny? Strange women."

"I'm sorry," Anne tried to get control of herself. "You're absolutely right. It's just...would you mind if I smoke? I'll roll down the window."

Maya was convulsed.

"What's wrong with you, Maya? Are you hysterical?" Edward spoke sharply.

"No, no, I know I shouldn't laugh. It's just so weird. Typical questions: the Mafia, the bomb, can I smoke?" Maya smothered her laughter, leaned out the window and flipped off her scarf.

"Of course, it's horrible, Edward," Anne lit a cigarette and drew deeply on it. "We're just responding to the absurdity of the situation. I mean, really; you and Valeriano in a car that was bombed. It's too incredible." Anne pulled hard on her cigarette, filling her lungs. This was not what she had expected, she thought as she passed a tractor, which was inching along the narrow road—Maya in hysterics, Edward with a broken arm, Valeriano with half a leg. No, the summer was not starting off at all the way she had thought it would.

CHAPTER ELEVEN

"In Leo Steinberg's book, <u>The Sexuality of Christ</u>, he
focuses on the controversial motif of the veiling and
unveiling of Christ's genitals in Renaissance sacred
painting. He argues that these images are justified
within contemporary theological sermons on Christ's
humanity. You can't do that with Caravaggio,
can you? His 'Youth with a Ram' may contain
certain symbols associated with John the Baptist but
this charming, erotically posed young man is about
as spiritually oriented as the ladies displaying
themselves on the pages of Playboy or Penthouse."
(Edward Donant)

Maya was tired of Edward's whining. Men were such babies when
they got hurt, she thought as she dressed. She needed to get out of the
apartment; she'd been waiting on Edward since they had returned from
Florence three days ago. She was supposed to meet Anne for drinks later
that afternoon and she had decided to go to the Forum beforehand. Maya
hoped Anne wasn't going to be as irritable and touchy as she had been the
last few days. Anne really wasn't as much fun as she used to be.

As Maya descended the stairs to the courtyard, she saw the woman
who lived in the apartment across from hers. A big, fat lady, she was
standing in the courtyard, holding an umbrella and wearing a huge, red,
tent-like dress with dozens of beaded necklaces draped around her neck.
Not wanting to speak to her, Maya waited in the shadows on the staircase
for the woman to leave. She laughed to herself, thinking of this woman
walking through the streets of Rome with her umbrella, like some great
Felliniesque figure. An umbrella! For goodness' sake it hardly ever rained
in Rome.

To Maya's surprise a man appeared and, stooping, kissed the fat lady
on each cheek. He was wearing dark glasses and Maya couldn't see him
well from the staircase but he seemed somehow familiar. The two of them
looked in her direction and she felt uncomfortably certain they could see
her. Maya stepped closer to the shadowed area by the curving stone wall
and they turned away, the fat lady swinging her umbrella with one hand
while the tall man took her other arm.

Maya frowned. Now, where had she seen that man before? She crossed
the courtyard and passed beneath the portico. It suddenly occurred to her

that the man she had seen with the fat lady reminded her of the mime in Florence. There had been something about the way he stood, slightly hunched over, the way he gestured with his hands. How very curious. So the mime was friends with the fat lady. Maya giggled at the thought. It was like something out of a circus show.

She walked down the Via del Aracoeli that opened onto the wide space that formed the Piazza d'Aracoeli. What an assortment of emotions she experienced as she wandered the streets of Rome again. She loved the sights and sounds and smells; they were absorbed by her as though through osmosis and were reproduced as dirty feet and sweat-stained armpits; the flattening of her stomach and browning of her thighs the physical products of a surfeit of sensuality. She crossed the busy Piazza Venezia and continued down the Via dei Fori Imperiali, past vendors of bottled water, postcards and plaster images of Michelangelo's "David."

Maya paid for a ticket and an audiotape but, even with the map and the tape, she found it nearly impossible to discern the remnants of temples and buildings, which Tom had pointed out to them long ago. The forum was all a jumble of stone and broken columns, interspersed with the occasional bits of cobblestone road and Spartan sprigs of wild fennel and acanthus whose mass of spring green was stripped to tough beige by the intense Roman heat.

She spread her red scarf on one of the stones near the Arch of Titus and sat down. It was here she had met Aldo, nineteen years ago. She had noticed him watching her. Their eyes had met several times and she had looked away only to find herself irresistibly drawn back. Separating herself from the group, she had pretended to look more closely at the relief sculpture representing the spoils of the Temple of Jerusalem when he had approached her, his fawnlike eyes and black mustache reminding her of Giancarlo Giannini. "Che bella," he had murmured reverently, his eyes caressing her as he stood next to her. She had blushed but had been pleased, lowering her eyelashes in what she had hoped had been a shy but irresistible gesture. A waste of time, Maya thought. He hadn't been interested in shyly irresistible young women. He'd wanted sex and money and had managed to get both, leaving her the loser in every sense. 'You little vamp, you,' Maya grinned ruefully at herself.

A small green lizard skittered up the rock next to her, heedless of her bulk, her looming capacity to destroy it. She watched it, mesmerized, its brilliant chartreuse scales turning purple in the shadows of the crevices. She had always believed in the possibility of portents; that reptiles and weeds, humble rocks and broken sticks could foretell the future if only she had the vision to read the signs. Sadly, though she lived close to the edge through which psychic vision was unleashed, she lacked the ability to turn such power to her advantage. Her extreme sensitivity fit her only for a life of intense physical sensibility whose parameters were marked by frustration and desire rather than revelation and wisdom. Disillusioned but not disappointed, she had accepted her fate with equanimity, determined to compensate by living as hedonistically as her financial and physical conditions allowed. Still, there were moments like this when she realized that hers was the more transient of choices and she regretted her limited prospects.

As Maya left the forum, a group of gypsy boys holding large, metal sheets appeared from the Sacra Via. Like warriors, they approached her, their shields glinting in the white light, their oddly unfocused eyes the eyes of murderers or zealots. Knowing that this was an oft-used ruse to steal unsuspecting tourists' purses, Maya was prepared for them as they came scrambling around her, pressing the sheets about her waist, crying out in their shrill incomprehensible tongues. Imperiously she shoved them aside, dismissing them in rapid Italian. "Eh via! Brutti mascalzoni! Ma che fate...lasciate mi. Su via, via! Andatevene cretini! Go away, leave me alone, stupid kids." Lithe and wary they dispersed, laughing mockingly.

Her adrenaline on high, Maya walked briskly to the bus stop, keeping her eyes open for any sign that the boys might return. While she was waiting for her bus she saw one of them, probably no more than eleven or twelve, shove his way into the line to climb onto the bus. Maya eyed the boy suspiciously as he pushed an old lady out of his way, forcing his way onto the bus in front of her. "What a little jerk," Maya thought and then she saw him take the old lady's wallet out of her pocketbook, which she had left unzipped and hanging down her back. Looking straight ahead, the boy stood on the bus, holding onto one of the seats. Maya's blood boiled as she jumped onto the bus and confronted him.

"You took that woman's wallet," Maya hissed at him in Italian. He looked at her, furious, and shook his head, vehemently denying her accusation. "I saw you!" Maya looked around and noticed that everyone on the bus was either regarding her with disapproval or were looking away, pretending not to notice what was going on. The bus pulled up to the next stop and the boy started to get off but Maya grabbed his arm and blocked his exit. Three men who had been watching them, came up at that point and asked the boy if he had taken the old lady's wallet but again he denied it. All this time the old lady continued to sit in her seat, looking straight ahead as though none of this had anything to do with her.

Maya turned to her, "Do you have your wallet, Signora?"

Suspicious, the lady looked in her bag and screamed, "No, my wallet is gone!"

With that, two of the men grabbed the boy but not before he dropped the wallet on the floor. Angry and humiliated, he bent down to pick it up and handed it to the woman, muttering that it must have fallen out. She snatched it from him, returned it to her purse and continued to sit in her seat, staring straight ahead.

"Cretin!" Maya snarled at the boy as he got off at the next stop. He stared back at her out of dark eyes full of loathing.

***

Maya was not entirely surprised to see Sergei sitting at a table at La Dolce Vita. He invited her to join him and looked disapproving as she flung herself into a chair. She dropped her purse, ran her hands through her hair and impatiently called to the waiter who nodded and smiled as she breathlessly ordered a Campari.

"Why haven't you called me?" Sergei spoke peevishly, his blonde hair was seductively tousled, his beautiful chest encased in an open-necked white shirt, the sleeves rolled up over muscular forearms, his long legs in black jeans.

Maya pictured Sergei as he was followed by the mime on the piazza in front of Rivoire and smiled. She wondered again what he could have been doing in Florence. "You look gorgeous."

Slightly appeased, he leaned over to kiss her on the cheek. "Why didn't you call? I've been waiting for you."

"I don't think it's such a good idea for me to keep seeing you."

He snorted. "We've only seen each other once."

"It was enough."

"So, why are you panting like that?"

"It's not excitement at seeing you if that's what you mean," Maya said sourly.

Sergei stretched out his legs and eyed an elegant, dark-haired lady who was standing uncertainly at the edge of the terrace.

"Sometimes I think Italy can be such an awful country. People can be so mean, so..." Maya shook her head and took a sip of her drink.

Sergei looked at her and raised his eyebrows. "Someone was mean to you?"

"Oh, there've just been so many *disturbing* experiences. Like my purse was stolen in Florence."

"When were you in Florence?"

Maya waved her hand impatiently. "Just a couple of days ago."

"How did your purse get stolen?"

"Some man on a motorcycle snatched it."

"That happens all the time."

"I know but not to me and then there was the car bombing and then, today, I went to the forum and there were these gypsy boys who attacked me trying to steal my purse."

"Why do you carry a purse? You should get one of those belts you can wear around your waist."

Maya looked at Sergei, horrified. "Go around like a tourist? Wearing one of those things that make your stomach bulge out? They're so *ugly.* How could you even suggest such a thing?"

Sergei laughed.

"You can laugh but I don't see you wearing anything like that. And afterwards I saw one of these boys steal this woman's purse on the bus and if it hadn't have been for me he would have gotten away with it. No one else did anything!"

"I'll bet he wasn't too happy with you." Sergei looked amused.

"He hated me. I could see it in his eyes but I was *infuriated* with him. And do you know what? That old lady never said 'Thank you' or anything she just took the wallet and put it in her bag and stared straight ahead. And everyone on the bus looked at me like I was the weird one."

"The gypsies, gli zingari, they're all over the place. Gypsies and Africans. They're ruining Rome."

Maya rolled her eyes. "What about the Russians?"

Sergei ignored her and ordered two more drinks. "You know, now he'll find his friends and they'll look for you and, if they find you, they'll throw acid in your face."

Maya stared at him. "Oh, gee, really. Thanks."

"So, you were there when the bomb went off in Florence? I heard two men were in the car and that they were hurt."

Maya frowned. She looked at Sergei as he watched the elegant lady seated nearby writing postcards. Why didn't he tell her that he'd also been in Florence? Could he be mixed up in something criminal? He was very good-looking, but there was something cruel about him. He didn't seem to have any real feelings. Certainly the way he had treated her in his apartment had been incredibly insensitive. He hadn't even kissed her, just used her as a means of getting off and yet...he was awfully attractive.

Maya blushed suddenly as she reminded herself that she had decided to quit getting involved with these kinds of men. She and Edward hadn't had sex in weeks. She wondered sometimes if Edward really liked sex.

It was frustrating but then there were so many things about him that she liked. Maya studied her slender fingers as she slid them up and down the stem of the glass. She looked up to see Sergei staring intensely at her and she felt a rush of desire. His hand closed tightly around her arm and he pulled her to him. She turned her face away as his lips brushed across her cheek. "I want you," he murmured in her ear. Maya shivered and, laughing a little shakily, pulled away.

CHAPTER TWELVE

"Rosso Fiorentino was a prankster. He had a pet monkey that terrorized the monks at the convent of Santa Croce. Just look at the face of Joseph of Aramathea in his 'Descent from the Cross.' His face is that of a fanatic without redemption, like the faces of the wicked mocking Christ in Ensor's 'The Entry of Christ into Brussels in 1889.' Fiorentino was a modern man. Icy tones, slick surfaces, cynical chiaroscuro, he plays the cymbal in Christian iconology— claaashing theology and dramaturgy. His paintings are torn between utter despair over salvation and vicious pleasure in representing hypocrisy. Even the dead Christ smiles as though to say, 'They've bought it but they'll never gain from it.' Rosso would have made a wonderful addition to the ranks of the Theatre of the Absurd or, perhaps more appropriately, the Theatre of the Cruel."
(Edward Donant)

Valeriano lay in bed with his eyes open, his thighs covered by the hospital sheets. He hated hospitals, he hated the sick-person, dying, rotting smell that underlay the antiseptics sprayed in a useless attempt to mask the decay but that only made the atmosphere more nauseating. He hated the smell of the wretched food, the watery tomato sauce over limp spaghetti, the slimy minestrone, the white rolls that looked and tasted like Styrofoam. He had shoved his lunch away in disgust and in so doing he had discovered the tiny piece of paper folded next to his bowl of soup, which was now crushed in the fist of his left hand. His face was swollen, one ear was partially ripped, his chest was bandaged where he had received cuts from flying glass and shards of metal. When he heard the door open he closed his eyes and pretended to be asleep. Why couldn't they leave him alone?

"Signore Cerasi, mi scusi signore ma..."

It was Carlo of course, so happy to have the opportunity to interrogate Valeriano. Ever since he had been made a detective in the TPA where he was in charge of investigating art fraud, he had become even more impossible. Valeriano had known Carlo since he was a surly teenager and his cousin had come to work in Valeriano's gallery. He opened one eye and regarded Carlo wearily. "Carlo, what a pleasant surprise. Come to visit me again?"

Carlo smiled but his eyes were hard and speculative. Valeriano shrugged and shifted in the bed. "I see that you're determined to interrogate me in spite of the fact that I've repeatedly told you there's nothing I know that can shed a light on this bombing."

"That, Signore Cerasi, is hard to accept." Carlo pulled up a chair and sat next to Valeriano's bed. "You must have some idea why someone put a bomb in your car and who that person or persons could be."

Valeriano grimaced.

"You are interested in finding the person responsible for this attack, I assume?"

Valeriano remained silent. It was the fifth time the police had questioned him since the bombing three days before. Carlo looked with exasperation at his associate who was taking notes. "There's no question that it was not an accident, of course. The bomb was not an act of vandalism or the whim of some kid off the street. It was a sophisticated instrument wired below the chassis of the car by someone who knew what he was doing. It is our belief that this person never intended to kill you, only to maim you. Now, what do you think that suggests?" Carlo leaned closer to Valeriano, who rolled his eyes with a look of pained boredom. "It looks like it might be a warning of some type, wouldn't you agree? A certain pressure brought to bear on some little problem you may have. Now this leg, next time, poof, you're gone if…"

"If what?" Valeriano removed the sheets from his right leg, staring at the shortened limb with distaste.

"If you do not do something they want. I imagine it has to do with money."

Valeriano laughed. "Everything has to do with money."

"Perhaps you owe money to this person? Perhaps, you've not fulfilled a pledge, a promise? You will need to help us out if we are to find the people responsible. I think you must know that your life depends on our finding them."

Still, Valeriano said nothing. Carlo shrugged and motioned to the young man who closed his notebook. "There's also the question of the Piranesi drawing which disappeared from your gallery. I don't suppose there might be some connection between these two incidents?"

Valeriano looked thoughtful. "Perhaps there is a connection as you say. It certainly seems as though someone is trying to put me in a very difficult position."

Carlo shook his head and got up. "I don't admire your stoicism, or rather, your refusal to cooperate. You know as well as I that such an attitude will not help us find the answers."

Valeriano lay very still until the door closed behind them. Three days ago he had had both legs. Now, he was a cripple. Deformed, immobilized. He hated deformity, ugliness, abnormality. He stared again at the useless leg whose lower limb had disappeared like so many paper streamers: shredded flesh, splintered bone, living tissue of his body exploded like a black star disintegrating into the ancient paving stone. He could not accept it, he thought suddenly infuriated. He slammed his right fist against the bed, tears of frustration welling up. The pain seared his chest at the violent movement and Valeriano gasped, letting the tears roll down his cheeks unstopped until he regained a sense of calm. This was not like him, to be so undignified, so out of control. He wasn't going to survive if he lost his head.

Slowly, Valeriano opened his left hand and stared at the crumpled sheet of paper. He didn't need to read it again—he knew exactly what it said. And Lors had never been in Rome. The message at the hotel had simply been a ruse to make sure he took his car that night. He closed his eyes. The bomb had been a warning all right. He needed to get the money fast or he would be dismantled piece by piece. He had to sell the Caravaggio sooner than he had intended and the only way he could do that was to have it stolen as soon as possible.

CHAPTER THIRTEEN

"Color was very important to both Renaissance painting
and its food. But such a connection between visual and
savory delight is not at all surprising. After all, the
use of egg yolk and oil is basic to both painting and
cooking and, in Florence, the chefs and painters belonged
to the same guild. Just look at Domenico Veneziano's
'St. Lucy Altarpiece.' It makes your mouth salivate. You
want to suck on the limes and pinks, reds and greens like
those sour balls we used to eat as kids. And it *is* sour,
even the mouths of the saints and the Virgin and Child
seem to pucker as though the taste of life in this world is
too complex and bittersweet for these cool spiritual
figures who inhabit this ornamental space. It's as
though the artist realizes that the only way to grab our
attention is through artificial means. Again, there's that
connection between cooking and painting, hmmmm?
They're both the result of artifice."
(Edward Donant)

Anne entered the Ristorante dal Bolognese on the sidewalk beneath
the awning in the Piazza del Popolo. Already seated on the terrace were
fifteen men and seven women—all beautifully dressed with manicured
nails. Nine of the men had mobile phones—five were speaking into
them.

That morning Anne had gone to visit the Galleria Nazionale but it had
been closed. Afterwards she had intended to go to the Campidoglio but
instead of the Piazza Venezia she had gotten confused and ended up here
in the Piazza del Popolo. It was two o'clock in the afternoon, incredibly
hot and the city, outside of the busy cafes, seemed shut down. She stopped
at the first restaurant she came to where she was, of course, seated next
to the only single man on the terrace. He was not unattractive: swarthy,
a bit thick, with a dark suit, pink silk shirt, gold chains and a gold Rolex
watch. They glanced at one another when she was seated and then each
looked away, carefully avoiding further eye contact. Anne ordered a large
bottle of acqua naturale and, when it arrived, the gentleman offered her
some of his ice. She thanked him before a bucket of ice arrived at her table.
Anne was pleasantly surprised as she had never before seen ice presented
like that in Italian restaurants and it was refreshing in the midday heat.

Taking out her map she studied it, looking in some bewilderment for the Piazza Venezia. She had a terrible sense of direction and she often, like today, ended up in a place completely opposite to where she had intended to go. She noticed, for the first time, that the center of Rome, the part that fascinated her and most other travellers, was really rather small. She had remembered it as much larger, more overwhelming.

"You, uhhh, find Italy bella?"

Anne looked up in some consternation. The gentleman was trying to open a conversation with her. "Si, si, molto bella," she smiled and looked back at her map.

"You, aaah, you here sola?" He shrugged his shoulders and waved a hand in the air. "Ummm, lone, aaaah, my Inglese is....Spreken zie Deutsch?"

"Non. Vous parlez Francais?"

"Un peu. Io parlare Deutsch very good, not very good Inglese, Franchese." He shrugged and looked confused. They both smiled apologetically. Anne looked away from him.

She thought back to the bombing three days before. Edward said that Valeriano was to remain in the hospital for another couple of weeks and that they were preparing a prosthesis for his amputated leg. Anne shivered. Why would someone want to hurt Valeriano? And a bomb seemed such a...well, absurd way to get rid of someone. She forced herself to turn her attention to the pasta. Although a tiny portion, the mixed pasta was lovely; green tortellini stuffed with white ricotta, spaghetti graced with a deep red Bolognese sauce, there were three other pastas with colors varying from orange to plum—sixteen dollars for a plate the size of a saucer. Anne took a small bite and realized that she had made a mistake. It was far too hot to be eating pasta, even as light a course as she had ordered.

"Buono?"

"Si, si." Smiling, nodding, eating, and wishing she hadn't been seated next to the man, Anne looked past him to the huge piazza where people were reclining on the steps of the Church of Santa Maria dei Miracoli. The heat was intense—Roman heat; dry enough to be tolerable in the shade, stupefying in the sun.

"Va bene?"

"Si, si."

"La pasta e, ummm, buono?"

"Si, si."

The man continued to ask questions that were basically unintelligible to Anne though she was able to determine that they were centered around food. "Si, si," she smiled again, wondering if he was asking for her opinion of all Italian food or just her pasta. "Si, molto buono," she added. "Si, Italiano." He was asking her if she wanted to eat Italian or American. How odd.

He spoke to the waiter and they both looked expectantly at her.

"Pardon?" She was confused until she realized that they were waiting for her to make her choice for the second course. "Non, non," Anne fluttered, embarrassed. Everyone at the nearby tables had paused to listen to her response.

The waiter came next to her. "Gigot d'agneau?" he offered helpfully.

"No, no, niente, niente. Basta," Anne smiled politely and everyone looked disappointed. "I'm not very hungry," she explained apologetically but the waiter looked somewhat contemptuous and withdrew. She continued the fragmented linguistic conversation with her neighbor, interrupted occasionally by his unfolding his little, black telephone and shouting "Francesca, Francesca" into it. He always refolded it, explaining that Francesca was not there. His eyes were strangely unfocused, two light dots marking the cornea on either side of his nose.

Anne paid her bill with relief and smiling 'Arrivederci' she left the restaurant. It was only a couple of minutes before the gentleman caught up with her. Irritated and distressed she ignored him.

"Ummm, you go...dove?"

She sighed. "I'm going to see my friends."

"Your friends? You want to come with me to Sicily due giorni? I leave domani."

"Excuse me?"

"Sicily. E bellissima. La mer, mountains, the sun. You like il mare.. ummm, the sea?"

"Si, oui, yes but non, non, c'est pas possibile. Grazie."

"Tonight you ummmm, mangiare cena, eat dinner, con me?"

"Non, non est possibile, scusi, grazie."

"Perche no, why not?"

They were beneath a group of trees on the opposite side of the square and Anne found him facing her, the sun having moved slightly so that its light was directly in her face, back lighting him, turning him into a dark silhouette. Oh, good grief, she thought and she looked around the empty square somewhat desperately. "I'm meeting friends for dinner tonight. My boyfriend."

"Scusi," he was smiling at her, leaning toward her. "Non capisco." The light points in his eyes were disconcerting. He was incredibly tiresome. Sicily. She could only think "Mafia." Was he dangerous? Did he have anything to do with the bombing? This thought made her nervous and, for the first time, she noticed that the nails on each pinkie finger were extraordinarily long. She found this detail both fascinating and repellant and had a hard time taking her eyes from them.

"You want a coffee? Cappuccino? A gelato?"

"No, no." Anne shook her head. The whole situation was becoming exhausting.

He tried to put his arms around her, "La voglio baciare. I want to kiss you."

Anne pushed him away. "No, no."

"Si, si." He was blocking her, pressing her against the stonewall. "Uno. Then I go."

Wanting to get away with as little fuss as possible, Anne nodded. She stood on her tiptoes, kissed him lightly on the cheek and then she strode quickly into the piazza. The man followed her but she walked fast and he soon stopped. Anne continued down Via Ripetta until she reached the Church of San Rocco, which she entered. She took off her hat and sank onto one of the wooden pews. Closing her eyes, she allowed herself to disappear into the cool shadows of the interior. Once again she found herself grateful for the churches in Italy. She appreciated the blessed silence, the dimly lit basilica, chill in the midday heat, and she thought that churches were the only communal spaces left where she could experience a sense of privacy. That was another thing she and Edward shared, their love of churches and cathedrals. Charlie had hated churches. At least he had refused to enter them with her. She wondered now if it wasn't because he had felt her unworthy.

"Do you love me?" He had asked her.

"No."

He had laughed. "But you hate me and you can't leave. Is it that you hate me so much that you are always glad to see me?"

Anne had curled her lips in scorn, confused and hurt as usual. Charlie had led her through the streets near the Piazza Venezia, empty at two o'clock in the morning. He lived somewhere in some apartment with some parents whom she would never meet. He had been tall and thin so that when he pressed her to him he hurt her with his bones. He had had long, straight, black hair and black eyes. He had worn sunglasses even at midnight and had played his thin lips in a restlessly despising way. She had dreaded his painful kisses. She had stopped before a church and asked him what it was.

"A church."

"Yes, but what church? To what saint?"

"I don't know. I don't care. I haf to go now. You can get back if you take dis bus." He had left her at the corner of the Via Battisti and the Via del Corso from which she could see the Vittorio Emanuele Monument. No bus had come. Charlie had been no better than John but at least he hadn't tried to kill her. Anne pressed her head into her hands, running her palms almost painfully across her eyelids. Nineteen years ago John had tried to kill her. What would he do now if he knew that she was planning to betray him? Anne got up from the pew. By the time he found out it would be too late for him to do anything.

CHAPTER FOURTEEN

"It's the same old story, you know. 'Come to bed with me.'
'No, I can't.' 'Well, you're going to die, better do it while
you can.' Love effeminates man. By becoming involved
in love he loses his masculinity. Botticelli dreamed that
he was married and was so upset he walked the streets of
Florence until dawn, terrified that the dream might return."
(Edward Donant)

Maya looked at her watch. Anne should be here shortly. What could
she do about Sergei? She glanced up to see him staring at her. Leaning
forward, he put his hand on her knee. "Why don't we go back to my place
and make love?"

Maya removed his hand. "You're irresistible, Sergei, but I'm waiting
for a friend."

"What friend? A man?"

Maya shook her head. "What difference does it make to you?"

"How many men have you met since you came to Rome?"

"A few."

"Tell me about them. Did they try to kiss you?"

Maya laughed.

"Did they try to make love to you? Tell me."

"Well, of course."

"Did you kiss them?"

"Why are you asking me this?"

"I'm curious. I want to know."

"It's really none of your business."

"But it interests me. I want to understand these people. Why won't
you tell me?"

Maya was silent.

"I think maybe all of Rome wants to make love to you."

Maya laughed. "I know. Isn't it wonderful?"

Sergei looked at her, his eyes hidden behind the glasses. "And what
about the man you are in love with?"

"What do you mean?" Maya looked at him sullenly.

"You told me you didn't want to have sex because you were in love."

"It's true. I can't help it if other men want to make love to me." She
shrugged.

Sergei laughed. "Watch out for gli zingari," he said as he leant over to kiss her. Relieved to see him leave, Maya leaned back in her chair and crossed her legs. 'A vain display of virginal retreat,' she thought sardonically. At thirty-nine who would be taken in by her ruse? She watched a man and a young woman seated separately at nearby tables. The woman sniffled, the man sipped his soup. 'If you blow your nose you've blown your chance to seduce the other,' Maya thought. The man was holding the collar of his white shirt so that it would not get soiled as he ate. The woman's belly hung out over her hip-hugger pants, not fat, just youthful flesh uncontrolled by an exercise of will and posture.

The waiter approached her with a glass of sparkling wine. Bowing, he deposited it before her. "From the signore at the table by the door." Maya turned to see a short, fat man smiling at her. Suddenly two palms, cool against her cheeks, were pressed across her eyes, the thin fingers blocking her view. "Oh."

Anne laughed. "Hi. Did I scare you?"

"Yes you did. I'm very jittery these days. It seems like everyone's out to get me."

Anne removed her hat and sat down at the table. "Whatever are you talking about?"

"Don't look in that man's direction. He just sent me this drink. I don't want to encourage him."

The waiter arrived.

"Let's order a bottle of good Prosecco." Maya spoke to the waiter in Italian and he bowed and left. "You know, I always thought Italian sparkling wines were sickeningly sweet like the Asti Spumante they export to the States but I've had some wonderful sparkling wines since we came here."

"What man?"

"Oh, don't look. It doesn't matter."

"Is that what you're worried about? Is he out to get you?" Anne looked doubtfully at the little man who raised his glass and winked.

"What? Oh, no, I'm being followed by a band of gypsy boys who want to throw acid in my face."

"Maya, what *are* you talking about?"

"Never mind. Ah, here's the lovely liquid. A toast. To friendship."

"To friendship," Anne said dryly.

They drank, the water in the fountains splashed, and the sky turned a deeper blue as if in acknowledgement of their pledge. Two middle-aged men stopped before the cafe and set up a music stand. One of them, in black jeans and a white shirt, played the accordion, the other, wearing cut-off jean shorts, a ragged sweatshirt and a baseball cap, its beak slanting backwards, sang. "Volare, oh,oh, cantare, oh,oh,oh..."

Maya closed her eyes and stretched her arms. "I love this song, it makes me believe that romance really exists."

"Oh yeah, back in the fifties," Anne said.

Maya ignored her. "And it goes so perfectly with the wine. This is marvelous wine, don't you think?"

"Yes. What's this song about? I've always liked it, too, but I have no idea what they're saying."

"It's about flying, flying into the blue sky, the blue painted of blue, something like that. And he's so happy to be up there but then he's in love with his sweetheart whose eyes are also blue. It ends where he's happy to be down here, on earth, with her. Well, it's something like that. Anne," Maya leaned forward and touched Anne's arm. "Do you think that Edward loves me?"

Anne lit a cigarette. "Not that again. Why wouldn't Edward love you? And why would he ask you to marry him if he didn't love you?"

"You know as well as I do that marriage isn't always equated with love."

"Why are you asking me this? I thought you were madly in love with him and that everything was hunky dory."

"I do love Edward, and I think everything's fine. It's just...well I confess that I've met some other men. I mean they don't mean a thing to me, but well it could be taken wrong if Edward were to find out and, oh, I don't know. I guess I'm just a bit scared that I'm going to lose him."

Anne tapped the cigarette against the ashtray. "I wouldn't worry. He'd be a fool to let you go. And anyway, why do you see other men if you're so in love with Edward and so afraid of ruining your relationship?"

"I don't know." Maya sipped her drink. "It's like some sort of addiction. I need men to tell me I'm beautiful, that I'm desirable, that I'm wonderful or I just lose all confidence. And Edward telling me isn't enough. I'm very insecure as you know. I want both and besides...oh, forget it. It's nothing. I'll work it out." Absently she flipped the end of the fork against the tabletop. "Why weren't you more impressed with the Caravaggio?"

Anne put out her cigarette. "I don't really know why I think there's something wrong with the painting, but I do." She lit another cigarette.

"I thought it was exciting to see it. I don't know, of course, but it seemed pretty good to me."

"Yes, yes, it was well-done but still, there's something...that's just not right. Hasn't Edward said anything else about the painting?"

"No. But, of course, with the bombing afterward...." Maya and Anne were both silent, thinking of that night.

"How's Edward doing? How is his arm?"

"Oh, he's much better. The doctor said his arm is improving. He's driving me crazy with his whining."

"That's good, I mean that he's getting better. Do you remember the mime?"

"I'd hate to have him follow me." Maya uncrossed and then re-crossed her legs. Two men walking by angled their gaze in her direction.

"I have to agree with you. There was something rather sinister about him. Maybe it's that mask. People who wear masks are always a little creepy."

"I find my thrill on strawberry hill..." the singer's Italian accent grated across the notes.

Maya made a face. "I *hate* this song."

"An awful man tried to pick me up at lunch today." Anne didn't know why she brought it up. "He was from Sicily. He asked me to go with him to Sicily."

"After lunch? Wow. That was fast. He's probably with the Mafia."

"That's what I thought." Anne laughed. "And I don't even know his name. He had these really long, manicured nails on each pinkie finger, just those nails. I kept staring at them. And I kept thinking he might be involved in the bombing."

"Ooh. How sinister. 'Unghia.'" Maya waved her fingers delicately in the air.

"What's that?"

"That's the word for fingernail."

"Of course, he's probably just some businessman involved in some perfectly legitimate enterprise."

"Oh dear. That would be disappointing." Maya sipped her sparkling wine.

"Yes, I suppose it would be in a perverse sort of way. Now why would we think that?"

"Because there's something sort of sexy or exciting about men who have a violent edge. That's why women are always attracted to the 'bad' boys."

"I totally disagree." Anne shuddered at the memory of the night with John on the roof of the hotel. "I think if you really were in danger you wouldn't find it at all exciting or erotic. It's really just...oh, I don't know, horrible and humiliating. In fact, I wouldn't be at all attracted to a man who was violent. And I don't think you would be either. You can't tell me that you found the bombing the other night erotic."

"That's not what I mean at all. Maybe 'violent' isn't the word I want. But you must admit there's a connection between sex and violence. I don't agree with de Sade or anything. I'm not a sadist or a masochist, but there's that cutting edge—that place where you want the man to take you. If you're attracted to him, that is."

"You mean being seduced by forceful persuasion. It reminds me of something Milan Kundera said in The Book of Laughter and Forgetting, about the woman always saying 'No, no, no' and meaning 'Yes, yes, yes.' It's far too simplistic. There've been many times when I was with a man and I wanted to have sex with him but I knew I couldn't or, rather, that I shouldn't, and the more he tried to persuade me the more I said, 'No, no,' not because I wanted to be forced, not even as a statement that had anything to do with him but because I needed to remind myself, will myself not to succumb."

"Well, okay, I know what you mean, but there's also the fact that there's always an edge to male/female confrontation. It's like a good argument."

"So that's why you're attracted to Edward." Anne laughed. "He argues about everything."

"Oh, Edward. That's different." Maya knotted her napkin distractedly. "I suppose that is one reason that I'm drawn to him and, yet I don't know. I can't get to know him fully, which is kind of tantalizing except..."

"Except that it becomes an awful bore." Anne finished her glass. She was annoyed at how often Edward intruded into their conversation. They talked like a couple of women who had nothing else to think about.

"It can become awfully *frustrating*. You know, he goes off on these trips for days. I don't know where he is or what he's doing. He tells me but I don't think he tells me everything."

Anne shrugged. "I've been there, you know. Do we really have to keep talking about Edward all the time?"

Maya flushed and re-filled the glasses. "That's a barrier now, isn't it? Between us? Whatever I say it will come back to your relationship with him. I'm an intruder, you mean."

Anne looked at her, surprised because, for once, it wasn't at all what she had been thinking. But then it was so typical of Maya. "It sounds like you mean that I'm the intruder. You mean that whatever I say about Edward and my relationship with him, you'll think it's a comment on your relationship with him."

"No, that's not what I mean."

"It's really not about you, Maya, though naturally I relate what you say to my own relationship with Edward. And I am still angry, but I'm angry with myself for ever having married him and really, for ever having fallen in love with him. It bothers me that he thinks he's so superior to everybody. It brings out this immature side of me where I just want to prove him wrong."

Maya looked at her somewhat bitterly. "I didn't think that bothered you. It's not like you and he aren't equals. You're not like me. I don't have any diploma proving my brilliance like you do."

"Like the scarecrow in the 'Wizard of Oz,' you mean?" Anne laughed. "All you need is a piece of paper to prove you're intelligent."

"Well, it does make a difference when you don't have it. It's easy to say it's meaningless when you do."

Anne lit a cigarette. "Yes, I guess you're right."

The two musicians launched into Eric Clapton, "Darling, you look wonderful tonight."

"What did you mean about the acid boys?"

Maya laughed. "I'll tell you later. What're you doing tonight?"

Anne felt a little embarrassed. "I'm meeting Antonio."

"Ooooh, Annnntoooonnio. A romantic soiree?"

Anne smiled. "Maybe."

"I don't suppose you want me to stick around?" Maya grinned. "I hope your Antonio proves worthwhile. I must meet him." She reached out and took Anne's hand. "Maybe he won't find you cold."

Anne took a deep breath. Could Maya really have no idea how irritating she could be? "I hardly know him, Maya," she said coolly. "This is only the second time I'll be seeing him."

"Well, that doesn't mean anything. Time is relative you know. Oops, speaking of which, I've got to go. I promised Edward I'd meet him for dinner and it's already seven-thirty." Maya kissed Anne on the cheek and crossed the piazza, tightening the red belt about her slender waist. Anne watched people watching Maya, their heads turning as she passed, before she disappeared down the Via di S. Agnese in Agone raising one slender wrist as though to wave good-bye.

She was really a stunning-looking woman, Anne thought and yet, it was true that she had a hard time keeping any man interested in her for very long. It had always been that way with Maya. She attracted dozens, hundreds of men, but rarely did her relationships last longer than a year. She was too narcissistic, too shallow to keep anyone's interest for long. And now here she was confiding to Anne of all people her concerns about Edward. Anne wondered if Edward wasn't becoming a bit bored. She stood up for a moment to relieve the ache she got whenever she sat for too long.

Looking around the piazza, she was struck by the exquisite lines of the buildings and monuments. The straight horizontals, rising and falling, were broken by the facade of Borromini's church, whose rhythmic cadence of concave and convex formed a baroque backdrop to the more austere Renaissance buildings. The sun splintered at the apex of the cupola, its rays spilling over onto Bernini's Fountain of the Four Rivers, itself a marvel of movement. An organic tangle of upraised arms, crossed legs and sinuous plant forms set off the rear end of the horse whose body plunged into the carved walls of the stone grotto. The obelisk rose out of the massive representation of the four great rivers of the world—what were they? Anne could only remember the Nile and the Danube. The tiles of the rooftops formed a dentelle between the limpid blue sky and the ochre walls. Delicate antennae rose from the roofs echoing the tips of palm fronds that graced some hidden rooftop garden.

Casually, Anne shifted her gaze to the Bar Tre Scalini. Standing on the terrace before the cafe was the very man she had been seated next to at lunch that day. She quickly sat down and shaded her face with one hand. She looked again and was relieved to see that he had not noticed her. Curious, Anne watched him. He wore a pale cream suit that looked almost pink in the early evening light. He spoke briefly into his phone, which he folded and replaced in his pocket. Anne laughed. The inevitable portable phone, the new phallic extension. He raised his right arm as though in greeting and Anne saw another man emerging from the cafe, dressed in a rumpled linen suit, his white hair pulled back in a ponytail, his arm in a sling. Edward!

CHAPTER FIFTEEN

"Beccafumi's 'Stigmatization of St. Catherine' is,
although represented in a traditional realistic technique,
an almost post-modern deconstruction of Christian
motifs. The artist has worked his picture out through
a maze of theological and philosophical references
that, although often ambivalent, are not meant to
hide but to reveal the mystery of faith. St. Catherine
kneels on a beautifully inlaid floor which dissolves
into an almost Northern European landscape. The piers
support a dome which is really the dome of heaven from
which the Virgin Mary and the baby Christ look down.
Two rather spastic angels mar the vision but we are
perhaps prejudiced in our perspective, hmmmm?"
(Edward Donant)

Anne frowned as Edward and the Sicilian walked off together, deep in conversation, toward the opposite end of the piazza. What on earth could Edward have in common with that awful man? They couldn't possibly be friends, though here Anne was reminded of the many odd people Edward knew. This man was from Sicily, a part of Italy she always found suspect. She remembered wondering if he was connected to the Mafia. Suddenly Anne put her hand to her mouth. She had thought he might be somehow connected to the bomb in Florence but it had only been a passing thought. Now she wondered if it wasn't true. And the Caravaggio had been discovered in a church in Sicily. Maybe the Sicilian had something to do with the painting. Anne stared across the piazza, puzzled. What did Edward think of the painting? Was it a fake? Could there be a connection between the bomb, the painting and this man?

Distracted by her thoughts Anne gazed at the pigeons pecking for breadcrumbs around the tables. Surreptitiously, she pushed a peanut over the edge of the table so that it fell in front of one. Simultaneously, a waiter arrived, shooing the pigeon away with large gestures and loud cries. Anne blushed, feeling that she was being scolded for having encouraged it.

She saw Antonio crossing the piazza and she pushed her hands nervously through her hair. He was really very attractive, too attractive to be interested in her, Anne thought. Why on earth did he want to have dinner with her? She watched him, realizing that she had become one of those people who saw only the negative in everyone.

Antonio leaned down to kiss her on both cheeks. "I'm sorry I'm late. Have you been waiting long?"

"I came a bit earlier to meet a friend."

"I see. What would you like to drink? May I suggest un aperitivo?"

"Yes, please," Anne smiled. "Something different from Campari would be nice."

"How about Aperol? You'll like that I think." Antonio ordered for them. "You seemed deep in thought when I arrived. What were you thinking about?"

"I was...wondering why you wanted to have dinner with me." There she had said it. Anne regarded Antonio, a cigarette poised between two fingers.

He laughed and leaned forward to light the cigarette. "What a strange thing to say. Why were you thinking that?"

Anne shrugged, regretting that she had said anything. "I just was."

He looked at her, his eyes warm and amused. "Because I like you, I find you attractive and stimulating. Besides, we share so many interests. We both teach, we're interested in art, we know similar people."

Anne dragged on the cigarette. "We do? Who is it we both know?"

"Well, Edward for one, Valeriano for another."

Anne was surprised. "I didn't know you knew Edward!"

"Oh, yes, I've often worked with Valeriano and I've met Edward several times."

"What do you do with Valeriano?"

"I write catalogues for exhibitions, things like that. At the moment I'm involved in writing a treatise on drawings by Piranesi and I've been working closely with the collector who lent several drawings to Valeriano's gallery for an exhibition he mounted on drawings of the Renaissance. Including the one that was stolen."

Anne continued to stare at Antonio. "Oh, my goodness, I had no idea you were involved in that." The cigarette burned down between her fingers and she dropped it with a brief exclamation. "I burned myself," she said, smiling sheepishly at Antonio.

"Are you all right? Here, put your fingers in some ice water." He signaled for the waiter.

Anne wondered what Antonio knew. "Do you have any idea who might have stolen the drawing?"

"I'm looking into a couple of possibilities."

"Looking into? You mean like investigating? Don't tell me you're a detective as well." Anne thanked the waiter and dutifully dipped her fingers in the glass of ice water he brought.

Antonio laughed. "No, my cousin is an official, a detective, who specializes in the investigation of art fraud and theft. I've had several opportunities to work with him before and, as I'm really indirectly involved in this..." He shrugged.

They sat together in silence, watching the fashionable Italians and backpacking tourists as they strolled through the piazza. The waiter placed two glasses before them. They were half filled with a pale, orangish-rose liquid and cubes of ice. The drink was garnished with an orange slice and a crust of sugar coated the rim. Anne took a sip. It was not as bitter as Campari or as strong. "That's nice," she said appreciatively. "Do you know Valeriano's son, John?" Anne asked the question casually as she watched a group of young, American girls walk by. They were wearing long dresses, tennis shoes and backpacks, twittering and giggling, looking around to see if any men were watching them. She thought they looked utterly ridiculous yet she appreciated the fact that they were so young and un-self-consciously enjoying themselves. It reminded her of when she had first come to Italy.

"I've met John once or twice."

"What do you think of him?" Anne turned to look at Antonio.

He shrugged. "It's unfortunate that he was disfigured by an accident he had a long time ago. It's affected him in more ways than just looks."

Anne raised her eyebrows. "Such as?"

"He drinks—he drinks way too much and he's not involved in anything productive. I don't think he ever even finished college. I know these things have made him, well, I think Valeriano is disappointed in him." Antonio looked at his watch and then across the piazza.

"So what? He was always like that. He was always drunk." Anne felt dissatisfied, which made her want to be mean. Whatever Antonio said, he clearly wasn't interested in her. He appeared preoccupied.

Antonio looked at Anne. "You know John? How do you know that he was always like that?"

"We were both in Rome on a study program together." She spoke shortly. She wondered if Antonio had any idea that it was John who had stolen the drawing. But even if Antonio suspected something he wouldn't be likely to share such a suspicion with her. So, he investigated art theft, he knew Edward and Valeriano, what else was there about him that she didn't know? Anne leaned forward and stared at him.

"What?" Antonio smiled at her. "Why are you looking at me like that?"

"I'm just curious. I hardly know you."

"What do you want to know about me?"

"Well, for instance, do you have any children? Are you married?"

Antonio laughed. "I assure you that I'm not married nor do I have children. All right?" He reached over and covered her hand with his.

Anne was shocked at the sensation of his hand on hers and jerked her hand away. "Of course it's all right. I was just curious is all," she blushed.

An elderly, twisted hunchback in a wheelchair rolled up and stopped in front of a couple several tables away from Anne and Antonio. Pulling a sheet of music from a tattered bag, he began to sing "La donna e mobile" from "Rigoletto." His voice quavered, rising and falling in uneven tones. Anne laughed, covering her mouth with her hand. Antonio smiled at her. A tall, thin woman, a long green scarf loosely wrapped around her neck, joined the hunchback as they sang "O soave fanciulla" from "La Boheme." Antonio softly sang the words to the song and Anne asked him what they meant.

"It's a love duet," he explained. "Between Rodolfo and Mimi. They've just met and they've fallen madly in love. Rodolfo tells her 'Oh, sweet face bathed in the soft moonlight, I see in you the dream I'd dream forever' and Mimi says, 'Ah. Love, you rule alone.' In the end, Rodolfo kisses her and says 'You're mine.'"

Anne blushed again and, annoyed with herself, laughed. "The dangers of a kiss."

The couple stopped before Anne and Antonio's table and the man began to sing the English version of "Oh Sole Mio." Anne smiled fixedly, embarrassed for them but Antonio joined them, singing lustily. "It's now or never, my lovely one. Kiss me, my darling, be mine tonight" and everyone around them applauded. Antonio gave the couple some lire and the two moved away to another table. Anne felt chastised, as though she had been remiss both in the pleasure of the moment and in a generosity of spirit. Antonio called the waiter and Anne pulled out her wallet but he waved her away impatiently.

"Let me pay," she said, smiling prettily.

"No, no," Antonio frowned. "Soi in Italia. You do not pay."

Anne giggled. She was feeling tipsy and silly, her earlier irritability replaced by a sense of light-heartedness.

Antonio paid the bill. "What's so funny?"

"It's just funny for you to say that I don't pay in Italy. When I was here, ages ago, I met two guys, young men, who asked me out, and when we got to the bar they told me that I had to pay. 'In Rome,' they said, 'we always go Dutch.'"

Antonio looked surprised.

"Which I thought was pretty unfair. I mean, *they* asked *me*. Anyway, it was all right because I hadn't brought any money. They were mad but they had to pay." Anne laughed; she was definitely feeling good. "I'm sorry. Scusa."

"No, no, you are happy. Va bene. How are your fingers?" He took her hand and gently kissed each of her fingers.

Anne shivered at the touch of his lips on her flesh and pulled her hand away. "They're fine. Grazie."

He took her by the elbow.

"Are we walking?"

"No, I drove." He escorted her to a rather battered-looking BMW. "I have two cars. I use this one to drive in Rome because, well, you see." He gestured at the dented body. "The way people drive in Roma."

Anne spent much of the evening laughing. Her typical reaction, she thought, to laugh at things that made her feel uncomfortable. Antonio was so sober, so difficult to interpret. He was disconcerting. He looked as though he should be quietly masterful but he seemed unsure of himself, and yet, he had surprised her twice in the evening. First, when he told her about his involvement with the stolen drawing and again when he sang with the street performers.

They were seated at a table at "Er Grottino Trattoria Pizzeria"in the Campo dei Fiori. It was brilliantly lit with lamps that hung from the beams on the terrace. Anne allowed Antonio to order for her. The definitive odors of garlic and rosemary punctuated indeterminate scents that Anne vaguely identified as roasted vegetables and meats made pungent by stewing in herbs and wine.

"We shall have a typical Roman meal." Antonio was enthusiastic. "We Romans eat very well. We don't eat quite as much as we used to but I think you will find it sufficient. We must start with one of the wines from the castles around Rome: the vini dei Castelli. I think a dry white Frascati."

"Whatever you think is best," Anne said. She looked at the people talking, eating and drinking all around them. Beyond the arc of light projecting from the café, couples strolled around the piazza, passing in and out of spheres of light and shadow as they moved closer to or further away from the cafes. Anne was reminded of the movement made by a curtain shifting in a breeze and imagined the people in the piazza being gently blown around a timeless circle by some giant, invisible fan. Totally unaware, they were unable to break the pattern it created—the idea of the Divine reduced to the mechanics of a rotary apparatus. That was nothing new, of course, she reminded herself. Wasn't it Newton who had defined God only as something that set the world in motion and left it to continue without divine intervention? It was similar to what Anne had done. She had set into motion a series of events that would affect John and her in some as yet unknown but fundamental way. Whatever happened it would be better than the way things were now. Anne shuddered slightly, pulling her sweater closer around her shoulders. It was dangerous to play God, she thought but it was too late to worry about that. She looked at the plate set in front of her on which were what looked to be wads of fried paper flowers.

"'Carciofi alla Giudea.'" Antonio said. "Jewish artichokes."

Anne had completely lost her appetite. "They're very good," she said dutifully tasting one.

A young wedding couple sitting at the far end of their table with an entourage of joyous drinkers sent pieces of their wedding cake down to Anne and Antonio along with two glasses of champagne.

"What a nice thing to do," Anne exclaimed.

"They think we're lovers," he said, smiling.

Anne blushed.

Antonio leaned toward her and stroked her arm lightly. "Why aren't you married?"

"I was married. It wasn't what I wanted."

"What do you want?"

Anne lit a cigarette, leaning forward to take the flame from Antonio's cupped palm. She sat back. "I want what most people want. To meet someone I can love and, more important, trust. To have a life that makes you happy rather than one that makes you miserable."

"The fact that you were unhappily married doesn't mean that you can't find what you want from marriage."

Anne sipped her champagne and looked at him. "Why aren't you married? Do you think you can get what you want from marriage?" Antonio shrugged and said nothing so she continued. "I think marriage, the idea of marriage as a romantic liaison, is doomed to failure. You have to accept it as a socio-political institution."

"And financial."

"Of course, especially for the woman. And it's rather interesting that, as women grow more financially independent, they're the ones who often instigate divorce. I have several friends who married young and now that they're successful they're leaving their husbands. I think the idea that women want to get married is just a myth perpetuated by men to save their egos. In my experience it's usually the man who wants to get married."

"Maybe you're right but there are still a lot of Italian women who've never heard that they don't want to get married."

"Oh, a lot of women are still insecure if they're not possessed by a man."

"But not you."

Anne relaxed her guard and smiled at him. "I know I sound like I think I'm superior but that's not really what I mean or how I am. In a lot of ways I want all of the traditional romantic stuff—I want to be swept away and I'm not talking about the film by Lina Wertmuller. Just, you know, the idea that there's one man who adores me and whom I adore." Anne sighed and then she looked up to see Antonio regarding her with a blank expression. "Sorry, but you did ask." She grinned at him. "I certainly don't expect you to adore me though, of course, you can if you like."

Antonio smiled. "I'll keep that in mind."

"The moon in the sky like a big pizza pie, that's amore"... A group of musicians had set up in front of the cafe. Anne laughed and stretched her arms above her head. "Everywhere in Rome there's music. Isn't there a song about that?" She brought her hands down and ran them through her hair. She was feeling very sensuous and relaxed. She realized that it had been a long time since she had felt that way and she smiled gratefully at Antonio.

"There should be. Let's make one up."

"I can't sing." Anne finished her champagne. "It's so lovely to drink champagne. I know that song. 'The night they invented champagne...'" she sang a little out of tune as they left the restaurant.

"Would you like to go somewhere for a cappuccino?" Antonio steered her through the crowds toward his car.

"Not tonight. I've got to give a lecture tomorrow."

He nodded. "I'll drive you to your hotel. Would that be acceptable?"

"It would be very nice, grazie."

They drove in silence and Anne stared through the window at the lights, the families out for midnight strolls, the young girls in tight pants and high heels.

"What are you thinking about?" Antonio asked her.

"About how funny it is that you know Edward and Valeriano and that you're involved in the exhibition of drawings, the one where the Piranesi was stolen."

"Why is that funny?"

"It all seems a bit strange. That I met you the way I did and that you're a professor in the school I came to teach at and, now, I find out you know the same people I do."

"Ah, si, I see what you mean. There do seem to be a number of rather extraordinary coincidences and yet, when you realize that we're both involved in the art world and that Rome is really a small city, it's not so unusual."

Anne blew out a stream of smoke. "I'll bet you didn't know that it was Edward I was married to before."

"No."

"What do you think of him?"

"Edward? I don't really know him. He knows a great deal about art and he's a talented artist from what I've seen. Why?"

"Oh, just curious. You don't suspect him of having anything to do with the stolen drawing, do you?"

Antonio glanced over at her. "Why would you ask that?"

"I don't know. You said you were involved in looking into the theft and that you knew Edward and I just assumed you'd check everyone who had anything to do with Valeriano's gallery." Anne shrugged. "I didn't really think you would suspect him, of course."

They drove the rest of the way to the hotel in silence. Antonio got out, circled the car and opened the door for Anne. It was impossible to tell what he was thinking, his dark brown eyes regarding her pensively behind the chic, round lenses.

"Well, thank you for a lovely evening." Anne held out her hand.

Antonio took it in his as he helped her out of the car. "It was my pleasure. I hope we may do it again sometime soon." He pulled her toward him and kissed her lightly on the cheek. Anne trembled when he released her and she walked wearily into the hotel, limping slightly. The wound in her pelvis had suddenly turned into a throbbing ache. Paolo was waiting for her in the lobby. He was one of the brothers who ran the hotel. It was Paolo who let late guests into the hotel.

"You had a nice evening?"

"Yes, it was very nice."

"Do you want to join me for a drink?"

"Not tonight, thanks Paolo. I'm really exhausted." Anne smiled at him briefly and went up to her room where she sat on the edge of the bed and stared at her face in the mirror. How stupid of her to talk about marriage and wanting to be adored. Antonio wasn't interested in adoring her. He had probably been given the onerous job of keeping her entertained while she was visiting Rome. She remembered doing that with visiting professors at Agnes Scott.

Anne washed her face and brushed her teeth. No wonder Edward had dumped her for Maya, the beautiful, beautiful Maya. Anne lay back on the bed, her eyes wide open, watching the rhythm of the fan as it turned slowly above her head. The light from the street framed the curtains, seeping in around the edges, the light's diameter growing momentarily wider as the motion of the air caused the curtain to sway. The mechanical God was everywhere: in the piazza, here in her room—the ubiquitous fan. It seemed arbitrary but, of course, it was not. The fan turned at a certain constant speed and each time the current of air came in contact with the material of the curtain it shifted in almost exactly the same direction, with almost exactly the same movement. Anne found herself mesmerized as she stared at the relationship between fan and curtain. So far apart and yet so touched by one another although, really it was the curtain that was touched by the fan, the fan simply turned, impervious to its impact on the objects and persons in the room.

Anne had been seven when her father had left. Her mother had been bitter, angry and Anne had loyally comforted her but all along she had desperately wanted him to come back, had secretly hoped that he would come back. And he had come back. One day, just a few months after he had left. Her mother had made Anne promise she would not speak to him, not let her father talk to her or see her and Anne had promised but she had been so glad to see him and she had let him into the house. He had picked her up and hugged her, told her how much he missed her, how much he loved her, how it was her mother's fault that he had left and she had believed him, or half believed him anyway. He had told her he just wanted to look at some pictures and take some of his clothes and she had made him a cup of coffee while he had begun rummaging through the house, taking things which he should not have taken, things which weren't his to take. He had carried these to his car and, kissing her good-bye, he had left her, holding the cup of cold coffee in her hands.

Anne began to feel as though she was also under the fan's power, pulling on and pushing off the coverlet as the air circled in warmer and cooler cycles. Was there some Fateful spirit who had set her life into motion and, if so, what would be the outcome? 'And yet I can always turn off the fan so I'm the one who's really in control,' Anne told herself but she didn't turn it off, of course, and under the spell cast by the motion and the pencil-thin strips of light which animated the room, she finally fell asleep.

CHAPTER SIXTEEN

"Ah. Masolino's 'Founding of Sta. Maria Maggiore.'
Christ and the Virgin sit in a sphere like the wicked
witch in the crystal ball, floating on a cloud as flat as
a pancake followed by a series of other flat clouds.
Pope Liberius looks for all the world like he's out for a
round of Sunday afternoon golf. But they didn't play golf
then. Our twentieth century cynicism blinds us to the
most sacred moments, hmmm? Perhaps this is the most
poignant loss of all—the inability to see beauty anymore—
instead we have faith only in the ugly and the mutilated."
(Edward Donant)

"Recently Discovered Caravaggio Disappears Once Again." Valeriano accepted a copy of "Corriere della Sera" from John and read about the theft with some amusement. He was once again settled in his own home, an opulent apartment overlooking the Piazza Navona. After ten days in the hospital in Turin he had insisted on moving back to Rome.

"A recently discovered painting of the Crucifixion, which is believed to have been painted by the Northern Italian renegade artist, Michelangelo Merisi da Caravaggio, was stolen yesterday as it was being transported for further tests regarding its authenticity. The painting had been crated in the Palazzo early the evening before under the supervision of Signore Frati who has sworn that the painting was in the truck when it left the Palazzo. Upon arrival the next day, however, it was discovered that there was no painting inside the crate—just the frame. There has been no statement from either the government or from Valeriano Cerasi, the prestigious gallery owner who discovered the painting.
"Signore Cerasi was involved in a car bombing just a few days prior to the theft and authorities are interested in the possibilities that the two events might be connected."

Valeriano leaned back in the chair and closed his eyes. His leg or, more accurately what was no longer his leg, was throbbing. It was one of the oddest and most annoying aspects of the mutilation: the fact that he had imagined pains where his leg no longer was.

"Interesting article, isn't it?" John stood next to the window overlooking the Piazza, a glass in his hand. The region around the temple on the right side of John's face was grossly deformed. Deep, irregular scar tissue had hypertrophied and contracted around the empty eye socket whose glassy replacement struck a disturbingly smooth note in the midst of such violent disfigurement.

Valeriano hated looking at his son's mutilated face. He knew that John exposed himself like that on purpose, just to annoy him. "Quite."

John swirled the amber-colored liquid in his glass. "Nice cognac, papa, do you want any?"

"Per piacere." They would never be able to tolerate each other. Valeriano had never been able to feel anything even close to affection for John. Brought up by his mother in America, John had many of the mannerisms and habits that Valeriano had detested in Caroline. It had been a mistake to leave him with her but it was too late to do anything about it now. And the drinking, John drank just like his mother had—compulsively, obsessively, without any restraint.

"Grazie." Valeriano took the glass and set it on the table next to the paper.

"So, who do you think stole your fabulous painting?" John perched on the edge of a Chippendale armchair.

"Don't sit on the edge of the chair," Valeriano snapped.

John stared at him blankly out of his one good eye. He took a sip from his glass. "Do you think it's the same people who put the bomb in your car?"

"I leave all that to the police. How am I supposed to speculate on such issues? I'm just an art dealer."

John began to laugh. "Maybe it's the same people who stole the Piranesi. Where's Gianni? He was supposed to meet me here this morning."

Valeriano shrugged. "Why do you hang around with such a person? He's disgusting. He has no integrity, you can't trust him."

"You certainly don't mind doing business with him."

"That's different. As you say, I do business with him, I don't socialize with him and neither should you."

John gulped down the rest of the cognac. "I'm going out." Without a backward glance John left the room, slamming the door behind him.

"John!" Valeriano called peevishly after his son. "John! Aspetto." He grimaced as he looked around for his crutches. He had to pee. "Bastardo," he muttered. He called for Claudio but then he remembered that Claudio wouldn't be back for another hour. Valeriano saw his crutches leaning against the far wall. John had put them there on purpose. He had meant to make it difficult for Valeriano. Now he'd have to crawl over to get them. "Bastardo!" he repeated as he pushed himself out of the chair and eased onto the floor.

CHAPTER SEVENTEEN

"Pisanello's 'Study of Hanged Men' in the British Museum is
a gruesome reminder of one of the more popular pastimes
during the Renaissance. The Campo dei Fiori, which means
'field of flowers,' rather ironically became a piazza notorious
for executions. And they were such fun. Ladies in the
seventeenth and eighteenth centuries paid money for a little
refreshment while they watched a hanging or a drawing
and quartering from their windows."
(Edward Donant)

"Rome smells. The heady aroma of garlic, basil, cat piss, exhaust fumes
and the stench from the Tiber combine to create an indefinably irresistible
perfume. It's a city of mysterious beauty; old, knowing, corrupt, cynical
and yet eternally young."

Anne scribbled over the references to smell and decay. It was too
personal, too hostile for such a group. After all, these students were in Rome
not so much to imbibe its invisible structure as to immerse themselves in
a foreign culture, unwilling or unable to see that what they feared most
lay on the other side of seduction—losing their comfortable identity only
to find a disturbing figure staring out at them from Narcissus' ancient
pool. She sketched out her lecture quickly on the small notepad she always
carried with her. She needed to hurry if she was to meet her students on
time at the Borghese Gallery.

"Like Paris in the late nineteenth and early twentieth centuries,
Rome, from the fifteenth to the eighteenth centuries, was the
center of artistic activity. All of the great artists came to Rome
to study. Goya had to pay his own way—he traveled with a group
of matadors, Rubens came and Velasquez, Poussin, David. They
all saw what there was to see of the forum, of course, and the
Palatine, the Colosseum and the Basilica of Maxentius. But it is
here, in the Villa Borghese, that we find one of the most compelling
reasons for the foreign artist's interest in Rome. It's the exciting
new surge of expression and power associated with the Baroque
and epitomized in the work of one man, Gian Lorenzo Bernini,
the father of modern Rome. Aside from the ruins of antiquity and
Michelangelo's Sistine Ceiling, it's Bernini's works that provide
the nuclear impression of Rome; the Fountain of the Four Rivers

in the Piazza Navona, the Ecstasy of St. Teresa in the Cornaro Chapel, the great throne and baldacchino within the Basilica of St. Peter's and the colonnade around the piazza before St. Peter's— these works, like Rome's heady perfume, remain embedded in the visitor's memory.

"Thus we find ourselves here, in the Villa Borghese, before a work of the young Bernini that epitomizes the schizophrenic character which underlies Roman history; the statue of Daphne and Apollo executed for Bernini's patron, Cardinal Scipione. In this work the power of desire and the excitement of conquest is contrasted with the rejection of desire and the frustration of conquest. The incredible grace of the two figures and the respective faces of anguish and frustration increase the onlooker's sense of empathy and fascination. Daphne's toes turning into roots, her fingers curling into twigs, her beautiful hair metamorphosing into leaves are all details in which Bernini revels in his exceptional technical skill. Walk around the group, feel the power of this twenty-five year old sculptor whose image is represented in the head of Apollo. The lust for Daphne can be equated with the ambition of the young Bernini who, perhaps, recognized that age-old anxiety which the Greeks termed hubris—the fall of those too proud before the gods. He prophesied his own fall from favor after his death, a prophecy culminating in the nineteenth century with Ruskin's contemptuous declaration that it 'was impossible for false taste and base feeling to sink lower.'"

It was noon when Anne left the Villa. It had been somewhat unnerving having so many people stop to listen at the edge of the group, and she had found herself experiencing the situation on two levels; the present in which she was discoursing, with apparent authority, on these great works of art and the past in which she had also slipped into groups, listening intently for the speaker to make a mistake, comparing what they said to what Tom said, curious as to their backgrounds, their knowledge, the reason that they were lecturing.

The sun was hotter than the day before, and yet the light was clear, not hazy with the humid heat of the tropics. Always conscious of the sun's effect on her skin, Anne put on her large floppy hat and crocheted gloves. She was going to meet Maya and Edward for lunch on the Via Veneto.

She passed a man sitting on the sidewalk in the Piazza Barbarini, begging. He had only half a body—he was cut off at the trunk and had long, dark bushy hair. Anne was horrified and she felt torn, as she always did, between pity and loathing. She hurried past him, ashamed that she gave him nothing but too disturbed to stop to leave him a few coins. She arrived at the Via Veneto where a group of young boys accosted her, teasing her, making sexual remarks, trying to touch her. Disgusted, Anne walked on, trying to ignore them but they followed her, surrounding her, laughing. She turned on them, haughtily dismissing them in French. In desperation she climbed the stairs to the Church of Santa Maria della Concezione. The boys remained on the street but continued to taunt her as she entered the church. Anne removed her hat and put on a jacket over her short-sleeved dress. Briefly she dipped at the central aisle before the altar. She was not a practicing Catholic though she had not completely denied the possibility that there was a deity whose presence was evoked in the echoing stillness of these huge cathedrals.

She sat in one of the pews and looked around the interior. She had never been in this church before and she wondered how she had missed it. Off to one side she noticed a large painting that she recognized as Guido Reni's painting of "St. Michael Trampling on the Devil." There was the image of the beautiful angel in powder blue armor, his short skirt flying, his sword raised as he prepared to plunge it into the coarsely muscular body of Lucifer who lay writhing beneath St. Michael's implacable foot. The angel stood against an ashen sky, his fair beauty contrasting with the dark brutality of the hellish landscape and the devil's face. Sparse hair covered Lucifer's skull, a black beard and moustache framed his face, which was supposedly a representation of Innocent X, a Pamphili pope hated by the Barberini family. As Anne walked over to look more closely at the painting, she was struck by the resemblance between Lucifer's face and Edward's—the pointed ears and nose, the eyes gleaming with unremorseful defiance and demonic humor. Edward, too, she thought, like Innocent, was a man of many facets who would not question his decisions in relation to any moral structure. Again she wondered what he knew about the Caravaggio and how he was connected to the Sicilian. Anne couldn't shake the sense that whatever Edward was involved in it wasn't legal.

CHAPTER EIGHTEEN

Goya is very expressionistic, he's often called the
Father of Romanticism. Goya is a philosopher. Rembrandt
and Caravaggio are marvelous psychologists, eh, but Goya
is a philosopher. He's the first artist to be really politically
involved. Before Daumier, before Courbet."
(Edward Donant)

Edward and Maya were already seated at the "Cafe de Paris" when Anne arrived. She kissed each of them on both cheeks.

Edward took off Anne's hat and ran his fingers through her hair. She stepped back and shook her head, frowning at him. "Stop it, Edward!"

"But that's so much better." He smiled at her complacently.

He ordered a bottle of Ferrari Rose, Anne asked for a Campari. She told them about her experience with the young boys. "If it weren't for the sanctuary of the churches, Rome would be intolerable," she finished.

Maya shook her head. "You don't dress properly, Anne."

"I must agree with Maya. You look like one of those awful matrons Caravaggio painted as Madonnas."

"Oh, thank you very much."

"Don't get angry, love." Maya leaned forward to kiss her affectionately. "It's just that you're so beautiful but you dress so boringly. It's almost as though you want to look dowdy."

Anne sipped her Campari and regarded them stonily. "Let's say you're both right, so how should I dress and how would this change the problem?"

"Remember how we used to dress when we were students? How we wore jeans and gypsy skirts and no bras? And how the worst men were always chasing us and following us in the streets?" Maya leaned back, one of her golden arms stretched along the back of Edward's chair where she lazily ran her fingers across the nape of his neck.

Anne thought that Maya was an awfully touchy, feely kind of person. She wondered why she had never noticed how annoying this was before. "I remember."

"I figured it out," Maya continued. "What's respected here is a sort of expensively luxurious style, not too casual, not formal, sexy without being cheap. You must dress provocatively without looking like a whore: short skirts, revealing necklines but not too much. Your hair has to be properly styled and your makeup subtly sensual. Then, when you know you look wonderful, you can go anywhere and instead of having kids insult you, you have charming younger men murmur compliments and older ones press their hands over their hearts in a gesture of reverence."

Anne shrugged. "And you don't think that I've achieved this delicate balance?"

"Well, the hat needs to go and the crocheted gloves, really, darling."

The waiter brought them their food.

Anne cut into her carpaccio. "Still, how am I to attain this impossible paragon of feminine desire and unapproachability? I can't just change who I am and besides, I don't really want to."

Edward smiled at Anne. "We would never propose that you change the way you are, would we Maya?"

"Of course not. I was just suggesting ways you might avoid being picked on by boys."

"You mean, like boys who go around wanting to throw acid in your face?"

Maya flushed. "You don't even know what I was talking about."

"What?" Edward looked curious. "What boys are these? What have you been doing, darling, to warrant such attention?"

"I saw a boy steal a woman's wallet on a bus and I confronted him and he hates me. That's all." Maya looked triumphantly at Anne. "It had nothing to do with the way I dress."

Anne raised her eyebrows. "Very noble of you but what makes you think he's out to throw acid at you?"

Maya shrugged. "It's just something I heard. I'm not really worried, of course."

"Well, it was a nice thing for you to do," Anne said with grudging admiration. "And I'm sure that what you heard is just some sort of urban myth or something."

"Of course." Maya laughed as she took a bite of her salad.

"As to the way I dress, well, I like the way I dress." Anne knew she sounded defensive. She tried to soften her tone. "And, anyway, I'm not beautiful like you, Maya. With your looks and the way you speak Italian they probably think you're one of them. They never bother their own women the way they do foreigners."

"Anne! You're far lovelier than I. At any rate you look much more Italian than I do."

"Ah," Edward poured wine into the three glasses. "We must be careful putting thoughts into the heads of the Italians. They've got enough thoughts of their own. We must be perceptive of, we must be careful with those things, you know. There are so many different people in each country.

People do get around with their genes, you know. There are blondes in Italy all the way down to Naples."

"Edward's *so* politically correct." Maya leaned toward Anne conspiratorially.

"It has nothing to do with political correctness. It has to do with understanding human nature."

"Human nature meaning rape and pillage." Maya took a bite of Edward's fettucine.

Anne searched for her cigarettes in her purse.

"You make too many assumptions." Edward said as he leaned back in the black chair with orange plastic webbing.

Anne wondered why the Italian cafes she frequented always had some glaring tasteless note, such as the fake flowers at "La Dolce Vita." It reminded her of her mother who had had a penchant for pink glass figurines and plastic roses.

Edward made an expansive gesture with his hand. "I rather appreciate the coarser side of humanity—what would we do without those wonderful sly characters in Flemish and Italian paintings, not to mention the lovely lascivious nudes?"

"Lust and gluttony isn't always quaint, Edward, art historical citations notwithstanding." Anne picked up a Tribune, which was lying on the table.

"No, but they remain the base of the social pyramid. We haven't moved that far from the hot quarters of an incestuous bed though we like to buy our sheets from Gucci."

"Oh, dear, Edward, that really is taking poetic license with Freudian theory." Anne opened the journal.

Maya smiled at Anne. "All of my sheets are hand-me-downs."

"Voila." Edward kissed her. "I love Maya's honesty."

Anne ignored them, pulling out a cigarette. Suddenly she gasped and held up the paper. "Have you read this?"

"Of course." Edward looked at her affectionately. "That's why I bought the paper. Oh, excuse me." He held out a lighter and Anne leaned forward, cupping his hand to draw on the flame.

"Aren't you in the least upset?" Anne felt cheated and angry.

Edward shrugged. "The Caravaggio's been stolen. I'm surprised but not upset."

Maya sipped her drink. "Why would he be upset? It's not like it belonged to us or anything. I guess Valeriano's pretty angry about it."

"It didn't belong to him either," Anne said irritably. "And that's not even the point."

"Why are you so upset?" Maya asked.

"Because, now, we'll never know for sure whether or not it was a fake. I really wanted them to finish testing it."

"You think that the painting wasn't genuine?" Edward poured more wine into Anne's glass.

"That's right," she looked at Edward. "I'm positive it was a fake and now we'll never know for sure and that frustrates me!"

"But there are a lot of paintings around that may be fakes, right, darling?" Maya looked to Edward for confirmation. "Just look at the Mona Lisa. When she was stolen and returned to the Louvre after they'd made those copies of her no one could really be sure that the real one was returned."

"May I?" Anne had barely touched her carpaccio. She passed her plate to Edward. He twirled a large piece of the almost transparent meat carefully around his fork. "Which is ridiculous. The forgers in the early part of this century weren't up against the sophisticated equipment we now have to detect fraud. However, it all leads into the question of the value of the originals. The issue between fraud and authenticity is really one of technology. It's no longer an issue of 'art' or 'taste' or 'intuition.' They might as well exhibit fakes since most people are perfectly satisfied as long as they think they're the originals." He transferred the meat from the fork to his mouth.

"You certainly have a lax attitude towards crime." Anne turned to Maya. "Have you noticed that? Makes you wonder if he doesn't have a criminal mind."

"Oh, I don't think there's any question of that." Maya grinned at Edward affectionately.

"You deeply offend me." Edward wiped his lips. "I do not have a criminal mind. It's just that I find fraud fascinating. And it's not only because of the issues of authenticity and the market but because the production of fakes also reflects the human fascination with and desire for proof of magical and miraculous events. Look at the Victorian assertions that fairies really existed. When those two little girls faked photographs of fairies people, like Arthur Conan Doyle, who wanted to believe in fairies, leapt at the chance to publish them as a vindication of their own beliefs. And because people wanted to believe in these things there were plenty of pragmatic individuals willing to provide evidence of their existence. The most amazing objects of fraud are religious relics, which are quite astonishing in their proof that human reason will always be prey to human gullibility. Look at the Shroud of Turin, which has recently been proved to be a genuine fourteenth century fake."

"Yes, all right. So what? You think that the fakers are pragmatists and the believers gullible, therefore the fakers are somehow superior?" Anne found herself irritated, as usual, with Edward's smug point of view.

"I find it sad that faith and belief require such ridiculous compendiums. Like the appreciation of the aesthetic of a painting, faith should rely on knowledge, experience and internal understanding, not on the hysterical adulation of trinkets."

"Actually, that was well put." Anne picked up her gloves and laid her share of the bill on the table.

"Did you think that I put that well?" Looking puppyish, Edward sighed and leaned his chin on Maya's shoulder.

"Ow, you're hurting me." She pushed him away. "I don't know that that means you don't have a criminal mind. But never mind, darling, it's all part of your endearing charm. Don't you agree, Anne?"

"Oh, definitely." Anne made a show of putting on her gloves and hat. "I can't think of anything more charming than an endearing criminal. But I'm still not satisfied in spite of all your pretty talk."

Edward picked up the bill. "You always were difficult to satisfy, Anne."

Anne smiled sarcastically. "Ooh, touché."

Maya slipped her hand through Anne's arm. "Can I walk with you? Edward's got another appointment this afternoon, as usual."

"Oh, Edward," Anne pulled her arm from Maya as they were leaving the café. "I almost forgot. I didn't know that you knew Antonio Tani."

"Yes, why do you ask?"

"Did you know that he was writing about Piranesi? And that he's involved in the investigation of the theft of the drawing?"

Edward shrugged. "I didn't know but it doesn't surprise me. How do you know him?"

"He works at the American University."

"Of course. Actually, it's interesting that you mention him. He's one of the guests I've invited to dinner tonight. If I had known you knew him I would have included you, Anne. I'm sorry."

Anne shrugged, slightly piqued that she had not been invited anyway. "That's all right."

"Don't forget to buy some flowers, Maya."

Maya held on to Anne's arm as they left the café. "Come with me to the Trevi Fountain. I haven't been there since we were here with the Emory program."

Anne hesitated. "Sure, why not? It's the way I wanted to go anyway."

"Edward's been very mysterious about this dinner tonight. I don't know anyone he's invited. Well, not until he mentioned your friend. And I did ask him to invite you but he said that tonight wasn't a good time. You don't mind, do you, Anne?"

Anne shook her head and smiled. "Not at all. I've got to prepare for a lecture I'm giving tomorrow."

They walked down the Via Liguria, turning into side streets until they reached the Largo di Tritone. Maya fanned her hand before her face. "It's so dreadfully hot, even in the evenings. Do you still wear socks to bed at night?"

Anne laughed. "Yes."

"I remember when we roomed together at Emory I couldn't believe it when you put on ankle socks before you went to bed."

"My feet are always cold." Anne jumped out of the way of a speeding motorcyclist.

"Grazie," he waved a hand.

They turned down the via della Stamperia which opened onto the Piazza Trevi. The fountain, made famous by the films, "Three Coins in the Fountain" and "La Dolce Vita," crawled up the rear of the neo-classical building, the carved rocks and foliage appearing to grow out of the walls like some sprawling fungus. A giant, rather ungainly figure of Neptune stood upon an oyster shell while two winged horses, held by two mermen, reared up from the rocks. Anne felt a pang of sadness. She remembered throwing coins in the fountain and wishing fervently that she would return to Rome but then she had had no idea how difficult it was to ever really go back.

"Do you remember when we threw the coins in the fountain? It took a long time but it worked. Here we are, back again and yet we'll never experience it the way Anita Ekberg did, standing in the water in the magically empty early morning hours." Maya sighed wistfully.

"You know they actually filmed that scene at 'Cinecitta.' It was all a fake."

"Oh no, how disappointing," Maya pouted. "I liked it better when I thought they did it here."

The square was crowded, as usual, with tourists eating cones of gelato and Italians watching the tourists. Maya immediately attracted the attention of a good-looking, sleazy man who began to converse with her in Italian. His companion, a fair-haired, muscular individual wearing tight, striped pants and an orange vest over a checked shirt sidled up next to Anne.

"Hello."

Anne tried to ignore him.

"Hellooo." He leaned over and stared into her face, grinning, two gold teeth prominent at the front of his mouth.

"Hi." She turned away.

"You like the Trevi fountain?"

Anne sighed. "Yes."

"What do you do?"

"I'm a professor. I teach."

"Reeeally." He sneered at her. "What do you teach?"

"Art history." She held her head high and withdrew her hand, which he had taken.

"So. Art history. Do you know who designed this fountain?"

"Of course." Anne turned away. She hadn't the vaguest idea who had designed the Trevi fountain.

"Really? Who was it?" He followed Anne as she walked away.

"Why should I tell you? I don't wish to talk to you."

"I know who designed it."

Anne began to walk faster.

"You don't know." He hooted after her.

"Yes I do." She laughed.

"You don't know," he called after her again.

"Maya, come on." Anne pulled her friend unceremoniously away from the man she was talking with.

"What's the matter?"

"I can't stand that offensive man who was following me."

"Why? What did he say?"

They turned onto the Via Sabini Crociferi.

"He challenged me about who designed the fountain." Anne laughed. "I have no idea but I insisted I knew and he saw right through it."

Maya preened, "I know who designed it."

"You're kidding. I've never met anyone who knew. Who is it?"

"Nicolo Salvi. It was completed in 1762. Evidently he died during construction."

"I'm impressed. How did you know that?"

"That guy I just met told me."

They laughed as they came out onto the Piazza Colonna.

"Who would ever think of that as a pickup line?" Anne searched through her bag for her cigarettes. She noticed a group of young boys standing before a gelateria, smoking cigarettes. They were staring at Maya and her and talking amongst themselves.

Maya moved closer to Anne. "Those boys are watching us."

Anne shrugged. "There are boys all over Rome watching women and making fun of them. Who cares?"

"It's what Sergei said. It's made me nervous."

"Who's Sergei?"

"Nobody, well, just some man I met."

"What did he say?"

"He's the one who told me about those boys looking for me and throwing acid in my face."

"I thought you said you weren't bothered by that."

"I'm not but it still makes me nervous whenever I see a group of boys watching me."

Anne lit a cigarette and blew smoke out in a thin stream. "I don't think you should worry about those boys but I do understand. I've got things that haunt me, too. I suppose it's waiting for something to happen, wanting to make something happen, that's hardest. You just want closure. You want to move on, to not obsess about something over which you have no control."

"But that's precisely the problem. How can you control the crazy people? How can I anticipate something that's totally ludicrous and that's motivated by something that's completely unfair?"

"Maybe that boy who stole the wallet feels like you acted unfairly. Jumping on him like that. Maybe he feels like he's struggling to survive in a hard, unfeeling world, doing the best he can and that you step in from your privileged position of wealth and security, and you take away from him what he feels he's owed."

Maya stared at her. "You don't actually think that I should have let him get away with stealing that woman's wallet?!"

"No, of course not. I'm not saying that he would be right thinking that, I'm just suggesting that sometimes fairness depends on your perspective." Anne stopped. If it really depended on perspective then there wasn't any way to judge whether something was right or wrong. She shook her head. There were some things that could never be justified, never be forgiven. "No, I think you did what was right. I was just arguing for the sake of argument like I always do."

"That sounds just like Edward and, by the way, why did you say that you think he has a criminal mind?"

"Oh, I don't think he's done anything actually criminal. It was just something I said." Anne looked curiously at Maya. "But it wouldn't surprise me if he was ever involved in something illicit would it you?"

"Yes it would." Maya looked surprised. "I thought you were just joking. In all honesty I *would* be surprised if he really did something illegal."

"Do you remember the Mafia man with the long fingernails I was telling you about yesterday?"

"You don't know he's with the Mafia, Anne."

"Yes, yes, but anyway, I saw Edward with him in a café on the Piazza Navona after you left."

Maya stared at her. "That's weird."

"Isn't it? I thought so. Why would Edward know someone like that?"

Maya frowned and then laughed. "Oh, it's probably nothing, just one of his many business contacts. You're right, it was a strange coincidence but you know Edward. He has lots of strange acquaintances." Maya looked at her watch. "Oh God, I've got to go. I've got to shower and change for this dinner tonight, make myself beautiful, you know."

"Right," Anne said dryly.

"I really wish you were coming, darling. You honestly don't mind?"

"I couldn't come anyway. I've got to work on this lecture," Anne smiled but she felt a hollow tightening in her chest. So Antonio was going to be there. He could have invited her if he had wanted to see her.

"Edward's been so mysterious about his guests. There's someone other than Antonio coming but he won't tell me who it is."

"Maybe it's the Mafia man."

Maya laughed. "Wouldn't that be funny?"

CHAPTER NINETEEN

"Rutilio Manetti's 'Andromeda liberata da Perseo' in the Villa
Borgese is an example of how terrible artists can be...
even before the twentieth century. Those awful globular
breasts, her legs primly crossed at the ankles as though she
were at some British tea party. One arm raised, manacled to
the cliff. Sweat, oh, excuse me, tears are dripping off of
her face. Perseus is sailing above the sea like a figure in a
Disney cartoon. The monster looks rather tired and definitely
off course. He's actually heading straight into the cliffs
behind her. Perhaps there's a tastier morsel back there, hmmm?"
(Edward Donant)

Maya twisted and turned on the bed, angered by her desire, fantasizing about Sergei. Her lips were like the inside of blooms so sensitive to touch that they opened and closed at the most minute sensation. Desire turned her to a hothouse flower seeking warmth. Trying to analyze passion, desire was an exhausting process because wherever she began—with the lingering gaze searching for confirmation yet protectively veiled, with the first tentative kisses that became burning insistence, with the touch of hands and arms and tongues that broke the boundaries of respectability— it all circled back to an overwhelming need for closure, for relief.

"Good God, give me satisfaction," Maya muttered as she ran her hands across her body. Nothing satisfied her, she had only arid, infertile fantasies. She threw the sheets off with a curse and tied on her bathrobe. Edward would be here shortly with his mysterious guests.

After her shower, she dressed carefully, putting on the short black dress, which was so successful, a simple strand of pearls and dangling pearl earrings. Maya looked approvingly at her reflection—if she couldn't find sexual fulfillment at least she could have the satisfaction of knowing that she aroused desire in others.

She made martinis, which she disliked but Edward adored. "A martini is like the notes of the saxophone," he had said once. "It's the elixir by which you transcend the humdrum routine of the everyday. The olive, rolling like polished jade in the clear liquid; it's a universe in a glass. And the martini glass..." Edward had insisted on packing his set of Waterford glasses. He considered them the perfect martini glass, their lines, their lips, the stems just heavy enough to grasp easily, slender enough not to interfere with the bowl.

Maya heard steps and voices in the hall. She identified Edward's voice as the door opened. Checking her face quickly in the mirror, she turned to greet him with a smile that promptly froze on her face as he stepped into the room followed by two men, one of who was Sergei.

Edward crossed the room and kissed her warmly on the cheek. "My dear, let me introduce Antonio Tani from the American University here. You remember Anne mentioned him today at lunch."

"Yes, of course. How do you do?"

Antonio took Maya's hand and, bowing, kissed it delicately. "Mi piace to make your acquaintance, Maya. Edward has spoken often of you."

"I hope he only mentioned my good qualities." Maya laughed nervously.

"I've heard only good things," Antonio smiled.

"And this is Sergei, a model whom I met posing for Aristide. I'm thinking of using him myself in my next painting. A perfect Adonis."

Sergei crossed the room and kissed her on both cheeks. "Buona sera, Maya."

"Sergei." She spoke coolly.

"Well, how extraordinary." Edward looked from one to the other. "You already know each other. I do think that's very neat."

Maya thought that he sounded slightly triumphant. She smiled stiffly, "Yes, Sergei and I have met before in the Piazza Navona." She turned away. "Can I offer anyone something to drink? I've made martinis but I must warn you they're quite strong."

"I would love a martini," Antonio smiled at her again. "Especially when it's made by a hostess as charming as yourself."

Maya smiled at him gratefully. Sergei took a glass of Pinot Grigio like herself. They all raised their glasses in a toast. "Salute." The conversation continued rather desultorily, with Sergei staring insolently at Maya while Edward and Antonio discussed art. The rich, meaty smell of roast lamb filled the apartment, complemented by the pungent odor of anchovies in the sauce for the crostini. Almost overwhelmed by the stronger odors was the subtle scent of lavender, a bouquet of which Maya had arranged in a vase on the table. They nibbled on nuts and olives. "Anne tells us that you're involved in investigating the theft of the Piranesi drawing," Edward said to Antonio.

"Yes, that's right."

"Have you found out anything? Do you have any suspects?" Edward winked at Sergei and Maya. "We're all fascinated."

Antonio shrugged. "As a matter of fact we do want to question a couple of people who have connections to the gallery and the exhibition. They're not necessarily suspects but their testimony may prove to be of value. In fact, one of them lives in your apartment building."

"Really?!" Maya's eyes shone. "Who?"

Antonio smiled at her. "I'm afraid I can't tell you that."

"How unfair. Now I'm going to suspect everyone I meet."

Antonio re-filled Maya's glass. "I hear you were also at the exhibition in Florence. I'd be curious to know what you thought of the Caravaggio."

"Quite impressive." Edward answered for Maya as he brought in the abbacchio alla cacciatora(baby lamb) and a green salad with lemon and freshly pressed olive oil.

"I believe Antonio was directing the question to me, darling," Maya frowned at Edward but he didn't notice.

"Well," Antonio said diplomatically. "I was asking both of you. I guess what I was really wondering was if you thought the painting was authentic."

Maya shrugged. "I don't know much about art but it certainly looked genuine to me. It looked old at any rate. Edward's really the expert."

"What did you think?" Antonio turned towards Edward.

"I haven't made up my mind."

"And now we'll never know," Antonio said. "It's really a shame."

"That's exactly what Anne said," Maya sipped her drink. "Have the two of you been discussing this?"

Antonio shook his head. "It's only natural that the theft of the painting would raise the question of validity especially if it was, if it is, a true Caravaggio. If so, it's a great loss."

"Well, perhaps the painting will be recovered." Edward's mouth turned up slightly in a smile as he helped himself to more salad. "We owe the delicious olive oil to a rustic winery in the Tuscan hills. I received it from a friend."

Antonio took a bite. "I'm quite impressed that you made abbacchio. It's one of my favorite dishes."

Maya made a pretty moue. "I have a certain resistance to eating babies of any kind; lamb, veal, chicken. I prefer to think that my food is more mature and simply came to a timely end."

Sergei snorted. "They're all coming to a timely end as far as I'm concerned." He cut up pieces of the lamb and ate it aggressively.

Edward smiled at him indulgently. He took Sergei's plate, his fingers lightly brushing Sergei's hand. "Some more for the beautiful boy?

"And what did you think of the Salone dei Cinquecento?" Antonio turned again to Maya.

"It's a beautiful room," Maya smiled brightly at Antonio. What was Edward up to this evening? He was actually flirting with Sergei and he was treating her as though she was an idiot. Maya glared at him.

"Yes, though it's really a shame that neither Leonardo's nor Michelangelo's frescoes remain." Antonio accepted a second helping of abbacchio. "I commend your culinary skills, Edward."

Edward bowed. "And now we have the pleasure of Vasari's boring interpretations of Duke Cosimo I's reign. It just shows how mediocrity can triumph over brilliance. If only Leonardo hadn't insisted on experimenting with his medium." Edward dribbled a bit of wine down his chin, which he deftly removed with a swipe of his napkin. "Almost as deadly as a bomb."

"Ah, yes, the bombing. You were lucky you weren't seriously injured." Antonio filled Maya's glass again. She smiled at him.

"You mean, like Valeriano." Edward said.

"Actually, from what I hear, he's also lucky. At any rate, there are far too many bombings in Italy. We really must do something about these people."

"What people?" Maya picked at the meat on her plate.

"The Mafia, dearest," Edward said. "They're usually behind these attacks though in this case it's hard to see why they would target Valeriano."

"Maybe it wasn't the Mafia," Sergei said. "Maybe it was just someone who had a grudge against Valeriano."

Edward shrugged. "We'll probably never know."

"But to put a bomb in someone's car," Maya said. "I don't understand that at all. I mean, don't they care who they hurt? They could hurt anyone, not just the persons in the car."

"These aren't nice people, darling. They're not even brave people. There's something inimically revolting about bombs. You're right—they're so indiscriminate, so destructive. There's nothing in the slightest of either intellectual or aesthetic appeal in a bomb. Unlike the crossbow, the sword, the pike—just look at the beautiful design of the Scythian dagger." Edward opened another bottle of wine and brought in a tray of cheeses and fruit.

"In a way, you could say it's sort of like contemporary art."

Sergei unfolded his legs and held out his glass for more wine. "What do you mean?"

Antonio glanced at Sergei. "I was referring to Edward's comparison between bombs and art."

"You mean they self-destruct leaving nothing for posterity." Maya spoke slowly. "Like that piece by the French sculptor, Tinguely. Something about New York."

Edward cut a chunk of Taleggio cheese. "It's an interesting point, Antonio. Much of the twentieth century has been spent in trying to produce the 'final' painting, the ultimate work of art and in so doing artists have competed trying to create something so banal, so average that it will no longer be marketable. Since Dada, artists have been seeking the ultimate denial of art as a collectible object so, in a sense, you're right—art, in the classical sense, is in danger of being destroyed. But, it's kind of backfired, at least for the art market. In seeking to destroy the object artists have only succeeded in creating a market where the least interesting objects have become goldmines for unscrupulous artists and dealers."

Sergei peeled the skin from a pear. Maya watched, fascinated, as the opaque flesh descended in curls from the fruit. "But you don't paint like that," she said. "Your paintings are much more traditional."

"Classical," Edward corrected her. "Yes, I'm interested in the concept of beauty in the classical sense. For instance, don't you find Sergei beautiful? In the classical sense, I mean and by that I'm referring to the ideal established by the ancient Greeks."

Sergei cut a slice of the pear and slid it into his mouth, watching Edward who smiled at him. Edward turned to Maya. "I saw him at Aristide's and I thought, 'Wouldn't he make a fine addition to any room' so, of course, I wanted to invite him here where I could see the two of you together. Two beauties adorning my room. It's like having living works of art."

"Don't be ridiculous, Edward." Maya spoke irritably, "You sound like one of those mad collectors in one of those awful short stories who decides to add human prey to his rooms of treasure."

"Do you think that's mad?" Edward smiled amiably.

"It's definitely inviting trouble." Antonio ran his hand absentmindedly through his hair. "There's a certain pleasure to be gained by viewing beauty when it's hung upon the wall. You don't have to worry about it growing old and fat and grumpy."

"Oh well, who's to say what beauty is anyway." Sergei poured the last of the wine into his glass.

"That's a very interesting point." Edward leaned back in his chair and crossed his hands on his belly. "It's fascinating to speculate on. Look at the eighteenth century. Their ideal is exemplified in one of those marvelous drawings by Watteau. Fashion certainly enters into it. For the eighteenth century, especially for Watteau, beauty's in all of those transitory, changing aspects of the human, including fashion. Fashion is always changing and so are the figures. And poor Watteau, when fashion shifted he was out of the picture. Left standing there, like Giles with his arms dangling helplessly by his side. Oh, beauty, the idea of beauty, is cruel. Once you're past your prime you become an object of mockery."

"You're an object of mockery even before you're past your prime."

"When have you ever been an object of mockery?"

Maya rolled her eyes, "Oh, come on Edward. You know what I mean. You're making fun of me right now."

Sergei smiled sardonically and Antonio looked uncomfortable. He seemed about to say something when Edward spoke. "I certainly hope that's not how I come across. At any rate, I never make light of your beauty." He tilted his head as though in appraisal of Maya. "Look at Rubens' second wife, a wonderful strawberry blond. All of that radiant, glorious, abundant nudity wrapped round with a mink. I don't know if it's a mink. It's a specific idea of beauty. Not quite what we admire today. She tried to have the painting destroyed after Rubens died. She didn't think it was very proper. I wonder what we would consider proper today. You certainly wouldn't object to being represented in the nude." Again he smiled at Maya.

"You see?" Piqued, Maya turned to Antonio for support.

Antonio leaned forward. "I don't think it was the nudity Rembrandt's wife objected to so much as the intimacy. It's not exactly pornographic but it's a painting that was created clearly for the pleasure of the viewer, for the pleasure of Rubens, in fact, who shares his erotic delight in his wife with the whole world. That old idea of objectifying the female for the delight of the male."

"And do you feel that you're an eroticized object when you pose?" Maya looked challengingly at Sergei.

"I pose for the money. I don't have any problem being nude or having other people see me nude. I don't give a damn what they think."

"Bravo." Edward stood up and the others followed suit. They had coffee and cognac on the terrace.

"But we never finished our discussion of bombs." Sergei cupped his hands behind his head and leaned back in the seat.

"What more can you say about them?" Maya stared irritably at Sergei.

"Actually, I find bombs rather fascinating."

"Really!" Maya demanded. "And why would you say that?"

"They're products of our time and they're quite beautiful—all those flames, the noise, the excitement."

"And the death and destruction," Antonio added dryly.

Sergei shrugged. "Everybody dies."

"You find a bomb beautiful." Maya leant forward. "I hope you get the chance to experience the beauty of a bomb yourself some day."

Sergei poured himself some more cognac. "Many beautiful things are unpleasant."

Maya frowned at him. "Of course, beauty isn't always nice but a bomb isn't beautiful. No weapon of destruction is beautiful. I think you just say that to try to look cool."

Sergei grinned at her.

Antonio leaned forward, "I hear that you and Edward are planning on getting married."

Maya looked at him and smiled somewhat bitterly. "We've talked about it."

Edward crossed the small terrace to take Maya's hand. "Maya hasn't decided if I'm good enough for her," he said.

"Don't be absurd," Maya withdrew her hand and picked up a fan lying on the table next to her. "It's certainly not me who gives the impression that I don't care..." She stopped and leaned back in the chair with half-closed eyes. Staring at Sergei, she fanned herself slowly, almost meditatively.

"There," Edward waved his hand at Maya, "The language of the fan. That's a lost art. The beauty is in the social presentation, the performance, the whole psychology of the person. The flash of an eye, the animation of a face as it converses, the ineffable expressions of sweetness that play across the face. It's almost like the psychology of perfume. It has no beginning, no end; it floats past your senses. You can't grasp it as it floats past; it's quickly gone. Do you know they put a little manure in perfume in Paris? Just a pinch. Isn't it wonderful? You mix manure with roses and rosehips and whatever they put in there and it's suddenly delightful. I suppose you could make that into some kind of metaphor—beauty is always mixed with a little shit, hmmmm?"

CHAPTER TWENTY

"Goya almost speaks for himself, I think. It's almost a sacrilege
to lecture on him. Very macho man, like Caravaggio—
amours, fights, tavern scenes. He's got everything and
I think he knows it. Another curious thing about Goya and
Caravaggio—they don't fit anywhere—they ride the time box.
Goya was born way back in the time of Louis X, in the
time of the French regime. Spain is the strangest country.
I remember going to the museums. Ghastly, ghastly pictures—
unless you have a taste for it you know, like American
art historians who have a taste for those awful *primitives*
they parade around. And then, in the midst of it all
come those great names; Goya, Velasquez, Ribera."
(Edward Donant)

In Ostia, Anne and John had argued as they always did. She had claimed
that one could never really return to the past, never really understand how
people had felt, how they had lived. "History, art, anthropology, it's all
an illusion, an abstraction of reality," she had said. John had insisted that
it wasn't an illusion. "I live in the past," he had said. "It's more real than
the present." He had shown Anne his new watch: a Patek Phillippe—very
expensive, very gold. "It's a gift from my dad."

They had followed the group of students and their professor, Tom,
down the ancient streets lined with tufa blocks. The stones bore traces
from the tracks of wheels of carts from a culture centuries old. Turning
down a side street they had climbed the stairs to look down into what had
once been the main room of the Baths of Neptune. There, unprotected
from the intrusion of earth and sky, dogs and humans, were the remains
of a large and beautiful mosaic of Neptune. John had talked about the
people who had walked over this work of art, indifferent to the value it
would later hold for artists and historians. Anne had said that its cultural
meaning had disintegrated along with its human referents.

"There are few people who know who Neptune is, much less who care
about the connections between myth and culture."

"You don't need to know about the literary past to appreciate Bacchus,
though," John had said. "Like Christ you just have to have faith" and he
had smiled that lopsided grin and patted his pocket where he always
carried a bottle of whiskey.

"I don't think whiskey was one of the god's elixirs."

"Ah, but intoxication was. It's the essence of the cult; the beast that prowls on the verge of the conscious and the unconscious, that guards the realm between life and death."

***

As Anne stood once again before the Baths of Neptune, she regretted the fact that the stairs were now closed off. As Anne began her lecture, her students peered at the floor through an opening in the ancient walls: the Nereids and other sea creatures had become wavy and bumpy as the earth had pushed the tiny stones in different directions, warping and altering the original pattern.

"These baths were built on an even older complex of Roman baths. Begun during the Emperor Hadrian's reign, they weren't completed until 134 A.D. when Antoninus Pius gave Ostia the funds necessary for their completion. What you're looking at here, frustratingly fragmented view that it is, are the remains of the 'Triumph of Neptune,' which decorated the main room of the baths. On the other side is a mosaic representing Amphitrite, the queen of the sea. Imagine uncovering these beautiful mosaics from the sand and dirt and weeds that had overgrown so much of Ostia. As we walk through the ancient city you will see tantalizing bits still underlying the grass, which has yet to be removed."

It was extremely hot and Anne paused, as they walked down the road, to drink from her bottle of tepid water. She found the road much more difficult to walk on than she remembered it when she first came here. Stumbling on the uneven stones, she led her students past the Thermopolium (an ancient tavern) towards the Great Horrea (a warehouse). Anne recalled talking to John as they had followed Tom on a similar tour. Tom had pointed out the various brickwork that could be found on many of the buildings.

***

"Of course, the walls weren't just brick and stone as we see them today," he had said. "They were originally covered with smooth stucco. They used cement mixed with lime called 'opus coementicum.'

'Opus quadratum' is a technique of squaring off stones so that they can be fitted together without the use of mortar, 'opus verticulatum' is where stones are fitted together to create a diamond grid and 'opus testacaeum' is pointed brick embedded in cement..."

"'Opus testicularum,'" John had muttered to Anne.

107

"'Opus pornigraficum,'" she had responded, giggling.

***

Anne led her students back down the main street, the Decumano Massimo. She wanted to find the mosaic of the Via della Caserma dei Vigili. She remembered eating blackberries from tangled vines growing near this mosaic and she wanted to share the experience with her students. She was relieved to find it just as she had remembered it and that, though not wholly ripe, there was plenty of black fruit clustered on the vines.

There had been moments when she and John had been so close, when he had been so sweet. Of course that was why she had continued to be friends with him. Otherwise she would never have gone up to the roof with him. It was strange how often love could be so petty and mean. But surely that wasn't real love; it was more a sickness, a disease.

Anne reached out to search among the greenness of the leaves and the shadows of the thicket. Picking a handful of berries, holding each one in her mouth, she savored the burst of flavor and thought how lovely it was to eat fruit fresh from the vine. Sweetened and ripened by sunshine and rain, made intense by thunder and lightening, each berry represented a lifetime, an eternity of genealogical development. Popped into the mouth, they were consumed but still left that evanescent moment of immortality lingering on the tongue and in the memory. Anne thought that only handpicked fruit carried the seeds of generations, of cyclical nature. Fruit purchased in stores were, like packaged chicken and hydroponic tomatoes, flesh of the never born, the never dead. There was no connection between that exquisite combination of desire and destruction.

You altered that which you desired when you ate, of course, but also when you loved. Food, wine, sex; they all represented various acts of consumption resulting in different products; feces, urine, babies. What had da Vinci called people? "Sacks for food" and "fillers-up of privies." As with so many great men, there was no mention of vessels of birth. This aspect of creativity was discarded as something only women could fulfill, thus something of negligible or negative value. Or was it because they were the bearers of worthless humanity? Certainly it was something she would never experience.

Bitterly Anne thought of that night on the roof of the hotel. She could hear John's voice again, whispering in her ear, his hand pulling on her wrist. He had been drunk as usual. Anne reached deep into the thicket for a big, ripe berry. As she did so a thorn caught her cheek. "Ow." Anne retreated, vexed. She was hot and tired. "It's way too hot here and we've seen all we can see today. Let's go."

Her students expressed concern about the blood trickling down her cheek. "It's nothing, just the result of being too greedy." Anne smiled reassuringly as a droplet of blood, warm and salty, slid from the scratch on her cheek into the curve of her mouth.

CHAPTER TWENTY ONE

"Desire is one of those impish concepts—Cupid's bow
and arrow doesn't bring *love*, it brings the stinging rage
of desire. He's a mischievous little devil, always grinning
as he goes about wreaking havoc in gentle folks' lives.
A lot like advertisements today. They shoot us with the
barb of desire and, all oblivious to quality, beauty or
love, we rush to satiate our ungovernable greed."
(Edward Donant)

Maya opened her eyes. She was sleeping in a cool recession of the room, in a niche behind the arch that opened onto the dining room. She closed her eyes again so as to be able to hear more distinctly the noises of late-afternoon apartment buildings. The sound of sunlight so bright it squeaked down the glossy leaves of the philodendron and landed with a harsh jolt on the linoleum floor. That would be the kitchen whose windows opened onto the west where there were three or four obligatory pigeons cooing on the windowsill. The fat lady across the courtyard was calling her cat, an airplane droned overhead. Inside, the passing time was marked by primal cockroach scribbles in the dust, gnat's whirring wings, the restless settling of unprimed cogwheels as the mantle clock ground out the hours. There was a half empty glass of Soave by her bed, leftover from dinner the night before. Newspapers were scattered on the floor, the sheets loose and crumpled. Maya sat up, pulled on an oversized robe, brushed her short hair straight back from her forehead, and finished off the wine. She had slept until almost 4 o'clock. As usual, she was going to be late.

With a slight grimace Maya headed toward the terrace to see what the weather looked like. She moved slowly, languidly, her flesh dissolving in the patches of bright light, congealing in the chilly shadows. The phone rang. It was on the floor by the sofa, partially covered by an open magazine. Ignoring the insistent staccato chime, Maya opened the doors to the terrace and stretched her arms slowly above her head. Bringing them down and leaning forward she tapped her blood-red nails against the balustrade. The apartment belonged to Harry O'Connor, an Irish poet and friend of Edward's, who had leased it to him for the summer. The view from the terrace was fantastic; the dome of St. Peters gleamed in the distance and closer, the lovely sun-bleached, rose-tinted apartments that lined the Via dei Funari shimmered in the heat. It was another hot, glorious summer day.

Maya's nails were long and hard and sharp. Her eyes traveled from their scarlet tips to the window opposite where she could see the fat lady standing by her dining room table. She was flipping through papers, pausing occasionally to take a sip from a teacup.

Last night had been very strange. Why had Edward invited Sergei to dinner? Had he and Sergei met when they were in Florence? And why had Sergei pretended that he hadn't been in Florence? Could it be that Sergei was involved with the bombing? He had certainly made it clear that he was fascinated by bombs. Maya shivered. There was something going on that she didn't know about but she felt sure that Sergei, Antonio and Edward were all somehow involved. Maya thought that the Caravaggio was at the center of it all but she could not imagine how it tied in with these three men.

She showered, dressed, and brushed her fingers casually through her hair. She hoped Anne wasn't going to be in a bad mood again. Descending the staircase to the courtyard, Maya paused at the bottom of the steps to put her keys in her bag. She cried out and dropped her keys when someone grasped her around the waist and pulled her into the shadows of the portico.

"Oh!" Maya twisted around to face Sergei who pulled her close, caressing her and pressing her against his pelvis.

"Hey," she pulled away. "What are you doing?" Infuriated, she smoothed her skirt.

"What do you think?" He lolled against the wall regarding her with his insolent gaze.

"I think you're crazy, that's what. How dare you?"

"How dare *you*? What's your problem anyway? Why don't you make love with me? We could be up in that lovely bed of yours right now..."

"I don't want to make love to you. I've already told you, I love Edward."

"Oh, ha, ha. You didn't seem too concerned about that when I picked you up." Sergei reached for Maya's hand and pulled her close. She jerked it away.

"Well, I'm not interested now."

Sergei's eyes narrowed. "Don't tell me that old guy satisfies you."

Maya glared at him. "Don't tell me you could."

Sergei picked up his leather jacket. "You do realize what's going on, don't you, Maya? With your beloved Edward?"

"What do you mean?" Maya's sense of anxiety returned.

"He doesn't care for you. Oh, he likes to have you with him as a sort of ornament but he's into men. Didn't you hear him going on about me last night?"

"Oh, give it a break, Sergei." Maya laughed. "Edward appreciates beauty and, whatever else you may be lacking, you certainly are good-looking."

"That's not all. He was coming on to me the whole evening. Saying things, touching me. The guy's gay."

"That's absurd. Even if Edward did like men in that way he wouldn't be attracted to someone as stupid and boring as you. He's always preferred intelligent people."

"You bitch." Sergei grabbed her wrist and squeezed it.

"Ow, you're hurting me."

He laughed, bending her arm behind her back until she gasped and dropped to her knees. Twisting with pain, Maya looked up just as the fat lady brought her umbrella down with a loud thwack on Sergei's arm.

"Hey," Sergei released Maya and turned on the fat lady who pointed a pistol at him. "Are you nuts?" Sergei stood perfectly still. "What do you think you're doing?"

"I think the question should be reversed, young man. Don't you know that you should never hurt a lady?"

Sergei sneered. "She's not a lady."

"And you're not a gentleman." The fat lady puffed herself up and waved the pistol at Sergei. "Go away. Hurry up. Go away."

Sergei laughed as he turned to look at Maya. "I'll see you later, bitch." He stared coldly at her.

"Bastard!" Maya muttered, rubbing her wrist.

"Go on. Get out." The fat lady raised her umbrella again and shook it at Sergei who picked up his helmet and walked to the door.

"Go fuck yourselves, ladies." He disappeared.

"What a vulgar man." The fat lady turned to Maya. "Are you all right, honey?"

Maya stared at her in amazement as she massaged her sore arm. "Yes. I can't believe you stopped him. Do you always carry a pistol?" She had never seen anyone actually holding a gun before.

The fat lady returned it to her purse. "I find it very useful. You can never be sure with Italian men," she looked knowingly at Maya.

"He wasn't Italian," Maya said, somewhat irrelevantly.

"Ah." The fat lady narrowed her eyes. "Where's he from?"

"Russia." Maya turned to pick up her purse, which she had dropped. Her keys lay almost hidden where they had fallen between two cobblestones.

"Aha. Russia." The fat lady nodded vigorously and tucked her umbrella under her arm. "You should come back inside with me. Let me fix you a cup of tea. There's nothing like a cup of tea to soothe one's nerves."

Maya began walking a bit unsteadily toward the street. "No, thank you. I'm going out to meet friends."

"Are you sure?" The fat lady walked after Maya. "Don't you think you should wait a little bit? Your friends would understand."

"No, no, but thank you so much. I can't tell you." Maya's voice trembled and she bit her lip.

"Oh, honey. Now, you go ahead and cry if you want to. We women have to stand together." The fat lady put her arm around Maya's waist and walked with her. "Where are you going to meet your friends?"

"On the Via Veneto."

"Are you sure you should go there alone? At least let me walk with you to get a taxi. You are taking a taxi, aren't you? That awful man could be waiting around, you know."

Maya allowed herself to be led to a taxi stand. "Thanks again. Really. I'm Maya Kelly," she added and she held out her hand, which the fat lady pressed between both of hers.

"I'm Rose Williams. I know who you are. I live in the same apartment building as you."

"Yes, I know. I've seen you before," Maya said as she climbed into the taxi. "I'm leaving town tomorrow but I'd like to invite you over when I get back so I can thank you properly."

The fat lady waved her umbrella nonchalantly. "Think nothing of it. We must stick together," she said again. "You would have done the same for me."

Maya nodded even though it was difficult for her to imagine Sergei attacking Rose. It was hard for her to accept the fact that he had attacked her. She gave the driver the address and massaged her wrist. It was the same arm she had hurt in Florence. Sergei was a jerk...and dangerous as well. Maybe she should tell Edward or...maybe not.

Maya closed her eyes and leaned back against the seat. Rose had said that she knew who Maya was. That was strange, Maya thought and then she shrugged. Whatever the case, it had been an amazing stroke of luck that Rose had arrived when she had. She would invite her to dinner when she got back from Lyon. She wondered what Edward would say if he knew that Sergei had attacked her. Maybe he would just be amused. Maybe Edward hated her and didn't care what happened to her. Maya felt very sorry for herself. It was evident that Edward suspected that she and Sergei had met before and it was just like him to embarrass her by inviting Sergei without telling her so he could see their reactions. And, Maya didn't want to admit it, but Sergei had had a point. Why had Edward been so flirtatious with him? And why was he being so pushy about her visiting her stepsister in Lyon? It wasn't like she had ever been close to Ruth and yet Edward had insisted that she go.

"You must share the news of our impending marriage with Ruth," he had said the other day. "She's the only family you have and she'll be hurt if you don't tell her in person. And she can help you shop for your trousseau."

"How old-fashioned you are, Edward," Maya had said smiling. "Women don't shop for trousseau anymore."

"I've already booked your seat on the train. It'll be fun. Good for you to get away."

Waving aside her protests, Edward had handed her a first-class ticket. Now she thought that, whatever the reason he wanted her to go, he was right. She needed to get away—from him, from Sergei, from Italy. But she wasn't going to tell Ruth they were getting married. Not yet, anyway. She and Edward needed time to really talk first, to try to retrieve the love they had shared when they'd first been together. Maya rubbed her arm thoughtfully. One thing was certain, Anne had been right; violence wasn't at all erotic or sensual.

CHAPTER TWENTY TWO

"The fantasy seems to take flight—to show less and less
the way things are. This is the age of reason.
Everybody thought reason was going to save the world.
The encyclopedia, Diderot...But it only led to
disenchantment. That comes with a dream lost."
(Edward Donant)

Anne pressed the button for the elevator that led to the roof terrace. She had never quit trying to overcome her fear of heights. Still it was hard even after nineteen years. She glanced at her reflection in the mirror on the elevator door. She looked thinner than when she had arrived. Was it only twelve days ago? It seemed like weeks. The elevator doors opened but Anne stayed inside, her finger pressed against the open door button, looking out onto a large, flat terrace with terra cotta pots of bougainvillea and hibiscus, ivy and creeping fig. A large palm tree stood next to an arched awning that covered tables and benches. Directly across from her Anne could see the outer walls of the Vatican rising in blind self-assurance, the blankness of the medieval walls giving no indication of the wealth to be found within. The roof's edge was quite a distance away so Anne edged out of the elevator to the nearest table and chairs. It wasn't until she sat down that she realized how shaky she was. She steadied herself with her hands on the table. She closed her eyes and breathed deeply, counting backwards from fifty. When she opened them she felt calmer and took the opportunity to appreciate the quiet beauty of the garden.

How different this was from the Hotel dell'Antica where she had stayed on her first trip to Rome, where the rooftop had been covered in asphalt and the only decorations were TV antennae and ugly pipe ends. There was a lot to be said for money, for the ability to choose your place, your identity. Although it could also be fun to have others project their fantasies onto you. It was part of the excitement, the thrill of meeting a stranger, of attracting someone who was both intrigued by and ignorant of your character. That had been part of her attraction to Charlie. He had romanticized her in his perverse manner, turning her into a woman with secret power. She had done the same with him and with Edward and they had both turned out to be disappointing in much the same way she must have been for them.

***

"You look very mysterious. Right now you look like da lady off da Black Sabbath album." Charlie smiled at her. He knew she wanted to look mysterious.

Anne tossed her head, a gesture she realized would be lost on him due to the darkness of the night. "Don't be cruel Charlie. When you tease you're terribly spiteful."

"Si." He took her hand and led her back to the Volkswagen. "But you love it, don't you?"

"Come, come darling. Don't you think we've insulted each other enough? I really can't understand why I continue to go out with you." Anne was surprised to realize that she really didn't want to continue seeing him.

"Yeah, well, why do you?"

"You're so insecure, Charlie. You're really scared that someone will recognize how cowardly you are beneath your brutal exterior. So, you're twice as nasty as you think you should be and, because it isn't natural, you're uncomfortable and it comes across as boorish. I continue to go out with you because I want to discover what it is that you're so afraid of revealing about yourself."

Charlie sneered at her. "You talk like a book. How come you can't say nothing witout making it twenty pages long? You know what I think? It's because you don't really know what you talking about so you try to figure it all out at once and you don't make no sense at all."

She was hurt. "Well, that's just the way I talk. You know, we really don't communicate, Charlie. When I try, we only get farther and farther away from each other. So, I guess it's better if we don't see each other anymore."

"Sure." He sat back and looked out of the window. She turned away from him and stared through the opposite window. They drove back to the hotel in silence. Maurizio and Claudia talked cheerfully in the front seat. 'They're just too disgustingly happy,' Anne thought irritably. The car stopped in front of the hotel.

"Well, good bye, Charlie." She went inside, feeling relieved and pleasantly sorry for herself at the same time. What a jerk Charlie was! She was glad she wasn't going to see him again. She nodded to the sleepy doorman and, cursing the chairs and steps that tripped her in the dark, she opened the door to her room and flung herself upon the bed. Anne waited, curious, to see if she would cry or if she would celebrate by sneaking down to the kitchen (she and Maya often did that) to steal a piece of bread.

John knocked on the door, a bottle of whiskey dangling from his hand. "Come up to the roof and have a nightcap with me." She could see immediately that he had been drinking heavily. His breath was foul. "Let's make a toast to a wonderful shit of a city. A toast to us."

Annoyed with Charlie, Anne was pleased to see John. She took his arm. "How can you say that about a city as beautiful as this?"

"Yeah."

They climbed the steps to the asphalt terrace where the stars glittered brightly.

"My dad's a bastard."

Anne was silent. She was used to John's expressions of hatred for his dad. It probably wasn't true just like so much that John said. Feelings of his were always exaggerated by his infantile self-pity. He turned to her, his face pale and glittering in the moonlight. She realized that the shimmering effect was not produced by the moon but by tears running down his cheeks.

"Poor John," Anne murmured and she reached up and wiped away the tears.

Abruptly, he grabbed her wrist and pulled her to him. She tried to pull away but he jerked her close so that her head was level with his lips. She remembered how, when she first met him, she had wanted to kiss that sensuous mouth. She couldn't imagine now how she had ever found him desirable. He bent down so that his lips were touching her ear, his grip on her wrist was like steel.

Angry, Anne tried to jerk away. "Ow, you're hurting me, John. Let go."

"You bitch," he murmured in her ear. "You were out with that fucking Italian again tonight, weren't you?"

"Let go. It's none of your business." Again Anne tried to pull away but he held her tightly. "Really, you're hurting me!"

"I love you, Anne." John's face was close to hers. "I need you." Again the tears started in his eyes.

Appalled, Anne thought quickly. "I love you, too, John. I just don't love you like that anymore. Like being lovers, you know."

He gripped her harder and she twisted in pain.

"How do you love me? Show me."

"I can't." Anne cried out in a kind of gasp. "You're hurting me."

John relaxed his grip then and stared out across the rooftop. Anne tried to take advantage of this and get away but he immediately tightened his hold. "I want to die, Anne. What's the point in living? I hate my dad and you don't love me." He looked down at her, his voice slurred by drink.

"Oh, John, I'm sorry," she said, and she had really meant it.

"I'm sorry too." He smiled at her somewhat distractedly. "Haven't you ever thought of dying?" He began pulling her across the roof, the bottle of whiskey grasped in his other hand. He stopped to take a long gulp and he held the bottle to her mouth. "Drink some." He shoved it against Anne's lips. She jerked her head back and hit at him with her other arm. The bottle dropped, shattering on the roof.

"You bitch. You broke my bottle! " John hit Anne across the face and she felt blood welling up in her nose. She clawed and slapped at him with her free hand. "We're going to die together, Anne. We'll just jump over the edge, it's all easy, a clean, easy drop. Not so far and it's all over."

Suddenly terrified, Anne struggled to release her arm. "Stop it, John, you're scaring me. You don't know what you're doing. You're drunk."

John laughed, releasing his grip on her. Anne pulled her arm free and shoved him as hard as she could. Losing his balance, John had staggered back, crashing face first onto the shards of glass. Simultaneously, Anne had stumbled over the raised rail that defined the edge of the roof. Their screams merged. Briefly, she had scrambled with her fingers to hold onto the eave but she couldn't hold on.

***

Anne pressed her hands to her abdomen, the wound throbbed, she would never forget that moment of absolute terror as she had fallen and the shuddering, agonizing impact as the flagpole at the front of the hotel had stopped her fall, piercing her pelvis like a skewered piece of meat. Anne felt faint. She leaned her arms on the tabletop as tears spilled down her cheeks. Waiting for the spell to pass, she wiped her eyes with the back of her hand, glancing hastily around the terrace to make sure no one had seen her crying. She needn't have worried; no one was there but herself. An accident, the police had called it. A tragic accident, but it had not been an accident, Anne thought grimly and this time John was going to pay.

CHAPTER TWENTY THREE

"'The Entombment' is ambiguous. Pontormo's figures
slip and slide across the canvas turning into and out of
the picture plane. Like salt water taffy that's heating
up they streeeetch beneath those unreal pinks and
yellows. Shifting ambivalently on the surface,
they dis-link themselves from our assumptions of
real space through a kind of psychological disjuncture.
There is no connection between the figures and us.
We can't touch them just as they scarcely touch the
ground. That's mannerism for you. Carrying faith
beyond Renaissance rationalism into the Land of Oz.
'Follow the yellow brick road?' The mannerists laid the brick."
(Edward Donant)

Anne loved the Via Veneto. In spite of the fact that it no longer
drew the famous, the decadent, the beautiful like Elizabeth Taylor, Gore
Vidal, and Brigitte Bardot as it had done in the fifties and sixties, it never
ceased to arouse in her a sense of romantic anticipation and nostalgia. She
stopped the taxi driver just before the American Embassy. Here the street
curved enticingly, drawing her up in the direction of the Excelsior Hotel.
Just below the turn of the road was Santa Maria della Concezione where
she had seen Edward's face reflected in that of Lucifer. Anne tripped on
her high heels as she headed up the street and she stopped to readjust
her shoe. Two men passing by glanced at her with an air of amusement
and she imagined what they must think about her clumsy attempt to look
seductive. Her face red, she continued on to the Café Streca.

Few people were there when she arrived. She sat at a table for four
where she ordered "un bicchiere di vino bianco," a glass of white wine, and
lit the inevitable cigarette. She really couldn't afford to put off contacting
John any longer. She blew out a steady stream of smoke, firmly repressing
her revulsion at the idea of seeing him. Maya and Antonio arrived almost
simultaneously. Maya was dressed in a simple beige shift, her bare
shoulders satiny beneath the thin straps. "Anne. Antonio." Maya kissed
both of them on the cheek in typical European fashion. Antonio pulled out
a chair for her.

"Grazie." Maya sat on the edge of the chair, drawing a shawl around
her shoulders.

Anne saw Edward turning the corner in front of Harry's Bar.

119

"Anne," Maya leaned over and whispered to her. "I've got to talk to you. Can you spare me a few minutes? You can tell Antonio we'll be back shortly."

Anne raised her eyebrows. "How mysterious. But of course." She turned to Antonio. "Mi scusa, Antonio. I need to buy some more cigarettes. I hope you don't mind if Maya and I abandon you for a minute."

"I'd be glad to get them for you if you'd like." Antonio rose courteously from his chair.

"No, no, grazie."

Antonio sat back down. "Certo. It's not a problem."

Anne smiled and waved at Edward who was crossing the street towards them.

"You'll never guess what happened," Maya laughed a little shakily as they walked down the street.

"What?"

"Sergei attacked me. I mean really. He was waiting for me as I left the apartment this afternoon."

They entered a Tabaccheria where they stood behind a beautiful, young, black woman and a handsome, elderly gentleman.

"He attacked you! What do you mean he attacked you?"

"He was waiting for me in the courtyard and he grabbed me. That's what I mean. Isn't that unbelievable?"

The black woman and the man exchanged glances.

"But why would he do that?"

"Oh, he wanted sex. He was tired of waiting, I guess." Anne thought she detected a slight preening as Maya shrugged. The couple looked back at them as they left the store. Anne ordered two packs of Marlboro Lights.

"So, tell me what happened."

"I told him he was stupid and he grabbed me by the arm and I think he actually would have broken it if..."

Anne stopped in the middle of opening one of the packs. "Good God, Maya. Let me see."

Maya showed Anne the darkening bruises on her left wrist. "Luckily, there's this fat lady who lives in our apartment building and, she..." here Maya giggled.

"What?" Anne opened a pack and took out a cigarette. "What's so funny?"

"She hit Sergei on the arm with her umbrella!" Maya gasped as she leaned against a wall, laughing.

Anne stared at Maya. "That's not very funny. It's scary."

"You don't understand. You'd have to have been there. You see, she's quite fat, that's what I always call her, 'the fat lady,' and she had this umbrella and a gun..." Maya stopped. "That's strange isn't it? For her to have a gun? Isn't that illegal?"

"Well, thank goodness she had one. I can't believe it. You really need to be more careful. So," Anne smiled suddenly. "Were you excited by this dangerous encounter? Just what you like, sex, violence, even a gun."

Maya shook her head. "That's not really what I meant and I thought about what you'd said and I agree that you were right. Anyway, it's hardly erotic being saved by a fat lady in a flowered dress."

Anne stopped again before they reached the café and lit the cigarette.

"Anne, you do know that cigarette smoking is dangerous."

"It seems rather healthy compared to picking up guys like Sergei."

Maya laughed nervously. "You may be right."

"What are you going to tell Edward? How are you going to explain those bruises?" They had almost reached the café.

" I don't know."

"Why don't you just tell him the truth? You can't want to protect this guy."

"No, I just don't want Edward to know that I saw him. I don't want to talk about it at all with him. I know it was partly my fault that Sergei expected me to have sex with him and I'm afraid that Edward suspects something...not that there was ever really anything between Sergei and me."

"But what if he comes back? He sounds like he may be one of those dangerous stalker type guys. And he knows where you live. Don't you think it would be better for Edward to know about this?"

"I don't know. I have to think about it. Let's not say any more about it right now, okay?"

Anne shook her head as they arrived at the table. Edward and Antonio stood up. "So, what have you girls been talking about?" Edward smiled genially at them. "Women's stories? Make-up, shoes, manicures?"

Maya pouted at him. "Very cute, Edward."

"I thought that was what you always talked about. Did Maya tell you that she's going to Lyon tomorrow?" Edward turned to Anne.

"No." Anne accepted a glass of wine from Antonio whose fingers lingered on hers as he passed the glass. She glanced at him, but he was already pouring wine for Maya. "Why are you going to Lyon?"

"Edward thinks it's important for me to see my step-sister."

"Is that why you're going? Just because Edward says to?"

Maya shrugged. "I guess I really should visit her."

Anne looked thoughtfully at Edward who was talking with Antonio.

"It seems evident that whoever stole the Caravaggio was somehow involved with the exhibition," Antonio was saying. "I don't think that it will take them long to find out who was responsible for the theft."

"Oh, I think you're right. I wouldn't be surprised if they discovered the culprit fairly soon." Edward saw Anne looking at him and raised his glass in a mock salute.

Anne smiled somewhat acidly at him. "Nothing seems to surprise you Edward."

"And what is that supposed to mean?"

"I mean that you never seem surprised by anything that comes up about the Caravaggio—not the fact that it was discovered, not the fact that it was stolen, not the fact that you think the thief will be easily caught."

Edward raised his eyebrows. "And how exactly should I react when I get these little news tidbits? Open my mouth in shock? Jump to conclusions and wave my arms in the air?"

Anne shrugged. "I don't know, none of those things, of course." Edward, Antonio and Maya looked at her curiously. Anne flushed. "Why are you looking at me like that? It's true, he's never surprised by anything."

"But that's Edward's character," Maya said, sounding perplexed.

"That's also true." Anne ordered another glass of wine. Edward knew something about the Caravaggio, Anne was positive of that and she was equally positive he'd had something to do with the bomb though she didn't know how he was involved in either of these things. As soon as she could see Edward alone she would ask him. She also wanted to know what relationship he had with the Sicilian because, if anyone was the type to be involved in a crime, she was certain that it would be the Sicilian.

CHAPTER TWENTY FOUR

"The scapegoat is a familiar figure in folk tales, probably
deriving from the sacrificial kings made famous in Frazier's
book, The Golden Bough. By the time they've come down
to us they've become tragi-comic figures; comic in the sense
of Divine comedy. They have a universal, anti-historical
appeal. It's not such a great leap to Christ as the scapegoat,
represented in the guise of a clown or buffoon."
(Edward Donant)

Maya pulled her bags off the train in Turin. It was two o'clock in the
afternoon and she had two hours to wait before she could catch the train to
Lyon. She remembered passing through the station once before. It was still
ugly, still totally unappealing. She straightened her dress, hoping that her
thigh-high stockings were not visible beneath the short skirt. Placing her
bags on a cart, she wheeled them to the little fenced-in area that fronted
the cafe within the terminal. Plastic plants in planters had been set around
in a futile attempt to make the place more attractive. Black vinyl covered
the floor, opaque white glass hid the leaden sky through the clerestory.

She sat at a table somewhat removed from the others and ordered
a cappuccino. A thin, rather attractive man in khaki pants and a white,
button-down shirt was standing outside the barrier, staring at her. She
looked at him, wondering if he was going to try to approach her, but he
looked away. The waiter brought her drink. Looking up again, Maya
noticed the young man staring intently at her only to look away each time
she glanced in his direction. He had pale, expressionless eyes and his head
was shaved. He wore a white cap pulled low on his forehead. There was
something unpleasant about him, something sinister. Maya felt uneasy
and looked around to see if there were any Polizei nearby. She saw none.
She would just ignore this man, she decided, and perhaps he would lose
interest.

Maya grimaced as she took out Kazantzakis' Zorba the Greek. Her
wrist was still sore and the bruises very noticeable in spite of the makeup
she had used to try to camouflage them. She wished she could talk to
Edward about the incident. Would he understand? Would he sympathize
with her, want to protect her or would he detest her, suspect that she had
encouraged Sergei? She would talk to him when she got back from Lyon,
Maya decided. She would tell him everything, well almost everything,
and they could start afresh. It was all this suspicion and distrust that was

123

ruining their relationship. Feeling somewhat relieved that she had made this decision, Maya began to read, glancing up occasionally to see the young man pacing outside the fence watching her. She felt more and more uncomfortable and, looking up once, she noticed that he was kneeling outside the fence staring at her legs. She blushed and shifted her short skirt, which she realized was not long enough to cover the tops of her stockings when she was seated. Why didn't this man go away? Frowning, Maya looked at her watch. An hour and a half before the train was to leave for Chambery.

She wished that he would leave. She felt as though she were contributing to some weird fantasy about an older woman with thigh-high stockings. And the situation was incredibly unfair. He could stand there and stare at her apparently without embarrassment whereas she was in the defensive position of having to ignore him even though she was curious to see what he was doing. Maya noticed a second man was now watching her. He cocked his head suggestively whenever she happened to catch his eye.

She tried to focus on the novel. She looked up again and found the two men standing at opposite ends of the fence, staring at her. She sighed. 'Perhaps this is a torment peculiar to Turin,' Maya thought. 'It's not at all the same as when other men have stared at me. Usually that's exciting, slightly erotic, but this is unnerving. I feel somehow as though I were under judgment.'

Maya looked at her watch again, feeling somewhat desperate now, simultaneously hoping the train would arrive at any minute and dreading the moment when she would have to leave the security of her table and the fenced-in area which seemed somehow sacrosanct, the barriers of which these men were unwilling to cross. She ordered a cognac. I need something to help me relax, she told herself.

The man in khaki disappeared. Good, Maya thought though the next time she looked up he was back in place. He was strange, sort of mean-looking. She made a face at him as she took another sip of cognac. Two more men had appeared who were also looking at her. She wondered if she were only imagining the attention. Looking around at the other people sitting on the terrace she saw that they were all watching her curiously. I must be the most interesting spectacle in a very boring place, she thought. She felt stripped naked, shamefully exposed in the same manner she imagined it must be like to be a beast in a cage or a fish in a glass bowl.

Maya needed to go to the toilet but the effort of rising from her chair, of making her need visible by heading toward the restroom always represented a moment of discomfort which was intensified, this time, by the unrelenting attention she was receiving. She was torn between her need to relieve herself and her fear of exposing her need. She would wait. Her train should arrive any minute.

Finally, she saw her train pull in. Maya stood up and pushed her cart beyond the little, fenced-in terrace. She could feel the other occupants in the cafe watching her. Of course they were curious to see if she would be allowed to make her way to the train unmolested. She strode firmly across the terminal, not breaking her stride even when she heard steps behind her and someone call out "Si. Ferma!"

Anxious and eager to reach the relative safety of the train, Maya moved more quickly. She pushed the cart ahead of her towards Binario 13 where the train had stopped. Suddenly, the second man who had been watching her stepped in front of her cart and stopped it with his hands. Shocked, Maya cried out and stepped back, only to find herself in the grip of the other man with the shaved head.

Infuriated, she shook her arm free and began to curse him. He looked at her, then, reaching into his pants pocket he produced a badge, which he held up in front of Maya's face.

"Signora Kelly." The other man stepped up next to her and spoke quietly. "Con permesso, sia tanto gentile di venire con noi. I would appreciate it if you would come with us." His English was excellent and Maya felt slightly off balance, as though she had stepped out of a boat expecting to find firm ground only to realize that her feet were sinking into shifting sand.

CHAPTER TWENTY FIVE

"Piero della Francesca's 'Madonna and Child with Saints' is in
the Brera Gallery in Milan. What a surprise. That single
ostrich egg dangling in perfect stillness over the figure of
Mary. The ostrich egg was associated with virgin birth
because the ostrich leaves her eggs to hatch in the sun, sort
of like Aristotle's theory that certain worms and insects
were generated spontaneously. A little less appealing to
have a worm hanging over Mary's head, hmmmm?
Have you ever eaten ostrich? I had it in a restaurant in
The Hague once. It was kind of tough, a sort of red meat
fowl served with cranberry sauce. Good potatoes, too.
Those Dutch can do a thing or two with potatoes. They
mostly fry them—very Northern European, like the Belgians.
What a mistake to call them 'French' fries. They eat 'em with
mayonnaise. Gobs of it. But you must try it you know.
Like raw herring from those stands in the streets
throughout Holland. You can grow quite fond of them."
(Edward Donant)

Anne replaced the receiver. She felt numb. What was she to do now?
So this was how John had intended to get the drawing out of Italy. But
why had he called the police? What on earth was the purpose of that?
Anne stood for a moment staring at the phone and then she exploded.
Damn him, damn him! What was he up to? Everything she had planned
was ruined. Anne squeezed her fists so tightly her fingernails dug into the
palms of her hands. She waited until her rage receded before she relaxed,
the indentations in her palms aching soothingly. She needed to remain
calm. She would have time to think on the train to Turin. Maybe John had
become suspicious of her and decided he wanted to do things his own way.
Irritable and nervous, Anne threw some clothes in an overnight bag. She
bought a ticket at the station for the 8:35 train. Anne left a message for
Antonio on his answering machine. At least he would be happy to know
that the drawing had been recovered.

Anne had almost thrown away the letter John had written her
requesting her help, but then she had realized that he had given her the
perfect opportunity to avenge, in some measure, the pain he had caused
her. He had stolen the Piranesi drawing from his father's gallery. He had
written to Anne asking her if she or Edward knew of anyone who would

126

be interested in purchasing it. Anne had told him they did, though she had never mentioned any of this to Edward, of course. She had thought up a fairly simple scheme. All she had to do was to pretend to cooperate with him. She knew it was all a bit absurd; the idea that she would betray John at the moment he brought the drawing to the "purchaser," but still, if he hadn't called the police, it should have worked. Anne wondered again why John had written to her at all…after all those years.

Now, of course, she would need to revise her plan. She could hardly expose John without revealing her own role in the attempted smuggling and why would anyone believe that she had intended to turn John and the drawing over to the police? Clearly she was going to have to think of something else.

***

It was after ten when Anne arrived in Turin. She hailed a taxi and went directly to the police station where she tried to explain to the corpulent policeman sitting at the desk who she was and whom she wanted to see. The only thing she said that he seemed to understand was "Maya Kelly." Picking up a phone he spoke rapidly and then motioned to a young policeman with a shaved head standing nearby whom he called "Luca." The man nodded at Anne and said in broken English, "Follow me." They walked through a metal door, down a hall and into an office. "Si siede. Aspetta qui, per favore. Sit down, wait here."

Anne sat nervously on the edge of an Aluminum folding chair before a small, bare desk. For the first time the enormity of the situation hit her. The little room was so exactly how she had pictured police stations to be: impersonal, cold, contemptuous as though the mere fact of being there was already confirmation of guilt. What was she to do now? How could she tell the police she knew who had stolen the drawing without being implicated as an accomplice? The door opened and Luca escorted Maya into the room. He leaned against the doorjamb, his arms folded across his chest. Maya didn't move toward Anne or express any overt emotional anxiety, but Anne saw that she was very pale and her lips trembled slightly. Anne rose from her chair and, crossing the room, put her arms firmly around Maya, holding her until Maya leaned into her with a short sob then pulled away.

"I took the first train that left for Turin after you called. Are you all right?"

"Oh sure. Nothing like being ogled in the train station, stopped in front of everyone, taken off in a police car..." Maya's voice cracked. "Do you know what this jerk did when we got to the police station?"

"Luca?"

Maya looked at Anne curiously. "How do you know his name?"

"That's what the man at the desk called him."

"Oh. Well, anyway, he was going through the contents of my bag and he dropped my keys right next to my feet. He bent down to pick them up and I realized he was looking up my skirt. Then, almost before I was aware of it, he stood up and ran his hands across my bottom." Maya clenched her teeth. "The bastard!"

"What?! You must be joking!" Suddenly Anne laughed. "Imagine. You're accused of stealing a very valuable drawing and yet you're still the object of illicit desire."

Maya frowned. "It's all the same really. I'm always the fool being set up by some man. Oh dear, that sounds really adolescent cliché or something doesn't it? But it's true. I'm an idiot, I'm afraid." She sighed and sat down on the chair where Anne had been sitting. "I can't believe this is happening to me." Maya looked as though she was going to cry and Anne reached out and took her hand.

"I know. We'll find a way to do something." 'This is ridiculous,' Anne thought. 'I should just tell Maya that John stole the drawing. No, I have to wait. She'll be all right. I'll take care of it as soon as I have a chance to figure out what to do.' "How on earth did the police know you had this drawing anyway?"

"Someone called, obviously! I've been set up very nicely indeed."

"How bizarre! But who would do such a thing?" Anne looked at Luca and held up a pack of cigarettes. "Can I smoke? Posso fumare? Grazie. Why didn't you call Edward?"

"I did. He was the first person I called." Maya began to cry. "He wasn't there. He's never there and then...then I began to think." She choked on a sob.

"Oh, Maya, what? What is it?"

"I began to think that there's only one person who could have done this. Edward knew that I was going away. He insisted I go to Lyon, he bought the ticket and everything and he knows Valeriano and that's where the drawing was stolen—from Valeriano's gallery. Who else would have the opportunity to steal it? And have the opportunity to put it in my purse? And then, and then..."

"Edward! But it couldn't have been Edward! Why would Edward do something like that?" Anne had to control a sudden, hysterical impulse to laugh. "He loves you. He may be unethical but he'd never do something like this. I know he wouldn't."

"I don't know. He's been acting so strange lately and then the way he behaved when he invited Sergei over. I began to wonder if he knew about Sergei and maybe about Stephen."

"Stephen? Who's Stephen?"

"A man I met in Amsterdam."

"Good grief, Maya, if you love Edward so much why do you keep picking up these men?" Anne pulled on the cigarette and blew out a plume of smoke.

"I know, I know. You think I'm a terrible person, but Edward doesn't really seem to care about me any more and he's been so sarcastic lately and I never see him and he never wants to make love and what am I to do? And what if he really did do this and I don't want to believe it but who else could it be? I've been torturing myself with guilt and regret and suspicion." Maya wiped away her tears.

"No, I don't believe it. Edward wouldn't do something like this." Anne spoke slowly, wondering how to deal with this unexpected turn of events. "There must be some other explanation. It must be some kind of mistake."

Maya looked at Anne in some exasperation. "Mistake? Someone mistakenly put a stolen drawing in my purse and then called the police?"

"No, of course not"

"It doesn't make any sense. I mean to steal a valuable drawing only to set me up." Maya shook her head.

"But what happened? I couldn't quite put it all together over the phone. They've accused you of attempting to smuggle the Piranesi drawing out of the country?" Anne tapped her cigarette into a Styrofoam cup on the table that was half full of a grayish liquid.

"Yes." Maya smiled sadly. "Can you imagine? I was taken to this station where the police made me open my bag and they tore through it. Of course, I was very angry and certain they'd made a mistake. You really can't imagine my surprise when they ripped open the lining and then they pulled out this drawing and I just stared at it in complete disbelief. It's a rather beautiful little drawing, by the way." Maya fell silent.

Luca stepped forward and took her arm. Maya jerked loose and glared at him. "Aspetto, per favore."

He shrugged. "Una minuta."

"Anne, what am I going to do? I'm frightened. I'm really frightened. I never stole this drawing, you know that I wouldn't do anything like that, but what if I can't prove that it wasn't me? I could be in real trouble and it's all so humiliating and I've never been in jail before."

Anne shook her head. "Of course. You must be scared. I've left a message with Antonio, I'm sure he knows a good lawyer. I don't really know what else I can do right now but I know you're innocent and I'll make sure you don't have to stay here long. You must trust me on this." Anne felt like she had to say something. Maya looked skeptical but she nodded. "Who did you talk to when they brought you to the station? Who do you think is in charge? Maybe I could talk to him."

"I only know that it was someone called 'Carlo.' He's the one who asked me questions. I can't really say though, I was so confused and upset."

"It's all right," Anne patted Maya on the shoulder sympathetically. "I'll see this man, I'll talk to him. I'll find a way to help you. I promise I won't leave you here for long."

Luca tapped his watch and motioned to Maya.

"I've got to go. Thanks, darling." Maya hugged Anne tightly and Anne felt her trembling.

"Don't worry, don't worry," Anne murmured. "And don't worry about Edward. I'm sure you're wrong about that." Anne waited until Luca returned.

"You can go." He was curt. "You can go," he said again when he saw that she didn't move.

"No, I don't want to go. I want to speak with Carlo."

He shook his head and looked her up and down. "Non credo che sava possibile. Not possible."

"It's important. I need to speak to him. E importante. Tell him," Anne remembered a line familiar from the many mystery novels she read. "Tell him I have something important to discuss. Something which may be helpful to the...the case."

He looked skeptical. "Asppetta qui."

Anne wandered aimlessly about the room. Now what was she going to say? Should she tell this man about John? Should she tell him about her plan and hope that he would believe her? Even if he didn't wasn't there such a thing as immunity in exchange for cooperation? It was so difficult to know what to do now. Where was this damned Carlo anyway? It seemed ages before she heard the door open. She glanced at her watch. It had only been fifteen minutes since Luca had left.

Anne sat down quickly behind the desk. She wanted to look calm, to give the impression that she was in control. Unfortunately, she moved so quickly the chair slipped beneath her and she had to catch herself on the edge of the desk, which, in turn, tilted dangerously on its feet. Regaining her balance and replacing the desk firmly in its position Anne looked up to see a tall, slender figure regarding her from the shadowy recess of the door. She thought he was smiling and she frowned. "Are you Carlo?" She stood up and smiled as politely as she could. "Parlate Inglese?"

The figure stepped forward and Anne's mouth dropped open in surprise. The dark hair, the dark glasses, the bony structure of the face, the strong hands. She knew this man. It was Charlie.

CHAPTER TWENTY SIX

"Antonello da Messina. Here is the consummate Renaissance genius—he just *appears* out of Sicily where they hadn't painted anything since the middle ages. Look at his 'St. Sebastian,' his 'St. Jerome.' What masterpieces of psychological representation. He places the figures in an architectural setting but the feeling is surreal. It's as though they are figures in a dream—their inner spiritual state is far more real than their external environment. The 'Virgin Annunciate' is one of those lovely peasant girls you see sometimes in Sicily before they grow fat on babies and gossip. In her eyes you behold centuries of suffering—she knows the agony of being chosen to bear Christ and she raises her hand as though to say she doesn't want this fate but she will accept it. She's not like one of those ladies who sell detergent on TV. No, she's imbued with the spirit of something greater than clean clothes though you'd hardly think it listening to the excitement engendered by the properties of Fab. Maybe there *is* a correlation—cleanliness is next to Godliness, hmmmm?"
(Edward Donant)

Anne remembered the night Charlie had approached her on the Spanish Steps. It had been hot, like tonight, but she had been so excited to be in Rome that the heat had seemed only a minor nuisance. Now she was sweating, her armpits felt slimy, her palms greasy. He still hadn't said a word. "Hello, Charlie. You don't recognize me do you?"

Charlie stepped forward and smiled. "Of course I recognize you."

"It's Anne."

"Certo, I remember you."

"Your English has improved." Anne laughed nervously.

"Thank you."

Anne reached in her bag. She needed another cigarette. She couldn't possibly tell him about John. She had never trusted Charlie. "What on earth are you doing here? I never expected to see you."

He stepped forward to light her cigarette, then lit one of his own, cradling it in the palm of his hand. "I'm in charge of cases such as these."

"Such as what?"

"Such as smuggling valuable artworks out of Italy. Valuable, stolen artworks."

"You're talking about the drawing that was found in Maya's purse?" Anne took a deep pull on the cigarette. "Maya never took that drawing. I'll swear to that."

"Would you?" Charlie tilted his head slightly to one side. "How do I know that you would be telling me the truth? Maybe you'd say anything to defend your friend."

"She's not my friend," Anne said sharply.

"Really. Then what are you doing here?"

"She called me. I was the only one she could think of to call. I couldn't leave her like this when I know." Anne stopped.

"Si?" Charlie's eyes were hard and Anne felt uncomfortable.

"When I'm sure she's innocent."

"And why are you so sure of that?" Charlie was teasing her just like he used to do.

"Because the whole thing is ridiculous," she snapped.

"I'm afraid that her position is far from ridiculous. There's the matter of the drawing in her purse. It's called proof."

"Really Charlie. It could also be called 'planting something on someone to make her look guilty.' Surely you're aware that these things happen." Anne spoke sarcastically.

He shrugged. "Of course, the possibility has occurred to us though it's rather difficult to imagine the motive."

"Oh but that's what it is. Surely you don't want to hold her here if she's innocent. Just think you're letting the real thief escape."

Carlo shook his head, smiling slightly.

"But can't you do something? Maya could come back to Rome with me, I could guarantee that she wouldn't leave or anything."

"Now, that's an interesting idea." Charlie spoke slowly, watching Anne. "Why are you so concerned when you're not even a friend of hers?"

Anne flushed. "Because I feel...sort of responsible for her."

"How strange. You're not by any chance involved in this operation, are you?"

Anne turned pale, then flushed red. "What?! Why on earth would you say something like that?"

Charlie smiled and shrugged. "Well, perhaps you know a good lawyer. I think that would be the best thing you could do for your friend."

"You could do something. You're in charge and you're responsible for finding the real thief. You don't want to look foolish by prosecuting someone for a crime they didn't commit." Anne stood up, nervously pulling her sweater around her shoulders.

Charlie smiled coolly at her. "What do you think I can do for her, Anne? It doesn't look like she's innocent."

"But, of course she is." Anne stopped. If she continued to insist then she would have to say why she was so sure. If Charlie decided to help Maya it wouldn't be because of any lingering tenderness he felt toward Anne. She shrugged. There was nothing more she could do for Maya right now.

Charlie moved closer to Anne and looked down at her through his dark lenses.

"Why are you looking at me like that?" Anne pushed her hands self-consciously through her hair.

"You've changed."

Anne frowned, immediately defensive. "Yes," she snapped, "I've gotten older like all of us."

Charlie smiled. "And more beautiful."

Anne stared at him suspiciously.

He took her arm. "I understand your concern for your girlfriend but I'm afraid there's very little that can be done at the moment."

"Why did you ask me if I was involved? Why would you say something like that?" Anne's curiosity outweighed her better judgment.

"Because you're so certain that Maya is innocent and yet you tell me you're not friends. I just wonder if there may be something you're not telling me."

Anne turned away from him to pick up her purse.

"Tell me honestly, who do you suspect could have put the drawing in Maya's purse?" Charlie put his hands on Anne's shoulders and turned her to face him.

Anne stared dumbly at him. "I...I don't really know." She shook her head and said more firmly. "I do have an idea, but it would be wrong of me to guess about something like this now. Without being sure..."

Charlie released her and put his cigarette out in the coffee cup. "Well, if you don't want to say anything now, perhaps you'll change your mind tomorrow. You must be exhausted. It's almost two in the morning and I know all of this must be stressful for you. Now, if you'll follow me I'll get Luca to take you to a hotel nearby."

He led her to the front desk. "I'll call you in the morning. Perhaps I will have something more concrete to tell you."

Anne nodded. Her hands were shaking when she got into the police car behind Luca. Anne shivered and pulled out her cigarettes. She didn't light one, just held it between her fingers, thinking about the events of the evening. Everything was happening so fast. And on top of everything else, it was Charlie who was in charge of smuggling and art theft! 'He must be involved in the investigation of the theft of the Caravaggio as well,' she thought. Anne leaned back wearily and closed her eyes. She thought of Maya, having to spend the night in jail, scared and lonely or worse, with other criminals, with prostitutes and thieves. The fact that she was an innocent victim wasn't going to save her but Anne could, she could tell them what had really happened but then...how could she be sure they would believe her? Maybe Charlie would put her in jail. Anne couldn't bear the thought of that.

This was all John's fault. She should have known that John couldn't be trusted. He deserved whatever happened to him. Anne sat up straight in the seat. At least now she was sure that she had been right. There was no need for her to regret anything she had planned. She just had to find another way to prove John's guilt.

CHAPTER TWENTY SEVEN

"Gaze on Raphael's 'Sistine Madonna.' She radiates beauty and grace. You can imagine, if you can get beyond the sacred taboo, taking her hand for an elegant waltz. A waltzing madonna, not like a waltzing Mathilda, hmmm? She's more like one of Signorelli's ladies. You can't imagine waltzing with *them*. More like a square dance or a box step—those awful rectangular torsos and flat rear ends. He just never got it, did he? Sort of boxed Pollaiuolo, you might say."
(Edward Donant)

Anne had slept quite deeply, so deeply that when she woke she wondered what had taken place the night before that caused her to feel so drained. She always had trouble orienting herself when she woke up in a strange room and it took her a moment to remember that Maya was in jail and that she was in a hotel in Turin. And that she had seen Charlie again.

The Hotel Genio was a block from the train station—pleasant, efficient, and surprisingly expensive, Anne thought, as she paid the bill. She decided to walk to the cafe where she was to meet Charlie. He had left a message for her saying he wanted to see her. She felt calmer this morning. It was true that she was in an awkward situation but it wasn't without its benefits. She didn't have to worry about how John had planned on getting the drawing out of the country nor about it being returned. The only thing she needed to do now was to make sure Maya was cleared without drawing suspicion on herself. Anne smiled wryly. That might prove to be a bit difficult.

The wide boulevard in front of the hotel was packed with cars and pedestrians waiting at bus stops. Anne passed men with newspapers tucked under their arms engrossed in conversation, women with strollers and babies, and a few women in suits, also with papers under their arms. The whole feel was decidedly northern, cooler not only in temperature but also in style. The glances were veiled here, there were no overt attempts to touch her or come on to her. For the first time since arriving in Italy, Anne realized that she didn't feel on the defensive as she walked down a street. She enjoyed the sense of anonymity. It was a relief not to attract attention, not to worry about whether or not she was attractive.

Anne arrived at the Café Agnelli a half hour before she was supposed to meet Charlie. There was plenty of time to read the article in the paper she had tucked under her arm, "The International Herald Tribune," the

136

only journal she read while she was in Europe. It was a short article on the Caravaggio painting, which had been written by Maria Peretti before the theft. Anne remembered meeting Maria when she had attended the conference on "Sexual Ambivalence and Renaissance Humanism" at Berkeley.

"The somber hues of the painting are appropriate for a late Caravaggio and the composition with its focus on the three figures; Christ on the cross, Mary Magdalene at the foot of the cross and Joseph of Almathea a little behind and to the right, is perfectly in keeping with Caravaggio's increasingly isolated compositions..."

Anne frowned and lit a cigarette. Had she been the only one to think that there was something wrong with the painting? And what could she do about it now?

Charlie arrived punctually at 10:30. Anne rose and he kissed her on both cheeks. "How is Maya?" Anne asked.

Charlie shrugged.

Anne drew on her cigarette. "So why did you want to see me?"

Charlie looked around the piazza then turned the dark lens back to Anne. "You're hiding something from me, Anne. I know this because, among other things, you never were very good at hiding things."

Anne blushed. "I'm not hiding anything."

"Why are you so certain that Maya didn't take the drawing? How do you know she isn't involved?"

"I know Maya, that's all. She has her faults but she didn't steal this drawing," Anne laughed lightly. "It's really impossible."

"But she could be an accomplice to someone who stole the drawing," Charlie said quietly. "That wouldn't take any skill, she'd just have to cross the border into France as she was doing and meet her partner or someone set up by him and pass on the drawing."

Anne looked at a couple seated next to them. "It's ridiculous. I don't think she had anything to do with it."

Charlie ordered an espresso. "I've talked with Antonio."

Anne raised her eyebrows. "You know Antonio?"

"He's my cousin."

"Good grief," Anne pressed her hands through her hair so that it fell loosely across her shoulders. "That's why he reminded me so much of you." She frowned and then looked at Charlie. "Oh, of course, you're the cousin he was telling me about who investigates art fraud."

"Si. He doesn't believe that Maya had anything to do with the theft either. He agrees with you…that she's been set up."

Anne smiled uneasily. "Just what I told you." She finished her cigarette and put it out on the sidewalk. She wondered what else Antonio suspected. "So what happens now? Did Antonio tell you why he thinks that?"

"Yes, he did."

Anne sighed. "And you're not going to tell me what he said."

Charlie smiled and shook his head.

"But are you still going to keep Maya in prison? In jail, oh, whatever? What happens to her now?"

"Well," Charlie took out his pack of Marlboros and lit one. "I've decided that your idea of having Maya return to Rome, under supervision of course, is a good one. I'm going there tomorrow and I'll take her with me. She'll be able to stay in her apartment. Someone will be watching her at all times. Whatever she does, wherever she goes. We'll see who she visits and who visits her."

Anne twisted the cup between two fingers. "Couldn't that be somewhat dangerous for her? If someone did set her up?"

Charlie shrugged. "I've discussed it with Maya and she understands the situation. As I said, we'll have someone watching her."

"So, is that it?" Anne rose to go. "I have a train to catch at 11:30."

"You don't have any plans to go anywhere this summer?" Charlie said as they both rose.

Anne looked at him, surprised. "No. Why?"

"I think it would be a good idea for you to stay in Rome until this is straightened out."

"Oh." Anne frowned. "I don't have any plans to go anywhere at the moment."

"Good." Charlie insisted on driving Anne to the train station where he waited on the track until the train pulled out of its berth. Anne sat in the seat trying to sort out all the ramifications of this turn of events. The fact that John, it could only be John, had called about the drawing in Maya's purse, the fact that Charlie was a detective, that he and Antonio were cousins, that Antonio had reason to believe that Maya had been set up. What did Antonio know? What did he suspect? And why did Charlie care what Anne did or whether she remained in Rome or not?

Looking across the aisle of the train, Anne saw a middle-aged man staring at her. Anne looked hurriedly away. When she glanced in his direction again he smiled at her. Embarrassed but pleased, Anne smiled shyly back at him then lowered her gaze to the book lying in her lap. She suddenly wanted him to talk to her. She feared growing old and unattractive, another thing she hated about herself. It was a weakness to cling to youth and youthful beauty. She wanted to be one of those women who lived comfortably with themselves and all of the changes that age brought. She wanted to grow old gracefully. What was it Edward had said? "My dear, after forty one gets the face one deserves—all your vices show up there."

She thought of the last night they had been together, just over a year ago now. She had not wanted to go to the party. It had been at Edward's editor's house, in celebration of the publication of his second book: a discourse on the similar roles played by art in the seventeenth and twentieth centuries. She had spoken coldly in response to his chatter, thrown on her coat with a sulky disdain. He had been withdrawn and unaware of her restlessness. On the way home she had accused him of having fallen in love with Maya. She had gazed out of the window; the cool, winter air pouring into the car swirling eddies of heat from the radiator in delicious contrast around her legs and nose. She had circled her lips around the butt of her burned-out cigarette.

It was useless to try to recover all of their lapses. She wasn't sure exactly why their marriage had failed. She had been so in love with him when they had married and she had believed that their love would be a union in which they would share a depth of understanding that spanned the hypocrisy of words, the failure of physical communion but she now realized that it had been just another false door, another myth.

The sun glittered through the window as the train clattered past a field where two men toiled. A dog slept on the bed of a pickup truck, cypresses suddenly blurred the view. The train moved swiftly on the tracks back to Rome. Anne needed to think, she needed to find another way to have John convicted of the crime.

CHAPTER TWENTY EIGHT

"What?! Are you just going to walk right by? He's laughing
at you. Get in there and outguess him. Here Uccello's
turned Albertian perspective on its head or, more accurately,
against itself. The whole thing pivots around that spiral
banister exposing the fatal flaw. Art is a riddle based
on illusion—don't let yourself be deceived."
(Edward Donant)

Curious to see Edward's reaction when she told him about Maya, Anne arrived early at Rosati on the Piazza del Popolo. Edward had asked her to have dinner with him after Maya had left for Lyon. Anne wondered how she should play the episode with Maya in Turin. It would serve Edward right to sweat a bit knowing that Maya suspected him. Anne knew she would eventually have to tell them both the truth but for the moment there was nothing she could do and she had to admit she got a certain satisfaction out of watching them squirm. Not a nice side of her character, she told herself.

It was still light, the sun set very late in Rome in July. Several elegantly dressed ladies were seated at one table, a single beauty was sitting at another, her slim legs crossed, her mobile phone lying prominently on the white tablecloth. Anne was seated at a corner of the terrace near the hedge that surrounded it. A vase of fresh flowers graced the table. A smiling waiter took her order for a bottle of sparkling mineral water. She had brought Light Thickens by Ngaio Marsh, which she was close to finishing. She had almost reached the end when she felt someone bending over her and lips pressed against the nape of her neck.

"Hello, Edward." Anne spoke without looking up and, carefully marking her place, laid the book on the table.

"Still reading mysteries, Anne?"

She smiled. "It's an addiction."

"Don't you think that says something about your character?"

"Oh, this should be interesting."

Edward picked up the book and read the synopsis on the back cover. "'Macbeth is dead. Run through by brave Macduff. But the real tragedy is unveiled after the final curtain when Macbeth's grisly fate turns out to be all too authentic.' Do you want to know what I think?"

Anne took the book back and put it in her purse. "No."

"I think one of the reasons people like murder mysteries is so they can participate in a violent act without taking any of the risks, without doing any of the bloody work or suffering any of the consequences."

Anne shrugged. "Well, of course, all reading is, to an extent, about vicarious participation."

"Yes, but have you considered that you are, therefore, an accomplice? There's collusion between murderer and reader. Without the reader the murder, literally, wouldn't take place."

"I disagree. I'm not interested in the gory aspects of the murder itself. I'm interested in the successful investigation and resolution of the crime, thus the ultimate vindication of justice. I think that's what most people look for."

"That may be, but you can't have the gratification of seeing justice triumphant without some act of violence which results in the need for justice. The poor murder victim becomes the scapegoat for our need to affirm a sense of universal order and meaning. You're a participant in the sacrifice by desiring the resolution and thereby you are a participant in the crime. I don't see how you can escape my brilliant conclusion."

Anne rolled her eyes. "I don't see how anyone can escape your post-modern reading. Trapped by the text, even the act of reading becomes a revelation of my guilt." She stopped and frowned down at the table.

"Isn't guilt a subversive little devil?" Edward spread his hands as though to rid them of the affliction. "But it's a perfect foil to your particular beauty."

Anne looked back up at him. "Which is…?"

The waiter arrived to take their orders.

Edward studied her. "You have the quiet beauty of a Raphael Madonna."

"The other day you said I looked like one of Caravaggio's dowdy matrons."

"You wear your clothes like a Caravaggio, but you have the features of a Raphael."

"As they're both often associated with peasant women I'm not certain how to take your comment."

"Take it in a post-Marxist sense. Raphael was beyond his time. Out of time like yourself."

Anne smiled. "Ageless you mean?"

"Exactly."

Anne lit a cigarette. "Going back to the idea of guilt, guess where I was last night?"

"In some gentleman's bed?"

The waiter removed the vase of flowers, placed a peach cloth over the white tablecloth and replaced the vase of flowers.

"No. I was in Turin trying to get Maya released from jail."

Edward looked sharply at her. "What kind of joke is this?"

"It's no joke, Edward." Anne told him of the preceding day's events.

"But why didn't Maya call me?" Edward seemed genuinely upset.

"She did but you weren't home."

"Where is she now?"

"Still in jail as far as I know."

"I have to go to her." Edward rose but Anne stood up quickly and put her hand on his arm.

"There's nothing you can do. And Charlie's bringing her back to Rome so you'll be able to talk to her tomorrow."

Edward looked at Anne, then nodded and sat back down. "All right. I'll call her later. Who's Charlie?"

"Oh, he's a man I met ages ago when we were students here. He's some sort of detective now. He's in charge of this investigation."

"Ah."

"Anyway, I should tell you that part of the reason Maya's so upset is because she doesn't entirely trust you."

"Doesn't trust me. What do you mean?"

"I mean she thinks that there's the possibility that you hid that drawing on her so that she could smuggle it out of the country for you."

"You can't be serious. She actually suggested to you that she thought I would do something like that?"

Anne shrugged. "You did insist that she go to Lyon, Edward. Who else knew that she was going? Just Antonio and me. It does look a bit suspicious."

"This is really ridiculous," Edward looked extremely annoyed. The waiter returned with a bottle of wine that he opened and poured into Edward's glass. Edward continued to talk as he took a sip and nodded his acceptance to the waiter who proceeded to pour a glass for Anne. "Just because I want her to visit her sister in Lyon she suspects me of doing such a nasty thing. Which means that she also suspects me of stealing the drawing!" He shook his head and drained off a good deal of the wine in his glass. "I don't suppose you stood up for my character?"

"I did, in fact, say that I thought the idea was absurd. Oh, and speaking of your mysterious character, I saw you the other day in the Piazza Navona with a Sicilian in a white linen suit and a pink shirt."

"It sounds like a character out of a James Bond movie. Is this the time to raise the quizzical eyebrow?"

"I think it's about that time." Anne spoke impatiently. "Who was he? What were you two talking about?"

"He's a business acquaintance. Why? How do you know him?"

"I don't know him, but I've met him."

"How interesting." Edward sipped his wine. "Where?"

"He tried to pick me up when I was having lunch. That very day I saw you with him. I think he's very shady. He invited me to go with him to Sicily."

Edward laughed. "His name is Gianni Cattanei. He's a very skilled restorer of Renaissance paintings. Quite harmless, I assure you. Though he does have a penchant for beautiful ladies."

"Like you?"

"You know I still adore you Anne. But it never worked between us. We're just too competitive."

"It wasn't just that." Anne looked at him coolly. "You acted like a bastard. You're always so infuriatingly smug and contemptuous. You can't just treat people as though they're nothing and expect them to respond amicably."

Edward looked surprised. "I didn't mean to treat you abominably. It's just one of the side effects of my character."

"A character flaw you mean."

"Well, it rather adds to my bon vivant personality, don't you think? Anyway, we must all struggle along with the flaws of our loved ones."

"My father never did," Anne spoke contemptuously.

Edward leaned back in his chair. "Why do you always blame your father? How do you know it wasn't your mother's fault?"

"I thought you said he was supposed to accept her faults. Besides, he's the one who left her."

"Maybe she was impossible to live with. Maybe he tried to live with her but he couldn't take it."

"She was ill. It wasn't her fault." Anne was shaken. She pulled out her pack of cigarettes.

"She was a hypochondriac, Anne, and she couldn't stand for you to be away from her."

"That's not true. She let me come on that trip to Italy." The waiter was by Anne's side in an instant with a match.

"She was always trying to control you. Remember when you met me?"

"She didn't approve of you." Anne smiled her appreciation and the waiter withdrew.

"She didn't want you to move away from Greensboro."

143

"And look what happened to us."

"Are you suggesting that your mother was right? Or is it just that you can't stand to be with any man? Did you ever contact your father? Did you ever let him know that you loved him and that you wanted a relationship with him? You're a fascinating woman, Anne, but you're not perfect and you're not the only one to be disappointed by someone you love."

Anne smashed her cigarette in the ashtray. "I never claimed to be perfect. *You're* the one who's always right. *You're* the one who's always forcing your opinions on others. You're impossible to live with!"

"There, you see?" Edward smiled placatingly at Anne. "You left me but it was really all my fault. Proves my point."

Anne laughed, a little irritably. "Anyway, I'm perfectly happy on my own."

"Really? You'll forgive me if I suggest that you're not being completely honest."

"Are you and Maya happy?"

Edward frowned thoughtfully. "I love Maya, I admire her beauty and give her a certain amount of freedom to indulge in her need for adoration. She gives me her love and the freedom to explore my artistic interests without demanding explanations. We don't ask too many questions," he added wryly, "so we're both happy in our own ways. Or so I thought. Evidently that's no longer the case."

"Edward, what are you up to? I know you didn't plant that drawing in Maya's bag, but I wouldn't have been surprised if it *was* you."

"Anne! I would think that you, at least, would know how incapable I am of such a thing."

Anne laughed. "Oh, my God, Edward, actually, I think you can be rather a cad when it comes to endangering those you love or, should I say, who love you."

"You can't be serious. I never hurt you. I don't want to hurt anyone. Certainly not intentionally."

Anne accepted her insalata miste in silence. The waiter deposited Edward's penne al pomodoro e basilico. "Buon appetito, signori."

"You insist that you're not involved in anything illegal or unethical?"

"Anne!" Edward pressed his hand to his heart, looking very hurt. "I'm not a character in one of your murder novels. Can we enjoy our dinner now?"

Anne sighed. "Yes, I'm starving." She didn't believe Edward but then, she wasn't being honest either.

The young woman at the table nearby looked at her watch, obviously annoyed. Her phone rang and she picked it up with one discreetly jeweled hand. "Pronto." She spoke quickly into the phone and Anne was unable to follow her conversation.

"She's angry with a young man," Edward leaned forward conspiratorially and Anne flushed. "He was supposed to meet her for dinner, but he has evidently been detained on urgent business, something which she does not believe."

The young woman waved to the waiter, who hurried to her side. They watched her pay and pick up her purse.

"She's quite attractive. But it's not enough to keep the gentleman interested."

Anne shook her head. "Cliché, Edward."

"But true, as you well know. It takes intelligence, an ability to challenge and stimulate the mind as well as the body to engage the other for a period of time."

"Of course. But that's true for men as well as women."

"I agree. In this case I was simply pointing out the failure of the young lady. I am certain she will, in her turn, discard some heartbroken man. Cliché again, but again, true."

CHAPTER TWENTY NINE

"Look at the figures in this painting—Caravaggio's
'Fortuneteller.' They're all shifty—the very essence
of shiftiness, I think. None of them trusts the other.
The old pimp lady, the bravo pose. A bravo is a
ruffian, a soldier. Each one of these is a type, a
caricature. You couldn't say that with a Murillo,
could you? He's much more subtle than that."
(Edward Donant)

Valeriano finished writing a short letter and sealed it in an envelope.
John must be out with Gianni again. He had never understood why John
spent so much time with that man. He would never have thought they were
particularly compatible. He wondered...Valeriano shook his head. Perhaps
Gianni actually liked the boy. He called for Claudio.

"Post this, per piacere. Domani."

Jan had received the Caravaggio and stashed it in his gallery
warehouse in Amsterdam. The buyer (American, of course, Valeriano
thought scornfully) had agreed to pay Valeriano's price and Valeriano
should have access to the money within three days. He had stressed to Jan
the overwhelming importance of time. The money must be in his account
in Lichtenstein before next Saturday. He wouldn't think about what would
happen if it were late. Valeriano knew there was no guarantee for his
safety as long as he hadn't paid. And even then...he pushed aside that
possibility and wheeled away from the desk over to the window where he
looked out on the Piazza Navona.

The gallery could no longer afford to represent Edward, of course.
Edward must have realized that this was going to happen sooner or later.
His paintings weren't selling; the clients to whom Valeriano had been
selling Edward's works were, to put it mildly, no longer buying. Valeriano
wondered what Edward would say if he knew that his brief success was
only the result of a scam, a means of laundering dirty money.

He looked at his watch. Where was John? The damned boy was always
off at some bar or, more likely, drunk in a gutter in some side street.
They'd brought him home twice like that since he'd moved to Rome. Such
a nuisance.

The bell rang and Claudio answered it. Valeriano wheeled back to
his desk where he had left his crutches. He didn't like to receive anyone
sitting in his wheelchair.

Edward entered the room carrying a briefcase. He nodded to Valeriano, "Buona sera."

"Buona sera." Leaning on his crutches Valeriano swung himself across the room to a leather chair. "Claudio," he called. "Could you bring something to drink for our guest? What would you like? I'm sorry that I can't offer you a martini. I recall that you are fond of them."

Edward shook his head. "A cognac will be fine. So," Edward set the briefcase down next to his chair. "How are you doing? I haven't seen you since you came out of the hospital."

"I'm doing better." Valeriano grimaced slightly and moved his stump on the chair. They were both silent as Claudio set the drinks in front of them. "I need to thank you for pulling me from the car." Valeriano said this reluctantly, his right hand resting lightly on his truncated thigh.

Edward waved his hand dismissively. "Think nothing of it."

"And you? I see you're looking quite fit."

"I'm fine."

"And the beautiful Maya? And Anne?"

"Maya's...doing well," Edward said slowly. "And so is Anne. I just had dinner with her."

"Ah. That's good." Again there was silence. "So, Edward, what did you want to see me about?"

Edward took a sip of his drink. "About my work, of course."

"Ah, your paintings," Valeriano shifted uncomfortably. "I think it's best if we speak directly, don't you? I'm sure you realize that your paintings have, how shall I put it? Lost their market. They're no longer selling as they were."

"Yes, the sales certainly seem to have fallen off." Edward smiled evenly at Valeriano. "Why do you think this has happened?"

Valeriano shrugged. "These things happen in the art market. Buyers can be fickle. You know that. There's nothing specific we can point to, however," he waved his hand gracefully. "We're all having problems. Since the market plummeted in eighty-nine, the galleries have been struggling to stay afloat. I'm going to have to close the gallery in Baltimore. And I'm afraid that I can no longer represent you. I will compensate you, of course. After all, you've been with the gallery for five quite profitable years."

"Quite," Edward smiled again, pleasantly. "What did you have in mind?"

Valeriano looked at him. "Well, when we consider the length of our relationship and my respect for your work, I'm quite willing to continue to show your paintings until the gallery closes in December. This will give you a chance to look for another gallery to represent you. I can, in fact, suggest a couple of galleries in Europe and in America that are interested in the kind of figurative realism you do. And I'll be glad to offer you a sum of money to help tide you over until you've found a new gallery."

Edward leaned back in his chair. "What sum of money were you thinking of?"

"Knowing that the galleries and myself are struggling to keep afloat, I think you'll appreciate my offer. I'm able to give you twenty thousand dollars now and we can work out a series of payments of, say, ten thousand a month, over the next three months. That should be more than sufficient to keep you going until you get established again. Of course," he added when Edward said nothing, "these are just round figures. It's possible that we might be able to work out something a bit higher but we have to face facts. Since the market crashed, money has gotten tight and there's really not much leeway. You have to admit that I'm being quite generous, especially considering the fact that the market's so unstable right now." Valeriano sipped his drink, watching Edward, who was swirling the cognac in his glass.

Edward said nothing, continuing to regard the contents of his glass. Then he leaned down and picked up his briefcase. "I've brought you something that I think will interest you. It's a photograph of a painting I've done. I'm sure you'll re-consider the idea of discarding me after you have seen it."

"Edward, please," Valeriano raised his hand and sighed wearily. "I don't want to offend you but, sometimes the market changes and an artist who has been popular just loses his popularity. You know that happens and I'm afraid that you'll have to accept it."

Edward opened his briefcase and removed several photographs. He got up and handed one to Valeriano. "That's the painting. I feel sure you'll recognize it."

Valeriano stared at the photograph, his face emotionless, his fingers still on the glossy paper. "This is a photograph of the Caravaggio." He shook his head. "You could have taken this photo anywhere and claimed that you painted it. It's meaningless." He held it out but Edward didn't take it.

"Keep it. I have plenty more. Not just the finished painting but a record of the whole process—from the canvas I bought in an antiques market in Amsterdam to the mixing of the pigments, to the process of painting the work. I can easily prove that I painted it and that therefore, what you discovered was a fake. Not only useless financially but a blow to your reputation as well wouldn't you say?"

Valeriano's mouth had tightened and his eyes flickered to Claudio who was standing impassively by the door. "Why have you done this? I've done nothing but support you and this is the way you repay me. Trying to blackmail me into keeping your lousy paintings in my gallery!" His voice rose slightly in self-righteous indignation.

Edward passed over several other photographs. "I know what you were doing, Valeriano. Did you think they were only going to contact you?"

Valeriano fingered his glass of cognac.

"I received a visit one night and it was damned scary, I'll tell you. Imagine my chagrin. I had no idea that anything was wrong, no idea that you had been using my paintings to launder dirty, fucking, Mafia money— suckering it to these clueless Russians and what happens? I'm working in my studio late one night and I get a visit from two very unpleasant gentlemen who inform me that my paintings are worthless, that they feel very annoyed at having been taken advantage of and they never want to see my work on the market again." He finished off his cognac. "I suspect it was the same group who were behind the bombing in Florence but then I also suspect that you know that already."

Valeriano said nothing.

"I'm an artist, Valeriano. I'm a damned good artist, one that even deceived you and I've been threatened with death or worse if I continue in the only profession I care about. I don't accept your proposition. Why don't we see what else you can offer me?"

CHAPTER THIRTY

"What an enigma. Piero della Francesca's paintings are
never straightforward, never easy to understand and
yet how brilliant they are. In the 'Flagellation,'
Christ's humiliation and suffering is relegated to the
background. We almost miss it so striking are the
three bizarre figures in the foreground. Are they
from three different eras, three different nations?
Do they represent three different philosophical or
religious perspectives? Whatever their purpose they
instill the painting with a sense of calm rationality,
of rhetorical discussion which contrasts with the
physical injustice of the flagellation. Perhaps they are
contemplating the mysteries of the universe or of a God
who would allow his only son, his children, to suffer."
(Edward Donant)

Anne left Edward and walked to the Piazza Rotunda where she was
to meet Antonio. The numbness she had felt the night before had been
replaced with a headache; the momentary satisfaction at seeing Maya and
Edward in positions of mutual distrust had been replaced by a weariness
for the fallacies of relationships. Edward had no idea how awful her father
had been, no idea what she and her mother had gone through after he had
left them. But it was just like him to express his opinions, to accuse her of
being the one at fault when it was so clearly her father. Anne stopped at
the edge of the piazza to regain control of her emotions. Looking across
the piazza she saw Antonio sitting alone at a table on the terrace facing
the Pantheon. He was going to want to talk about Maya and the drawing,
of course. What else did he want to tell her? Anne took a deep breath,
wondering what she should say to him.

Antonio looked in her direction, staring straight at her. Anne stiffened
before she realized that he could not see her due to the shadows of the
street. She stepped out into the light and waved. He hesitated and then
stood up, smiling warmly. Anne walked quickly to the table where Antonio
embraced her, more passionately than was usual. She was thrown by this
reception and found herself at a loss for words.

"Come stai, cara? How are you, darling?" Antonio asked tenderly,
taking her hand in his.

150

Confused, Anne stumbled over her words. "I'm...I'm fine. Grazie. How are you?"

"Bene. I'm sorry about what happened to Maya."

Anne realized that he was being solicitous because he thought she was upset about Maya. "It was awfully nice of you to help her," Anne said as she pulled out a cigarette. Leaning toward her, Antonio steadied her hand and held a match to the tip of the cigarette. Anne drew on it and pulled her hand away. "I was surprised to find out that you and Charlie are cousins and that he's the one you were talking about being involved in investigations and stuff."

Charlie?" Antonio looked puzzled.

"I mean Carlo," Anne said. "I knew him as Charlie."

Antonio looked questioningly at her.

"I met him years ago...when I first came to Rome with the Emory Art History program."

Antonio nodded as though that resolved everything.

"What do you think about this whole episode with Maya in Turin?" Anne asked, deciding to change the subject. "Isn't that the strangest thing?"

"Very strange."

"Did you know that Maya had her purse stolen in Florence? It seems like bad luck has followed her ever since she arrived in Italy."

"Do you think it's due to bad luck?"

Anne looked away from him. Charlie was right. She wasn't very good at disguising her thoughts. "What do you mean? What else could it be?"

Antonio shrugged. "The police know about Maya's purse and, though they have no concrete evidence, I believe they suspect that the person who stole her purse was also the person who put the drawing in the lining of the purse."

"Really? Is that what Charlie meant? When he told me you didn't think Maya was guilty?" Anne frowned and looked across at two young men sitting on the steps around the obelisk in the center of the piazza. They were dirty and unkempt. One had long, black hair and a beard. The other was muscular with tattoos on his biceps. He had stringy, blond hair and a book by Kierkegaard at his side. She wondered why they were where they were, how they had become like this and she found herself thinking of the fall of Sebastian in <u>Brideshead Revisited</u>.

"Ah, well, it's something like that," Antonio looked pensive. "Carlo's investigating the theft of her purse among other circumstances surrounding the theft of the drawing that we think may have a bearing on Maya's involvement. None of them clear her yet but Carlo's confident he'll get the real culprit soon."

Anne smoked nervously. "The real culprit." Maybe she needn't do anything, maybe the police already had reason to suspect John. But then John would certainly try to implicate her. "Do you think that Edward has anything to do with all of this?" Anne tried to appear concerned and curious.

Antonio took Anne's hand. "We believe that Edward's very much involved so be careful what you say when you are with him."

She looked closely at Antonio. Was he teasing her?

"What's wrong?" Antonio stroked the palm of her hand and Anne trembled, wishing he would just take her in his arms and kiss her—her lips, her neck, her breasts. She flushed scarlet. "Nothing's wrong," she said irritably. "I just don't believe that Edward had anything to do with Maya's arrest."

Antonio misunderstood her. "Don't worry. He's not dangerous and I know he wouldn't want to harm either Maya or you."

Anne put out her cigarette in the ashtray and spoke slowly. "Charlie's in charge of the investigation of the Caravaggio painting as well, isn't he?"

"Si."

"Was Edward involved in that?"

"What do you mean?"

"I just wondered if Edward might know something about the painting is all." She sipped her tea. "Who does Charlie work for?"

"It's a government organization, the 'TPA.'"

"What's that?"

"It stands for Nucleo Investigativo Tutela Patrimonio Artistico. You wouldn't be familiar with it."

Anne looked again at the two men, the blonde guy with the Kierkegaard book was staring at her. He grinned suddenly, two gold teeth flashing, and Anne realized that he was the same man she had talked to at the Trevi fountain. "Do you also work for...for that group, Antonio?"

"Only peripherally, when Carlo needs some information that I can provide."

Anne took out another cigarette. Antonio leaned across and lit it for her, his fingers brushing across the back of her hand as he did so. Anne felt a sudden skeletal charge to the inner passion zone: from flesh to tendon to bone. She was surprised that such simple contact could elicit that kind of reaction...and disturbed. She withdrew her hand with a sharpness that registered as rejection. "How close are you and Charlie?"

"We're pretty close. His mother's my mother's little sister. We kind of grew up together though he's five years younger than me so it wasn't until we were older that we found we had much in common."

"And what would that be?"

Antonio shrugged. "Valeriano was a good friend of my father's, I began working in his gallery when I was fifteen. He taught me a good deal about art and the art market and it was, in part, because of him that I went to the university to study art. As you know, Carlo's also interested in art. We share that and, if I may say so, we also share an interest in beautiful women. You, for instance."

Anne laughed shortly. "Ah, there I think you're wrong. I know Charlie's not interested in me."

"You seem to know Carlo fairly well. Do you still like him?" He leaned back in his chair.

"I met him a long time ago. When I first came to Rome. I was rather... fascinated at the time. I was young and he seemed mysterious and rather sexy. No, that's not the right word—he seemed vulnerable in some perverse way. And, no, I don't like him. I never did. I didn't really trust him."

"Did you sleep with him?"

Anne was irritated. "No, and it's none of your business."

Antonio put his hand on her arm. "I would like it to be my business."

Anne felt embarrassed and annoyed with herself. How this man could manipulate her emotions. She began to pull her arm away when, leaning forward, Antonio cupped his hand under her chin and pulled her close. Anne disliked public displays of affection so she yielded somewhat nervously to his embrace but, as his lips pressed gently against hers, she forgot her concern, feeling as though a shield of intimacy enclosed them. She returned his kiss passionately, his breath was sweet and his soft, curly hair shivered like silk through her fingers. Antonio ran his lips across her cheek and whispered in her ear, "How long I've waited to do that."

Anne pulled back, frowning at him. "Why *did* it take so long?" The shield had disappeared. She noticed a couple nearby smiling, watching them.

"I prefer to take things slowly. I find myself attracted to you on many levels and I want to make love to you on many levels. It's much better that way." He pulled her towards him again but she shook her head.

"People are looking."

"It's Italia, amore mia. No one glances twice at lovers. On the other hand," he murmured as he motioned for the bill, "There's something to be said for the complete freedom gained in privacy." They stood up and he handed her her cardigan. "Would you like to join me for a drink in my apartment?"

Anne stared at him, she yearned to be in his arms, she ached to be loved. It had been so long. Anne wrapped her cardigan more closely around her shoulders and smiled at him. "I think a drink sounds just the thing." Putting his arms around her shoulders, Antonio led her to his car.

CHAPTER THIRTY ONE

"What a revelation, standing before Masaccio's fresco
of Adam and Eve in the Brancacci Chapel. The
superb line and even more superb expression of
emotional and intellectual grief, of spiritual and
physical alienation from God's presence. Just
contrast this wrenching depiction of the expulsion
from the Garden of Eden with Masolino's
representation of the temptation. Masolino's dainty
figures would never suffer the extremity of shame
and self-conscious remorse that Masaccio's figures
endure, ehhh? How sad to think that he died at the
age of twenty-seven, carried off by the plague
like so many of his contemporaries."
(Edward Donant)

Maya rode back to Rome in the same train compartment as Carlo and
Alberto, the policeman who had been assigned to "protect" her in Rome.
Carlo read from a folder of papers he took from his briefcase, Alberto
worked crossword puzzles, Maya stared out the window watching the
scenery and wondering what would happen next. A Fiat was waiting for
them when they arrived at the train station in Rome and they drove to her
apartment. She wondered if Edward was going to be there, waiting for
her, but the apartment was empty. Maya stood a little distant from Carlo
as Alberto looked through all of the rooms, checking behind doors and
windows.

"Va bene?" Carlo asked him.

Alberto nodded. Carlo turned to Maya. "Are you going to be all right?
Alberto or another policeman will always be nearby. If you ever feel you're
in danger you can use this." He handed her a whistle.

Maya giggled. "Like calling a dog." She covered her mouth with her
hand. "Oops, mi scusi." It wouldn't do to alienate her "protector."

After Carlos and Alberto left, Maya removed her high heels and sank
down onto the sofa where she stared through the French doors onto the
terrace. There were those same palms and lilies, which she had contemplated
so often and, once again, they reflected a different mood from that which
they had seemed to express before. This time they seemed cold, unfeeling
and impervious to her. Someone had called the police, someone wanted to
hurt her, she had been arrested and humiliated for something she hadn't

155

done, and now she was a virtual prisoner under Alberto's regard. Maya's body began to shake and tears slid unchecked down her cheeks. It wasn't fair. None of it was fair. First, there had been the man on the motorcycle, then the gypsy boys, then Sergei, and now this. And she didn't even know what role, if any, Edward had played, was playing in all of this.

Maya walked out onto the terrace. There was a slight chill in the shade of the awning. She felt it climb from her bare feet through her knees to her chest where it saturated her heart, slowing her pulse until her head cleared and the tears slowed to a single drop which slid gracelessly down beside her nose. The scent of pasta and garlic rose from the landlady's apartment below. Every day she cooked pasta with what Maya imagined to be gargantuan amounts of garlic. She allowed the sensual mix of garlic and the odor of roses from her terrace to calm her nerves. "I will not be defeated by all of this," she told herself. "At least I'm back in my own apartment and I know there's no one I can trust. At least that much is clear."

Maya poured herself a glass of wine from a bottle of Chianti that was open on the counter. She thought back to the summer when she and Anne and Edward had come to Italy with the Emory Art History program. It had been 1973, the year of Watergate and Nixon's resignation, the era of Bob Dylan and the Rolling Stones, of Santana and Black Sabbath. The year that the "Roe vs. Wade" decision assured women's legal right to abortion. And yet, all she remembered was falling in love with Edward, falling under the spell of Rome. Slightly stocky, handsome in his pedantic way, both Maya and Anne had had a crush on him but he had paid them hardly any attention. And now, nineteen years later, he and Maya were engaged and she suspected him of having her arrested. She laughed shortly. They weren't even married yet and Edward wanted to be rid of her.

But what could have been the purpose of calling the police? She could see why Edward might use her to smuggle something out of the country—she would never have known about it and no one would have stopped her if there hadn't been that phone call. But why would anyone make such a call? Why would Edward have done such a thing? What did he think he would achieve by having her arrested? Maya shivered. It couldn't have been Edward; it just didn't make any sense. None of it made any sense.

She looked at her reflection in the gilt-framed mirror that hung above the plaster-molded mantel of the fireplace. When she was ten years old, she had gone swimming at the neighborhood pool. She had bought a grape Popsicle at the concession stand and, on her way back to the pool, she had been surrounded by a group of teen-age boys. They had towered over her and one of them, with pimples and acne scars, his big ears standing out from his head, had leaned toward her. He had reminded her of Dopey in Walt Disney's "Snow White." "Wanna shack up?" He had sneered at her. She hadn't understood what he meant but he had scared her and she had grasped her Popsicle to her chest, the grape staining her new, white bathing suit. Then, a bigger boy, obviously the leader of the group, had pushed Dopey away and said, "Leave her alone." She had run down the sidewalk to the pool, breathless and frightened.

Maya studied her face. She was always fascinated by how lovely she looked. She had her father's body, her mother's face. It had been two years since her mother had died. Emaciated and weakened by the cancer, her mother had let Maya cradle her head against Maya's chest. She had tried to comfort her mother's fears and had prayed for a peaceful passing and her mother had seemed to resolve her fight with mortality and had died with an air of serenity, but Maya had been left frightened and lonely. She experienced a spasm of loss so intense tears sprang to her eyes. She leaned her head against the palm of her hand and watched as the tears trickled down her cheeks. She should have told her mother about those boys. Now she could never reconcile the secret vulnerability and the guilt.

CHAPTER THIRTY TWO

"They call Brunelleschi a 'paper architect.' He worked
from ideas of the greatest simplicity. To take an idea
and to turn it into a three-dimensional object—
that's magic. Taking a mystery and revealing its
essence. It's not like *solving* a mystery, it's more like
returning to the origin; the beautiful simplicity of
Darwinian evolution. What could be more magical?"
(Edward Donant)

Anne stood nervously by the door inside Antonio's apartment. He
turned to her, smiling and, pulling her close, kissed her on the mouth.
Anne stiffened and Antonio released her.

"Would you like something to drink?"

"Yes," Anne said, grateful for the opportunity to put off the inevitable.
It wasn't that she was shy, it was just that she dreaded the finality of
physical intimacy, of discovering the limitations of fantasy in the reality
of intercourse. It was so often disappointing, a quick, sweaty, self-centered
orgasm for the man, leaving her with nothing but stale feelings of a bitter
deja vu. She didn't want it to be that way with Antonio, she didn't think it
would be but she was still nervous.

Antonio poured two glasses of wine and, taking Anne's hand, drew
her down on the couch next to him. "Allora," he smiled at her. "To the first
of many nights together."

Anne blushed.

"Are you all right? You do find me attractive, don't you?"

"Yes, oh yes, of course. I just, it's just that it's been a long time," Anne
took a deep breath. She was committed to go through with it. "I know that
it sounds ridiculous but I'm nervous is all."

Antonio took her hands in his and kissed her again. He kissed her
harder and deeper, sliding his hands down the back of her dress, pressing
his knee between her thighs and Anne felt a sudden release, a sudden
passionate desire for him that swept away all of her doubts and fears. She
wrapped her arms around his neck, drawing him to her, sucking at his
lips, at his mouth as though her life depended on her ability to merge
her body with his. He peeled off her dress and caressed her, murmuring
endearments in Italian that made her laugh with pleasure and catch her
breath with desire. "I want you inside of me," Anne murmured urgently
and she moaned with the exquisite sensation of pleasure and pain as he

penetrated her. Afterwards, they lay intertwined, breathless and sated, Antonio on top of her, softly kissing her face, her hair as she clung to him, not wanting him to leave her, not wanting him to move. It had been marvelous, so much better than it had ever been with Edward, so much more than she had ever imagined it could be.

"Oh my love," Anne murmured, overwhelmed with warmth and gratitude and then she pressed her hand across her mouth in shame. How could she have said such a thing, she thought but Antonio didn't seem at all bothered. Instead, he rose slightly above her, smiling down with such tenderness that Anne felt reassured by his warm regard.

"Cara mia," he said.

They made love again, slowly and passionately and Anne fell asleep in Antonio's arms. She awoke to find him looking at her. She stretched and smiled into his eyes. "You have a beautiful body," she said, looking admiringly at his tautly muscled chest, the subtle ripple of muscles on his biceps as he perched over her.

"It is you who is beautiful," Antonio said. His eyes slid to her belly and he reached out to gently stroke the scar that stretched from her pubic hair down her thigh. "How did you get that?"

Anne watched as he traced the line of the scar. "It's a memento from an old lover," she said, unable to keep the bitterness from her voice. "It's the death of future generations of Langlais."

Antonio raised one eyebrow and looked at her intently. "How did it happen?"

"I fell from a roof." She spoke flatly. "Here in Rome. It was a long time ago."

"You fell?"

"Yes." Anne pulled the sheets up around her in a protective gesture.

"How did you fall?"

"I...I lost my balance," she slid to the edge of the bed, pulling the sheet with her like a long cotton train.

"Where do you think you're going?" Antonio put his hands around her hips and drew her back to him, folding her into a tight embrace. Anne resisted briefly and then turned her head, eagerly seeking his mouth. "Wherever you want to go," she breathed, yielding to her desire and pressing her body against his.

CHAPTER THIRTY THREE

"What we're dealing with, of course, is an *un*definition
of realism. There is no such thing. A still life by one
of those high fidelity Dutch painters where the light
intrudes between you and reality. It *appears* to be
real but there's a trick, hmmm? Visible reality
takes second place to *visual* reality."
(Edward Donant)

Anne picked up the phone in her hotel room, hoping it might be Antonio calling about the night before. She had felt restless since he had dropped her off that morning, wondering if he regretted having made love to her. Did he find her scar repulsive? He hadn't seemed repelled but he could be skilled at hiding his emotions. So many people were, Anne thought with a sense of resignation. Her whole body trembled at the memory of their love-making and she picked up the phone torn between a sense of eager anticipation and fearful that it would not be him. "Pronto."

"Anne? It's John," he sounded extremely angry. "I've got a few questions I want to ask you." His voice was slurred.

Anne's heart began to beat rapidly. John was drunk as usual. "Give me your number. I can't talk on this phone."

Anne scribbled down the number and walked to the phone booth around the corner from the hotel. She slipped her phone card into the slot and dialed the number.

"John? It's Anne. You have a few questions to ask me? Well, I've got one for you," she spoke hurriedly, eager to express her anger in retaliation for his. "Why did you call the police in Turin?" There was silence at the other end of the line. "John. I know it was you. Tell me why you did it!"

John spoke slowly. "That's why I was calling you."

"What?"

"I was going to ask why *you* had called the police."

CHAPTER THIRTY FOUR

"Have you ever been to a bullfight? Look at this bull in
Titian's "Rape of Europa." How beautiful. He really
steals the show from that hefty girl with her cellulite thighs
waving her scarf as though she wants her girlfriends to
admire him. We all admire him. What a shame to imagine
him in a bullring, bleeding from the sword stuck into his
shoulders, struggling across the arena, falling to his knees.
But isn't that what theatre, what good theatre is all about?"
(Edward Donant)

Anne and Antonio entered the courtyard of Maya and Edward's apartment building. Anne reached for Antonio's hand and pulled him into the shadows of the portico. "Kiss me," she demanded, putting her arms around his neck and pulling his face down to meet hers. He pressed his lips against hers and she opened her mouth to take him with a sense of almost desperate desire. If John hadn't called the police, who had? Who else could have known about the drawing in Maya's purse? Who else knew about her? "Let's not go to Edward's and Maya's," she whispered snuggling into Antonio's embrace. "Let's just go back to your apartment and drink wine and make love and forget everything and everyone else."

Antonio held her tight. "That would be very nice, cara," he said tenderly. "But we're already here, let's just have dinner with them and then go to my place." He put his finger under Anne's chin and raised her head. She made a face and he laughed. "We have forever and ever to make love, Anne."

"Do we?" She turned away from him and began to walk toward the stairs.

"Certo." He caught up with her and took her arm. "All I want is to make you happy."

Anne looked at him, pausing next to him on the stone staircase. Tears welled up in her eyes as she reached out to stroke his face.

"What's wrong, carissima?" Antonio gently wiped a tear from her cheek.

Anne shook her head and smiled at him. "Nothing, it's just…wanting to make someone happy is such a transient thing. It's nice but it can't last."

Antonio stroked her arm. "Just because you feel like other men haven't been able to make you happy, it doesn't mean that…"

"What? That you can?" Anne caught herself. She hadn't meant to sound so hostile.

"Caring for someone is more than just making the other person happy, Anne. You almost seem to want to push me away."

Anne ran her hand down his chest and, leaning close to him, pressed her lips softly against his cheek. "Does this look like I want to push you away?" she murmured.

Antonio laughed. "I'm not talking about physical desire. I'm talking about your distrust of men."

Shocked, Anne backed slightly away from him. Edward had said the same thing the day before. Antonio put his arm around her. "Come on. You'll see," he smiled at her as she reluctantly accompanied him up the stairs to the top apartment where Maya and Edward lived. "You need to relax, Anne, and let go of the past. Otherwise, how will you ever be free to experience the joys of life?"

Edward opened the door. "Buona sera, Anne. Antonio. Come in." He kissed Anne on both cheeks. "I've prepared a small appetizer and chilled a bottle of Ferrari Brut. We must all gather about Maya tonight. She's feeling, perhaps understandably, a bit paranoid."

Maya came in from the terrace, a glass of wine in her hand. "I'm afraid it's true." She looked at Anne affectionately, "I'll never forget that you came to Turin when I called you, Anne."

Anne looked for the cigarettes in her bag. "It was nothing," she said irritably without looking at Maya. She hoped Antonio wasn't going to turn out to be like all the others. Always telling her what she should do.

"It does seem as though half of Rome were after you, Maya." Antonio accepted a glass. "And Torino as well. I hear that you were well taken care of by my cousin."

"What? By who?"

Anne held up her cigarette and accepted a light from Antonio. "I haven't had the chance to tell you that Charlie's Antonio's cousin," she said.

"Charlie?" Maya looked puzzled. "Who's Charlie?"

"That's another really bizarre coincidence. Carlo is Charlie, you remember, the Charlie that I met the first time we came to Rome. I realized it the minute I saw him in Turin. And Antonio's been working with Charlie on investigating the theft of the Piranesi. It was probably all because of him that Charlie let you come back to Rome."

"Really," Maya lowered her eyelashes provocatively. "How lovely of you. Grazie, Antonio." Maya put her arms around his neck and drew him down to kiss him briefly on the lips.

"Prego."

He held her lightly around the waist and she laughed, twisting to look at Edward. "Edward thinks that I'm not grateful enough for what others do for me. So I'm changing my approach."

Anne pressed her lips together. "Changing your approach? I wonder what that means."

Maya grinned at Anne. "That I'm going to show my gratitude. Especially when the recipient is a handsome man."

"Oh right," Anne said. "That's a big change."

"What about me?" Edward made a face as he poured the sparkling wine.

"You're on probation," Maya sniffed at him as she held out her glass.

Anne took Antonio's arm and drew him down onto the sofa next to her. "What's the name of the organization that Charlie works for, Antonio?"

"TPA," Antonio said.

"Oh yes. It stands for a long, complicated name that actually means he's in charge of going after smugglers and art forgers and stuff." Anne accepted a glass from Edward. "Doesn't that sound fascinating?"

Edward raised his eyebrows. "I'm sure he is superbly qualified."

"I thought you'd find it interesting," Anne reached for an ashtray. "Considering your fascination with fakes and fraud."

"As I've told you, I'm fascinated with the concepts relating to the human predilection for deception. This hardly suffices as a reason to become involved in the exposure of criminals. You must try some of these olives. I put them 'sott'oglio' myself."

Antonio took one. "But surely you're interested in whether an artwork is genuine or not. That's a part of every historian's job. Take the Caravaggio that was stolen. Do you think that it was authentic?"

Edward popped an olive pit into his hand and dropped it into an ashtray on the table. Maya frowned at him. She hated the way he did that. "Authenticity is an academic question," he said. "Both in terms of philosophical and aesthetic issues."

"Oh good grief," Anne said. "You're always turning fraud into some sort of philosophical observation."

"Well, it's in the philosophical sense that fraud interests me. Whether the work is determined to be legitimate or not, it's only the work itself I care about, not the legitimacy of the persons connected with it."

"That's nicely ambiguous," Anne said sarcastically. "Of course it's the work that's important."

"Though it's the forgers who are sought by the police," Antonio added, looking at Edward.

Edward shrugged. "Perhaps they should be more interested in the corrupt dealers and collectors who create a market for forgeries."

"That's true," Antonio smiled. "But it's often easier to arrest the forgers."

They went to "Le Volte," one of Edward's favorite restaurants, where they dined on alici marinate, penne all'arrabiata and frito misto di mare. Afterwards they walked to the nearby Piazza Navona. Maya and Anne walked ahead of Antonio and Edward.

Maya smiled at Anne. She took her arm confidentially. "You've slept with Antonio, haven't you?"

The question irritated Anne. "Yes, why?"

"I'm just glad for you. I'm glad you and Antonio are together. I'm glad you're happy."

"Who says I'm happy," Anne was annoyed at Maya's presumption.

"Well," Maya looked confused. "I just thought…"

"You just made the assumption that I'm happy because I've had sex with Antonio."

Maya pulled her arm away from Anne's. "You've really become awfully sharp and bitter, Anne."

"Oh please, Maya. I don't need your analysis of my character, thank you very much."

"And I don't need your contempt." Maya stopped to confront Anne, her face flushed. "Ever since you've come to Rome you've treated me with contempt. You've been cold and sneering about everything!"

Anne stared at her and then laughed. "What did you expect, Maya? After all, I do have some reason to feel bitter toward you."

"What did I do? What do you mean?"

"Oh, nothing," Anne hated herself for letting go like this. What, in fact, had Maya done? Why was she so irritable and edgy?

"What you mean to say is you resent the fact that I'm with Edward. That's not fair. You told me that you and Edward were through."

"What was I going to say? When it was obvious that he was infatuated with you. I thought you were my friend."

Maya stared at Anne, shocked. Her eyes filled with tears. She turned and strode away. Edward and Antonio caught up with Anne.

"What's wrong with Maya?" Edward asked.

"I don't know. She's just stressed I suppose." Anne felt a commingling of regret and relief. Maya didn't really deserve to be the recipient of all of Anne's anger and yet she hadn't been a good friend and Anne was tired of pretending that she had been. Antonio put his arm around Anne's shoulders. "Oh my God," Anne pointed. "There's that mime again and he's following Maya. She's not going to be happy about that."

The three of them watched Maya she walked past the tables crowded onto the piazza. People turned to stare after her, laughing as the mime followed her, mimicking Maya's unconsciously flirtatious gait, the way she held her head, the movement of her hips. Anne felt a flicker of sympathy for her. Maya was taking care not to look around her though it was obvious to Anne that she was distraught, wondering why people were laughing at her.

Anne, Edward and Antonio followed the mime. As Maya entered the Bar Tre Scalini, the people at the tables were laughing at her openly. She arrived at an empty table and turned to indicate it with a triumphant flourish of her hand only to confront the mime. He made her a sweeping bow, the black holes in his mask watching to see how she would respond. Maya turned away from him, her face flaming red, and sat down.

As the mime left the café, Anne made him a deep bow to which he responded in kind. She bowed even deeper and the people in the café applauded her bravado. As she turned to go, the mime spoke to her in a low voice.

"I need to talk to you."

Anne turned around slowly. "What? Are you speaking to me?"

"I must talk with you. When can I see you?"

Anne stared at the expressionless mask. "But I don't know who you are."

"Oh, you know who I am," the mime said.

Anne's eyes opened wide. "John?" she whispered.

He nodded.

Anne looked away from him. "Not here, for God's sake."

"Thursday night at 9, at 117 via Argonale." He, too, spoke in a whisper. "Mi scusi, signora," he said loudly. "I mistook you for someone else." He turned quickly and left the café.

Anne slowly walked back to join the table at which the other three were already seated. Now what could John want? She considered her options.

"What were you talking about with that man?" Maya was looking curiously at Anne.

"What? Oh, he just thought I was someone else." Anne stared thoughtfully after John as he followed a group of giggling girls.

Maya shuddered. "He gives me the creeps. He certainly knows how to pick up on peoples' weaknesses. Talk about being an object of mockery."

Edward looked surprised and then he smiled. "We were talking about beauty the other night," he explained. "And I questioned Maya's assertion that she was ever an object of mockery."

"I don't think he was mocking you, Maya," Anne rummaged through her purse for her cigarettes.

"Really? What do you think he was doing? Setting someone up to make fun of them by pointing out their weaknesses isn't mockery?"

"But what weakness do you have?" Antonio ordered everyone an espresso.

"Vanity." Maya said with a rueful smile. "He picked up on my cheap vanity."

Anne shook her head. "I think that you're right, actually."

"What do you mean?" Maya asked sharply.

"I mean that there's definitely something creepy, something sick about him." Anne lit her cigarette. That was an understatement, she thought.

"Vanity's only a weakness when it's misplaced." Edward said. "In your case, my dear, you have every reason to be proud of your looks and there isn't a person here who would argue with that."

"That's sweet, Edward," Maya smiled at him. "Though clearly not pertinent to the issue."

Anne drank her espresso slowly as she glanced across the crowded café. She felt Maya's fingers tighten on her wrist as Maya leaned toward her and whispered. "Anne, Sergei's over there."

Anne looked around. "Where?"

"That tall man leaning against the wall over there. Wearing the leather jacket."

Anne looked at him curiously. "Isn't he the man the mime followed in Florence? Did you know him then? Why didn't you say anything?"

"Please suggest something to get us out of here. I don't want to speak to him or for him to come over here."

Anne hesitated and then nodded. "I'm tired," she said rising from her chair. She realized that it was true. She was exhausted. "Could we go now?"

"Of course." Antonio put his arm solicitously around Anne's waist. As they made their way past the tables, Maya put her arm through Edward's. Anne glanced back to see Sergei watching them. For just a moment their eyes met but she could read nothing there.

The streets were thronged with people; men on motorcycles circling in search of available women, women with arms linked waiting for the men to approach, children running between Fiats and scooters, elderly men and women returning to their homes or taking the air, strolling down the streets. The four of them turned onto the Via dei Funari leading to Maya and Edward's apartment. As usual, it was darker there and silent with the eerie stillness of night in an unpopulated urban area. Maya moved closer to Edward, who was discussing the neo-classical painters with Antonio and Anne. As they approached the door leading to the courtyard of their apartment, Edward took Anne's arm and tucked it into his other elbow so that the two women flanked him.

"It's so wonderfully quiet here, like the fine tranquility of a Poussin landscape although clearly we have an urban landscape entirely filled with the unnatural lines of high rise buildings and paved streets. No classical ruins or bucolic sheep, and yet, it's still full of the possibility that myth gives to life, like the academic serenity one finds in Poussin's works. These are not exciting streets but they're inspiring in that subtle, romantic way imagination has of infusing even the most rational vision."

They had already entered the portico when Anne heard a tiny, sharp sound and Maya staggered under the weight of Edward who had released her arm and fallen against her chest.

"Edward! Stop it. What are you doing?" She tried to push him off but he only leaned more heavily against her.

"What's happening? What was that noise?" Anne turned to Maya who had stumbled to a sitting position under Edward's weight. Edward stared up at Anne, his face gray in the lamplight.

"I think I've been shot." He looked puzzled and rather resentful. Maya and Anne stared at him in disbelief.

CHAPTER THIRTY FIVE

"Veronese's 'Feast in the House of Levy' is an astonishing
setting for the most diverse characters; monkeys, buffoons,
soldiers, dwarfs, servants and noblemen all set upon a
grand architectonic stage before a backdrop of pale, ghostly
edifices. Originally titled a 'Last Supper', Veronese was
called before the Inquisition to explain why he had peopled
the sacred meal with such vulgar and unacceptable
characters. Calling upon poetic license he had defended
the painting but, in the end, he changed the title of the
work, thereby affirming my thesis that what we see and
what we're told we see may be beautifully manipulated
according to our own prejudices and limited vision."
(Edward Donant)

Maya continued to sit on the paved floor of the courtyard as she
watched Antonio support Edward into the shadowy foyer. Anne followed
them, her black hair merging with the dark shadows made by the colonnade
so that she looked like some pale figure with gigantic strands of hair. 'She
looks like the Medusa,' Maya thought vaguely and her eyes shifted to
register the moonlit faces of the sculptures that lined the courtyard walls.
'The Medusa who turns men to stone.' Maya giggled. She pressed a hand
across her mouth, stifling her laughter. She was becoming hysterical. But,
of course, none of it was funny. Maya rose stiffly to her feet.

Anne stared at Maya when she entered the apartment. "Maya! Were
you also hurt?"

Maya looked at her, confused. "No, I'm fine. Why?"

"Your face, your arm," Anne gestured at her and Maya turned to look
at herself in the mirror. She gasped. Her mouth was bloody and a patch of
blood had seeped into her dress around her bosom. She looked down at her
hand. It, too, was stained with blood.

"Oh," she said faintly.

Anne found a towel and used it to gingerly wipe at Maya's face and
dress. "Does anything hurt?"

Maya shook her head, looking helplessly at Anne.

Anne sighed. "It's all right. I think you just got bloody when Edward
fell on you."

Maya nodded, speechless. She looked at Edward who was sitting in the armchair with a towel wrapped around his upper arm. Maya walked over to him. "Is this where you were shot?"

"Apparently," Edward tilted his head in the direction of his wound.

Maya removed the towel and stared at the bloody shirt. "But I didn't hear anything," she muttered, turning pale at the sight of the darkly opalescent tear in Edward's upper arm.

"I thought I heard something," Anne said. "Just a tiny sound."

"He used a silencer." Antonio was on the phone to his personal doctor.

Anne crossed the room with a snifter of brandy. "How melodramatic. You'd have to think it was all planned then, wouldn't you? Not like someone just showing up and deciding to shoot at us."

"But why would anyone shoot Edward?" Maya was pale.

"Are you all right, Maya?" Anne took Maya's arm as she began to sway.

"Blood makes me feel faint," she said, allowing Anne to help her to a chair. Suddenly Maya clenched her fists and cried out. "I don't understand what's going on! I don't, I don't! What have we done to deserve this? Is everybody crazy in this country?"

"Don't get hysterical, Maya," Edward looked a bit faint himself as he glanced down at his arm.

"'Don't get hysterical.' 'Don't worry.' Don't wonder why on earth someone put a bomb in Valeriano's car or a stolen drawing in my purse or why someone shot you."

Anne lit another cigarette from the butt of her first. "Maya does have a point, Edward. Why would anyone shoot you? You must have some idea."

"But I have no idea." Edward leaned back in the chair and closed his eyes.

Maya bent over, her head between her knees. "But surely darling," she mumbled from her upside-down position. "You know something. These kinds of things don't just happen out of the blue."

"Lots of things seem to be happening out of the blue," Edward remarked without opening his eyes.

There was a knock at the door and Antonio went to open it. It was Alberto. He spoke briefly with Antonio.

Maya lifted her head. "So where was *he* during all of this? I thought he was always on the job."

Antonio turned to Edward. "Alberto told me that he chased the man who shot you. Alberto's sure he shot the man in one leg but he got away. He had a motorcycle."

"No kidding," Anne blew out a shot of smoke. "There's some man limping around Rome who shot at us? It's just like in a movie." Edward sighed and looked pityingly at Anne. "Well, it is."

The doctor arrived at the same time as two carabinieri. While they questioned Maya, Anne and Antonio, the doctor dressed Edward's arm. "Non e molto grave. It's not so bad," the doctor said. Edward looked a bit disgruntled. "The bullet tore through the deltoid at the edge of the arm then exited. As you see there's only some lacerated flesh, no muscle tissue or ligaments were destroyed. It should heal nicely. I recommend rest and a more prudent outlook." The doctor gave him a shot for the pain.

"It's not always easy to anticipate thugs." Edward was irritable.

"And no heavy lifting." The doctor said as he closed his bag.

"Ha." Maya poured herself a small amount of brandy from a snifter on the table beside the sofa. "Edward never lifts anything heavy."

One of the policemen had established himself at the dining room table, delicately pushing the vase of lavender out of the way before placing a pad before him and twisting a pen between his thumb and forefinger.

The second policeman pulled up one of a pair of Hepplewhite wing chairs and placed it in front of the sofa. Maya frowned. She didn't like anyone to move the furniture. Oblivious of her sniff of disapproval, he addressed her. "I understand that you were recently arrested in Turin for the attempted smuggling of a stolen drawing and that you have been released under the condition that you do not leave Rome."

Maya's mouth dropped open. "What on earth does that have to do with my fiancé being shot?!"

The policeman raised his eyebrows. "It raises the question of motive. Perhaps the two incidents are related." He looked around the room. "Do you know of any reason someone would attack the four of you? Mi scusi, signore," he turned to Antonio. "Ma dobbiamo fare queste domande a' tutti coloro che erano presenti."

"Why should you apologize to Antonio? What makes him so different? The fact that he's Italian?" Maya folded her arms and looked defiantly at the policeman.

"Antonio works with Charlie who's with the police, remember?" Anne whispered.

Maya rolled her eyes.

The policeman spoke to her again. "There could be someone who was perhaps unhappy that you had taken the drawing? Perhaps you know of something that might help us track down this man?"

"I never took any drawing so I can't imagine how there could be any connection."

"Va bene. We assume that you are innocent. Still, someone wanted you arrested and that person may be unhappy that you are still, apparently, free. So, have you any idea who might have put the drawing in your purse?"

"If I did, I would certainly have informed the police when I was in Turin."

"Excuse me but I don't understand why you're questioning Maya when it was Edward who was shot," Anne interrupted.

"Because, signora, there has been a theft in connection with the young woman. And it is my understanding that you were all very close together when the assailant shot the gentleman. It is certainly possible that the attacker was aiming at any one of you and that Signore Donant was not the intended victim."

Maya turned pale. "I don't understand," she said stiffly.

Anne looked at Maya. "It's just that we hadn't thought of that," Anne turned back to the police officer.

"It's a possibility," he said with a slight shrug.

"Well, whoever he was shooting at we were lucky that nothing worse happened," Anne said.

"Oh, yes, just a bullet harrowing my flesh and blood. Don't worry about old Edward."

"Oh, my poor darling," Maya rose and went to Edward. Bending down she kissed him lightly on the cheek. "I'm so sorry. Of course, we're concerned about you."

The policeman addressed Edward. "Allora, and you, signore. Do you have any idea why anyone would want to shoot you?"

Edward took a sip of brandy. "I've been pondering that very question and I'm afraid that I cannot come up with a single reason. Baffling, isn't it?"

"Well, signore, perhaps not. What is the purpose of your visit to Italia?" The policeman at the dining room table was silently taking notes.

"I'm writing a guidebook to great works of art in certain Italian museums."

"And how long do you intend to stay in Italy?"

"I'm not sure—another month or so. Why? What does this have to do with my being shot by some miscreant?"

171

The policeman bowed slightly in Maya's direction. "Since you have arrived in Italy, signore, signora, there have been several incidents in which one or the other of you have been…involved. There was the bombing in Florence, there has been the attempted smuggling of the drawing, and the theft of the Caravaggio…"

Maya stared at the policeman. "The theft of…? I can't believe you'd even bring that up. How could you possibly think that we had anything to do with that!"

"We are simply looking into the possibility that there may be a connection between these incidents and the attack tonight. All of these incidents suggest a level of involvement in something illicit. If you see our line of thought."

Edward grimaced. "I'm very tired gentlemen. Perhaps that's why I fail to see the relevance of any line of thought that you have produced tonight. You actually seem more interested in speculative questions concerning our supposed criminal activity than in tracing the person responsible for attacking me."

"Ah, but we are interested in all lines of inquiry that may lead us to knowledge of the recent crimes. Until we get some answers from you on these I believe it will be difficult for us to find out what was the motive for the attack tonight."

"'We? Who's 'we'?" Edward shifted irritably. "The fabulous Italian polizia? I understand that the person who attacked me may have been shot. Can't you check the hospitals?"

"I know my job, signore, grazie," the policeman spoke genially. "However it's unlikely that he'll go to any public institution."

"Well, that's about the best I can offer. That being the case I wonder if I might retire."

The doctor gave Maya a small bottle of pills. "For the pain. No more than four a day. No alcohol." He shook a finger at Edward, who finished off his glass of brandy. The four of them signed copies of their testimony, which had been taken down as they talked. The two policemen waited until Antonio returned from assisting Edward to bed.

"Signore, a questo punto, credo che sia tutto. That is all for the moment," the officer turned to speak to Anne.

She nodded. "Do you think there's any possibility of catching this person?" Anne walked with the two policemen to the door.

"Not considering what we have to go on." The first policeman nodded to the second who opened the door.

"You mean you don't really care," Maya spoke up from the depths of the sofa into which she had sunk.

"As you wish, Signora."

"Buona notte, officers e grazie." Anne closed the door and turned to look at Maya. "Why did you say that? Are you trying to antagonize them?"

"They were practically blackmailing us. Offering to help find this person only if we could give them information on a bombing, for God's sake, and the theft of that painting, as though we would have any idea."

"How are you feeling?" Antonio put his arm around Anne and kissed her on the forehead.

She looked at him. "Actually I feel like I'm going to be sick."

"It's been a trying night for everyone. Let me take you home," Antonio pulled Anne close to him.

She sighed, allowing herself to be drawn against his chest. "I'd love that but I think, well, I wonder if maybe Maya wouldn't need me here."

They both looked over at Maya who was sitting on the sofa, staring at the terrace doors.

"She'll be fine," Antonio said firmly. "There's nothing you can do."

Anne nodded and, walking over to Maya, put her hand on her shoulder. Maya reached up and covered Anne's hand with her own. "I'm really sorry, Anne," Maya's voice quavered. "I'm sorry I yelled at you tonight and that I've been so blind and selfish. Of course you were upset about what happened between Edward and me. I've not been a good friend, but I'm still your friend, I still love you no matter what you think of me."

Anne stood silently beside her. Maya gripped Anne's hand and turned to look up at her. "Thank you anyway, for helping me in Turin, and for trying to…trying to..." She stopped and released Anne's hand.

Anne patted her awkwardly. "It's all right. I'm sorry too. We're both a bit stressed."

Maya laughed shortly. "That's putting it mildly."

"Well," Anne sighed. "Antonio's offered to take me home. Are you going to be all right?"

Maya shivered. "Oh please, Anne, I don't want to be alone tonight. I just can't bear it. With Edward lying in there and I don't know who's waiting outside or what will happen." She looked up at Anne, her eyes huge in her pale face. "Would it be terrible of me to ask you to stay with me? Just for tonight, I'll be better tomorrow."

Anne hesitated and looked at Antonio. He shrugged and reached for his jacket.

"I'll see you tomorrow, cara," he said. "Try to sleep, Maya," he said gently to her and, bending down, kissed her on both cheeks. "Everything will be all right," he added.

Anne walked with Antonio to the door. He kissed her deeply. She felt his arms tighten around her waist and she grasped him, running her hands down his back. After a moment, Antonio disentangled himself from her embrace and she reluctantly let him go. "A domani, carrissima."

Anne walked to the windows leading to the terrace where she watched the night dissolve to early morning. A pale wash spread across the sky like a fine muslin sheet over a black board. Wanly bleeding through the white, a faint rose tinted the rooftops. A sparrow hopped onto the balustrade of the terrace and began to twitter.

Maya spoke wearily. "It's very late isn't it? I hear the birds."

"Or very early."

Maya stood up. "I should check on Edward to make sure he's okay." She returned a few minutes later. "Those pills must work because he's sound asleep."

Anne glanced at her watch. "It's almost five o'clock and I have to give a lecture this morning. I've got to go to sleep, too and so should you. I guess we'll just have to wait and see what happens. Maybe they'll find the person who did this today. Maybe it'll be the same person who set off the bomb and called the police in Turin and everything will be neatly resolved."

"That would be nice." Maya looked doubtful. "At least we have to admit that it hasn't been boring since we came to Italy, right?"

Anne wondered again what John wanted to tell her. "No, I guess I'd have to say that it's not been boring."

CHAPTER THIRTY SIX

"The black figure of Satan points to the cities and lands
Christ will govern if he will denounce God. Christ repeats
Satan's gesture, the two figures parallel on the landscape
almost as though Satan were Christ's shadow, his darker side.
Duccio has represented one of the enduring themes of
Western art; the duality of man—light and dark, good and
evil. Christianity recognizes this, of course. The
temptation of Anthony, the temptation of Christ though
there was wide divergence between those who thought
Christ was truly tempted or not. The whole issue of Christ's
humanity contradicted the doctrines of the Gnostics and
the Manichaeans. 'He really suffers.' 'No, he doesn't.'
'Yes, he does.' Humanism won out, of course."
(Edward Donant)

Anne had dreamed that she was in her house in Atlanta and that her cat, Pinkham, had climbed on to the bed where he was kneading the covers. She opened her eyes and tried to orient herself. She wasn't in her hotel room—there was no fan and the window wasn't in the same position. It wasn't Antonio's apartment—she distinctly remembered a tall wardrobe next to the bedroom door with books piled on top. Gradually she realized she was in the guest room at Edward and Maya's apartment. With that she recalled the events of the evening before. Anne groped for her watch, which she had left on the table next to the bed. It was almost ten o'clock. She dressed and went into the kitchen to find Maya already up and preparing coffee.

"Did you sleep well?" Maya kissed Anne on the cheek.

"Deeply. How about you?"

Maya shook her head. "I couldn't sleep. Edward's up and complaining like a baby."

"Well, he *was* shot." Anne took a bottle of water from the refrigerator.

"Tell me about it."

Edward called fretfully from the dining room. "Is the coffee ready and do you know where those damned pain pills are?"

Maya nodded in the direction of the toaster. "The pills are on the counter over there if you don't mind."

"Good morning, Edward." Anne gave him a pill with a glass of water.

"Thanks." Edward was wearing a white kimono with a long, black scarf wrapped about his waist. The kimono was arranged so that the shoulder and wounded arm were left free. His skin showed pale and fleshy above the dressing of gauze and tape.

Anne looked at him contemplatively. "You look a lot like Caravaggio's 'Bacchus' you know. You've got the perfect decadent face and then all wrapped up like some pagan god from antiquity…all you need is a beautiful glass of claret."

"I could use a glass of something strong right now." Edward swallowed the pill with a grimace.

Maya brought out coffee and put a loaf of bread and a block of butter on the table.

"How are you feeling now, my love? Do the pills help?"

Edward grimaced. "Not much. Not yet anyway. You know what I think would really help? A small glass of brandy."

"You're not supposed to drink alcohol with those pills, Edward. And it's only nine o'clock."

"I'd like a glass please, dear, and I'm really not concerned what time of day it is."

Maya poured a large portion into a glass. "Go ahead, kill yourself." She handed it to him.

He took a sip, "Well, there you have it. The simplest resolution of the human condition—kill the other."

"Speak for yourself."

"You're not being fair Edward. It's your own choice," Anne buttered a thin slice of bread.

"I'm not talking about that. I was thinking of last night when someone shot me, in case you've both forgotten."

"What do you consider the human condition?" Anne poured a cup of coffee.

"Why, loneliness of course, isolation, the feeling that no one understands you and the paradoxical certainty that you know what's best for everyone else. Lethal combination. Take last night. I'll bet the person who shot me is incapable of empathizing with others."

"You think that you were shot because this person was lonely?" Maya buttered a slice of bread. "Boy, are you back in form. It doesn't take you long."

Edward took a sip of brandy. "Not lonely. Isolated in his own sense of virtue or injustice—completely blind to others' points of view. I don't think it would be difficult at all to persuade you that I'm right."

"It sounds like you're talking about psychotics," Maya said, "not regular people. They're a little different you know."

"And you think that shooting someone is something a 'regular' person would do?"

"Hmmm, well, I guess not."

"Anyway, you're quite wrong. They may not be motivated by the same thing but they're frequently related. The 'psychotic' often has the same mentality as 'normal' people."

Anne pointed her piece of bread at Edward. "You say there's no difference between normal people and psychotics or between fraudulent and legitimate works of art and I'll bet you'd argue there's no difference between love and desire. Well, you're wrong. It's very important to distinguish between those persons who are crazy and those who have some moral sense just as it's important to distinguish between true love and lust, between the real and the fake. Their legitimacy lies in their difference."

"Oh, there I must stop you. I never said that there was no *difference*. Just that most people can't recognize the difference and isn't recognition, knowledge, understanding what we're talking about? If I place a work of art before you and you don't think it's well done or has any value and then I tell you that it was painted by Leonardo da Vinci and you change your mind and think it's wonderful, what has been accomplished? What does that say about the artist or the work of art? It's only a sort of fraud in that the work becomes valued beyond its intrinsic worth where it joins the legitimate community of frauds. If I then turn around and tell you that it was never painted by Leonardo but by a pupil and poorly done at that you feel betrayed. You think that I've been unfair but, in fact, you should be happy, joyous to discover that, after all, this great artist never created such a mediocre work.

"The fraud is not in the painting or the work of art itself but in the falseness of viewers, in their hypocritical desire to look knowledgeable when, in fact, their opinions are always based on the subjective observations of others. Oh no, when you say that fraud is the responsibility of those in authority I must disagree. Fraud takes place in people's hearts, in their souls."

"Oh, yes, you would take that petty, elitist view. I can't believe you'd argue that people who know nothing about art shouldn't have the right to expect the experts to give them opinions that are as honest as possible. After all, I know nothing about electricity or plumbing but I expect the electrician or the plumber to know their metier and to do the job properly."

Edward shook his head and smiled gently. "I'm disappointed in you, Anne. Art is not plumbing or electricity. As you well know, it's a highly subjective genre, one in which fraud may take place on any level: that of authenticity, of credibility, of technical proficiency, of aesthetic or historical merit. Good God, love, just look at the contemporary market."

"Well, I admit the argument's weak but I believe there's a place for honesty and faith. Just as in a love relationship. If one person loves another and the other doesn't love them in return but pretends to do so with all the trappings of tenderness and concern, of avowed devotion, etc. and the one who loves believes all this then she's got the right to feel disillusioned and disappointed when she finds out that she's been deceived." Anne stopped, flushed.

"Another poor analogy." Edward cradled his arm. "Of all relationships the one between two lovers should be the most transparent. No matter how one tries to conceal dislike or disaffection it's evident and simply means that the lover's trying to convince himself of continued affection where he must be quite aware of the change. No, no, that's really not very persuasive."

"And what, may I ask," Maya interrupted, "does any of this have to do with your being shot?"

"Nothing that I can see. It's only Anne's perverse nature. She likes to argue with me about everything."

"I've got to go." Anne rose. "I've got to meet my students at eleven."

"There Edward, you're so persuasive Anne's going to leave."

"Oh, Anne makes up her own mind. That's one thing I'm sure of. Like those sturdy pioneer women she just shoulders the burden and moves ahead. Right across that old prairie."

"Oh, God, Edward, what are you talking about? Bye, darling. Are you going to be okay?" Anne kissed Maya.

"I'm fine."

Anne leaned over to give Edward a kiss on the cheek. "I need to talk to you, Edward," she whispered. "Alone."

Edward looked up at her. "Call me later." He grimaced as Anne's hand brushed his shoulder.

CHAPTER THIRTY SEVEN

"In Caravaggio's painting, 'Magdalene,' there's a splendid,
literal kind of realism as opposed to this painting by Rembrandt,
'The Flayed Ox;' a very repugnant theme. Rembrandt uses
that subject that causes physical repulsion in us as an
expression of what paint can do, can express. The literal aim
of Caravaggio is full of expressive interpretation versus the
non-literal commentary of Rembrandt who chooses this
subject. Rembrandt is experimental almost like Pollock
or de Kooning who let paint speak for itself."
(Edward Donant)

Valeriano put down the phone and sat quietly, his mind working back over the past few days. What a mess. And after he had arranged everything... He heard the door open. "John?" Valeriano wheeled his chair about to face the door. "John, veni qui, per favore."

John limped into the room. He looked sullen, the ravaged area around his eye more inflamed than usual, making him more repellant than usual.

"Do you know who just called me?"

John shrugged.

"It was Edward."

John limped over to the bar and poured himself a large scotch. "Good old Edward," he mumbled as he took a gulp. "What did he want?"

Valeriano spoke in slow measured tones. "It seems that someone shot him last night."

John slouched on the couch and stared at Valeriano. "So?"

"So," Valeriano emphasized the word. "I just wanted to ask you if you knew anything about this.

"Why would I know anything about someone shooting Edward?"

"Because Edward said he thought it was you."

"Why would he think it was me?"

"He says he saw you."

"It was dark. How could he have seen me?" John giggled.

"So it was you. Why did you do such a thing?"

"It wasn't me." John looked slyly at his father out of his one good eye. "But then what's the point of me denying it. You've judged me and found me guilty."

"Why are you limping?

Ignoring Valeriano, John got up to re-fill his glass.

"Answer me! Edward told me that whoever it was had been shot. Is that why you're limping? John! Don't you see how serious this is?"

John gulped down the scotch and smiled wickedly. "Serious? I don't see what you mean."

"I don't understand you." Valeriano shook his head in disgust.

John laughed. "Understand me. That's a joke. You never even tried to understand me."

"Did you shoot Edward?"

John got up to pour some more scotch. "D'you want some?" He waved his glass at Valeriano.

"No." Valeriano pressed his lips together. "Why are you limping? How did you get hurt?"

"Why do you keep asking? Do you care?" John grimaced as he sat down again on the couch.

Valeriano looked at him thoughtfully and sighed in exasperation. Suddenly he wheeled the chair rapidly across the floor and came to a stop directly in front of John. Startled, John spilled some of the scotch. "What're you doing? You almost made me drop my glass."

Valeriano spoke in a low voice. "I want to know where you were last night. I want to know why you're limping. And I've about had it with your drinking."

"Ah, you do care." John grinned and Valeriano wheeled back from him. "Can't stand to see my lovely face, can you, dad?"

"You drink too much," Valeriano said contemptuously.

John drank all of the scotch in his glass before throwing it almost nonchalantly on the floor where it shattered. "You can't threaten me, you bastard. I know everything that's going on, I know what you're involved in. I know why that bomb was planted in your car. You think that I don't listen? That I don't have friends? That I'm too *stupid* to figure anything out? You don't know anything about me. You have no idea…" he stopped, suddenly plaintive. "I've been shot and you don't even care. All you care about are your stupid deals." Tears welled up in his eyes. He turned and picked up another glass.

"John," Valeriano controlled his voice and spoke as gently as possible. "Please don't take another drink. Let me get a doctor for you. We'll get you taken care of. You're stressed out. It's all right."

John filled the glass and sat down heavily on the couch. He set the glass on a table and pressing his head into his hands he began to cry, ragged, harsh crying, his breath coming in short gasps. After a few minutes, he stopped and looked up at Valeriano who was watching him with an expression of extreme distaste mingled with sorrow. "You can't imagine how much I hate you," John spoke slowly. "How much I hate her."

"Who?" Valeriano shrugged irritably. "Your mother?"

"I loved my mother," John screamed at him and stood up. "Fuck you. Fuck all of you." He limped out of the room, slamming the door behind him.

"John! Merde." Valeriano shook his head. What a fool. It was time to do something about John. He picked up the phone.

CHAPTER THIRTY EIGHT

"'One day, entering the church of the Madonna del Pilero with some
gentlemen, one of them, most cultivated, stepped forward in order to
give him some holy water; Caravaggio asked him what was the
purpose of it and the answer was that it would erase any venial sin.
'It is not necessary," he replied, "since all my sins are mortal.'"
(From Le vite de'pittori messinesi by Francesco Sussino in
Caravaggio, Howard Hibbard, Harper & Row, (1983) pp.386

John felt dizzy as he descended the stairs from his father's apartment.
He stopped to lean against the wall and wipe the sweat from his forehead.
He clung to the railing for support until his vision cleared and he began
to go down more slowly. The pills he had taken for the pain caused by his
wound must be mixing badly with the scotch he had drunk at Valeriano's.
He was convulsed by a sudden pain in his stomach and felt as though he
were going to vomit. Gasping, he staggered out the door into the Piazza
Navona and bent over, waiting for the retching feeling to stop. When it
subsided he continued to cross the piazza. He had missed Anne but at
least he had wounded that bastard Edward. Everything in his life was like
that. It was so unfair. Haggard and exhausted, John sat down on one of the
benches, heedless of the stares that his uncovered face provoked. What
was he going to do now? He needed the money—why had Edward called
the police about the drawing? John groaned and pressed his hands against
his face. He was sitting in the same position when he felt someone tap him
on his shoulder.

"Go away," he muttered without looking up.

"Signore Cerasi?"

John removed his hands from his face and squinted up at a man
standing in front of him. The man squatted before John and flipped open
a discreet leather folder disclosing a police badge. "Would you mind
accompanying me to the police station, signore?"

John smiled grimly. "Are you sure you don't want my father?"

"Are you John Cerasi?"

"No." John smiled with satisfaction at the puzzled look on the man's
face.

"But you are Signore Cerasi's son, John?"

John shrugged. "Si."

"Allora, there are a few questions we would like to ask you, signore."

John raised bloodshot eyes to the man's face. "Why? What questions?"

"I'm afraid I can't disclose that information here, signore. If you would just come with me."

John spat onto the ground and rose painfully. "Oof," he complained as he limped stiffly next to the police officer.

"Is something wrong, signore?"

"No," John said shortly. "I just hurt my knee is all."

John was taken to a small office at the police station where he was given a seat before a desk. "Would you like anything to drink, signore?"

John looked at the man with a glint in his eye. "D'you have any scotch?"

"We have coffee and water," the man spoke patiently.

John laughed and shook his head. "Water then, per favore." He closed his eyes. He just wanted to curl up and go to sleep. Someone entered the room.

"Buon giorno, John."

John opened his eyes. "Oh God," he closed them again.

Carlo pulled up a chair next to John's. "I would like to ask you some questions, John."

"So I've been told."

"What were you doing last night?"

John looked at Carlo. "Why do you ask me that?"

"Because there was a shooting. There are witnesses who would swear that the perpetrator of this crime was you."

John grimaced. "Witnesses? Like who?"

"Where were you?"

"I was at the Piazza Navona, like every night."

"And afterward, between 12 and 12:30?"

"I was walking around. You know." John shrugged.

"Piero told me you had hurt your knee. Have you had anyone look at it?"

John stared at Carlo. "It's just a pulled muscle. Why?"

"You're limping. I'm concerned. We have a doctor here who can have a look. He can take care of you."

"I don't need one of your doctors, grazie." John's hands shook as he picked up his water glass.

"You seem a bit shaky, John. Are you sure you don't need a doctor?"

"Quite sure," John said sulkily.

"So," Carlo leaned back and crossed his legs. "How is your father doing?"

John shrugged.

"How is he getting along since the accident?"

"He's all right," John muttered.

"You're not too fond of each other, are you?"

John's eyes flashed then lost their luster. He shrugged. "We're okay."

"That's not what I hear," Carlo said genially.

John stared at the floor.

"I hear that you hate each other, that you'd like to see your father ruined."

"Bullshit," John's voice quavered.

"Why did you shoot Edward, John? Is it because he works with your father? Is it because your father prefers Edward to you?"

"What?!" John laughed. He rocked back in his chair and laughed mirthlessly, "Ha, ha, ha. My father dumped Edward. He set him up and dumped him. Edward hates his guts. I think *he*'s the one who'd like to see my father ruined. Why don't you question him?"

"So you shot Edward in order to keep him from ruining your father?" Carlo adjusted his sunglasses and glanced toward a corner of the room.

"You can't trap me," John said, looking at Carlo cunningly. "I didn't shoot Edward. Even though he deserves to be shot. He's a thieving, lying bastard!"

"Why do you say that?"

"Because," John stopped suddenly and shook his head. "You're not going to trick me. I'm not telling you anything."

"Oh John, John," Carlo said gently, returning his gaze to John's face. "I'm afraid there's no point in denying it. All I want to know is why you shot him. I want to know what Edward has been up to. I want to know what you know about Edward."

John caught his breath on a sob and reached up to wipe his good eye. He looked around the room and then at his feet. His shoulders sagged and he slipped down in the chair until he was curled against the seat like a comma. "Why do you ask me about these things? I didn't shoot Edward. I didn't shoot anybody."

Carlo stared at John and then smiled. "Well, I appreciate you coming down to answer my questions." Carlo stood up and nodded at the man standing at the door.

John looked up at Carlo, confused and suspicious.

"You can go," Carlo said to John. "Just make sure you're around the next few days. We'll want to talk again."

John rose heavily to his feet. He staggered a bit as he walked out of the door. He turned at the door and spoke again. "Just one other thing. You might want to ask Edward what he had to do with the Piranesi drawing. You might want to ask him why he called the police in Turin."

"Just a minute," Carlo spoke crisply. "What do you know about the drawing? Why do you think Edward had anything to do with it?"

"My dad told me it was stolen, he told me someone called to say that the drawing was in Maya's purse. She's engaged to Edward and Edward's looking for ways to make money now that my dad's thrown him out of his gallery. It looks pretty clear to me."

Carlo stepped close to John. "If that's the case, why would Edward want Maya arrested and the drawing returned?"

John's face crumpled with perplexity. "I don't know," he muttered. "That's what you should ask him."

Carlo nodded. "Grazie, John. You've been very helpful." He nodded at the policeman standing by the door.

John looked nervously around the room. "That's it then? I can go?"

"Certo," Carlo smiled coolly. He watched John as he walked cautiously down the hall. John turned once and, when he saw Carlo watching him, John grinned and waved to him. He disappeared and Carlo turned back to the policeman standing next to him. "I want you to keep an eye on John. I don't think we can entirely trust our American friend. Any of our American friends," he added.

CHAPTER THIRTY NINE

"Christianity is a story about the *in*version of desire—not seeking to
fulfill oneself but seeking to be fulfilled by fulfilling another."
(Edward Donant)

"You must imagine, of course, what the artists of the Quattrocento
and Cinquecento came out of. The Plague or the Black Death had
swept through Europe devastating populations and altering urban
landscapes. In one hot summer of 1347 it wiped out fifty to eighty
percent of the populations of Siena and Florence and with it went
the adventurous spirit of artists such as Bernardo Daddi, Andrea
Pisano and Pietro and Ambrogio Lorenzetti. We could compare
it, on a much different scale of course, to the awful toll AIDS has
taken in the last thirty years. Again, legions of brilliant artists and
creative individuals have succumbed. Death, the grinning skeleton
with its merciless scythe, cuts people down indiscriminately; the
young and the old, the beautiful and the ugly, the good and the
bad, the noble and the greedy, the brilliant and the dumb. However,
despite a brief conservative return to the rigid spiritual imagery
of the Byzantine period, defiant individuality creeps in. By the
time of the Early Renaissance the focus shifts from consolation
in a spiritual afterlife to the physical and intellectual pleasures of
earthly life.

"Out of terrible suffering the Renaissance emerges in praise
of human endeavor and individual genius. Except for Trecento
works such as Traini's 'The Triumph of Death,' Renaissance
artists in Italy rarely focused on the literal corruption of the flesh
or the physical suffering and disintegration of the human body.
Even when they're depicting the Deluge or the Last Judgment the
focus is on the soul in a world where dignity is defined according
to a stoic acceptance of fate. The damned are confused, lost,
refusing to believe they've been damned, struggling against the
fate they've brought upon themselves through their choices and
actions. Following the precepts set out in Dante's <u>Divine Comedy</u>
the artists portray individuals who have damned themselves. They
may represent these sinners with some compassion, just as Dante
did, but there's no question that justice is meted out and that those
who are damned must have known they would be damned.

"We must all die, of course, we will all become corpses eaten by snakes and worms but our souls are our own. It's this that distinguishes the Italian Renaissance image of Hell from that of Northern Europe where monstrous demons torment and terrify human beings. The external monsters of Bosch are internalized in the somber realization of Michelangelo's 'Last Judgment' where he represents himself in the hideous flayed face of St. Bartholomew which he holds in one hand while brandishing the knife of his martyrdom in the other. The demons tormenting this sagging empty skin come from inside and are all the more horrifying."

As required by the guards in the Sistine Chapel, Anne gave her lecture before taking her students into the chapel itself, which was less crowded than she had feared it would be. Although she had often lectured on Michelangelo's frescos in her classes, she had not seen them since 1973, years before their recent cleaning. Curious and a bit nervous, she entered the chapel at the head of her group and waited until she was well within the room before she raised her eyes to the magnificent ceiling. She caught her breath, stunned by the brilliance and clarity of the colors. She remembered being overwhelmed by the melancholy beauty of the darkened frescoes many years before but now she felt uplifted, transformed by the powerful figures, clothed in the acid limes and yellows, pinks and blues that swept across the Biblical landscape from the stories of "Creation" to the "Drunkenness of Noah."

Turning toward the altar, Anne surveyed the great "Last Judgment" and for a moment she reeled before the awful vision through which Michelangelo turned human figures into symbols for the good and evil possibilities that had tormented humanity for centuries and that was far from being reconciled or redeemed in her own. Anne stared into the tortured face of Bartholomew and shivered. Was she only to see visions of hell when she looked into the mirror, into the past, into her heart? Did she really think that Antonio could love her? Or that love had redemptive power? How foolish and naïve it all seemed to seek such transient happiness when faced with these images of eternal despair.

Anne left her group at twelve-thirty. She felt so exhausted she decided to forgo her usual walk, taking a taxi instead across the Tiber to the Piazza Navona where, once again, she found a table at La Dolce Vita.

She ordered a salad and opened her notebook. There were so many questions she wanted answered. First and foremost was the question of who had called the police in Turin about the drawing in Maya's purse. Only John had known that it was there. At least…Anne frowned—obviously someone else knew—John hadn't been faking his anger in his belief that she had made that call. That meant that John must have told someone else. That meant there was someone she didn't know about who knew about her role in the theft of the drawing. That meant that the whole situation was beyond her control. Anne ran her hands through her hair. And to make things more confusing, Edward had been shot and she had no idea who could have done that or why.

Anne looked up as a shadow fell across the page of her notebook. It took her a moment before she recognized him. The Sicilian she had met at lunch. 'Gianni,' Edward had said. "Oh no," she muttered as he bowed slightly.

"Signora. Est-ce que I sit? Permesso? Posso sedermi un attimo?" He pulled out a chair and seated himself. "Come stai? How are you?"

"Fine. And you?"

"Bene. Scrive sempre? You write, umm, always. You are intelligente. Si, si. Edward tells me."

Anne sighed pointedly and put down her pen. "What do you want? If you will excuse my bluntness. And how did you know I was here?"

"Scusi? Oh, you are, ummm, occupata. Mi scusa. Si. I want... You cenare, diner con me sta sera. Tonight you have dinner con me."

Anne shook her head.

"Si, si. You will find it interessante. Ho informazione of Edward. Molto interessante."

"What?" Deeply curious and more than a little suspicious, Anne lifted her sunglasses and stared intently at Gianni. "What do you mean? If you have something to say, tell me now."

"Non. Sta sera. You cenare con me. E molto importante." He chuckled and, reaching for her hand, he kissed it. "Bellisima," he murmured.

Anne jerked her hand away. "I don't know."

"Ma, come signora?"

"Peut-etre. Forse...maybe."

"Si. You come. Si venga. Le Cave di S. Ignazio on the Piazza di S. Ignazio. La conosce?"

Anne shook her head.

Gianni took a napkin and drew a rough map on it that he handed to Anne. "Alle nove. At, come si dici? Nine o'clock."

"But what can you possibly have to tell me? Why are you being so mysterious?"

Gianni shrugged. "Non capisco." His phone rang and he began to talk rapidly into it.

Anne drained her glass of water before pouring more. She felt better after she had drunk three glasses of water. So, Edward was up to something. She had known it all along. Despite her distrust of Gianni, Anne was eager to find out what he knew. The waiter brought her salad and she ate, ignoring Gianni's lengthy conversation. 'Now I look just like all those other women sitting with men talking into their mobile phones while they eat,' she thought. 'Disgusting. And those nails!' She couldn't keep from staring at his long pinkie nails.

He closed up the phone, apologizing for having spoken so long. Or that was what Anne assumed he said. "How did you know I was here?"

"Oh, si. I…a passeggio. I see you sempre, always Piazza Navona."

"Oh." So much for returning to the same old places.

"Allora. La cucina est, ummmm, buona? Le piace?"

Anne sighed. "Please, Gianni. I'm tired and I need to work. Would you mind?"

"Ah, si. Va bene." He stood up. "A sta sera. Arrivederci." He strolled confidently across the piazza while Anne watched him. He was a strange man. What on earth could he tell her about Edward? And what role did Gianni play in all of this? Anne picked at her salad. Gianni knew Edward. Could it have been Gianni who had shot Edward? But why would he do that? What could be going on between them? Anne pursed her lips, tired and uneasy. She sighed. She would meet Gianni for dinner, of course. The way things were going, how could she not?

***

When Anne woke it was already evening. She had fallen asleep while she was reading in bed and she felt rumpled and dirty. A sign of advancing age, she told herself as she showered and studied the clothes she had laid out on the bed. She did not want there to be any question of romantic interest on her part but she also didn't want to look dowdy because she was meeting Antonio that evening after her dinner with Gianni. She chose a short, plain black dress and a long gray cardigan. She put on lip-gloss and blush and brushed her hair straight back into a chignon.

The night was warm and the lights glowed along the Tiber. The streets near the Piazza di S. Ignazio were crowded with couples and families, laughing and talking and gesticulating. The restaurant was also crowded. There were several long rows of tables set out on the piazza's paving stones. Anne wandered along the shadowy edge of the lit café, looking for Gianni among the throng of diners but he wasn't there. A waiter seated her next to a group of Japanese ladies who were eating an assortment of pastas, passing them around and laughing good-naturedly. When they smiled at Anne she said, "Buona sera" and they responded in kind.

She looked around the tiny piazza. The building on her right facing the church was typical of the traditional Renaissance buildings in Rome with its pilasters and pediments over the windows, but it broke from the norm with its curving shape, designed to fit the piazza. Anne liked it; it reminded her of the Flatiron building in New York City.

She ordered a carafe of the house white wine and lit a cigarette. Sitting there sipping her wine, caressed by the Italian language rippling and singing, rising and falling in waves of sound underlined by laughter and a passion and joy in life and all of its pleasures, it struck Anne that she had forgotten the pleasure that could be had from simply enjoying life. Shocked at this revelation, Anne stared across the table at the laughing group of ladies. That was what Antonio had said. Did he really think that was true? Why couldn't she be like those ladies? What was wrong with her? Was she really a cold, unfeeling person as Maya said? Or incapable of loving anyone as Edward said? Anne's flesh felt clammy in spite of the warmth of the evening. She drew her cardigan close around her shoulders.

"Buona sera, bellissima." Gianni bent down and kissed Anne on each cheek, three times. He was smartly dressed in a black shirt and black pressed trousers, the thick gold chain exposed on his bare chest. Anne frowned. She had to admit that he had a nice chest. "Scusa, se sono in ritardo for being, ah, late, ma…" he waved his hand in a general expression of an inability to finish the phrase but in the hopes that she would accept his apology.

"No, no, niente. It's okay." Anne looked at her watch. "But it is late and I have to go shortly."

He stared at her almost full plate of pasta and the empty carafe of wine. "Ah, peccato. Too bad." He sat down.

"So, what did you want to tell me about Edward?"

"Non ora, not yet. Prima, mangiamo." He rubbed his stomach and smiled at Anne. "Ho molta fame."

"Oh, good God, Gianni." Anne pushed her plate over to him. "Mangia questa and tell me what you know. You're very late, after all," she added accusingly.

"Non capisco." Gianni grinned again and called the waiter. He ordered what seemed to Anne a rather extensive meal. "Ancora del vino? You want more wine? Rosso? Bianco? Rosso," he said to the waiter who hurried off before Anne could say a thing.

"Allora," Gianni turned back to her. "You have a…come si dici? Nice day? Una buona giornata?"

"Yes," Anne said shortly. She finished off her wine and accepted more without another word.

Gianni talked expansively, answering his phone on occasion and winking at her as he spoke into it. After he had finished her pasta, he leaned forward. "So, about Edward. You are molto curioso, no?"

Anne smiled. Oh, please, please, let him tell me so that I can go. "Si," she nodded.

"Ah, well, Edward ed io siamo amici, I think we are friends. I help him, he helps me, capisci? He tells me, per esempio about some paintings, some paintings that might be good for me, paintings that I can restore, paintings that I might be able to sell afterwards for more money. And, recently, he tells me about a very interesting painting in a church that might be worth a lot of money."

Anne stared at Gianni, forgetting the wine, her cigarette burning down between her fingers. The Caravaggio—of course. "Si? Go on. Per piacere."

Gianni took her hand and brought it to his lips. He kissed it gently, turning her palm over so that his lips pressed the soft inner flesh. She resisted the impulse to jerk her hand away. What an odd way to seduce someone she thought. Gianni's cunning, brown eyes were looking at her over the palm of her hand. He lowered it but kept holding it, stroking her flesh with his thumb. Anne stiffened involuntarily and pulled her hand away. She wanted to wipe her hand on her napkin but was afraid of insulting him. "And?" she prodded him. "So? A painting in a church. That's nothing much."

"Oh, penso che tu capisca, I think you understand. Non e un pittore normale ma..."

"You're telling me that Edward was the one who told you about the Caravaggio—where it was originally discovered?"

Gianni nodded.

"And it was you who told Valeriano." Anne spoke slowly, trying to figure out the ramification of this bit of news.

Gianni said nothing but wiped his lips on his napkin.

"Why are you telling me this? Perche?"

He smiled genially at her. "Edward tells me tu sei molto interessata nel Caravaggio. Allora..." he raised his eyebrows.

Anne spoke slowly. "So, Edward wanted Valeriano to discover this painting. Now why would he want to do that?"

Gianni watched her, his eyes glittering. Was he amused? Anne thought so. Or perhaps it was a calculating look... "If it was truly an original painting, why would Edward want Valeriano to have the honor of discovering and exhibiting it?"

Gianni shrugged.

"It wasn't an original, was it?" Anne looked up excitedly. "Edward knew it wasn't original, he knew where it was, he told you to tell Valeriano…that means." She stopped…frowning. What did that mean? "What else did Edward tell you about this painting?"

Gianni drank his wine. "Non e importante. Penso che tu sei gentile ma…" he waved his hand dismissively. "I give nothing more."

"Oh." Anne stared at him. "I see," she spoke shortly.

Again he shrugged and poured some more wine into his glass. "Come va la signora? Edward's wife?"

"Fiancee, fidanzata," Anne corrected him. "How do you know Maya?" Anne stopped. Of course, through Edward. "She's fine, I guess."

"I hear she was, come si dice? Arrested in Turin." Gianni's eyes were dark and opaque.

Anne looked at him sharply. "Yes."

He smiled. "E mysterioso, non? How these things happen? Ancora del vino?"

Anne shook her head. "Why do you ask? Perche?"

"It seems so," Gianni waved his hands helplessly. "So bad that she is accused…and Edward doesn't help her."

"Why do you say that? What could Edward do? He had nothing to do with it." Anne felt more and more annoyed by this man.

"Non capisco." Gianni held out a lighter to Anne's cigarette.

"What do you know about all of this anyway?"

"Ho una amica, a friend." He leaned close to Anne, his eyes glittering. "She lives in the same building as Edward and she knows a great deal about this drawing. I know Maya didn't take the drawing because I know who did."

Anne stared at him. Her heart was beating very fast. Did he know about John? And if so…did he know about her? How could he know? But then…she remembered John's phone call. He had been all excited thinking that it had been Anne who had called the police in Turin. Anne frowned and leaned forward. "It was you who called the police in Turin." She spoke intensely, certain that she was right.

Gianni smiled and shook his head. "Non capisco." He chuckled gently and Anne thought his understanding of English was awfully convenient for him.

"It was John who told you about the drawing, wasn't it?"

"John?" Gianni was watching her. "No, ma it seems as though you know a good deal about this drawing as well." He poured more wine into Anne's glass. "Now that we know so much about each other we can be friends, eh?" He winked at Anne.

She shook her head. She was confused. He took Anne's hand and pulled her toward him. "Voglio baciare, bellissima," he murmured, his eyes hard.

Anne pulled away, uncomfortable and repelled. "What do you want?" she demanded. "Why are you telling me these things? What good does it do you?"

"Confession is good for the soul. Sono una buona Cattolica," he smiled solemnly. "I want to know you better. Is that so strange?"

Anne looked at him appalled. "I'm sorry. I don't know what you want but I don't want to make love to you."

He shrugged. "Dove vai sta sera?"

"I have to meet someone." Anne answered him stiffly.

"Ah. Not nice. After I meet you sta sera, per il cena." Gianni shook his head, his eyes dark and impenetrable. "Il conto, per favore." His phone rang again. He talked swiftly and Anne could understand very little. She felt embarrassed. He had invited her to dinner. But he had practically blackmailed her into coming. She took out some money to pay for part of the bill but he waved her away impatiently, still speaking into the phone. He folded it up. "Allora."

Anne rose. "Mi scusa, Gianni, I have to go. Ummm, devo andare."

"Si, capisco." He walked with her to the edge of the restaurant where he suddenly took her by the shoulders and kissed her on both cheeks. "A piu tardi."

Anne walked off slowly. She had been right. Edward was definitely involved with the Caravaggio. Anne pondered the implications of this as she walked down the dimly lit street in the direction of the Pantheon. She turned onto via Pastini and walked towards the Piazza di Rotonda. Preoccupied, she almost ran into a man who was blocking her path. She looked up, startled.

"Mi scusi," she said automatically. The man grinned at her and, bowing, let her pass. She recognized him as the fair-haired, tatooed man with the copy of Kierkegaard from the Trevi fountain. Why did she keep running into that obnoxious man? She felt as though he was following her. Anne rounded the corner and entered the noisy Piazza della Rotunda. She stopped and turned to see if the man was still behind her but she couldn't see him. As she looked over the crowd at the Café, she spotted Antonio sitting with Maya. Anne stared in amazement. Maya had her hand on Antonio's arm, she seemed to be saying something intimate to him, Antonio had his head bent towards hers as though listening. Anne watched them, outraged. What was he doing with her? Anne strode forward, unable to keep the resentment and anger from her voice. "Buona sera, Maya." Anne ignored Antonio. "What are you doing here?"

Maya raised a pale face to Anne. "Oh Anne, we've been waiting for you. Edward was arrested today."

CHAPTER FORTY

"Fragonard's 'Strawberry Ice-Cream Girl' I always call her,
like Renoir's 'Breck Shampoo Girls'—do you see that kind
of eroticism in Goya's Maja? I think not, hmmm?"
(Edward Donant)

"Edward was arrested today?" Anne repeated the words stupidly. Antonio stood up and pulled out a chair for her. Anne sat down, shocked and confused. "Tell me what happened. Does this have anything to do with the Caravaggio? Did the police find the painting? Do they think Edward had something to do with it being stolen?"

Maya stared at her. "Good grief, Anne. You really do jump to conclusions. Where did all of *that* come from? It doesn't have anything to do with the Caravaggio. Does it?" Maya added anxiously, turning to Antonio.

Antonio shook his head. "Let me clarify for you, Anne. Edward's not been arrested. He's been detained for questioning."

"About what?" Anne lit a cigarette and drew deeply on it.

"Apparently the police believe he's involved in the theft of the Piranesi drawing."

"It was Edward who called the police in Turin," Maya added, tears welling up in her eyes. "I can't believe he actually did such a thing."

Anne's mouth dropped open, the cigarette fell to the terrace from her fingers. "What?! You think Edward called the police in Turin?" She laughed. She saw the bewildered expressions on Maya and Antonio's faces and she covered her mouth. "I'm sorry but that's just ridiculous."

"What is wrong with you, Anne?" Maya snapped at her.

"Do you think Edward called the police?" Ignoring Maya, Anne directed her question to Antonio.

"I don't know," Antonio said. "Carlo told me they have reason to suspect it was Edward. That's why they want to talk to him."

"But why would they suspect it was Edward?" Could John have told Edward about the drawing? Anne gasped with the sudden realization. John thought that Edward knew about the drawing. Anne had told him that she and Edward were both involved in setting up the illegal transaction. "Did someone accuse Edward?" Anne asked the question almost casually as she pulled out another cigarette.

"Yes. He insists he's innocent of course."

"It was John," Maya leaned closer so that she could whisper to Anne and Antonio. "The police questioned John this morning because Edward says he recognized John as the man who shot him and John denied it but he said that whoever did shoot Edward had every right to do so because Edward was a thieving traitor. John's the one who told the police they should talk to Edward about the drawing."

"John thinks Edward called the police." Antonio waved to the waiter for the check.

Anne laughed. She shook her head, pushing the tendrils of hair from her face and laughed helplessly, wiping her eyes as she saw the looks on Maya and Antonio's faces as they regarded her.

"Are you all right, Anne?" Antonio reached out to take her hand.

"I'm fine." Anne choked on the tea she had ordered. "Pardon. Mi scusi but that's funny. That's really funny. So John thinks Edward called the police and Edward thinks John shot him. John must think Edward betrayed him. Oh my God, this must come as a surprise to Edward."

"I'm sorry, Anne," Maya spoke stiffly. "I don't see what's so goddamned funny. None of it's funny."

"Well, yes, it is. Or it would be if you knew what I know."

"So what is it that you know? Why are you laughing like a hyena? If you know something different tell us what it is, for God's sake," Maya's voice was strained. She looked pale and nervous.

Anne realized that she was going to have to tell them everything. She hesitated. "I know that Edward didn't betray John. I betrayed John. Or rather I planned on doing that."

Maya stared at Anne. Antonio squeezed Anne's hand. "You're not making much sense, cara. What are you talking about?"

Anne looked at him. "What reason did John give for Edward making that call?"

"He didn't give a reason as far as I know."

"Edward wanted to get rid of me," Maya said flatly. "Why else would he have called?"

"But that's not true," Anne exclaimed. "I'll swear that Edward knew nothing about that drawing..." Anne stopped. Could it be possible that John really had contacted Edward without telling her and that Edward, not knowing the real purpose for her involvement with John, had wanted to save her from going through with a criminal act? Was this why John wanted to see her? But taking that kind of risk was so out of character for Edward.

"What are you thinking? What were you going to say?" Maya leaned forward.

196

Anne shook her head. "I...I don't know." She looked at Antonio. "What would happen if someone accused me of...of being an accessory, an accomplice to a crime?"

Antonio raised his eyebrows. "I think it depends on what you mean."

"I mean, let's say that I know who stole that Piranesi drawing and that I offered to help this person sell it on the black market. Even though there's no proof of this, even though the drawing's been recovered, would I still be in trouble? With the law here in Italy?"

Maya gasped. "Anne!"

Antonio stared at Anne. "You're telling me you were going to help sell this drawing." Antonio looked coldly at Anne. "Who was this person who stole the drawing?"

Anne bit her lip and looked anxiously at both of them. "No, no, you don't understand. I did know about the drawing but I had a reason for doing what I did. I was never going to sell the drawing. I was just trying to get it back. It was a good plan," Anne ended lamely. "It just got screwed up."

Maya continued to look at Anne in horror. "You knew about the drawing? You knew who stole it? You knew it was in my purse? All this time?!! How could you? Oh!" Maya drew back from Anne in disgust. "You knew when you came to Turin! It was you who called the police!" She was breathless with anger and indignation.

Anne shook her head vehemently. "You're way off, Maya. That's not how it happened at all. I didn't know who called the police, I still don't know. In fact, it may very well have been Edward. Only he can tell us that. No, let me explain. John contacted me after he stole the drawing. You know that Edward and I are both involved in buying and selling works of art. John said that he stole the drawing on impulse. He was angry with Valeriano so he took the drawing. It was easy evidently and then he panicked. He didn't know what to do with it and he contacted me asking if Edward or I knew someone on the black market who would buy it. I never told Edward, I realized that I could use this opportunity to retrieve the drawing. So, I suggested that John smuggle it out of Italy and I would meet him with a buyer—of course there was no buyer—I was going to have the police there when we made contact." Anne looked at both of them. "It seemed like such a good plan. I thought, that way, you know, John would be arrested for the theft and the drawing would be returned. All very simple."

"But why did you use me?" Maya demanded angrily. "Why didn't you carry the damned thing across the border?"

Anne sighed. "Because John doesn't trust me. He doesn't trust me any more than I trust him. But I didn't suggest he 'use you.'" Anne looked at Maya. "He refused to tell me how he was going to get the drawing out. He said I would find out. After you called me in Turin I realized that it must have been John who stole your purse in Florence and hid the drawing inside the lining. God knows who called the police." Anne shrugged helplessly. "Everything just went wrong," she muttered. "I guess I'm not very good at exposing criminals."

Antonio took Anne's hand. "You'll need to tell this story to Carlo."

Anne crushed her cigarette out on the terrace. "Do you think he'll believe me?"

Antonio frowned. "Of course. Other than being contacted by John you've really done nothing at all. I think that's what you need to tell Carlo. That John told you he'd stolen the drawing and was going to smuggle it out of Italy and he asked if you or Edward knew of anyone interested in buying it. That's all you need to say."

"But won't he wonder why Anne didn't tell the police right away?"

Anne looked at Antonio. "Maya's right. I'll have to explain why I waited. That I was afraid the drawing would simply disappear if I didn't look as though I were cooperating with John. That no one would ever be able to trace the theft to him or recover the drawing unless I set it up so that John thought I was working with him."

Antonio shook his head. "I don't think it will be much of a problem, really."

Anne slumped in her chair, her chin in her hands. Suddenly she drew herself up. "I'll talk to Edward tomorrow. Where is he?"

"He's being 'detained,'" Maya spoke bitterly.

"He can receive visitors, can't he?" Anne stood up. "I'll see him tomorrow and I'll find out."

"Really," Maya watched her. "And why would Edward tell you everything if he hasn't told me."

"Because I already know what's been going on and he'll see that what I say makes sense. Oh don't be sulky, Maya, it has nothing to do with you and Edward." Anne turned away, impatient and tired. "I'm going home."

"I'll walk with you," Antonio also rose. "Maya?"

Maya shook her head and, leaning back in her chair, closed her eyes. Tears slid unchecked from beneath her lids. "Come with us," Antonio said gently, reaching down to take Maya's hand. "I don't want you going home alone. Not with all that's happened."

"I've always got the loyal Alberto," Maya spoke contemptuously then she sighed and rising, she walked silently next to Antonio. Distracted by her thoughts Anne didn't realize that she almost ran into the muscular, gold-toothed man again as they were leaving the piazza. "Oh," she exclaimed. The man held out his hand to Antonio and spoke rapidly to him. Antonio fished in his pockets and handed him some change. The man bowed to them sardonically, pocketing the money. Anne turned to look back at him as they walked on. It was strange that he kept turning up.

CHAPTER FORTY ONE

"The ultimate mystery for the Renaissance Roman Catholic
artist was God's humanity and God's grace. The mystery
of the Host, of the Eucharist, of the Incarnation. But they
weren't above witchcraft either. Parmigianino quit painting
when he was older and got interested in the black art of
alchemy, the black science of alchemy. When he died he
wanted to be buried naked in the ground with a cross of
cypress wood on his chest. Makes you wish you could
get him on a psychoanalyst's couch. Of course, he was
never devout in the sense that Fra Angelico was. He was
too fascinated with his own image, with the twisted
and contorted figures he fashioned through the convex
mirror of his particular narcissism. High Mannerism
I suppose you could say about Parmigianino, hmmm?"
(Edward Donant)

Anne was nervous as she waited for Edward. A policeman had led
her into a small room with a desk and a couple of chairs. She wondered
what Edward would say. She wished she could be back in Antonio's bed,
with his arms around her, her head against his chest. She shivered at the
memory of their kisses that morning and she smiled in anticipation of
seeing him later.

The door opened and Edward entered. He smiled at Anne. She stood
up and Edward hugged her tightly with his one good arm. Surprised at this
reception, she drew back from his embrace. "You seem in good spirits,
Edward."

"As do you. What causes you to sit there grinning like an idiot?"

"How sweet you are, Edward."

"That I am. How is Maya? I'm really concerned for her. I fear my being
detained by the police has proved too much for her on top of everything
else."

"I think what upsets her most is the thought that you would have called
the police in Turin."

"I can't say I blame her except, of course, for the fact that I never
made that call, just as I never knew a thing about the theft of that drawing.
In fact, I'm rather at a loss as to why I've become so interesting to the
police."

Anne stared at him, thoughtfully. You never knew when Edward was telling the truth. Could it be that he hadn't called the police?

"But it's good of you to visit me, Anne. Did you bring me a cake with a rasp hidden inside so I can work my way out from behind bars?"

"Oh very funny. No, I just wanted to ask you a question. You see," she hesitated, searching in her bag for her cigarettes. "Oh God, it's the last one." Anne removed the slightly creased cigarette and crushed the pack. "Well, I guess there's nothing for it but to ask you outright. Did you call the police in Turin because you talked to John and you knew he thought that I was party to the theft and you didn't want me to be an accomplice to a criminal act?"

For the first time in her acquaintance with Edward Anne saw that he was speechless. He stared at her as though she had just said something totally incomprehensible. Anne lit her cigarette and watched him, impatiently. "Can you say something, Edward? I just want to know if you were telling the truth when you said you hadn't called the police in Turin."

Edward shook his head and reached for his glass of water. "I hardly know what to say. I don't even understand the question. You think I called the police in Turin because I talked to John who…what did you say?"

"Who thinks I'm working with him, well, he actually thinks you and I were working together with him to smuggle the drawing out of Italy to be sold."

Edward continued to shake his head. "I'm mystified, darling. Where did he get this idea?"

"From me," Anne said somewhat defiantly.

Edward looked amused. "I had no idea you were a criminal, Anne."

"I'm not," Anne said indignantly. "You haven't given me a chance to explain."

"Don't get defensive," Edward put his hands up in a protective gesture. "You're the one who described yourself as being involved in a criminal act, I'm just repeating it in order to ascertain if I understood correctly."

Anne stared at him and then nodded. "Oh, right, I see what you mean. I'm not putting this very well. Let's see. Did you make that phone call to the police in Turin about Maya?"

Edward took a deep breath and rolled his eyes upward in a martyr's gesture. "I have no idea whoever came up with this ridiculous idea but I had no knowledge of any of this until yesterday when I was 'requested' to come in for questioning in relation to the theft. So, to answer your question fully, 'No, I did not call the police in Turin.' Now, why did you ask me that and what exactly are you involved in with John?"

Anne explained her plan to him. "John contacted me—out of the blue—when we were living in Pittsburgh and you and I were going through our divorce. I thought it was a perfect opportunity to...to make sure the drawing would be recovered and to see that John would be arrested. Justice you know, after all these years." Anne broke off.

Edward reached for her hands and took them in his own. "You have to stop thinking about that accident, Anne. And, yes, it was an accident. Whoever was at fault, whatever the emotions that engendered that moment, it's over now. John has suffered all these years, too, you know. You're not the only one. He's dreadfully disfigured, he's hated by his father, repellant to others, he's a drunkard. Do you think anything you could do would erase your suffering...or his?"

"I don't care about him," Anne muttered. "He's a thief and a murderer. Or at least he meant to kill me and he's never been punished for what he did that night."

"Yes he has, Anne. More than you can ever imagine. Let it go, for God's sake. Move on with your life." Edward released her hands. "What's the point of harboring these grudges? Against your dad, against John..."

"That's not the point, is it?" Anne spoke acidly. "The point is my plan failed because someone, I don't even know who now—I thought it was you—called the Turin police. Someone knew the drawing was in Maya's purse. I can't even prove it was John who stole the stupid drawing and that was the only reason I gave him the impression that I would cooperate with him."

Edward touched his wounded shoulder. "Let me see if I have this straight. John was under the impression that you and I were working with him to sell this drawing to some corrupt collector. He had arranged to have it taken out of the country in Maya's bag. Since neither he nor you called the police in Turin you assumed I did. Why did you assume it was me?"

"Because John thought you were involved and if he knew it wasn't me then the natural assumption would be that it was you and then it occurred to me that maybe John had talked to you about the plan since he thought you were involved and, realizing what was going on, you called the police to keep me from..." here Anne faltered. "Well, it doesn't matter, it wasn't you."

"No, wait." Edward looked amazed. "You actually thought I would put Maya in such a position in order to protect you? Anne, you stun me. Not that I don't care about you, darling, but really."

Anne blushed deeply. "I hadn't really thought it through." She looked down at her hands, confused. What was it Gianni had told her? Regaining her composure, Anne raised her eyes to meet those of Edward who was staring at her thoughtfully. "I met Gianni last night," she said.

Edward waited.

"He wanted to tell me something about you and he also told me he knew about the drawing and Maya. He said some woman told him all about it and that she lives in the same building as you and Maya." Anne looked questioningly at Edward but he shook his head. "I did think he was the one who called the police but he denied it and, to be honest, I can't think why he would have."

Edward shrugged. "I confess I can't imagine why he would do such a thing either."

"He told me that it was you who told him about the painting in the church. That you wanted him to set it up so that Valeriano would think he had found a masterpiece."

Edward nodded. "That's right."

Anne raised an eyebrow and adjusted her cardigan about her shoulders. "Why? If it was a fake, why would you want Valeriano to think it was an original?"

Edward waved a hand dismissively. "It's not important. I was the one who painted it and I had my reasons for wanting Valeriano to think it was a Caravaggio. Let's just say that it amused me to see him make such a mistake."

"It amused you?!" Anne stared at Edward. "My God, Edward. What about the Italian government exhibiting it and the police and all the time they've spent trying to find the thieves who stole it? I mean, I know you're an egomaniac, but do you really think you're justified in creating such turmoil?"

"Don't be so self-righteous, Anne. What were you doing playing around with John and that stolen drawing?"

"That's different," Anne said haughtily. "I was trying to get the drawing back."

"Well, well, let's not quibble over niceties," Edward chuckled. "Anyway, I've told the police about my role in the whole affair. I've confessed to having painted it. It's Valeriano who doesn't come out of this looking so good. I'm almost certain he's the one who had the painting stolen."

Anne thought for a minute. "I see what you mean. He must have found out it was a fake and wanted to get rid of it in order to protect his reputation. He probably had it destroyed."

"Oh, I don't know about that," Edward smoothed his hair. "Valeriano's desperate for money. I think he sold it to some unscrupulous collector on the black market. Someone who believes it is one of Caravaggio's lost works. What a disappointment when I publish the facts about the provenance."

Anne looked puzzled. Edward told her about the money laundering scheme and the Russians who had come to his studio. "Valeriano had miscalculated. He was too sure that he couldn't be touched. It was one of them who planted the bomb in Valeriano's car. And that was only the beginning. Valeriano needed to pay them off and the Caravaggio was the only way he could get enough money."

"What?! How could he be so stupid? And to use your paintings for something like that," Anne looked up, suddenly realizing what this had meant to Edward, how he must have felt when he found out what Valeriano had been doing. So this was why he had wanted to expose Valeriano. She laughed.

Edward looked at her quizzically. "What's so funny?"

"You. What gall you have lecturing *me* on getting on with my life and forgetting the past. 'You're not the only one who's suffered. Why can't you let go?'"

Edward had the good grace to smile. "I see your point."

"So now what happens?" Anne said, looking vaguely around the room. "Are you going to be imprisoned for forgery or whatever they do to people like you?"

"Well, it's an interesting question. The painting has disappeared, I've provided proof that it's not an original and I'll be shortly publishing an article with accompanying photos. There doesn't seem to be a whole lot of interest in prosecuting me. At any rate, Maya has been gracious enough to put up bail so I'm free to go until my trial. I'm actually looking forward to it. It should be fun."

"What happens to Valeriano? And John? And what about Gianni? Wasn't he an accomplice or something?"

"Oh, I imagine Gianni's been involved in pretty much all that's taken place but if I know Gianni it will be very difficult to pin anything on him. And Valeriano, well, you can hardly arrest someone for being duped by a forgery or for being the victim of a car bombing even if he is ultimately the catalyst for both incidents."

"What about John? I'm not going to let him get away with this. Not again."

"Just leave John alone, for God's sake. He's crazy and he's dangerous and it does you no good to continue obsessing over him. Christ, you'd almost think you were still in love with him."

Anne eyed Edward coldly. She sat in the chair, her hands pressed between her thighs, tendrils of her hair curling across her cheek. Absentmindedly, she pushed them back from her face.

"Leave him alone, Anne. He'll destroy himself. People like that always do."

Anne stood up and smiled sweetly at Edward. "Yes, I suppose you're right."

CHAPTER FORTY TWO

"Raphael's 'Transfiguration' is surely one of the great
monuments of the Italian High Renaissance.
When the artist was dying, at the age of thirty-seven,
he requested that it hang above his bier in the Pantheon.
Not only did the works he produce during his brief
lifetime symbolize the idealistic aspirations of the
High Renaissance but his dramatic use of foreshortening,
the spiraling figure, and his exaggerated utilization of
darks and lights influenced the Baroque, particularly
fascinating the youthful Caravaggio when
he arrived in Rome almost seventy years later."
(Edward Donant)

Anne walked quickly towards the Pantheon. She crossed the piazza, looking for the address John had given her. Anne paused before the building, touching the cassette recorder she had hidden in her bag. She looked around nervously. Really, this was an absurd idea, meeting John by herself, hoping to get his confession on a tape recorder like some B movie detective and yet what else could she do? And what could John want from her? Why did he want to see her? She wished she could have asked Antonio to go with her but, of course, John would never have accepted that. Taking a deep breath, Anne stretched out her hand to turn the knob on the door. It was one of those small doors cut into a much larger one (what had originally been the old carriage door) that so often presented blank faces to the passerby in European cities. The door opened easily and Anne stepped over the threshold into a narrow courtyard. It was quite dark and she had to wait a few minutes before her eyes adjusted to the darkness.

"John? John, where are you?" Anne whispered.

She heard someone giggle then there was silence.

"John. Please, I'm not in the mood to play games. Where are you?"

John struck a match and lit a candle that he was holding in one hand. The flame illuminated the smooth white mask of the mime. "Good evening, darling."

"Why did you confront me on the piazza the other night? Why didn't you just call me?"

"I needed to speak with you. I had to see you. Besides, I thought," here he giggled again. "I thought it was more fun to surprise you."

206

"More fun!" Anne took a deep breath. "All right, so here I am. Let's talk."

Anne put her hand in her purse and nervously pressed the record button.

"Not here. Follow me." John turned away, holding the candle high so that its light splashed eerily against the walls of the stairwell.

"Why not here? I'm not going anywhere, John. This is as good a spot as any."

John continued to climb the stairs.

"John!" Anne bit her lip. 'Bastard,' she thought. She took a few deep breaths and began to climb behind him. "Couldn't you just use a flashlight like a normal person?" Anne asked irritably as she followed him.

"I'm not a normal person," John answered.

'That's an understatment,' Anne thought. 'And he's drunk. As usual,' she added. She glanced around her, noting the dingy, dirty walls, the peeling paint. It was all too shabby, like John, like this preposterous position in which she had put herself. Anne realized that John was panting and limping slowly as they climbed the stairs.

"Why are you limping like that?"

"I hurt my leg." Again there was the unnerving giggle.

Anne remembered that Edward thought it had been John who had shot him. She hadn't believed it but now, she wondered.

They climbed five flights of stairs before they arrived at a door. The wound in Anne's pelvis ached. When John opened the door, Anne expected to see the interior of a room; instead she saw moonlight glinting off an asphalt-covered roof. Anne stopped at the door leading to the roof and looked back down the dark stairs. "Why did you bring me up here, John? You know I'm afraid of heights." In her hyper-nervous state she imagined she could hear the sound of the tape whirring in the machine. She stepped back from the door and pressed herself against the wall of the staircase.

John put the candle down on a small table on the roof and removed his mask. When he turned to look at her, the flame exaggerated the grotesque vision of his ravaged face and Anne forced herself not to look away in revulsion.

"I wanted, I wanted," John's face screwed up and Anne was afraid he was going to cry. He drew a deep breath and stepping forward took hold of Anne's hand. "I wanted to talk to you about us."

Anne was aware of the sense of déjà vu that enveloped them as she stood in the doorway, John's hand on her wrist. As he looked at her, she felt only disgust for him and a kind of pity. Suddenly she wanted Antonio to be there, more than anything she wanted him to be at her side. "I'm not going out on that roof with you John," Anne's voice grated through her parched throat.

"Yes, you are," John's hand tightened on her wrist as she held onto the door. He jerked impatiently at her hand and Anne stumbled onto the dark surface of the roof. A full moon lit the surrounding roof edges and aerials with eerie clarity. Anne tried to steady her nerves as she looked at John. She was so frightened that it was impossible for her to speak. She tried her trick of closing her eyes and taking deep breaths. She had to remain calm.

"What are you doing?" Anne opened her eyes to see John's face close to hers. "Why did you close your eyes? My beauty overwhelms you, is that it?" His tone of voice had changed and his grip had hardened on her wrist.

Anne winced. "Don't be absurd, John." Her voice sounded muffled and strange. She struggled to gain control. "Naturally, since that night with you when I fell from the roof, I've been afraid of heights. I have a habit of closing my eyes and taking deep breaths. It usually helps."

John grunted and relaxed his grip.

"You know the police have arrested Edward for trying to smuggle the drawing out of Italy?" Anne tried to speak distinctly. She hadn't thought this through but it was quite clear that John was not going to just let her walk back down those stairs. There was something he wanted that she hadn't anticipated. She didn't know what it was but whatever it was, he wasn't going to just talk to her and let her go. She looked around for something she could use against him if he attacked her.

John smiled. It made his face look even more grotesque. "Yes, that was a fortunate twist, wasn't it? Since the whole plan was washed up," he added bitterly. "What I want to know is why he called the police." John released Anne and reached into his pocket. He pulled out a flask and took a long drink. He offered it to Anne but she shook her head. He drank from the flask again. "Kind of reminds you of another time we were together, doesn't it?"

Anne watched him warily.

"I never intended to hurt you, Anne. You must have known that. Why did you push me away?"

Anne stared at him. "You tried to kill me!"

"But you pushed me away." John ran his hand over the scarred remnants of his face. "You were always doing that. Always pushing me away. You didn't have to push me away. I never intended to jump off that roof with you. I was just acting funny to scare you. Did you think I was crazy?"

"You did scare me," Anne spoke quietly, grimly, suppressing a desire to run from him. "And you were crazy, you were acting crazy. And it wasn't funny."

John laughed harshly. "But it's funny, now, don't you see? I was just joking around with you, you know that, and it was you who fell off the roof because you pushed me away. And I fell on that fucking broken bottle. It's very funny because I never intended to hurt either of us. I just wanted to scare you." John glanced over Anne's head, apparently lost in thought. "Since mother died, I've only thought of you. We share so many things, Anne. We're both scarred, we've both been unlucky, we both hate our fathers—yours abandoned you and my dad hates me. He always has," John laughed briefly and then he pulled Anne's hand to his face. Paralyzed, she allowed him to press his cheek against her palm. "Why shouldn't we support one another? I know, I know," he looked down at her and smiled. It was a terrible smile. "I look horrible but that's not important is it? Not when two people love each other and you do love me, don't you, darling?" John emphasized the 'darling' and Anne shivered at the sarcasm in his voice.

"You know I don't love you, John," she said nervously.

"Don't you, darling? It couldn't have anything to do with the way I look, now could it?"

Anne took a deep breath. "Don't be absurd, John. I don't know why you're going on about this anyway. I came to talk to you about the drawing and about what happened to Maya and to Edward. You know he didn't call the police in Turin so you must have told someone else about the drawing. Someone else must have called."

John looked at her slyly. "That's what he says, is it? And you believe him?"

"Yes, I do." Anne spoke firmly. "But that's not really the point any more, is it? It doesn't really matter who called the police. What matters is that you stole the drawing and other people are suspected. It's not fair."

John looked away from Anne. "Didn't it ever occur to you that it was a bit strange, me contacting you again after all these years?"

Anne hesitated. "Yes, I wondered about that."

John turned back to her, almost lazily taking her wrist in his hand, turning it over, stroking her palm. "Wouldn't it make you wonder why someone you had mutilated like me would ever want to see you again? Did you really think I would call you for help?" His eyes narrowed as he leaned toward her.

Anne tried to pull away. "I…I didn't know," she stammered. "I thought you wanted me to help you find a buyer…"

"That I would call someone who I knew hated me." John laughed and jerked Anne closer to him. "You must think I'm a complete idiot, darling."

"John, you're hurting me." Anne tried to keep the hysterical edge out of her voice.

John grinned. "Good." He twisted his fingers on her wrist so that Anne cried out.

"John, this is ridiculous. And anyway," she spoke quickly, panting from the pain in her wrist. "The drawing's been returned. What difference does it make now?"

"Why do you think I contacted you? Answer me!" John shook Anne.

"Because you had no one else to turn to?" She knew this wasn't the answer. She suddenly knew that he wanted to destroy her as much as she wanted to destroy him.

"Dammit, you're either incredibly naïve or you think I am. You probably believe that I still love you, that I contacted you because I wanted us to be together again." He laughed harshly.

Anne trembled. "Why did you write to me?"

"Because I want you to pay!" John leaned closer to Anne, his lips drawn back over his teeth.

"Pay?" Anne said stupidly, cowering back from him. "What do you mean?"

Suddenly John grabbed Anne and pulled her close to him. She tried to turn her face away; his breath reeked of scotch, the proximity of his one-eyed face made her feel faint. "Look at me! Do you like the way I look now? You did this, you fucking bitch." He leaned closer to Anne so that his tongue almost licked her ear. "You broke my bottle of scotch, you pushed me away. All I wanted was for you to love me." He was breathing heavily. "Who would want me now?"

"*I* broke your stupid bottle, *I* pushed you away!" Anne forgot her fear, turning furiously to face John. "How dare you! How dare you accuse me? And now you want to make me pay..." she laughed, realizing that she was starting to sound like John. "You really are insane."

John was shaking his head. "I didn't know what I was doing. I was desperate, I was drunk. If you had only listened to me, if you had only cared. That's all I wanted, that's all I ever wanted." He began to cry, tears seeping out of the still-seeing eye.

Anne looked coldly at him. "How could you have ever thought that I could love you?" she asked quietly.

He sucked in his breath, staring at her. "I never meant to hurt you. I never meant to hurt Edward. Oh, everything's always been against me. I can't go on, I can't." John suddenly released Anne and sat down, his head in his arms and began to rock slowly back and forth.

Anne stared at him, repelled and fascinated. "Why did you shoot Edward?"

John looked up at her, his mouth widened in a sickening grin. "I wasn't aiming for Edward."

Anne was shocked. John had tried to kill her; he had actually tried to kill her. She turned and ran toward the stairs. Suddenly she tripped, her ankle caught in a vise-like grip and crying out, she fell, her face grinding against the asphalt terrace. Anne was terrified, her face pressed against the roof, John's body hard and heavy as he heaved himself on top of her. He grabbed her by the hair and jerked her around to face him. "You're… you're hurting me, John," Anne said through swollen lips. "Let me go."

"Let you go." John smiled at her with his wolfish grin. "Let me tell you what I was planning to do to you until that fucking jerk called the police. I had it all planned out. I was going to set you up, I was going to have you arrested when you picked up the drawing. The police were going to be there."

In spite of her fear, Anne laughed. They had both wanted to set the other one up.

"You laugh," John said pressing his heavy body against hers so that she had to gasp for air. "You think it's funny, do you? And why not? You survived pretty intact, didn't you? You still look pretty good, you don't repel everyone you meet." His eye glinted as he suddenly flashed a knife before her eyes. "I hate to do this, darling," he sneered, "but I think the only way I can forgive you is to give you the face that's made me who I am. I'm sorry dearest but I'm only doing this because I love you."

Unable to scream, Anne threw one arm up, trying to shield her face as the knife slashed into her cheek. She felt a sharp pain as the knife slid into her flesh just below her eye. Suddenly John's body lifted off of hers. She heard John snarling and then an animal cry. Anne rolled to her side and tried to rise but her knees buckled under her. She wiped the blood from her cheek with one hand and looked up. A familiar-looking, muscular man was standing over John. His arms twisted behind his back, John was moaning. Anne wasn't even surprised to see that this was the same man with the gold teeth she had met at the Trevi fountain. Brutally, he attached handcuffs to John's wrists and then he looked down at Anne. He smiled briefly, flashing his gold teeth. "Buona sera, professore."

Anne pressed her hand to her bloody cheek and continued to stare at him. She couldn't even organize her thoughts to ask him what he was doing there. It was all too absurd. The man jerked John to his feet and turned to look back at the door leading to the stairs. Anne followed his gaze and saw a light rising up the walls of the stairs as though someone were carrying a torch in ascent.

He turned back to Anne. "I was assigned to follow you," he said as though he had read her thoughts. "But I lost you once I entered the building. And I had the devil of a time trying to find you. Fortunately, I heard you cry out." He nodded at the open door.

"Following me?" Anne stared uncomprehendingly. "But why?"

"Who is this creep?" John looked no less terrifying in handcuffs. "And what right do you have to put cuffs on me, you bastard?"

The man looked at John. "You're under arrest for assault and attempted murder."

"That won't stick. I never intended to murder Anne. Just carve her up a little," John giggled and then swore as the man with the gold teeth jerked on the cuffs. "You don't understand," John muttered.

"What don't I understand," the man spoke impatiently.

"She's the one you should arrest," John said darkly, glaring at Anne.

Carrying a powerful flashlight, two men stepped through the door onto the roof. One of them came quickly to kneel at Anne's side. "Antonio," Anne mumbled. Surprised at the violence of her relief, she began to cry, pressing her head against his chest and twining her arms about him.

He lifted her to her feet and turned her face up to his. "Cara, mia," he saw the bloody welt across her cheek and the torn flesh where her face had been ground against the asphalt. "What's this?!" He looked up angrily. "How did she get hurt?"

The Kierkegaard reader nodded toward John. "He attacked her."

"He saved me," Anne said, holding onto Antonio. "That man saved me."

The other man was Carlo. He took John's face in one hand and jerked it up so that John snarled. "You didn't tell us the truth yesterday, John."

John stared at him, his face livid. "I don't know what you're talking about," he muttered.

"Oh, I think you do. You're under arrest, John."

John looked petulant, his shoulders sagged. "What for?"

"Anne told us that you were responsible for the theft. And that you stole Maya's purse. That you put the drawing in it."

"It's all a lie," John spat viciously. "Don't tell me you believe that bitch."

Carlo looked coolly at John. "You stole the drawing, John. You put it in Maya's purse. You shot Edward and there's a witness to your attack against Anne."

"Yeah, right," John sagged, his large body folding in on itself. "You don't have any proof of any of this." He retched suddenly.

Carlo turned to look at Anne who was standing close to Antonio, encircled by his arms. "Antonio told me what you told him, Anne. It's lucky for you that Leonardo was following you."

Antonio wrapped his arms tightly around her.

Carlo's sunglasses were dark and impenetrable in the moonlight as he released his grip on John's chin. "I'm curious as to who else you talked to about the drawing. Someone other than you and Anne knew about it."

"What difference does it make?" John stared at Carlo then let his head drop. "You've got your precious drawing back, haven't you?" he mumbled.

"That's true," Carlo said blandly. "Still, we're curious why someone tipped off the police in Turin."

John laughed bitterly. "What about Anne? What makes her such a favorite of the police? Why haven't you arrested her?"

"Anne's not a suspect in the theft of the drawing."

"Anne's not a suspect in the theft of the drawing," John mimicked Carlo's tone. "What a fool you are but...oh, I almost forgot, you were fucking her, weren't you? Is that why she gets such special treatment from the police? Have you and she taken up where you left off that summer?" John laughed, looking at Anne. "It's always nice to be able to prostitute yourself in exchange for immunity from the law. Ironic but nice."

Antonio tightened his arms around Anne. She held onto him, filled with hatred for this mangled man, the cut on her cheek burning.

"You always were a bit slow. Don't you see what's going on here? It was all Anne's idea, it was all her idea to smuggle the drawing out of Italy. She's the one who told me to steal the drawing," John looked slyly at Anne.

Carlo nodded at Leonardo. "This gentleman will escort you to jail. We'll find the person you talked to but, as you say, it's not really important."

"She's the only one who *is* important. I told her I had taken the drawing to make my dad look bad. She begged me to give it back. She was afraid for me." His voice cracked. "She's the only one who cares about me."

"And yet this person must have called the police. She doesn't sound like someone who cares a great deal for you to me."

John looked at Carlo. "She didn't call, she would never have called."

Anne suddenly remembered her conversation earlier that night. "Gianni told me that he knew about the drawing and that he knew who took it."

"Gianni?" John looked at her stupidly. "How could he know?"

The policeman with the gold teeth prodded John toward the door. John turned back. "But this isn't fair. Why don't you arrest Anne? It was all her idea, it was all her fault; everything was her fault." He glared at her.

Anne thought of the cassette recorder. She really hadn't needed to do any of this. She began to cry again, silently standing next to Antonio. She looked after John as he was led from the roof, a trickle of blood curving from the edge of her eye to her mouth.

CHAPTER FORTY THREE

"Don't think that Rembrandt is that easy to dismiss. He's
full of surprises. Look deep into the shadows of a
Rembrandt etching. It's not just a dark stain on the paper
but a world of unseen objects which come to light
only under the closest scrutiny; an unmade bed, an
overturned chamber pot—Rembrandt's crude humor
saturates his work as does his obsessive rendering of the
details that complete the scene. But don't ask him to make
it easy for you. You're going to have to really look,
you're going to have to work to get the whole story."
(Edward Donant)

Anne walked out of the police station into the early dawn. Shimmering veins of sunlight snaked across the cobblestones between the dark shadows thrown across the street by the surrounding buildings. She had spent the last couple of hours at the hospital where she had been treated for shock and for the wound on her cheek. She had had to sign a testimonial at the police station and a paper accusing John of assault and battery. Anne looked around the piazza for a Tabaccheria—she needed to buy some cigarettes. She was feeling very shaky. It was funny now to find out that the gold-toothed man was an undercover detective and that he really had been following Anne. No wonder he had always seemed to be around. He had stopped her in the police station to ask if she was all right and Anne had told him that it was Nicolo Salvi who had designed the Trevi fountain. He had looked momentarily mystified and then he had laughed and kissed her on her unblemished cheek. Anne had smiled, pleased that she had actually remembered the artist's name.

As she started down the steps she stopped. Gianni was standing at the bottom of the steps talking to a policewoman. They were laughing about something. Anne retreated into the shadows of the portico but then she saw Gianni kiss the woman goodbye and walk away. Without questioning her action, Anne followed him, moving quickly in order to reduce the distance between them. She knew that it was no longer relevant but she wanted to find out why he had called the police in Turin. Surely he would tell her now, she thought.

Gianni crossed the busy Via del Corso and Anne hurried to keep up. The cut on her cheek was sharply painful and her pelvic wound ached from the fall the night before. She was relieved when Gianni finally stopped before the door of a large industrial-looking building. Anne stepped back into the shadows of a recessed doorway, waiting to see what he would do. She wanted to light a cigarette but remembered that she had no more so she dug her hands in the pockets of her cardigan and leaned against the doorjamb.

Gianni pushed the door open and entered the building. Anne waited a moment before crossing the small piazza where she hesitated before the door. What if he had seen her, what if he were waiting for her and he attacked her. What if...she shrugged—she had come this far, she might as well go on. Opening the door she entered a dark, narrow hall. Anne stood for a moment, letting her eyes grow accustomed to the dim light. She looked down the hallway—there were three doors on this level and a flight of stairs that climbed to the next. Uncertain, she strained to hear something that might give her a clue as to where Gianni had gone.

Anne tried the handle of the door nearest her but it was locked. She tried the other two but they were also locked. She started up the stairs but she suddenly realized that it was foolhardy for her to confront Gianni in a place as vacant as this. She hurried to the front door but, just as she reached it, the door nearest her opened and two people stepped into the hall. One of them was Gianni, the other was a very large lady dressed in paint-spattered overalls and a low-cut T-shirt. She looked distressed and she and Gianni were speaking rapidly in Italian. They both stopped when they saw Anne. Unable to move or speak, Anne stared at them. Then Gianni smiled. "Buon giorno, Anne, che cosa fai? Umm, what are you doing here?"

Anne flushed. "I saw you outside the police station and I followed you. I wanted to ask you a question." She knew she must look and sound ridiculous. She touched the gauze bandage on her cheek and pushed her fingers through her uncombed hair. Anne made a little face and tried to smile as though her behavior was perfectly reasonable.

The lady looked between Anne and Gianni. Gianni spoke to her briefly in Italian and she nodded. She smiled at Anne.

"I'm Anne Langlais," Anne said nervously, holding out her hand. "Who are you?"

"I'm Rose Williams. I think I know what it is you want to ask. Would you like to come in?"

Again Anne hesitated. Gianni was watching her with a sardonic smile.

"It's all right. This is my studio. I'm an artist," Rose laughed and looked down at her stained clothes. "Gianni and I were just having some coffee."

Anne followed Rose in; Gianni closed the door behind them. The room was surprisingly large and light-filled, with skylights drenching the canvases and the dirty floor in filtered sun. Anne realized that it must have been built onto the building as some sort of addition; perhaps it had been a garage.

In one corner there was a small sitting area with an overstuffed sofa and two folding chairs. Gianni took Anne by the elbow and guided her to the sofa. She was surprised when he did not sit down next to her but took one of the chairs facing her. Rose brought out three cups of coffee and took the other chair. Anne cringed as she watched Rose settle on the fragile-looking piece of furniture but it was evidently sturdier than it looked. She was a beautiful woman, Anne thought. Her hair was long and black and curled in unexpected directions, her mouth was wide and when she smiled it creased her whole face. On some people this would be a distraction, on Rose it drew her face together like a line an artist would add to a painting that gave it an inimitable sense of completion. Rose's eyes were a remarkable green—they seemed to refract Anne's gaze even as they bored into hers. She was regarding Anne as closely as Anne was studying her. "Gianni tells me that you know John."

Anne was surprised. "How do you know John?"

"The same way I know Gianni, through Valeriano. Valeriano has shown some of my paintings in his gallery here." Rose shrugged. "What did you want to ask Gianni?"

"He told me he knew about the Piranesi drawing and I wanted to know if he had anything to do with calling the police in Turin and also I wanted to ask him about the Caravaggio painting which I now know was a fake. I wondered if there was anything else he could tell me about it." Anne paused.

"My, my, such curiosity," Rose said brightly. "Didn't you ever hear that it killed the cat?"

Anne smiled at her nervously and stirred her coffee. She looked at Gianni but he seemed preoccupied and was leaning back in the chair filing his long pinkie nails.

"Well, don't worry, I can tell you what I know if you would like. Let's see," Rose shifted and the chair creaked, its legs quivering. "The Piranesi drawing, well, that's fairly simple but sad." She shook her head. "First of all let me explain that John was a very lonely man, lonely and craving love. When he lost his mother and moved to Rome he became quite attached to me. I think he felt that I was the only person who really cared about what happened to him. Certainly his father didn't ever care." Rose leaned forward to offer Anne a cookie from a plastic package. Her voluptuous breasts shook beneath the overalls and T-shirt. Anne shook her head. Rose took two and ate them daintily. "John stole the drawing on impulse. He was angry with his father because Valeriano wouldn't entrust John with any task in the gallery even though John was eager to prove that he was responsible and so, like a child—and he's really very much like a naughty child—John took the drawing. Afterwards he didn't quite know what to do so he came to me and told me what he had done. I was concerned and told him he had to return the drawing, that he was going to get in trouble but he became quite adamant that he would not. He said he needed the money, he wanted to get away from his father, away from Rome but that he didn't have any money. Well, when he left, I called Gianni and told him what John had done. I asked Gianni if he could find a way to get the drawing back."

Gianni raised his eyebrows and looked smugly at Anne. She wondered how much English he really understood. She looked back at Rose.

"I was with John one day when we saw Maya coming down the stairs from her apartment. She stopped on the stairs, waiting for us to leave, I suppose, and the way John looked at her made me wonder what he was thinking. I suspected that he might have somehow hidden the drawing on her, I don't know why exactly, perhaps it was because he knew Edward and Maya seemed a likely candidate. When I confronted him with my suspicion he was so transparent in his denial that I was certain I was right. I informed Gianni of my suspicions and he said he would find out for me." Rose shook a finger at Gianni who raised his eyes to the skylight in the ceiling. "I didn't know until today how he had accomplished this. Evidently Gianni called the police as it was the most expedient method of discovering whether Maya had the drawing or not. If the drawing was found in Maya's purse it would be returned and if it weren't in her purse we would at least know that my suspicions were unfounded. It was a good idea and it worked but I'm very sorry that that sweet girl had to go through that awful experience. At least I hear that everything is all right with her now. Not," Rose's face expressed a deep sadness. "Not the way things have gone for poor John."

Anne sat in silence on the sofa, holding her cup of cold coffee untouched in her hand. "I see." She leaned forward to put the cup on the overturned crate that served as a coffee table. "Thank you."

"Is there anything else I can help you with?" Rose stood up and the chair cracked alarmingly.

"I don't suppose you know anything about the Caravaggio painting," Anne said without much conviction.

Rose shook her head, glancing at Gianni. "I know nothing about that."

"Allora, bellissima," Gianni spoke up, his eyes focused on Anne's face.

Anne flushed.

"Penso e tutto, eh?"

Anne nodded. Stumbling a bit as she tried to rise from the deep recesses of the sofa, she grasped her purse and held out her hand to Rose. "Thank you for talking to me. I just wanted to know what happened."

"I'm sorry to hear what took place last night," Rose said gently.

Anne looked at her, surprised that she would know anything about that, but then she remembered seeing Gianni at the police station. She started for the door when on an impulse she turned back to Rose. "You're the woman who helped Maya when she was attacked, aren't you?"

Rose looked delighted. "Yes, did she tell you about me?"

Anne smiled. She didn't want to tell this beautiful woman how Maya had described her as the fat lady with the umbrella. "Maya was ever so grateful."

"Give her my regards," Rose said.

Gianni bent over Anne's outstretched hand and brought it to his lips. He raised his eyes to meet hers and he smiled. Anne walked away from them toward the door.

"There is one other thing I'd like to ask you," Anne turned as she put her hand on the handle. "What do you think will happen to Valeriano now?"

Gianni and Rose looked at one another and when Rose spoke she sounded surprised. "But I thought you would have heard..."

"Heard what?" Anne pressed her hand across her pelvis in an attempt to calm the throbbing pain.

"Valeriano's dead. He committed suicide sometime last night."

CHAPTER FORTY FOUR

"Art doesn't just sit there like a pretty woman waiting
to be admired. Look at Paolo Uccello's 'Deluge.'
He takes Renaissance spatial logic and funnels it into
a psychological vortex. This is no topographical
survey; it's life and death in a world where God's
law is arbitrary and man must suffer. Look at that
extraordinary man standing, one hand raised (in
benediction?). He's damned but his character is noble.
There's no right or wrong in Uccello's depiction of the
flood, only the saved and the damned—a powerful
depiction of St. Augustine's bleak doctrine of God's grace."
(Edward Donant)

Maya waited for Edward at the Café de Paris. Tiled rooftops and
antennas sketched the skyline of the piazza against the brilliant blue of the
evening sky. Palm fronds waved gently from some hidden roof garden, a
man blew valiantly on a trumpet, two other men set up a stand in front
of the café. An old man in a dirty red velvet vest limped by, leaning on a
cane.

She ordered another glass of wine. Ever since she had talked with
Anne two days ago she'd tried to imagine what Anne had been thinking
all this time. Why hadn't Anne said anything when she came to Turin?
Anne could have changed everything if she had just told Carlo then what
she had told them now. Maya frowned. Had Anne actually been pleased
to see Maya in jail? She had said there was nothing she could do but that
hadn't been true. Maya drained her glass. The light caressed the buildings
around her. Ochre walls shifted from baked red to burnt orange to a
washed out gray.

A beautiful little gypsy girl with long, black hair and a dark, oval
face crossed the piazza. She was wearing a pink dress with a white lace
collar and carrying a bunch of roses. She looked like a miniature Carmen,
her brilliant eyes flashing, preening herself as she confidently played the
tables. Maya watched her. The little girl approached the man who was
sitting at the table next to Maya's.

"Ciao Stefano."

"Buona sera, bella regazzina. Che bei colori." Stefano grinned at the
little girl who proffered her flowers flirtatiously.

"Buy some flowers for a lady?"

"But I am not with a lady." Stefano gestured to the empty chair and picked up his paper again.

"Look, Stefano." The little girl darted over to Maya. "A lady." She slapped Maya on the shoulder.

"Oh." Maya didn't like this beautiful little girl.

The man smiled at her and Maya blushed.

"Buy the pretty lady a flower, Stefano."

"No, no." He smiled at them both and resumed reading his paper. The little girl shrugged and walked on. Maya felt even more dismal. So, he wouldn't even buy her a flower, she wasn't the beautiful woman around whom everything revolved. It seemed that all the assumptions she had made had been wrong. When she had walked through the streets, thinking that everyone was looking at her, admiring her, desiring her, she had been wrong; they had seen her only as prey, they'd only been waiting to pounce. When she had assumed that she had been the center of some ominous plot it had turned out that she'd only been a convenient victim, an afterthought whose feelings had been of no interest to anyone involved. She should be grateful, of course, that everything had been resolved and that she hadn't really been in great danger but Maya felt deeply shaken, deeply betrayed. She watched Edward as he walked across the piazza.

"Hello, darling." He kissed her. "How are you?"

"I don't know. I feel strange. I keep thinking about this whole thing between John and Anne. How are you?"

"I'm feeling quite well, thank you. The joyous feeling of vindication."

"Oh, well, of course, I'm happy for that," Maya said, feeling even drearier.

"Happy is a most inadequate description for what I feel." Edward motioned for the waiter and ordered a bottle of Ferrari Perle 1986. "I'm in the mood to celebrate. Have you had this sparkling wine before? It's truly wonderful."

"Don't you think what Anne did was kind of...weird?"

"What do you mean? Trying to have John arrested?" Edward chuckled. "I'd never have thought our little Anne would try to do something like that."

"Yes, that's what I mean. It seems so out of character."

Edward poured the wine and took a sip. "I think it unnerves you because you felt like you knew who Anne was and in reality neither you nor I have any idea how she really feels about anything. It makes you wonder how she feels about us."

Maya looked down at her glass. "Yes, I guess that's what bothers me. She hid all of this about John and the drawing and I have to wonder what else she's hiding. I'm sure she must hate me, the way she just ignored me all this time when I was so upset about being arrested. I mean, even if she didn't have anything to do with it she could have at least told the police that it was John who had stolen the drawing and put it in my bag. Why didn't she do that? What difference would it have made to say that then?"

Edward shrugged. "Maybe she was scared. Maybe she just didn't know what to do. After all, she didn't know that it wasn't John who called. She may have wondered what he was up to. She may have wanted to wait to see what he did next."

Maya frowned, dissatisfied. "I guess so," she said slowly. "It's all very strange."

"But everything has been nicely tied up," Edward said cheerfully. "We know who stole the drawing, we know who shot me. John's in jail awaiting trial. I think that's pretty good all things considered."

"But what about the Caravaggio? Was John connected to that?"

Edward laughed. "I suppose I should tell you, my dear, that the Caravaggio was a fake. I knew that from the very beginning because I was the one who painted it."

"You mean Anne was right?" Maya looked startled. "She always thought there was something wrong with the painting. But why would you want to paint something and try to make people believe it was somebody else?"

"It's rather a long, sordid tale. Basically I wanted to teach Valeriano a lesson."

Maya held her glass out for more wine. "Well, well, isn't this another interesting turn of events? Am I the only person here this summer who didn't have a clue as to what was going on?"

"It's quite a jumble of coincidences isn't it?"

"But why was the painting stolen if it was a fake?"

"I have reason to believe Valeriano was behind that little gimmick and I also think he actually succeeded in getting a pretty price for it. He wasn't too happy when I told him that I had proof I painted it and that I was going to write an expose."

Maya looked across at Edward. "What about the bombing? What does *that* have to do with all of this?"

"That's something none of us were directly involved with—except Valeriano. The police are pretty certain the Russian Mafia placed that bomb."

Maya turned pale. "Russian Mafia? Are you joking?"

"I don't make jokes about things like that," Edward said quietly.

She took out a small compact and applied lipstick. Could Sergei be a member of the Mafia? Could it have been him? And all this time...all that talk about bombs. Maya shuddered. "Valeriano was murdered, wasn't he? And I suppose it would be same person who was responsible for the bombing."

Edward shrugged. "It looks that way. You don't mess around with these people. You certainly don't want to be involved in deceiving them."

Maya shivered.

"What are you thinking about?"

Maya looked across the table at Edward. "I was just wondering...I was thinking about how awful bombs are and about how stupid I've been."

Edward raised his eyebrows. "Stupid? What do you mean?"

Maya waved her hands as though to diffuse the idea. "Oh...never mind. What did you and Anne talk about at dinner while I was in jail in Turin? About us? About me?"

Edward looked at her quizzically. "Anne and I? Umm, well, let's see. Of course we talked about you. She told me what had happened to you in Turin. What do you mean?"

"I don't know. I'm just curious now about everything Anne said. And what you've said. I guess I'm curious about what's been happening because, obviously, I've missed a lot of what's been going on."

"You're not jealous are you?" Edward raised his eyebrows as he poured more wine.

"No, not really. I'm just feeling sort of...depressed. I thought I knew Anne and I find out I don't. And I don't know you either and I don't think I can rely on you to tell me the truth. I feel like I've been living in a surreal world where nothing is what I think it is. For instance, I don't have any idea what you really think about me." Maya looked sadly at Edward. "And I know I can't rely on what you seem to think."

"Are you trying to say that you don't trust me?" Edward spoke solemnly but his eyes twinkled.

Maya clenched her fists. Even when she was trying to talk seriously with him he was judging her and finding her amusingly wanting. "Yes. Basically, I don't trust you." She spoke angrily. "I love you, but I don't trust you."

"You love me. Can you elaborate? Do you have any idea what that means?"

"Oh God, Edward, you're the most irritating person. And, no, I can't and won't elaborate."

"I ask since you just told me you don't trust me. Love without trust." He shrugged.

"It can happen." Maya was feeling more and more despondent.

"Obviously. But having opened the interesting issue of trust I must say there's some cause for me to question your unwavering devotion."

Maya stared at him.

"Interesting...the things I've observed since we've come to Europe." He looked at her blandly.

Maya crossed her legs nervously. "What do you mean?"

"The other night, for example, with Sergei. He was clearly attracted to you and it's so tantalizing to think that the two of you had met before."

"Is that why you invited him to our apartment? Were you hoping I might expose some unfaithful bone?"

"What an odd way you have of putting it."

"Well, talking about Sergei, he thinks you're gay." After she said this Maya felt ashamed. In part because she felt that she had somehow insulted homosexuality by throwing it out as an insult and in part because she feared she had insulted Edward and their relationship by suggesting that he was homosexual. To her relief Edward began to laugh. "I'm sorry," she said. "That was a stupid thing to say."

"Sex." Edward chuckled. "What a basis for a relationship. It makes much more sense to base relationships on mutual interests, mutual values, on love of country or loyalty to a philosophical ideal. But no, it's sex that draws us in, even to people with whom we fundamentally disagree."

"I don't think that's true with us." Maya was hurt and annoyed because sex was the last thing that attracted her to Edward.

"Really? What's true between us Maya? What is there that we can rely on as honest or genuine? Although 'truth' is hardly a very reasonable concept by which to determine the success or failure of a relationship."

Maya felt suddenly angry and saddened. "Why do you always have to abstract concepts and ideas in relation to people? Why can't we just talk about us and not include the entire world? It's like we're only a metaphor for lovers and it's very cynical. In every way—applied to us or the world nobody comes out looking good."

"And looking good is the bottom line, isn't it?" It was the first time Maya had seen Edward look genuinely distressed. She had missed this side of him as well. There were so many things she had never seen or wanted to see. She reached for his hand but he ignored her. "Everything's the same. We're only looking to fulfill the same needs as the lowest forms of life."

Maya withdrew her hand, hurt. "That's most unfair, Edward, and unjust to me. I understand now why Anne couldn't stay with you. You push people away. You've been pushing me away for a long time but I've been too stupid and naïve to accept it. I don't think you love anyone or believe in anything." She drank from the glass, the tears flowing down her cheeks. She didn't care if anyone saw her cry, she didn't care about anything anymore.

Edward looked at her and, reaching across, gently wiped the tears that were rolling down her face. "Actually, you're right, darling and I apologize. I can be a terrible cad but it's not true that I don't love anyone. I love you."

Maya just shook her head.

"I'll make dinner for you tonight, okay?"

She raised her head to look at him. "No babies."

"No babies." He smiled.

CHAPTER FORTY FIVE

"'Miracles happen after meditation, in silence, without
this hysteria.' 'It doesn't matter whether they saw
the Madonna or not. Italy's rich in natural and
supernatural forces. We all feel their influence.
If you look for God you find him everywhere.'"
(from Federico Fellini's "La Dolce Vita")

Her bags were packed, her passport and ticket were in her purse. Anne
sat on the edge of the bed; once again she gazed on her face in the mirror.
It was just as pale as the day she had arrived, the dark circles around her
eyes just as dark but she thought she looked less like an Audrey Flack
still life and more like a sinister figure from a Hollywood film. Raising
her hand she traced the line of puckered skin that was carved in relief
down the side of her cheek. So...she was alone again. Nothing really ever
changed. She was reminded of the mechanical world set in motion by
a distant, non-caring God. That was the world she lived in, she thought
philosophically.

Antonio had asked her to stay on in Rome. He had said that he would
help her find a teaching job or that she could just live with him and write
but she had refused. Anne wanted to stay, she hated the fact that she
wanted to stay so much she was willing to gamble losing her job, her
career, willing to risk everything just for the romantic hope that someone
loved her. Well, she wasn't going to do that this time. After all, she would
have to come back for John's trial and if Antonio really did care for her
then he would wait.

***

Anne met Maya in front of her apartment on the Via dei Funari at
five that afternoon. They were going to buy antipasti and sparkling wine
for their last dinner together. Dutifully, they kissed one another, Maya
carefully avoiding the raw scar on Anne's cheek. They walked in silence
to the Rosticceria. Maya shifted her bag from one shoulder to the other.
"I'm glad that Valeriano's dead. I don't care if that sounds callous—I like
it when the bad guys end up suffering the consequences of their actions.
Can you imagine having him for a father?"

Anne shook her head. "I don't think having a terrible father figure's
an excuse for the things John did."

They made their purchases and turned back to the apartment. "I met Rose yesterday," Anne said casually.

"Rose?" Maya frowned. "Oh, you mean the fat lady who rescued me from Sergei."

"I thought she was very beautiful."

Maya waved her slender wrist in the air. "I never said she wasn't beautiful, I said she was fat. And she is. So, what are you thinking now?" Maya stepped around a pile of dog droppings in the middle of the sidewalk.

Anne looked at her. "Nothing. Why?"

"I was just curious," Maya paused. "I was wondering if you were thinking about how stupid I am. I mean, I'm apparently the only one unable to see that everyone, including you, have been hiding things from me."

Anne stopped to light a cigarette. She drew on it and looked evenly at Maya. "I never thought of you as stupid and I never hid anything from you." She walked on.

Maya pressed her lips together and followed her. Passing the entrance to a shadowy courtyard, they both stopped to look inside. Iron lanterns flanked its massive stone portico. Inside, another lantern encased in a filigree cage, hung above the pavement. Behind it they could see the lower edge of a balustrade, below which ran an arched colonnade. Beyond the dark interior of this courtyard they could see the facade of a building on the street opposite the one they were on, its stone gleaming pink in the radiant light.

Anne gazed into the courtyard. "I do love this city," she said, more to herself than to Maya. "Just look at how evocative this courtyard is. We don't know who lives here or what it hides. And even though we can see through it to the other side, we're no more enlightened than if the other side was a blank wall. It's just pure poetry; the darkness and light, the hidden and the revealed."

Maya stepped closer to the courtyard. "It sounds like you're describing our relationship." She turned to face Anne. "You did hide things from me." Maya spoke slowly. "I guess I can see that you hated John so much you didn't care what happened to me."

Anne looked at her in exasperation. "Why do you say that? You know that I never meant for you to be involved. The whole thing in Turin was unfortunate, but it wasn't anything I had any control over. And why do you always think everything's centered around you, anyway?"

Maya stood next to the portico, running her fingers over a large, bronze ring that was embedded in the wall. "You're right," she spoke slowly. "I never really saw that side of myself until now. I've realized something after everything that's happened to me this summer. It's something I suppose I should have known about myself ages ago. I've always thought that everything that happened around me was because of me, because I was beautiful, desirable, irresistible or just because I was important in some inexplicable way. But now I see that I was really peripheral to everything that happened. John stole my purse so he could hide the drawing in it, Gianni called the police so he could find out if John hid it there, John shot Edward but he really wanted to shoot you—in fact, you were really the center of everything that happened to me. Isn't that funny? And there I was thinking only of myself all this time."

Anne looked curiously at Maya. "That's funny. I hadn't looked at it that way. But you shouldn't be so hard on yourself, Maya. The way things happened anyone would have thought they were the cause. And isn't it a relief that it turned out the way it did? I mean you and Edward are happy together after all and he didn't have anything to do with the whole incident so you can trust him again."

"Yes," Maya nodded slowly. "I still don't quite understand why you didn't tell me about John though."

Anne looked into the courtyard. "I didn't know what to do. I was only thinking of myself." She caught herself and laughed. "I guess we may both have that problem." Anne took Maya's arm and tucked it into hers. "Do you forgive me?"

Maya looked at her. "Are you making fun of me?"

"Maya!" Anne shook her arm a little. "You know I don't do things like that."

Maya looked away from her, tears starting in the corner of her eyes. "I suppose it's all right."

Anne realized that she no longer felt any anger toward Maya or Edward. Antonio had solved that. They walked on together, turning the corner onto the Piazza Mattei where Anne stopped next to the Fontana della Tartarughe. The figures of four lovely youths holding dolphins in one hand were helping four stone tortoises drink from the upper fountain basin. Suddenly, Maya cried out and turned to throw herself protectively in front of Anne. Running out of an alley a group of small boys squirted something at Anne who stumbled and fell. Laughing, they ran off down the narrow via della Reginella.

"Bastardi! Delinquenti! Stronzi maledetti! Ai mortacci tuoi, you stupid kids." Maya's voice subsided to a whisper as she wiped agitatedly at Anne's face with the corner of her dress. "Are you all right?"

Anne's hair was dripping and her blouse clung to her skin. She was pressing her hands against her face while Maya tried to dry her off. "Anne, say something, tell me you're okay. It's me they wanted."

Anne laughingly pushed Maya away. "What are you talking about? They just squirted me with water. It's nothing. Just a group of kids playing around."

"Are you sure?" Maya wiped Anne's face and looked at her doubtfully.

"Of course, I'm sure. But I'm afraid our starters are smushed." Anne stood up and held up the container of antipasto di frutti di mare on which she had fallen.

"Oh dear."

"I saved the bottle though." Anne was gripping it in her left hand. "I suppose you could say it's instinct." Laughing, she tried to pull her dripping dress away from her body.

"Or priority." Maya took Anne's arm, sheepishly. "I can't believe they did that. And just as I thought that all the menacing aspects of Rome had been taken care of. I guess you can't get rid of all the threats. Come on, darling, you really do stink."

Anne followed Maya up the stairs to the apartment.

"What happened to you?" Edward looked curiously at Anne's disheveled dress. He sniffed and made a face. "Good God, you smell like a fishery."

"Thanks." Anne pulled her dress away from her hips.

"She got sprayed by a group of boys. Why don't you go dry off? Or maybe you'd like to shower. You do smell, Anne. I'll take care of your dress. You can put on one of Edward's shirts while your dress is drying. They're hanging in the wardrobe in our room."

"Sprayed by a group of boys." Edward was drinking a martini. "That suggests all sorts of possibilities. I do wish you had been here earlier, Maya. Your martinis are so much better than mine but I simply couldn't wait."

"The virtues of patience." Maya sighed and removed the flattened remains of octopus and squid.

"What was that?" Edward peered over her shoulder.

Maya put the bottle of Contratto in an ice bucket. "Our antipasti."

"Did someone throw that at Anne as well?"

"She sat on them." Maya leaned over and kissed Edward on the cheek. "I'm so glad your arm has healed enough to make dinner. I've missed your wonderful dinners. What are you making for tonight?"

Edward puffed up. "A simple little repast. Though I see I shall have to whip up something to take the place of the antipasti." He began to rummage through the refrigerator. "Aha! Some prosciutto, some grissini. That will do just fine."

"That sounds good to me," Anne reappeared, drying her hair.

"That shirt looks good on you, Anne." Maya opened the sparkling wine and poured each of them a glass.

"Isn't that extraordinary," Edward took his glass. "Your final night in Rome and you're sprayed by a group of boys. Gypsies? No? How fortunate, right Maya?"

"It was close enough. I really thought it might be…oh, I was really scared."

"You really thought they'd thrown acid at me?" Anne felt torn between the absurdity of the idea and a dawning realization that Maya had tried to protect her.

Maya shrugged and looked chagrined. "Yes."

"She threw herself in front of me." Anne told Edward. "Just like she did that summer on the Piazza Venezia."

Maya blushed. "Well, I didn't, I couldn't let you…"

"Modesty and courage. Nobility indeed." Edward flourished his glass of wine.

Anne raised her glass to Maya. "Here's to friends." Maya smiled slightly as they touched the rims of their glasses. "You may make fun if it pleases you, Edward, but you can't deny that Maya is courageous."

Edward raised his hands in protest. "I wouldn't dream of denying such a thing. Of course, she's courageous." His eyes twinkled at Maya.

"Stop it, you're both making fun of me. Let's talk about something else." Maya walked out onto the terrace and Anne followed her. They stood together looking out over the rooftops, their arms around each others waists, the light from the living room behind them merging with the brilliant gleam of the moon and the lights shining from the apartments encircling the courtyard. They watched Rose as she crossed her living room. Drifting from her apartment came the strains of "La donna e mobile." Maya murmured the lines in English. "'Woman is wayward as a feather in the breeze, capricious in word and in thought, always a lovable, pretty face but deceitful whether weeping or smiling.' I hate that. How irritatingly typical of men."

Anne laughed and then stopped as her scar protested against the stretching of skin caused by her laughter. "The male defense par excellence. Hem us in with guilt over our flaws when it's really the human condition that defines the limits of our honesty."

"You're talking about me?" Edward appeared behind them, holding the bottle of Prosecco.

Maya held out her glass. "Of course. We're talking about how hypocritical men are and how they're always trying to project it onto the woman."

"Ho hum, cliché." Edward clinked his glass with Anne's and Maya's.

"Salute a Roma," Maya said.

"And to the most beautiful of women," Edward said gallantly. Maya smiled at him. "Are you feeling better, my love?" Edward leaned closer to her and whispered in her ear. Maya nodded.

Anne dropped into a chair, her glass in hand. She would miss Antonio. Had she made a mistake not staying here in Rome? Should she change her mind and take the risk?

"I don't plan on being away from Rome for long." Maya took a sip. "I rather enjoy the adventure, the unpredictability of daily life here."

Edward snorted. "You enjoy the number of men who are attracted to you, you mean."

Maya looked indulgently at him, forgetting her recent remorse over her vanity. "That's not it at all. You're so insensitive, Edward. You sound just like the song."

Edward laughed and put his arm around her.

"It's more the paradoxical quality of the every day," Anne said. "I feel as though I've lived, as though I could live forever when I'm here. You get a sense of immortality just walking through the streets—you can move from antiquity to the Renaissance, from the Baroque to the present just by turning a corner. It makes me feel almost as though I'm immortal or, at any rate, that I'm part of an immortal world."

"Grandpa singing 'Ave Maria' for a cigar, a statue of Jesus—hands raised in benediction—flown by a helicopter over the tenements outside of Rome, the pilots hovering above giggling girls sunbathing on a rooftop. 'They're trying to pick us up. They want our phone number.'" Edward poured more Prosecco. "There's the paradox captured in a nutshell. The genius of Fellini who depicts Rome in all of its eclectic sensuality."

Anne laughed. "Not to mention the bizarre spirituality. Caught somewhere between a coke commercial and the nativity."

"I think the most deeply religious moment in "La Dolce Vita" is when Marcello Mastroianni takes Anita Ekberg out in his car and he's looking at her with those wonderful fawn brown eyes and as he starts to kiss her she howls like a dog. He's surprised but he's not repelled. He warns her to be careful because the ground is full of holes. He's solicitous even though he's been discarded, replaced by dogs. That's really beautiful." Maya stretched herself like a kitten and fluttered her eyes at the two of them.

"There you have it." Edward turned to enter the apartment. "From the mouths of babes…" He disappeared into the kitchen.

About the Artist

Irene Belknap draws on symbols and rituals associated with human tradition, interaction and expression. Her paintings reflect a personal vision of beauty within the universal context of social and cultural constructs.

"Continuum" depicts the mysterious, sometimes absurd, sometimes solemn cyclical procession in which each of us play a part according to our heritage and character. It exemplifies what I wanted to explore in A Feast of Small Surprises, ie, the mystery, beauty, and illusion that surrounds the characters and affects their adventures in an unpredictable universe.

About the Author

Corinne Van Houten grew up in Atlanta, Georgia and received a Ph.D in Art History, Women's Studies and Literary Criticism from the Institute of the Liberal Arts at Emory University. She has lived in Amsterdam, the Netherlands and Paris, France and now resides with her husband and two children in Marin County, California. She has written reviews on contemporary art for several publications as well as a book on a contemporary Dutch artist, Rik van Iersel.

Printed in the United States
50702LVS00005B/124-264